To a very
Student! I am so
proud of you, Ozan! :)

Ruth Martin

Raven and
The Three
Dark Shadows

Raven and
The Three
Dark Shadows

Laura & Ruth Martin

Rev. date: 6/02/2015

To order additional copies of this book, contact:
Xlibris
1-888-795-4274
www.Xlibris.com
Orders@Xlibris.com
539087

CONTENTS

Dedication

Author: Laura Martin

I am dedicating this book to my wonderful stepmother, Ria Martin, who is an abundant source of love and support.

Also, to three terrific students who have given me valuable feedback and inspiration: Saajan Dekiwadiya–Patel, Emma Samuel, and Zachery Smith, I extend to them my deepest gratitude.

Lastly, I am dedicating this book to my fabulous sister, Ruth Martin who has written the book with me.

Author: Ruth Martin

I dedicate this book to:

Laurence Fishburne and Gina Torres, who have taught me to believe in myself, have mentored me, and who have encouraged me to fly. Thank you for believing in me when I didn't believe in myself.

Delilah Fishburne, who taught me how to follow my heart and my dreams.

Olga Brown, who has been my friend, my constant support, and my cheerleader.

Kenza and Kyle Taylor, who were there for me in one of the darkest moments of my life and who have continued to encourage me.

My stepmom and dad, Ria Martin and Bert Martin. I love both of you. Thank-you for your love and prayers. Ria, you are an inspiration to me.

Jennie Petko, principal of Keele Street Jr Public School, Toronto. Thank-you, Jennie, for encouraging me to believe in myself. I have learned so much from you.

Finally, I dedicate this book to my sister, Laura Martin, who has been my friend, my sister, and my encourager. I love you, and I am honored that we are sisters!

PROLOGUE

Raven and the Three Dark Shadows is the sequel to the first book *Raven's Promise*. The first book in the series introduces us to the character Sheila. Her mother had just passed away, and her father remarried. Sheila's new stepmother became cruel and bitter toward her. When Sheila's father was out, her stepmother abused her and treated her like a slave.

Unable to take it anymore, Sheila tried to escape. Unfortunately, she was found by the police and was returned home. As a result, Sheila's stepmother convinced her dad to lock her up in her bedroom for her own safety. While she was locked up in her room, she kept seeing a raven that visited her every night just outside of her bedroom window. Sheila saw the raven as her only friend and talked to it night after night. Not too long after, her stepmother brainwashed her dad into believing that Sheila was suffering from hallucinations and mental disorders as a result of her mother's passing away. He finally consented to placing his daughter into a permanent mental institution where she can get treatment.

Surprisingly, in the worst and most dismal of situations, Sheila's world took a turn for the unexpected and for a magical adventure. She met two friends named Molly Green and Stephen Comings. Molly's nickname is Snapper because she is very hyper and known to snap if she's angry or afraid. She is afraid of the dark and of being left alone. Stephen's nickname is Pen. When he saw his father drown, he stopped talking, and he chose to write instead of talk, which is how he got the nickname Pen. Little by little, as he began to trust his friends, he started speaking again.

All three began to have strange dreams of a woman with long blond hair, dressed in a flowing white gown, running through a stone gate. When the three children started a mission to investigate, they fell into a circumstance of strange events. Pen discovered a strange book with ancient symbols and depictions of animals. As he read from the book, he, Snapper, and Sheila were sucked into a mat. They reemerged through a field of grass into an alternate world.

This is a world that they've never seen before. It's a world where humans can change into animals at will and are ruled by a leader named Raven. Raven has the ability to change into a man or a woman. The children arrived at a very precarious time. A witch among them, Kalik, had become very power hungry and sought to overthrow Raven's rule. She struck terror into the people of that land and used her magic for evil and to control others. As punishment, Raven banished her into the forgotten valley. Unbeknownst to Raven, she found a way to enter the dreams of the children of the village as a helpless, frightened woman to lure them into the forgotten valley. Kalik held these children as her prisoners in the hope of exchanging them for her freedom.

Sheila, Snapper, and Pen were taken in by a family of two brothers, Hamza and Najata, and their wives Tameka and Remba, who can change into panthers. The three children were visited by Raven and given the power to be able to transform themselves into animals. Sheila is given the ability to transform into a raven, Snapper into a mule deer, and Pen into a panther.

The panther family trained Sheila, Snapper, and Pen for the mission to rescue the village's children from the witch Kalik. During their training, Raven gave Sheila the power to control the element wind, Snapper the element fire, and Pen the element water.

Pen miraculously regained his ability to talk as well. With their newfound powers, training, and abilities, Sheila, Snapper, and Pen were able to defeat the witch Kalik, free the village's children, and return to their own world. When they arrive back at the mental hospital, the three children are greeted by two unexpected visitors. Hamza and Tameka, who were their human/panther guardians in Raven's world, have crossed over into the children's world to adopt them as their own.

Raven's promise ends with Sheila, Snapper, and Pen pulling into the driveway of their new home, which is a cozy farmhouse of their new adopted parents, Hamza and Tameka.

CHAPTER ONE

Into the Wild

Sunlight poured through the open shutters of Sheila's bedroom window. It spilled out on to her wooden floorboards and slowly up her walls. It filled and saturated her room with its light and warmth. She felt it creeping up her blankets and brushing up against her cheeks with a gentle hand. She welcomed the sun like she was uniting with an old friend.

Sleepily, she gazed with half-opened eyes as they adjusted to the growing light of the sunrise. Tiny wisps of feathers and specks of dust floated in the air, illuminated by the sunlight. Waking up from dreams was wonderful. Waking up in a bedroom that was yours and to a family that wanted you was even better. There were times that Sheila would wake up wondering if everything was real and she wasn't still dreaming.

The last few months had flown by, and the nightmares of being trapped and locked up by her stepmother were beginning to dissipate. Sometimes she liked to lie in bed just for a few more minutes before getting up to reflect on everything that had happened. Sheila remembered the first time she stepped into her new house. Freshly cut yellow magnolia blossoms were the first things that welcomed her. They were beautifully arranged in a glass vase in the center of the kitchen table.

Almost everything in the house reminded Sheila of nature. Even the furniture was carved to mimic the branches of trees. There were paintings of waterfalls, mountains, forests, and oceans. Sheila couldn't quite put her finger on it, but the house had an almost ethereal presence, with its soft shades of watery blue. Patterns of silvery white budded vines were woven into the fabric of the gossamer curtains and the upholstery of the couches.

A slight breeze lofted into her room, causing the thin blue silky curtains to slightly flutter. Sheila yawned and slowly lifted her body into a seated position on her bed. Suddenly, she remembered that today Tameka and Hamza, who she now called Mom and Dad, had planned to take the family on an outing to the Skeena river park. Excited now, she dived out of bed and went in search of her brother and sister.

The majestic white-tipped peaks of the mountains stood like regal monuments. They etched themselves into a brilliantly clear blue sky. As Sheila stepped out of the car, she tingled with anticipation. Since returning to her world, she and her family had to keep a low profile. They hardly ever morphed into their animal forms. Only on rare occasions would the family venture out into a conservation area full of wildlife. Here, they would not be noticed changing into their animal forms.

Tameka wore a beautiful emerald green dress. It blended in with the lush green rolling hills and brought out her rich ebony skin. That morning, Tameka had braided Sheila's hair into two long silky braids. She had parted Sheila's hair in the middle, just the way she liked it. For these special occasions, Sheila liked to wear her beaded headband, which was denim blue with a zigzag pattern. When she wore it, it reminded her of her heritage, the Haida. She wore it proudly. It was given to her by her birth mother and by her mother before her. Tameka beamed when she wrapped it over Sheila's head. Each time, Tameka would whisper in her ear of how exquisite she looked. Sheila would blush, pretending to be embarrassed, but deep inside, she felt loved.

Snapper was very different from Sheila. Her hair was normally straight, but in the event that she was not persuaded to brush it after a shower, it would explode into a million wild blond curls bouncing in every which way. Her hair, oddly enough, resembled her personality. Snapper was never one to care about her appearance, as she was far too preoccupied with the acquisition of knowledge and adventure. In the bright sun, Snapper's blue eyes shone out from amid a sea of freckles.

Just ahead, a crystal blue river snaked its way toward the chiseled mountains. British Columbia boasted many beautiful parks full of flourishing wildlife, greenery, rivers, lakes, and mountain ranges. Many aboriginal tribes called British Columbia their home.

"Come on!" yelled Pen. While the girls were busy looking at all the scenery, Pen was already morphing into his panther form. He threw back his head and let out a deafening roar. His fangs flashed. Large catlike eyes replaced brown ones. Pen was a small boy. When he transformed into a panther, however, his whole body became enormous. Thick rippling muscles grew. They spread out down his neck, shoulders, and legs. As his hands became paws, they tripled in size. Sharp white claws overtook fingernails. Pen's clothes began to merge into sleek, black fur.

With a powerful swing of his long tail, he was instantly propelled into the air. Diving forward at least ten feet, his two front paws hit the ground simultaneously. Following shortly after, his two back paws pounded the ground. As he sped furiously through the grass, his muscular legs pumped hard. They gave him momentum and rocket-like acceleration. His breathing was deep and heavy. Charging past the two girls, he nearly knocked them over with his sheer power.

Tameka and Hamza shook their heads and laughed. "Our son, the show off," Hamza snickered.

"Well, what are you waiting for, girls?" goaded Tameka. "Go get him and show him what you girls are made of!"

With that remark, Sheila ran as fast as she could and fearlessly soared into the air. She remained in her human form for a few seconds, arms outstretched, hands pointed. Had she kept her human form for a second longer, she would have plummeted and buried her face on to the earth. But at the last possible second, feathers covered her arms. With one violent flap of her wings, she skimmed over the blades of grass and soared high into the air. Sheila had begun to perfect her transformation into a raven. She was able now to isolate the change to just her arms and keep the rest of her body in human form.

Longing now for more speed and height, she changed into a raven all the way. Feeling for the currents of air, she flapped her wings in their direction. Letting the air currents push her, she soared higher and faster above the forest floor. Her black feathers glistened almost blue against the bright sun. Purposely, she fanned her tail, allowing her to glide. Below her, the park stretched out for miles, and everything looked so small. Flying, she felt the strongest rush of adrenaline. Up in the air, she felt free.

"Well, I guess showing off runs in the family," remarked Snapper dryly. "I may as well join in the frivolity."

Hamza and Tameka shrugged their shoulders, bewildered. "Her vocabulary definitely doesn't run in the family," Hamza blurted out, half laughing.

"Another one of Snapper's words to look up in the dictionary, I guess," Tameka teased.

Snapper had a competitive side to her for sure. Mule deer were often underestimated, but Snapper knew how powerful they were. Snapper was nimbler than Sheila and Pen put together. Now that she could mutate into a deer, she was faster than any student at her school, even in human form.

Snapper narrowed her eyes. Without warning, she exploded into a lightning-fast sprint through the grass and over the rocky ground. Any onlooker would have just seen a blur of wind and not have thought for an instant that it was a girl. As she ran, her long curly blond hair steamed out behind her in the wind. Honey-brown fur, speckled with white spots, spread over Snapper's face. Then it covered her white shorts and tank top. Her ears became long and pointed, alert for any unfamiliar sound. White fur covered her underbelly and lay in a small patch just under her chin. Large black eyes and a small black nose shone out from her soft brown coat of fur.

To Hamza and Tameka's amazement, Snapper used her springlike momentum to catapult herself high into the air. She threw herself into breathtaking summersaults. Her parents gazed in wonderment as she flung herself into acrobatic twists from a fantastic height above the ground. Only lightly grazing the ground with her tiny cloven hooves, Snapper managed to catch up with Pen and Sheila in just a few short bounds.

"We should probably go after them, Hamza," urged Tameka gently.

"Tameka, you worry too much," chuckled Hamza "Let the kids be kids. We already restrain them enough from changing into animals. Why don't we leave our worrying for another day, and let's be panthers!"

There was a spark in Hamza's eyes as those words escaped his lips. He missed the feeling of adrenaline that coursed through his veins when he changed into his primal form.

Hamza tilted his head back and slowly opened his mouth. Two sharp white incisors began to slowly emerge from his gaping mouth. His eyes began to glow a fiery yellow, and large back pupils replaced the human ones. Sleek thick black fur took the place of the gray khakis and the white golf shirt he had been wearing. Black dreadlocks that hung just below his shoulders merged into the black fur at the nape of his neck. Sharp canine claws slowly grew where well-groomed and manicured nails had once been.

As the transformation continued, Hamza bounded forward on all fours. Now a massive black panther, he bellowed a deep and terrifying roar. It echoed through the forest, sending even the flock of birds noisily away from nearby branches.

And I wonder where Pen gets it from, mused Tameka. She had to admit that she liked seeing her husband as a black panther. He looked strong, mysterious, and powerful. He didn't look at all like the farmer that he disguised himself to be.

With a gleam in her eye, Tameka too changed into a large black panther. She sprang into the air and seized Hamza by the nape of his neck with her fangs and tossed him on his back.

Hamza turned his head, roaring, and pulled himself up instantly to face her. The two of them growled menacingly at each other. They bared their fangs. Circling closer and closer to each other, they extended their claws. Small creatures, such as squirrels and rabbits, scurried away from the violence of the two black panthers going head to head.

Hamza took a vicious swipe with his sharp claws at his wife. He narrowly missed her fierce face. She laughed darkly.

"So you want a fight, my darling husband," she growled.

"No, no, I surrender," he cried out with a touch of laughter in his voice.

Tameka had forgotten how much fun it was to play fight and how bonded she felt toward her husband. She knew that he had purposely missed her face with his claw. The exhilaration of the fight made her feel all the worry and stress she had melt away.

"Let's go for a run through the mountains," declared Tameka.

"Sure! If you can keep up!" Hamza retorted.

As swift as a scream the two black feline shapes sped up. Within seconds, they had slipped into the rolling hills and disappeared from sight.

CHAPTER TWO

The Dragon and the Druid

There was nothing like the feeling of flying, Sheila thought to herself. She knew if she had her way, she would fly every day. There was a small part of her that was resentful that her parents limited her freedom to fly. She thought back to the times she was trapped by her stepmom in that dungeon of a room. She had shared all her dreams with the raven at her window. Now she was the raven! The wind felt so delicious.

Sheila manipulated the wind to her desire. She swooped low over the tops of trees, gliding on the same level as the mountain. Her keen eyes were able to keep track of where Pen and Snapper were. The experience of flying was so spectacular that she slipped unconsciously into her daydream world.

A faint sound caught Sheila's attention. She cocked her head to one side as she flew. A large birdlike creature that she did not recognize approached her from a distance. She couldn't make out what it was at first. But the closer it came, the clearer she was able to see it take shape.

Almost falling from the sky, she screeched out in panic when she saw what it was. A giant, fire-breathing dragon was headed straight for her. If she hadn't seen it with her own eyes, she would have thought she was hallucinating. But there it was, soaring toward her, with its red and golden scales glistening in the sun. Bat-like wings flapped noisily like mighty waves crashing against rocks. Small wisps of grey smoke curled out from its large black nostrils.

When she looked down at Snapper and Pen, they had stopped moving and were staring up at her expectantly. They had seen the dragon too.

Descending cautiously, Sheila quickly transformed into her human form with a dramatic display. Grazing the ground one foot at a time, she gracefully dropped her arms down to her sides. She morphed her feathers into arms and the T-shirt covering them.

"It's a dragon!" yelled Sheila, "run!"

It was too late. The dragon landed noisily on the ground in front of them.

"Get behind me!" ordered Pen to the girls, still in his panther form. He stood between the dragon and his sisters, bearing his fangs. Pen's growls were terrifying. What could he possibly do to a dragon, though? Its thick, scaled armor was impenetrable to the sharpest sword.

Petrified, all three children prepared themselves to fight. "We need to get ready to use our powers against the dragon!" Snapper yelled out frantically.

"Who-o-o-o-a-a-a-a! Just wait a second!" exclaimed the dragon. "We haven't even met yet, and you want to fight me! What kind of a lousy welcome is this?"

Pen, Snapper, and Sheila stood dazed.

"I'm sorry," began Pen. "Would you mind telling us who you are?"

"Oh dear, I forgot to introduce myself! Why, I'm a druid!"

"What's a druid?" Pen asked, puzzled.

"You don't know what a druid is?" he asked.

Snapper interjected quickly. "Yes, I know that a druid is a type of wizard. The last time I checked my sources, however, druids were not twenty feet tall with smoke coming out of their nostrils."

"Oh!" exclaimed the dragon. "I apparently forgot to morph! Ha ha! My bad! Just give me one second, please."

The dragon raised its head and opened its large bat-like wings. With a giant downward swoop of his wings, he knocked the children off their feet and into the trees above. Slowly, the dragon shrunk and morphed into an old man.

Desperately flailing her legs, Snapper struggled as her bum was sticking out of a tree while her head was buried in the leaves.

Pen had also landed on the tree the wrong way. He was gripping the outmost branch by the end of his tail.

"Now what in the world are you doing up there?" the druid inquired.

As Sheila was the only one who could see properly, she looked down. Standing on the ground was an old man with a fairly round stomach, rosy cheeks, and a white robe that bulged in the middle. In the man's hand was a wooden staff, and in his eyes, a twinkle.

"Someone get me down from here!" yelled Snapper, her bum pointing straight at the druid. With a wave of his staff, Sheila, Pen, and Snapper were all suddenly standing in front of him.

"How did you do that?" exclaimed Pen, morphing into his human self. His black fur changed to dark brown skin and his hair into a short black afro. Snapper changed back into a girl as well.

"Elementary!" exclaimed the druid. "Now that's one of the simplest of spells that you had better learn! However, I don't have time to teach it to you. I'm here on a mission!"

"What is your mission?" muttered Snapper dryly, still embarrassed. "To hurl unsuspecting victims into trees?"

The druid giggled softly. "Actually, children, you are in grave danger. There are three sisters that, when together, possess dark and terrible magic."

"I think you are talking about Kalik," interjected Pen. "But we already killed her, so there are only two left."

"No, you did not," answered the druid quietly. "You merely vanquished her for a short time. Two of the sisters you have met, the third you will meet shortly."

The druid's face became solemn. "The third sister is the most frightening sorceress of them all. No one has ever fought against her and lived to tell the story. You must beware of her. Rumor has it that she feeds on the flesh of children and clothes herself in their skin." The old druid shuddered. "Be on your guard at all times. She can be anywhere."

Sheila, Snapper, and Pen looked at one another wide-eyed.

"But what do they want from us?" Pen asked again, anxious to get some answers.

"The three sisters have made a pact with dark magic to destroy the three of you, and to steal your powers. They will only truly be destroyed when all three of them are vanquished. To destroy only one witch just weakens them. As long as at least one of them is alive, the other two can be revived."

"But where can we find these witches?" inquired Pen, nervously.

"You won't need to look for them," replied the druid with a more somber tone in his voice now. "They will find you."

Suddenly, a dark feeling of fear gripped at Sheila's chest. Could the second witch be Marcella, her evil stepmother? She put it out of her mind. Sheila wanted to believe that her dad was safe.

"I do, however, have gifts for each of you," the old druid said, changing the subject to a much lighter one. "I hope that you will like them and find them useful!"

The druid smiled at Pen. "Now Pen, we'll start with you. I have a special gift for you." He handed him a small box with seven pens in it. "Since your name is Pen, I thought that you should have them!"

"But what do they do?" asked Pen curiously. "They just look like ordinary pens."

"Oh, but they're not!" The druid winked. "See, this pen that says *math* on the cap, is for math tests and homework. It does the writing for you, and always gives the right answers! Why, you can leave the pen with your homework and it will finish it all for you. Just make sure that when someone is watching you, you're holding on to the end of it so that it doesn't give your secret away. A pen that writes by itself would be a rather strange sight for some people, don't you think, Pen?"

Pen nodded, hardly able to believe his eyes.

"Now this pen here is for science, this one is for language, this pen is for math, this pen is for history, and this pen with the eraser, well . . ."

"What? What is it for?" cried Pen, unable to conceal his curiosity any longer.

"Well, my wife thought that I shouldn't give you this pen. But this one that says 'rewrite' on the cap is for rewriting any mark that you want."

"Why would I need that?" asked Pen curiously.

"Well, Pen, if you ever get a bad mark on a test, or on your report card, let's say—all you would need to do is use this eraser. It erases the mark on your test, and also on the teacher's records. It even erases it from the teacher's memory. Then you use the ink nib side of it to write down the new mark that you want. So as far as everyone is concerned, the only mark that exists, and has ever existed, is the new one that you created!"

"Wow!" cried out Pen, clutching at the box of pens and crushing them against his chest protectively. "Thanks a million! This is the best present ever! I can't wait to go home and change all my marks to A's!"

Snapper frowned disapprovingly. "Those pens should be outlawed!" she exclaimed. "Don't you know that good test scores should only come with hard work and good study habits?"

The druid giggled softly under his breath. "You sound just like my wife," he mused.

"And she's right!" snapped Snapper indignantly. "You clearly have no respect for the educational system and for honesty in school!"

The druid winked at Pen. A huge grin swept over Pen's face.

"And you should not be smiling at him, Pen!" exclaimed Snapper again.

Sheila didn't say a word. She was kind of jealous and had wished those gifts were meant for her. She was struggling with math and geometry.

"Now, Pen," the druid continued, "the sixth pen is the one with the silver tip. I am very fond of this one personally."

"What does it do?" asked Pen eagerly, trying not to be impatient. Pen pulled it out of the box.

"This pen is the perfect size for a travel-sized wand!" declared the druid proudly. "All that you have to do is to gently thrust it forward in the air and it immediately transforms."

"Wow!" whispered Snapper.

Pen gave it a little thrust. In a split second, a long shiny brown wand appeared in his hand.

"But how do I use it?" inquired Pen, staring blankly at it.

"Well, you use it to cast spells, Pen," answered the druid, in a matter-of-fact tone of voice.

"But I don't know any spells," answered Pen, a bit embarrassed.

"Well then, you learn, dear boy, you learn!"

"But who can teach me?" asked Pen again, impatiently.

"Well," the druid replied, slowly scratching his chin, "here's one to start you off. We will teach you more when you come. Now repeat after me." Pen nodded quickly. The druid continued. "Like smoke into dust, like fire unseen, take my essence as though I've never been."

Pen repeated the words after the druid. In an instance, he had disappeared from sight.

"Woah!" cried out Snapper. Sheila gasped in amazement.

Pen held up his hands to his face. There was nothing.

"Wow, you are completely invisible, Pen!" Sheila stammered somewhat nervously.

Pen didn't reply. He was tiptoeing silently as a panther across the grass to where Snapper was standing. He loved to tease the girls, especially Snapper. She always gave him such a good reaction. Leaning over to Snapper's ear, he took a breath and prepared to let out a scream.

Suddenly, Snapper reached out and grabbed his arm. "Don't even think of it, Pen."

Pen let out a yelp of surprise. "B-b-b-b-b-b-b-ut, Snapper, how can you see me? I'm invisible! I can't even see myself!"

"Did it slip your mind for an instant that I'm a deer?" asked Snapper with an attitude. "My hearing is better than yours and Sheila's put together."

Pen sighed, totally disappointed.

"Besides, invisible or not, whenever you become really quiet, I know that you're trying to play a trick on me or Sheila!"

The old druid grinned. "It looks like the girls have got your number, Pen! You'll need more than an invisible spell to trick them!"

Sheila laughed. "I'd agree with that, Pen!"

Pen let out another sigh, pretending to be defeated.

"Now when you want to be seen again, Pen, you just say, 'Let what is unseen be seen,' and it will reverse the spell."

The girls watched as Pen magically reappeared. He still had a mischievous twinkle in his eyes that told them that he wasn't done with his pranks on them quite yet.

"One more thing, Pen," the druid continued. "If at any time all three of you need to disappear, your sisters just need to hold on to you as you are saying the spell."

Pen and the girls nodded, eager to try it out later.

"Now thrust it backward, and it will change back into a pen."

Pen did this, and the same tiny silver pen appeared back in his palm.

"There's one last pen in that package that you haven't seen yet," continued the druid. "It's the seventh pen."

Pen reopened the package and looked inside. Sure enough, there was one more pen with no inscription. Pen pulled it out of the box and held it up.

"This pen is a very useful tool in times of danger. It writes out *danger* many, many times."

"Wow," gasped Pen. "That's really cool." He had not quite grasped the pen's complete and utter lack of usefulness.

Snapper threw up her hands and huffed in utter frustration. "This is the most stupid, ridiculous pen of them all! How on earth will that help us?"

The druid started chuckling. "I was just curious how red it could make your face, Snapper! See! There is more than one person here that can breathe out smoke!"

Sheila giggled.

The old druid had a mischievous little boy hidden inside of him!

"Okay, my dear Snapper, the pen doesn't write out danger one million times. Ha ha ha!"

He could barely finish his sentence; he was laughing so hard.

Snapper's red face was now purple with rage.

"Actually, Pen," continued the druid, trying to regain his composure, "this pen is a very unusual gift. It was given to me by a great wizard many years ago. It has the power to open up any doorway, anywhere, and let you walk through. The moment you enter, Pen, the opening will seamlessly close behind you."

"Cool!" exclaimed Pen, anxious to try it out. He rushed over to a gigantic oak tree that was close by.

"Now draw a door on the tree, Pen," suggested the druid.

Pen did as he was told. To his amazement, a door in the tree opened. Shuddering with glee, he stepped through the door and into the tree. The door behind him disappeared, and there was no evidence that Pen had ever been there.

"Okay, Pen!" called the druid, knocking on the outside of the tree. "Come back out now!"

The druid and Sheila and Snapper stared at the bark where the door had once been. Slowly, a new door reappeared, and Pen stepped out from the tree.

"That was so awesome!" exclaimed Pen, excited with his new gift. "I can walk into the coolest places now! I can hide practically anywhere!"

The druid smiled. "Now, my dear Snapper, this is for you!"

Hardly able to contain her excitement, Snapper tore the small box open. Inside the tiny box lay a delicate ring. It was white, and had an iridescent, pearl-like quality. "What is it?" asked Snapper, bewildered. She picked up the ring and held it up to the light.

"That, my dear, is a nothingness ring. It is very, very rare, so take good care of it. You won't want to lose this one."

"But what is it for?" asked Snapper, trembling with anticipation. "Oh dear, you don't know what it is?" questioned the old druid with a twinkle in his eyes.

Pen chuckled. "Wow, Snapper! We finally found something that you don't know anything about! I like this!"

"A nothingness ring is just that!" began the druid. "It means that you become like a ghost. You can go through anything. Nothing can stop you. If someone is chasing you, and there's a wall in the way, you can just go through the wall to the other side. And if they do catch you, you would just slip right through them, so they really didn't catch you after all. Also, if someone throws something at you, it would just go right through you. That's why it's called a nothingness ring. You become as weightless and uncatchable as nothing!"

"Wow!" Snapper exclaimed. She put the ring on her finger, and gingerly stepped over to Sheila. Putting her hand out, she reached right through her head and to the other side.

"Cool!" exclaimed Pen, a bit jealous of Snapper's new gift.

"That was totally gross!" groaned Sheila.

"Could you feel it?" inquired Pen, eager for any details.

"No!" barked Sheila, nauseated at the thought of someone's hand going through her face. "But why don't you let her try it on you, Pen, and let me know how fun the sensation is!"

"Yah! What a great idea!" shouted Pen.

Sheila rolled her eyes. Apparently, boys were immune to sarcasm, and her dry humor was wasted on Pen.

"Okay, here goes!" called Snapper stepping back a few paces. Taking a deep breath and closing her eyes, she made a fist, pulling it back and aiming it as hard as she could for Pen's stomach. Unfortunately, in her haste to make a fist as quickly as she could, the ring inadvertently slipped off her finger. Pen's unsuspecting face bore a wide grin. He couldn't wait to see this magic in action. As she let her fearsome fist fly, it met with Pen's unsuspecting stomach. The force of the blow that was meant to go through him knocked him off his feet and threw him into the air. Pen's once full cheeks instantly deflated! He fizzled like a popped balloon as he came with a thud to the ground. The druid, although eager to help, had fallen to his knees and was clutching his stomach, suffering from pangs of violent laughter.

"Pen, are you okay?" asked Snapper, her fist throbbing uncontrollably. "Oh! Look! Here's the ring! It must have fallen off my finger! It's okay, though, Pen. Can we try it again?"

Pen, who was lying on his back, still trying to catch his breath, put up both hands, wheezing. "Never again! Find another volunteer. Preferably one that's already dead!"

The druid, finally gaining his composure, stood up.

"Okay, okay! My turn!" shouted Sheila, more excited than ever to see her present now.

Smiling sheepishly, the druid reached deep into his bag. "Don't worry, Sheila! I have something for you too!" he said.

Producing a tiny package, he handed it to Sheila. Sheila carefully opened the wrapping. A delicate blue sapphire necklace with ancient white symbols carved on to it lay inside. It had a tiny mirror on its end.

"Wow!" said Sheila, gently lifting the necklace from the package. Snapper and Pen peered more closely at it. It was beautiful, and it shimmered in the sunlight. "What does it do, though?" asked Sheila, quite intrigued by her gift.

Taking the necklace from Sheila's hands, the druid tenderly placed it over her neck. "This is the only necklace of its kind that was ever made, Sheila. The little mirror on the end of the chain has the power to create a clone. Say for instance that someone was trying to hurt you. You could point the mirror at yourself and turn it clockwise. Each time you twist it, a new clone will appear. Why, you could create a whole army of yourself in seconds. The only drawback to this gift is that it is meant only to distract the person or persons who wish you harm. You can tell your second self what to do." Sheila's eyes became bigger. "And the best thing is that your second self isn't you. It's just a mirage, so to speak. An image or a copy. So that second self can't be hurt."

"Wow!" exclaimed Sheila speechless.

"So if you are in danger, and someone is following you, you can fight them with your second self, and you can't be hurt!"

"Cool!" called out Pen again.

"Try it out, Sheila!" Snapper said excitedly.

"One more thing, Sheila!" the old druid continued. "You can do something else with your other self that is a lot of fun. See, even though the second part of you is not really you, you can still feel the emotions if you choose to. You can live through her, so to speak."

"What do you mean?" asked Sheila, puzzled.

"Well, Sheila, let's say that you wanted to do something really extraordinary, but really dangerous. You wanted someone to test it for you first. Like, I don't know, riding on a shark's back, for example. Well, you could dive in to the water with your second self, grab its fin, and ride the waves. If he turned and tried to eat you, or even succeeded in doing that, you'd still be fine. You can always create a new self. And you had experienced the fun and danger without getting hurt!"

"No way!" blurted out Pen, unable to keep quiet any more. "Can I borrow your necklace sometimes?"

Sheila didn't even hear Pen's request. She had already begun pulling the mirror toward her. She turned it once. Instantly, another girl, in the exact form as Sheila, appeared. "Wow!" shouted Sheila, jumping back. "Now what do I do?"

"Well, tell her what you want her to do with your mind, Sheila! Just picture it in your mind, and she will perform it. If you want to feel what she's feeling, you can picture yourself in both bodies. Go on, try it out!"

Sheila thought for a moment. "Can you do math?" she asked her clone hesitantly.

"Why yes!" answered her clone excitedly. "I love math!"

"Wow!" said Sheila. "Do you like to do chores around the house? I mean like take out stinky garbage?"

"Oh yes!" replied her clone eagerly. "I love doing anything for you!"

Snapper and Pen stared at Sheila with their mouths open.

"That's not fair!" interrupted Pen emphatically. "You could literally sit back all day and drink iced tea, and your clones could do all the work. And Mom and Dad would never know the difference because it's still you doing it!"

Sheila ran over to the druid, and threw her arms around him. "Thank you so much! This is the best gift that anyone has ever given me in my life. Now I'll never have to take out another bag of garbage again."

"Oh! Just one more thing . . ." Sheila pondered. "Do you do dishes?"

"A-h-h-h-h-h!" yelled Snapper, who was utterly perturbed by this point. "Your gift isn't supposed to make you lazy, Sheila! Our gifts are for very practical uses, like self-defense in times of need."

Sheila wasn't listening to Snapper. She was thinking of all the chores around the house that her clone could do. "You might want to get rid of your clone now Sheila, reminded the old druid, chuckling.

"Oh yeah," said Sheila, pretending not to have noticed that she would need to make them disappear. "How do I get rid of it?" Sheila sighed.

"Turn the mirror counterclockwise and for each turn a clone will be sucked back into your necklace" he replied grinning. Sheila obediently followed his instructions, and sure enough, the second Sheila shrunk and dissipated like smoke into the small mirror.

The druid smiled. "Now, my dear children, I have to be off. The other druids are waiting for my return."

Snapper, Sheila, and Pen looked up at the old druid. They had grown fond of this wizard in such a short time.

"But when will we see you again?" asked Pen anxiously.

"Very soon, my dears. Very, very soon. We will have more gifts for you then."

The old druid lifted his head and raised his arms. Red and golden scales began to cover his body as he grew taller in height.

"What kind of gifts?" asked Sheila, eagerly.

The old druid didn't hear her. Before she could ask him again, he had sprung up into the air, his mighty wings flapping noisily on either side of him.

Within minutes, he became a small speck in the sky. And then he disappeared out of sight.

CHAPTER THREE

The Taunting Begins

The next morning came early for the three children. Tameka had packed their lunches the night before and had made them a hearty breakfast of bacon and eggs.

As Pen walked across the driveway, he was feeling more cheerful than normal. He even whistled a little tune.

"Hey, Pen, why so happy this morning?" grumbled Sheila, who was still clearly exhausted from the events of the previous day. "Isn't it a bit early to be whistling?"

Snapper looked at Pen with a look of disdain. "I'll tell you why he's so pumped, Sheila! Last night, when I knocked on his door to ask him a question, his math pen was doing all of his homework for him!"

Pen's smile was wide enough to crack his face. "Yup!" said Pen, happily. "It was awesome! You should have seen Dad's face when he saw my homework was completed. The pen even did all the bonus questions. It was totally cool."

Snapper shook her head angrily. "That, Pen, is what we call 'cheating.' Do you even know what that word means?"

Sheila, who hadn't said a word, looked up at Pen. "Hey, Pen," she began in the nicest voice that she could possibly muster up. "Do you think that I could borrow your math and history pen tomorrow? I have a big test, and I didn't really get a chance to study much."

"No problem!" replied Pen, generously. "But only if you swap your cloning necklace with the pens tomorrow. By the way," he asked her, puzzled, "why don't you just ask your clone to go in and write it for you?"

"Well," replied Sheila, "I have a bit of a problem. Even though my clones look like me, they don't always act like me. If I ask them to do my math test, they'll be way too excited, and I'll definitely be found out."

"Okay!" said Pen, a little bit amused. He pictured Sheila's clone in the classroom shouting "Me! Me! I want one!" when the teacher is starting to hand out the tests. Yup, Mrs. Nastiel would know for sure that there was a problem.

"I am disappointed with both of you!" Snapper finally blurted out, glaring at both Pen and Sheila now. "You should be ashamed of yourself, Sheila, for wanting to cheat on a test!"

"Yah, Sheila!" Pen lectured Sheila in a stern voice, pretending to be serious. "You should be ashamed of yourself! Go and write out forty math equations right now, young lady!"

"Thank you!" Snapper replied with a sigh of relief, obviously not getting Pen's humor at all. "Someone is finally making sense, and I had hoped that it would be you, Sheila!"

Pen and Sheila stared at each other in disbelief. The sad thing is that Snapper was really serious. She really thought that Sheila should do forty extra math equations as punishment.

"Anyway," continued Pen, determined to remain in his exceptionally good mood this morning, "I had an awesome night last night. I went downstairs and made myself a triple-decker sandwich with tomatoes, bacon, cheese, and the works. And then I started my homework!" He winked at Sheila, who was giggling. "Yup, I did my math homework, or at least I watched my pen write it for me. And then I took out my math test from last week that I got a D on. I erased my mark and replaced it with an A+. Then I wrote beside the mark: 'Well done, Pen! Your exceptional intelligence and hard work has earned you this outstanding mark.' It was pretty sweet!"

Snapper, who was sputtering uncontrollably now, was speechless for a minute. "I give up on both of you! If you ask me, the druid should have given me the cloning necklace. At least I could have cloned myself, and taught the other Snapper to be hardworking and dedicated to her studies. She could have furthered pedagogical and didactic approaches..."

Pen and Sheila stopped in their tracks. They had no idea what Snapper had just said in her last line, but the thought of having two Snappers was simply unnerving. They hardly knew what to do with just one. They looked at each other. Neither of them said a word, but they knew what the other was thinking.

"Don't ever let her get it!" Pen instructed Sheila solemnly. Sheila nodded slowly, just as seriously. They wouldn't even dare to think of the consequences of having two Snappers around.

Snapper huffed angrily, clearly unhappy with the two of them.

The rising sun felt so warm and inviting on their faces that it was impossible to remain angry. It wasn't long before the three of them were laughing about something else in a completely new discussion.

The light and happy mood quickly changed as the three children saw their school in the distance. Outside of school, they might have had awesome powers and gifts. But in school, they were just Pen, Sheila, and Snapper. They sighed as they neared the entrance.

Pen and Snapper arrived first at school. Sheila lagged a little behind. "Do we have to go to school today?" Sheila asked mournfully.

"Unfortunately, we do," replied Snapper sadly.

Ever since they had returned to school, they had been made fun of and tormented mercilessly. Word had somehow gotten into the school that Pen, Sheila, and Snapper had lived temporarily in the city's mental institution. Ever since that day, life had become a nightmare for the three of them.

As they entered the school yard, one of the boys approached Pen. Bumping into him, Pen's books dropped on the dirty pavement. Pen stooped down to pick them up.

"Hey dude. Take your meds today?" the boy scoffed sarcastically. The whole school yard erupted into laughter. "What should we call you guys anyway? The freak show?"

Snapper walked over to Pen. "Leave my brother alone, you bullies," she hissed at the group of children, who were clearly amused by the three of them. Putting her hand on Pen's shoulder, she pulled at his jacket lightly for him to come with them. "Let's just leave them, Pen. They're obviously immature," Snapper continued. "You know, in psychology books, I have read about the effects of insecurity and immaturity. One of the ways that you can always detect whether or not someone is immature is if they . . ."

"Is if they what?" demanded one of the girls standing close to the three of them.

"Come on, Snapper. How *do* immature people act?" she taunted Snapper, trying to get Snapper upset.

Sheila grabbed Snapper by the arm. "Ummm, Snapper, this is not exactly the time to spit out encyclopedic knowledge. Let's go."

Snapper looked at Sheila. "Sorry. I guess you're right. But you know," she continued, "they really do fit the profile of immature people. They can't really help the fact that they haven't mentally grown to the appropriate level of their age range."

Giggling, the three children walked across the school yard toward the double doors. They were early as usual. Tameka always made sure that they were right on time. After a hearty breakfast of eggs and bacon, she would send them out the door at 8:00 a.m. sharp. School didn't start until 8:30 a.m., and the children had tried again and again, in vain, to convince her that it only took fifteen minutes to walk to school. "It's better to be early than late," Tameka would reply every day.

As they approached the school entrance, three boys from Pen's class stepped in front of them, blocking their way through the doors.

The children recognized the three boys. Butch, Thane, and Brutus were the toughest kids in the school. Oddly enough, only the students knew this. All the teachers and even the principal thought these boys were well mannered. Probably the reason why the teachers were none the wiser was that no student who was ever bullied by them would ever report them in their right mind.

Brutus was the leader of the gang. Despite his age, he looked at least five or six years older. He towered over the rest of the children in his grade. His black hair was short and spiky. His dark eyes matched his evil grin. He was stocky and well built.

Thane and Butch were also tall, but thin and lanky. While Thane had long shaggy blond hair, and Butch had curly brown hair; they were both equally greasy and unkempt.

"Hey, freaks!" yelled out Brutus. "How's it going this morning? Did they let you out of the nuthouse today, or did you break free?" The other two boys started giggling. "Hmmm, and what's this in your hand, Pen?"

Grabbing his lunch box from his hand, Butch threw it to the other two. "Hey, Butch! Are you hungry?"

"No, I think I should leave it for Thane! Catch, buddy!" Thane grabbed the lunch box and dangled it in the air, just out of Pen's reach. As Pen jumped to get it, he threw it back to Butch.

"Give that back!" Pen yelled, rushing forward to reach for his lunch. Butch pushed him back, making Pen trip and stumble over a rock behind him. He landed on his elbow.

"Ouch!" said Pen, angrily.

Snapper and Sheila grabbed for his lunch box. "Give it back to him," Snapper protested, "or we'll tell the teacher."

"Oh no!" mocked Butch and Thane. They sneered. "She's going to tell the teacher on us!" Laughing, Brutus took the lunch box. "Okay, okay. Let's give him his lunch back, boys. We don't want to get into trouble or anything."

Holding it open, he tipped it slightly, just enough to let all of the food fall to the ground. Pen's apple rolled across the cement. Stepping forward, all three boys stepped on to the lunch. The apple split open, and the juice ran out under Brutus's foot. The liquid oozed from his juice box under his other foot. Thane and Butch stomped on the hamburger that Tameka had packed for him that morning. Opening the sandwich and kicking sand on to the meat patty, the boys picked up the hamburger, apple, and juice box. They placed those inside the lunch box and handed it back to Pen.

At this point, Pen was angry. He had just realized how hungry he was. Pen was always hungry. Looking down at his lunch box, Pen could feel his hot blood rising. He swung at Brutus. Brutus grabbed Pen's arm and once again pushed him backward.

Pen had to muster every ounce of self-control not to turn into a panther at that very moment. He fought the urge and forced his claws to retract back deep into his fingertips. Snapper saw his eyes change for a split second.

"Don't!" warned Snapper quickly under her breath.

"Don't what?" sneered Butch. He had obviously not noticed the slight change in Pen.

Snapper and Sheila screamed at the boys, "You bullies! Stop hurting our brother!"

Laughing uncontrollably now, Thane patted Pen on the shoulder. "Well, now you can't say that we didn't give you your lunch back, pal."

Still laughing, the boys opened the doors and walked inside the school. Sheila and Snapper put their arms around Pen.

"I'm so sorry, Pen," said Sheila. "They are nothing but bullies."

"We'll both share our lunches with you," Snapper added. "You know, I'm not that hungry anyway," she lied, feeling her stomach start to grumble. "Here, Pen." The two girls emptied their lunches into Pen's lunch box after taking out the dirty and stepped-on food inside. Let's go inside and tell a teacher what happened."

As they entered the school, Mr. Farkwart, the principal, was walking into his office. Their principal was a middle-aged man who wore thick black-framed glasses. His thin oily brown hair was combed over to the side in an attempt to conceal his balding head. What hair he lacked on top of his head was made up for by bushy eyebrows, which curled over the rims of his eyeglasses. A pencil-like mustache traced just over his thin pursed lips always made him seem to have an ill-humored disposition.

Pen tried to avoid staring at the large sweat stains that spread out under the armpits of Mr. Farkwart's long-sleeved buttoned-down white shirt. Lowering his eyes, Pen got an equally disturbing view of the small white buttons stretched almost at snapping point from the center of where a rather large stomach protruded. The cotton shirt could barely contain the enormous gut. Inevitably, around the center, where the buttons barely held on, there were gaps between the buttons. These gaps exposed glimpses of thick curly brown chest and stomach hair.

Suppressing the urge to gag, Pen finally decided that the only safe place to look at was the ground. Feeling agitated, Mr. Farkwart gingerly positioned his navy blue, pin-striped tie just over the bulge.

"Mr. Farkwart!" called out Snapper. "Butch, Thane, and Brutus just came and dumped out Pen's lunch. They smashed it and pushed Pen over!"

"Children," replied the principal. "Those three boys just came into my office to talk to me. They told me that you might come and tell on them. They said that they accidentally bumped into Pen, and he fell down. When he fell down, his lunch box opened and he fell on his own lunch. They're concerned because they say that you're always telling on them and making up stories. Do your parents know what's happening? The boys said that they feel sorry for you. Do you have any medication that you should be taking every day, Pen? Have you taken anything today yet?"

Pen clenched his teeth. He fought back against the frustration that was inside of him. Sheila wanted to go over and tell the principal off, but she knew that they'd really be in trouble then.

"You have to get this lying under control, Pen, or we're going to have a problem here. Do you understand, young man? We all understand perfectly well that you have had to spend time in an institution. We are trying to work with you the best way that we can. But we can't have you blaming other children, and telling on them for things that they have not done."

Pen narrowed his eyes but controlled his rage.

"Yes sir," Pen replied.

Snapper and Sheila were furious.

"Now are we going to have any more trouble around here, Pen?" demanded the principal.

"No, sir," answered Pen, still clenching his fists deep in his pockets.

"Then, that will be all," stated Mr. Farkwart. "You may leave my office now."

Without a word, the three children left and headed to class. "I hate Mr. Fart!" grumbled Sheila, under her breath. Snapper giggled nervously. "Don't say things like that, Sheila!" Snapper insisted. "We'll get into trouble if someone hears us! We're already not popular. Let's not make it worse for ourselves."

Pen walked to his classroom, while Snapper and Sheila headed to their class.

"What a fart face!" Sheila whispered to Snapper.

"We'll just have to go home and tell Tameka and Hamza what happened," stated Snapper, diplomatically. "They will have a solution to this, I'm sure." With that, the two girls walked into their classrooms.

CHAPTER FOUR

An Unexpected Whirlwind

"I'd like to beat up those boys!" whispered Sheila to Snapper. She had leaned across the aisle to where Snapper was sitting.

"Me too," seethed Snapper, leaning toward Sheila's desk as well, so that their heads were almost touching.

"Mom and Dad say that we are not allowed to use our powers at all here at school, but I'd love to send some wind at their butts. When I am finished with them, they'll be sorry," snarled Sheila.

"Hey, we're not allowed to use our powers here, remember, Sheila?" reminded Snapper. "Don't you think that I'd love to light their butts on fire? I can see them now, running in circles, trying to put the flames out!" Snapper laughed out loud at the image in her mind.

"Snapper and Sheila!" the voice of Mrs. Nastiel, the teacher, suddenly echoed throughout the class. "I have had enough of the two of you disturbing my class. I am giving you one more warning, girls!"

"Yes, Mrs. Nastiel," Sheila and Snapper responded in unison. The boys and girls sitting near Sheila and Snapper let out snickers of laughter.

Much like their principal, Mrs. Nastiel was rather plump and had a mustache, although not as well groomed as their principal or intended, Sheila presumed. She had a very round face, small squinted eyes, and a short puggish nose. Her shiny black hair was cut in the shape of an upside down bowl and looked a little too lacquered and plastic. The beige dress that was draped over her like a blanket made her figure look quite remarkably like a gigantic mushroom.

Snapper always squirmed involuntarily whenever Mrs. Nastiel came within a foot or so of her. Her hearing could keenly detect the high-pitched squeak of her teacher's tasseled leather loafers. As she moved, a vile, sour scent of foot fungus wafted from her shoes. Every day, she lathered her feet with astringent-smelling creams. "Snapper, why didn't you eat all of your lunch?" Tameka would inquire daily. "You know that there is barely enough meat on your bones as it is! Do you not like what I'm packing for you to eat?"

"My teacher, Mrs. Nastiel, always takes off her shoes when she supervises our lunch," explained Snapper. "She thinks that I can't see or smell what she is doing. She tries to hide them inconspicuously under her desk. Then she takes off her shoes to massage those bunions of hers." Holding her nose, Snapper continued. "The smell and sound of the fungus flaking off under her fingernails always makes my stomach turn, and I lose my appetite. I'm telling the truth."

"Now Snapper," Tameka would urge kindly, "you have to be tolerant of all types of odors, no matter how sharp your sense of smell is. She can't help it, you know," her mom would say.

"Yes, Mom," Snapper would reply obediently. But day after day, Snapper would return with her lunch only half eaten no matter what her mom would pack.

"Hey Snapper!" whispered Brutus, a few desks away from hers. "Do you think that Pen will have enough to eat today?"

"It's not funny!" snapped Snapper, angrily. "You boys had no right to squash Pen's lunch today!"

Mrs. Nastiel whirled around at glared at Snapper. She took pride in being in control of her class at all times. Snapper and Sheila had clearly disobeyed her rules and would pay for it.

"Well, well!" interjected Mrs. Nastiel. "It looks like you two girls are having trouble following the rules. Maybe you will find it easier to follow them from the back of the class!"

Snapper looked up at Mrs. Nastiel. "But Mrs. Nastiel, Brutus was teasing me about my brother."

"Me?" said Brutus, pretending to be all innocent. "Mrs. Nastiel, I would never do a thing like that. Why, I was listening to what you had to say. It was very interesting."

Mrs. Nastiel looked over at Brutus. She had a soft spot for him. He was one of her class pets who could do no wrong. "Oh, Brutus–don't worry, dear. I know that you would never do a thing like that. Sheila and Snapper have a habit of lying, don't you, girls!"

Snapper looked up at Mrs. Nastiel, her feelings hurt. "No, Mrs. Nastiel, I wasn't lying."

"Sheila and Snapper–I think that I asked you once before to go to the back of the classroom. If I have to ask you again, you will be spending the rest of the day in the principal's office."

Snapper and Sheila got up from their desks and headed to the back of the room. Snapper sat down softly on her seat. She was mortified that the teacher had thought that she was a liar. She felt terrible. She tried not to let her emotions get the better of her and held her tears back.

Sheila plunked herself down on a chair in the other corner of the room. "This is so stupid," she huffed under her breath.

"I'm sorry, did you have something else to say?" the teacher asked Sheila sarcastically. Snapper caught Sheila's eye, warning her to behave. Sheila sat up straight.

"No, I don't have anything to say for the moment." Sheila was seething. "But I'd like to see you spin in a hurricane," she whispered under her breath. Snapper, who had excellent ears because she was a deer, glared at Sheila.

"Stop it!" she mouthed to her. "You're going to get us both in trouble!"

"I'm sorry, Sheila, did you just say something else?" Mrs. Nastiel's voice suddenly startled them. "I thought that I heard something about spinning . . ."

Snapper's mouth dropped. *Mrs. Nastiel must have deer in her blood as well,* she thought. Sheila shook her head frantically, although she had meant what she said and wanted to spin her stupid wig off her head, and fling it around in a tornado.

"No!" answered Sheila defiantly. "I merely said that I like to spin."

The two glared at each other. Mrs. Nastiel was angry now. "That little brat," Mrs. Nastiel thought. She would think of a way to teach her a lesson.

"The problem with you two, actually three, kids in the school is that you're all from a mental institution. That makes all three of you a bit, well, different from the rest of us." A nasty, sarcastic grin crept on to Mrs. Nastiel's face. "What do you think of her, kids? If anyone has any suggestions for how we can help Sheila behave, please raise your hands!"

Tommy put up his hand immediately. He was a bit plump but was definitely more than just a bit of a bully. He reminded Sheila of one of those kids in a sausage ad. He had a little bit of a lisp when he spoke, and spit would always form in the corner of his mouth when he talked. It was very unwise to make him talk too much. When the corner of his mouth became too full from the saliva, strings of spit would fly out with every word that he spoke. Words with lots of vowels were the worst. You could most certainly expect a more concentrated spray of spit.

Sheila tried to slip a bib into his desk one day before school started, but Snapper had unfortunately intervened just before he walked in. Snapper was always worried about Sheila. She had a habit of drawing too much attention to herself. Sheila rarely cared.

"I think that we should ask them to leave our school," Tommy piped up. "After all, this isn't a loony bin. Those kids are crazy, you know!" The rest of the class exploded into laughter.

"Oh dear, don't say such things, Tommy," Mrs. Nastiel continued, pretending to scold him. "However, he does have a point, doesn't he, Sheila?"

Sheila glared back at Mrs. Nastiel. Her face was bright red now, but Sheila fought back furiously against any angry tears daring to make their way down her face. She grit her teeth, hating Mrs. Nastiel more than ever.

"Does anyone else have any suggestions that they would like to add?"

Jennifer put up her hand. She was timid and didn't speak much. "I think that Sheila and Snapper are both very nice," she said quietly. "I think that we should give them a chance." The rest of the class exploded once more into laughter.

Tommy put up his hand again and blurted out his thoughts before Mrs. Nastiel could even invite him to speak. "Sheila and Snapper are both stupid students, and they should leave our school now!" The class cheered. "Even Pen is retarded. They dress like they're retarded, they act like they're retarded. They're just retarded."

"Now, now," continued Mrs. Nastiel. "That's not very nice, Tommy. We have to try to be kind to our classmates, even if they're a bit strange. Now Sheila and Snapper and Pen, of course, are all a little strange. However, hopefully, they will learn from hearing their classmates' opinions. Right, Sheila?"

Sheila glared back at the teacher, unable to say a word.

"It isn't your fault if you and your family are a bit strange," continued Mrs. Nastiel. Once again, the students began to snicker in the classroom.

"Don't talk about my sister and brother that way!" Sheila suddenly blurted out. "You guys are all a bunch of bullies!"

Mrs. Nastiel turned and looked at Sheila. "I thought I had told you to sit quietly."

"Maybe they don't understand English," giggled Prisa, one of the girls sitting near the front of the class. "How did they talk to you in the mental institution? In animal talk?"

"Yah! Once crazy, always crazy!" chimed in Tommy. His classmates ducked for cover. They were used to the sprays of spit that would fly when he spoke. Tommy enjoyed bullying other students in the class. He loved seeing his peers become uncomfortable. He was most pleased when he sees another student actually cry.

"Well, we're trying to help you become normal, Sheila and Snapper." Mrs. Nastiel smiled. "However, I don't know if we'll succeed," she added.

"Yah! Maybe you guys are too messed up that we can't help you!" chimed in Tommy again.

Longer sentences were worse. Students grabbed their textbooks and used them as shields from the white spray.

Sheila glared back at Mrs. Nastiel in rage. She was so angry now that she was shaking, and her eyes were red because she was holding back her tears so fiercely.

A sudden gust of wind blew outside the window. It picked up leaves and twigs, flinging them around and around in circles in the air.

"That's strange!" exclaimed the teacher, suddenly shifting her attention from Sheila to the rising storm just outside their window. "I don't recall the weather man predicting a windstorm today!"

The students watched in amazement and then in horror as the wind picked up more and more speed and suddenly came crashing against the window.

"Oh dear!" shouted Mrs. Nastiel. "Everybody get under your desks."

Everybody rushed to get down on the floor, except for Sheila. Her eyes glistened as she controlled the wind's movement with her mind.

The windows rattled against the pressure of the wind. Mrs. Nastiel rushed over to the phone to call the principal's office. As she began to run toward the intercom, the wind suddenly sent a large branch smashing through the glass, sending pieces of the window flying everywhere. The wind picked up Mrs. Nastiel. Wide-eyed, she screeched, flailing her arms and legs in the air. Thankfully, she was wearing her long frilly pink panties because her dress was lifted over her head, and her wig was rotating violently beside her. Around and around she went, hitting the ceiling again and again.

Tommy started to giggle nervously at the strange sight in front of him. The more he giggled, the more drool leapt from the corner of his mouth. Without warning, the wind whooshed under his desk where he was hiding, picked him up by his feet, no less, and dangled him beside Mrs. Nastiel. He looked absolutely ridiculous and hilarious. His shirt was draped down over his face, and the wind was holding him upside down.

Mrs. Nastiel and Tommy were swung in circles, both of them flailing their arms and screaming. Around and around they went, hollering as loud as they could. Mrs. Nastiel was hanging upside down with her dress over her head, swinging her legs violently. Tommy was right beside her with his shirt over his face and his legs thrashing wildly in the air.

Gradually, the wind became a bit more forceful, and Tommy's pants ripped at the back, slipped down his legs, and fell on to the floor in a tiny heap. Bright yellow boxers with purple dinosaurs bearing the message *You're a big boy now!* in gold letters peered out at everyone. The class, although terribly afraid, started to laugh hysterically.

"Hey, look at Tommy's boxers!" shouted Chris, one of the boys who normally sat at the back of the class. "Aren't you a little old for dinosaur boxers?" The class exploded once more into fits of laughter.

Prisa, a tall red-haired girl, ran to the door, around the tornado, to try to open the door, but a gust of wind slammed against it. No matter how hard she tried, she could not open the door.

Snapper glared furiously at Sheila, trying to get her attention. Sheila, however, was having too much fun to notice Snapper. She was giggling to the point that she could barely breathe.

Finally, Snapper ran over to her and hit her arm hard. "Hey, what did you do that for?" responded Sheila angrily.

"You stop that this instant!" glared Snapper. "This is not funny, Sheila!"

"I think it's kind of funny," laughed Sheila. "Who knew that Tommy wore dinosaur boxers?"

"Sheila, I'm warning you!" threatened Snapper. "If you don't stop now, I'm going to call Mom."

"Oh my gosh. You're such a party pooper, Snapper!" whispered Sheila emphatically. "I'm just having a bit of fun!"

Tommy and Mrs. Nastiel suddenly crashed down on to the ground in one heap, leaves and twigs falling down on top of them. Mrs. Nastiel lay on the floor, her dress still over her balding head and her bum high in the air. Tommy lay crumpled over the desk. His teacher's black wig had landed mysteriously on top of his head. Helplessly, he lay in front of everyone with the words *You're a big boy now!* written boldly across his bum. It was a hilarious sight.

"There," sputtered Sheila angrily at Snapper, who was still glaring at her with her hands on her hips. "Are you happy now?"

Sheila pretended to sneeze. "Ahchoo!" Just as she brought her hand to her mouth, she faked a shocked expression when another gust of wind picked up Mrs. Nastiel's black wig and Tommy's ripped pants. It whisked them out through the window and placed them on top of the flag pole. Sheila snickered once more. Tears were running down her cheeks now, but not tears of sadness. It was the funniest sight that she had seen in a long time. Of course, Snapper was furious that Sheila had used her powers. However, the sight of Tommy's pants and Mrs. Nastiel's wig hanging from the Canadian flag was unbearably funny.

The 3:30 p.m. bell sounded not too long after the incident. Snapper and Sheila waited outside Pen's classroom until he had finished his work and put his books away.

Pen, Sheila, and Snapper opened the school door and headed across the school yard to go home.

"What in the world happened in your classroom today?" inquired Pen, wide-eyed. "We heard that a windstorm hit only your classroom. We had a lockdown for a few hours." Looking at Sheila suspiciously, Pen began "You didn't, right, Sheila? I mean, you wouldn't, right?"

Sheila didn't answer. She just smiled.

CHAPTER FIVE

Out of Control

There was silence at the dinner table as they ate. Snapper had her eyes fixed on her plate of fish and corn, nervous to look up, even for an instant. Pen liked to fidget when he was uncomfortable. His plan was to cut his fish into smaller and even smaller equal cubes until his plate of food looked like some sort of video game maze. Staring up from the table directly at her parents, Sheila was definitely the most brazen of the three children. After all, what did she have to be ashamed of? Why did she have to defend herself? Her cheeks flashed hot.

After what seemed an endless amount of awkward silence, Tameka, the matriarch of the family, finally spoke.

"So how was your day at school today, kids?" she asked. "Did anything new happen?"

Pen squirmed. Snapper stared harder at her plate. Sheila knew what it meant when her parents asked those two questions together. They were trying to offer them a chance to tell the truth—a way to clear their guilty conscience.

Sheila was stubborn and unremorseful. "No, not really," she replied, pretending to be absentminded.

Snapper shot Sheila a look that said "tell them please and let it be over and done with!"

Undaunted by Sheila's lackadaisical attitude, Tameka tried to bait her in the conversation. "So we heard there was an unprecedented windstorm that just targeted one classroom in the whole school,

Sheila . . . Yours! Very bizarre, wouldn't you agree?" Tameka looked at Sheila, waiting for an answer.

"Not mine!" Pen piped up, hoping to avoid any incrimination.

"I would agree," Sheila chimed in, feigning shock. "Very strange, Mom!"

Unable to keep silent anymore, Snapper caved. "Come on Sheila, they know. Let's just admit it!"

"Thanks a lot," snarled Sheila angrily at Snapper.

Glaring at Tameka and Hamza, Sheila blurted out sarcastically, "What did you expect us to do? Do you have any idea how we are treated at school?"

"Well, no, we don't," Tameka answered. "How can we know if you don't tell us?"

"Well, we are bullied from the minute we step into the school," Sheila continued, feeling her temper rising. "No, better yet, from the moment we step into the school yard!"

Sheila's chest was hurting as she stubbornly fought back tears. She slammed her fist on the table. The plates and glasses rattled violently.

"Sheila!" Hamza shouted at her. "Watch your tone of voice."

"And control your temper!" Tameka chimed in.

"Calm down, Sheila," Snapper said, nervously. Pen just stared at her, shocked.

"Did you know that Pen had his lunch taken by a gang of boys and had it crushed and tossed into the sand? Did you know that when we told the principal, he took the bullies' side?" Sheila was shouting loudly now. "Did you know that when we got to class, Mrs. Nastiel told us that we were a bunch of freaks that belonged in a mental hospital? We have been made fun of every day!"

Sheila was yelling now. Pen and Snapper stared at her with their mouths open. Tameka sat quietly, listening, with a pained look on her face. She had no idea that the other children were being so cruel to them. Hamza's face was becoming angrier by the moment as he heard the news of what was happening at their school.

"What is the use of having magical powers if we can't even use them to defend ourselves?" Sheila yelled as loud as she could.

Sheila's tears, though she tried as hard as she could to fight them, began to run down her face. Embarrassed, she wiped them away as quickly as she could with the back of her sleeve.

"They did what?" Hamza growled, rising to his feet, with his fists clenched.

"Calm down, Sheila," replied Tameka softly. She beckoned Hamza to sit back down. Hamza sat back down at the table, his eyes furious.

"I don't know why you've waited until now to tell us what has been going on, Sheila," Tameka continued. "What you did, however, is not the solution. Just because you have been given special abilities and powers does not mean that you are given the license to misuse them."

"What did you expect us to do?" Sheila blurted out. "Sit there and take it?"

"No, I'm not suggesting that," Tameka said, "but if you had told us sooner, we could have come to the school and talked to your teacher and to your principal. Remember the witch Kalik, Sheila? She had power and she used it for her own benefit and look what she became. Hamza and I want to protect you from making the same mistakes."

"By sending us to a school where we'd be treated like freaks and bullied every day?" cried Sheila.

"Sheila, Snapper, and Pen, you are all my children, and it is your father's and my job to protect you as your parents," reassured Tameka.

"But you are not our parents," scoffed Sheila.

"Sheila!" cried Snapper in shock. "How can you say that to our mom and dad?"

"But they are not our real mom and dad!" retorted Sheila angrily. "Are you blind, Snapper? Only Pen looks remotely like them. He's black and we're not. That's another reason why we are being made fun of over at school! Any fool can see we are adopted."

Tameka lowered her head. The words Sheila spoke seemed like they had gone straight to her heart like knives. Hamza leapt out of his chair and put his arms around his wife. He knew that the look on her face meant that she had been hurt by it beyond anything else that Sheila could have said.

"Sheila, you are out of line!" Hamza's voice was stern and low. It was the tone of voice you did not question. "You need to go to your room until you apologize to your mother and me."

"Fine!" Sheila yelled insolently. "I had a real mom once! It wasn't you!"

Snapper and Pen stared at Sheila, speechless.

"How dare you say that, Sheila!" Pen reprimanded her. "That is so mean! We are so lucky to have Hamza and Tameka as parents!"

Sheila ran up the stairs to her room. Snapper tried to follow her and calm her down. Before she could make it to the top of the stairs, however, Sheila had slammed the door shut.

Grabbing the books off her shelf, Sheila hurled and smashed them against the wall. Wild with rage, she reached for her jewelry box. She was just about to smash it on to the ground in a million pieces when she heard her dad's voice.

"Sheila!" called out Hamza. "You stop that this instant, young lady!"

Shaking with fury, Sheila managed to put it back down on the dresser. Opening her window, she morphed into a raven and dove outside.

Sheila flew through the air at top speeds. Her anger fueled her wings. They beat faster and faster. She whizzed past trees. She rushed by the hills and mountains beneath her. Other birds got out of the way, wondering where the demon bird had come from. Even an eagle decided to make for cover as Sheila hurtled past him through the sky. Finally, about three or four towns over, Sheila landed. She perched on top of an old oak tree, completely out of breath. Wheezing and panting, she looked around her. How far had she flown? Where in the world was she?

Jumping in the air once more, she hovered until she spotted her town, miles and miles away in the distance. Taking a deep breath, Sheila started for home. Before long, she flew through her bedroom window. Morphing back into her human self, she collapsed on to her bed, utterly exhausted. Within seconds, she was snoring soundly.

Wind fluttered through the curtains of Sheila's bedroom window. She stirred. Outside, the stars sparkled against the night sky. She shivered at the cool breeze. She didn't want to turn on her light. How long had she slept? Was it already nighttime? Getting out of bed, she walked softly over to her window. She felt the coolness of the wooden floorboards against her bare feet. Gazing dreamily at the moon and stars above her, she yawned and stretched out her arms.

Just then, out of the corner of her eye, Sheila saw something giving off a faint glowing light. Startled, she turned around. On her dresser, her jewelry box was radiating a pulsing, soft, warm light.

Curious, she walked over to investigate. Prying the box open, she found the necklace that the druid had given her. Peering more intensely now, she noticed that the source of the glowing light was the mirror at the end of her necklace. Scooping up the sapphire chain, she walked once more to her window ledge.

What she saw next gave her such an enormous fright that she dropped the necklace and jumped back. Dazed now, and not quite sure what she had seen, she grabbed the necklace again from the ledge and peered again into the shimmering glass. Sure enough, the image she saw staring back at her was Raven. She knew now that she wasn't dreaming.

Even though Sheila herself was a raven, the raven staring back at her in the glass was unmistakably different. That intense look of power, nobility, and strength set him apart. Raven was the ruler of the land where all humans had the ability to shape-shift into animals. He was no one's equal.

When Sheila first met Raven, she was terrified. But over time, she grew to love him. And the fear turned to respect. Raven had been the one who had given her and her brother and sister the power to turn into their animal forms. Through him, she had earned her gift to control the wind. Raven had also given her sister, Snapper, the power over fire, and her brother Pen, the control over water. Now here she was again, staring into his face in the tiny mirror, only this time his eyes were stern.

Without warning, the necklace flew up out of her hand. It suspended itself just above her. Blue mist poured out of the mirror. It darkened. First into indigo. Then into black, just like the night sky. The black smoke transformed into huge, black wings. Then slowly, they swept into an inky, black cloak.

It was Raven, in his male form. His giant figure almost took up her entire bedroom. His head was only inches under the ceiling. His long, silky black hair was gathered into one single braid that hung down his back.

To her, Raven looked like an Aboriginal chief. His mocha, reddish skin and high cheekbones were lined with black and red warrior paint. Raven feathers clung to his hair.

"Sheila!" his voice rumbled. "You have shamed me today. First of all, you deliberately did the one thing I commanded you not to do. You abused your power in the classroom. Secondly, you went to the very people I love and highly esteem, and you dishonored them. Your stepmother was cruel to you. I gave you the greatest mother of all. I gave you the gift of a new family."

"Now listen well, Sheila," Raven continued. Sheila froze. She didn't dare to speak or interrupt. "This is your consequence. Until you can represent me with honor and dignity, I am withdrawing my gifts."

"But, but . . .," pleaded Sheila desperately.

"Silence!" Raven commanded.

Sheila froze again.

"The other part of your consequence is that Hamza will decide if or when you will regain your powers. Remember, Sheila—these were privileges—not rights."

Without another word, Raven disappeared into the mist.

With that, the mirror's light went out, and all Sheila saw was her own reflection staring back at her.

All at once, Sheila heard a knock coming from the outside of her bedroom door. Jumping up from the floor, Sheila slipped the necklace into her pocket and quickly pulled the door open.

"What's going on in there?" asked Pen suspiciously.

"Come in," gestured Sheila, wiping her eyes.

"No way, you're crazy today!" muttered Pen. "What the heck is wrong with you anyway?"

"Are you going to yell at us like you did to Mom and Dad?" asked Snapper hesitantly. "And are you going to tell us that we're not your brother and sister either?" she demanded sarcastically.

"No, I'm so sorry," whimpered Sheila.

"Yah, I don't think that we are the ones you need to say sorry to," said Pen angrily.

"You're right," said Sheila feeling sheepish. "Where are Mom and Dad?"

"Downstairs in the family room," offered Pen reluctantly. "Are you sure that you are not going to bite their heads off again?" muttered Pen.

"No, believe me, I'm not," Sheila said. "Just please come with me."

Pen looked at Sheila suspiciously but followed her anyway.

Downstairs in the family room, Hamza had his arms wrapped around Tameka as she lay quietly beside him. Sheila slowly and quietly opened the door and peeked in sheepishly. Tameka looked up. Running, Sheila grabbed Tameka's hands and rested her head on her shoulder.

Between tears, she spoke. "I'm so sorry, Mom. I never meant to hurt you. I know you love me. I just got angry and scared."

Immediately Sheila felt Tameka's warm hand rubbing her back tenderly. "It's okay, sweetheart. I know you had a tough day at school. But you hurt me very badly. You hurt both of us very badly."

Hamza slowly raised his head. Although he was in his human form, his yellow panther eyes met Sheila's, and his voice growled deeply. "You may have had a hard day, but it's not okay to talk to your mom like that," he said, his voice stern and rumbling. "Do you understand, Sheila?"

Sheila nodded quietly. She knew that Hamza was upset. His deep voice sounded closer to a panther's warning growl right now. She knew what that meant. Hamza was deeply protective of Tameka. He would never let anyone hurt her—not even his own daughter. Hamza was clearly the alpha of this clan. Although Sheila was not a panther, she knew that this was a cue to submit. She hung her head.

"Your father and I are going to march into that school first thing tomorrow to sort out that bullying nonsense!" Tameka continued.

Hamza nodded slowly. Opening his arms, they embraced. Hamza's yellow panther eyes slowly faded back into his human dark-colored eyes. Pen and Snapper, standing close by, sighed a sigh of relief. It seemed that this ordeal was finally over. Sheila started to giggle and hugged Tameka again.

After hearing her story about her encounter with Raven, Hamza spoke. "My decision is that we will let you know when you have regained the privilege to have your powers. You need to prove to us that you can respect what Raven has given to you."

Submissively, Sheila nodded. She knew she had a lot of making up to do.

CHAPTER SIX

Calm Before the Storm

Tameka had a restless night. All night, she tossed and turned. Eventually sleep found her, and she was able to drift off for just a few minutes.

The sound of creaking jolted her out of her short sleep. Staring up in disbelief, she saw her beloved husband standing at the foot of their bed, bending his knees and rocking back and forth, ready to launch. It finally occurred to her from his drunken-looking sway that he was sleepwalking. Before the words "What on earth are you doing?" could escape her mouth, Hamza had already dismounted in perfect diving form and had landed with his claws embedded onto the bathroom door.

He was oddly still half in human form, with only his fangs, eyes, and claws that had changed. Speechless, Tameka watched as her favorite fluffy pink bathrobe that had hung on the door just moments before was shredded into tiny pieces in his mouth.

"Hamza," she finally yelled, "Wake up!" Startled by the familiar sound, Hamza retracted his claws and fell backward into the hamper of dirty clothes lying beneath him. Still clutching the fluffy pink bathrobe in his mouth, he looked dreamily at his wife whose eyes were now as wide as saucers. He opened his mouth awkwardly, and the bathrobe, which now looked more like a tattered wet handkerchief, drifted wistfully to the floor in a sad pile of pink slobber, string, and fluff. Clumsily lumbering out of the hamper and leaving a trail of tangled clothes behind him, Hamza made his way to the bed. "Well, Hamza, thank you for protecting me." Tameka sighed. "I always had suspicions of that bathrobe's ill intentions."

Wiping the pink fluff from the corner of his mouth, Hamza nodded playfully.

"Well I have eliminated the threat with my sheer and awesome power," he said as he yawned. "That bathrobe didn't stand a chance. Now you can get some sleep." Grinning, Tameka rolled her eyes and sat up beside him.

Resting her head on his shoulder, she sighed. "I don't understand, Hamza. I just don't understand. What is so wrong with our children that they are being made fun of in this way at school?"

Hamza put his arm around her reassuringly. "We faced a lot of difficulties back home, with Kalik, and everything that happened."

"But, Hamza, we have never ever heard of problems like these. Sure, fights broke out, as they do everywhere. But bullying at school . . . I didn't even know what that meant before we . . ." Tameka's voice faded away.

Hamza shook his head slowly. "I don't understand it either, honey." Hamza sighed.

"In any case," Tameka continued, "I'm going to go to the school tomorrow to speak with the principal about the way the children are being treated. Oh Hamza! My heart broke when the girls told me what happened to Pen. And when I brought it up to him, he just didn't want to talk about it. I've never seen him so down."

Once again, Hamza shook his head, unable to say a word. "And they're making fun of our children because they were admitted to an institution . . . for tragedies in their lives that they had no control over!"

Tameka's voice rose in anger again. "I don't get it! I just don't get it! If one of the children in any of our clans had lost his or her parents, all of the clans, or at least the members from that clan, would come together to help that child. Remember the time when Nbuka, the daughter of Nbelle from the deer clan, fell and broke her leg?"

Hamza shook his head, trying to remember what had happened.

"Oh, honey, don't you remember?" Tameka continued. "She had such a bad fall that she was knocked unconscious and lost part of her memory for a while."

Hamza nodded, suddenly remembering the incident.

"All of the children in the deer clan, including children from our own clan, helped her to and from school every day," Tameka reminded him.

Hamza smiled. "Yes," he added, "and remember the children took turns carrying her everywhere. There were fights that broke out because everyone wanted a turn to carry Nbuka and carry her books for her."

Tameka and Hamza smiled at the memory. Tameka sighed again. "Hamza, it's such a different world here. I don't know how to raise our kids in this kind of environment. I don't want them to ever become like the bullies in school, but neither do I want them to be hurt by the bullies."

The very word, *bully*, sounded so strange to Tameka. She wondered how these antagonistic children got that name.

"I still don't understand the word bullies," wondered Tameka out loud. "It just doesn't make sense. If that's a word for young bulls, then they don't know the animal kingdom very well, Hamza. A grown male alpha bull would never act that way. And if bully means a young bull, then they don't understand that young bulls don't act like that either." Hamza nodded.

"In fact, they don't seem to understand the animal kingdom at all, Hamza," Tameka continued, her voice rising again. "It's like the animal and human world have somehow completely broken off into separate kingdoms here. It's so strange. Why, just yesterday, a black bird flew to the top of a large oak tree, where quite a few women were standing. The bird cried out a warning call that a storm was going to approach. Hamza, they just stood there, continued to speak, and completely ignored the bird! I felt so bad. How incredibly rude and insensitive! I nodded at the bird and mouthed a thank you to him so that his feelings wouldn't be hurt. It was as if they didn't understand what he was trying to tell them. But how can this be, Hamza? How can animals and humans live together, I mean in the same home sometimes, and not be able to understand each other?"

Hamza shook his head again, at a loss for words. "I've tried to think it through myself, Tameka," Hamza finally said. "I've talked to Pen about it. I explained to him that an alpha hierarchy and a bully are two totally different things. We talked about my brother-in-law, Njata, and our relationship back home. Even though Njata was the alpha male in our clan, we respected each other deeply. Njata never once put me down. In fact, if he had ever done such a thing, it would have proven the opposite to everyone in our clan—that he was definitely *not* an alpha male."

Hamza paused for a second and then continued. "I think that Pen realizes that there is a big difference between the two. An alpha male never tries to ridicule another clan member. He just merely establishes his authority and demands respect because he has a responsibility to the rest of his clan. I don't want Pen to ever fight unnecessarily or ridicule anyone, Tameka. But on the other hand, I don't want him to be a victim of abuse. It's just really hard for me to decide how to advise him to handle this."

Tameka nodded, weary and exhausted from the long worrisome night. "Well," Tameka said warily, "whether I understand this strange society or not, these bull calves, or *bullites*, or whatever they're called, have got to stop hurting my son."

"Bullies!" corrected Hamza. "They're called bullies. Honey, please don't call them bull calves or bullites today when you talk to the principal. We need to try to learn their lingo as best as we can." Taking Tameka gently in his arms, he pulled her close to him. Tameka put her head on his shoulder.

The alarm clock sounded noisily. Kissing the top of her head gently, Hamza reached over and shut it off. "I guess we didn't need the clock to wake us up this morning, did we, honey?"

Tameka smiled. The weary couple pulled themselves out of bed. Hamza headed for his morning shower, while Tameka slipped quietly downstairs to begin making breakfast for the family.

After breakfast, Hamza went off to work. The sun was hot in the open field, and it was hard work harvesting the crops. Hamza didn't mind it, though. He enjoyed the physical exercise. "I don't have to run through the forests as I used to do every day," he would say, "so a bit of physical work keeps me on my toes! That way Njata won't be completely shocked when he sees me again. Hopefully I wouldn't have lost too much muscle tone."

Pen glanced mournfully at his spaghetti-string biceps. In the mirror, when Pen flexed, his arms looked as though as though his bulge was inverted. Thankfully when he morphed into a panther, he got the animal's muscular physique. He wished he could look muscular as a human too. "Don't worry," Hamza would say. "One day, the change will happen for you too. Your voice will squeak and go up and down.

You'll grow hair all over your chest and even under your armpits. Then the muscles on your arms will magically emerge."

It didn't help his masculine self-image when his sisters were mimicking gagging sounds in the background with an eruption of squeaky giggles. His sisters were particularly annoying when they presented to their mom a drinking glass with a black, smudged mark. This they handed to Tameka along with a black eyeliner pencil. Tameka tried hard not to laugh, and her cheeks turned beet red. "Why Pen," she cooed, "How manly you look with that thick, handsome mustache. It must have grown on your face overnight. However, if you insist on growing it so long, can you maybe try to wipe it off our dishes and utensils before putting them in the sink?" Pen blushed. The girls had even uncovered tubes of miracle grow manly hair creams and hair booster vitamins under his bed.

Hamza covered for Pen and had exclaimed, "Oh, that's where I left them! Thanks, Pen."

Tameka grinned and poked her husband. "Maybe if you used a little less of the hair-grow cream, our family could buy another house with all the money we would save on razors."

Hamza laughed his deep belly laugh, which rumbled throughout the room. He then gave Pen a noogie on his head.

The three children quickly packed their books together. Pen suddenly remembered that they had volleyball practice after school and ran upstairs to get their team outfits that Tameka had washed and left to dry. Hamza had managed to persuade them that it was important to keep themselves physically fit since they could no longer change into their animal forms at will. After the children had left for school, Tameka went upstairs and got herself ready to visit the school. She had not told the children that she would be speaking to the principal that day. She and Hamza had decided that it would just add extra stress to Pen and the girls, and they didn't need that.

After fastening the buttons on her pastel purple sweater, she made her way to the school. Tameka always looked her best no matter where she went. She looked like a model, each braid neatly woven and immaculately kept in place, fastened together by a stylish ivory clasp. She looked sophisticated and elegant. Tameka was a tall, slender woman, with radiant, black skin. She walked with a confident step. As she walked, everyone stopped and stared. Though she looked businesslike in her knee-length white pencil skirt and white silk blouse, the soft click of her beige high-heeled pumps echoed in the hallway.

Greeted by the secretary, Tameka politely requested the principal to be paged immediately. Mr. Farkwart entered the office. He had on a brown-and-yellow checkered shirt, which didn't quite match the dark blue pants he was wearing. Nevertheless, he walked with an air that told everyone in the school that he was in charge of this institution. Like a captain, he controlled the school as if it were a tightly-run ship.

His dark, black-rimmed glasses were nestled on his nose, touching his thick, curly eyebrows. He sniffed into the air, just out of habit, and held up his nose when he did so. He invited Tameka to enter his private office with him and motioned for her to sit at the chair on the opposite side of his desk.

Sitting down, he moved his papers to one side, looked at his watch, and twisted the dark green strap in place. Then folding his hands together on his desk and strumming his fingers together, he looked up at Tameka over his awkwardly-placed glasses.

"Yes, ma'am," he finally began, rather abruptly. "I understand that you are here with regard to Pen, Snapper, and Sheila." Readjusting his glasses once more to the end of his nose, out of the reach of his furry eyebrows so that he could clearly see her face, he continued. "I will have you understand that we have a predicament in our school. Our students have expressed the fact that they feel rather concerned, even threatened, with the presence of your three children—but especially your son, Pen. It would appear that your son suffers from *pseudologiafantastica*, otherwise known as *mythomania*."

Tameka stared blankly at Mr. Farkwart. He continued to strum his fingers together as he talked. "Are you aware of his condition, madam?"

Tameka, with a stunned expression on her face, shook her head. She had no idea what a pseudo . . . whatever was, but she was sure that whatever it was, Pen didn't have it.

Mr. Farkwart continued. "In case you are not aware of the meaning of mythomania, madam, it is quite simply defined as compulsive lying."

Tameka was speechless. She could feel her heart beating faster and irritation rising within her. "My son is not always an angel, Sir," Tameka finally blurted out, "but he certainly does not have an issue with lying."

"Oh, madam," consoled the principal, a bit mockingly, "that's what every parent says. However, the only way that you can give your son the help that he needs is to, first of all, acknowledge his disorder yourself and then begin with the appropriate treatment in conjunction with his illness . . ."

Tameka could feel her anger rising. "Mr. Farter!" Tameka interrupted. "My son is coming home repeatedly with tears in his clothing, scuff marks on his pants, and dents in his lunch box, not to mention a destroyed lunch that he is unable to eat. My husband and I will not tolerate this kind of abusive behavior. We don't know how this type of behavior is allowed to exist in your school, but I will have you know that my son and two daughters will not be subject to this!"

Tameka was hardly breathing between words now, speaking faster and faster with every syllable, and her volume rising more and more with each word. "And as for their medical background, that is none of your business or any student's business in this school! To my knowledge, you are not qualified to give a mental diagnosis nor have I authorized my consent for you to do so! I am not sure what planet my husband and I came to when we entered your town, but my three children will *not* be made fun of for any medical condition in their past. Do you understand me, Mr. Farter?"

"Mr. Farkwart," he corrected her, hardly daring to utter a sound.

Barely noticing his slight adjustment to his name, she continued. "I will have you know that if my children are disrespected, ridiculed, or physically hurt again, my husband and I are going to take action against you, against your school, and against all of your bullites!"

Mr. Farkwart had absolutely no idea what bullites were, but he decided that he should probably not ask and refrain himself from saying another word until she was finished.

When Tameka had finally made herself very clear, Mr. Farkwart took a deep breath. He couldn't quite understand why, but something inside of him told him that he probably shouldn't mess with this lady. He couldn't put his finger on it, but something had been slightly unusual. It had almost seemed as if her eyes had changed from a beautiful deep brown color to a slightly yellowish tinge.

"Yes, Madam. We will definitely implement a strategy to ensure that your son and two daughters are safe and out of harm's way."

Standing, he reached out and shook her hand. With that, Tameka left his office, quite satisfied that they had come to a very civil and acceptable agreement.

Staring from his office window, Mr. Farkwart watched Tameka leave the school yard. Scratching his head, he took a deep breath. She was serious and meant business, and he knew it. The strange thing is that he could have sworn that he saw her eyes flicker with a deep yellowish glow.

CHAPTER SEVEN

A Fateful Day

After volleyball practice, the three children stopped briefly in the change rooms, just long enough to pick up their belongings.

"I'm so tired," muttered Sheila gloomily. "I'm not used to running like you guys, you know, not even in my animal form." Pen laughed heartily.

"It is true that panthers always seem to be running," he chuckled. "That was hard to get used to at first."

"Deer aren't exactly slow animals, either," piped up Snapper. "I had to learn to leap pretty high when we were being chased by wild animals."

"You know, you guys aren't exactly making me feel better," sputtered Sheila. "It doesn't change the fact that I'm exhausted. And every time I tried to return the ball, somebody either knocked me out of the way, or I tripped trying to reach it." She sighed. "I wonder what Tameka cooked for supper tonight."

The wind was chilly this evening. The smell of fall was in the air as they left the school yard. Pen buttoned up his jacket and pulled his scarf tighter around his neck. The sun was beginning to set behind the clouds. Hues of pink, red, and orange filled the sky, as if a painter had hurriedly swiped a large brush across the horizon. Gorgeous shades of red, orange, and yellow from the fall leaves seemed to reflect the colors in the sky, creating a picturesque landscape.

The moon sat faintly in the sky like a pale, ghostly silhouette, reminding the sun that it was time for her to take her break for the night. The fall leaves crunched under the children's feet as they made their way home.

"Did you see my serve in the last game?" exclaimed Pen. "I just blasted the ball on to the other side. Nobody was able to return any of my serves," bragged Pen. "Did you see the look on Brutus's face when he missed the ball?"

"I did pretty well myself," Snapper cut in, with a satisfied grin on her face. "I jumped up and spiked that ball back on to the other side, exactly like a deer would have done it!" The three of them laughed heartily.

"Yeah, I guess we're all pretty good at the game," nodded Pen. "We've all had lots of practice dodging Hamza in the *predator and prey* Games!"

They got to the end of the sidewalk, and the three happy children, who seemed to be more and more like blood-related siblings, turned onto their street, Seventh Street. It was a long street, and their farmhouse was the very last house on the left side. Not many houses lined the road, making for a peaceful and quiet neighborhood with lots of space in between each house. Wind swept down the street toward them, pushing them backward and seeming to try to convince them to turn around and go back to the school. The lights from the previous house on the street seemed far away now as they walked toward the flickering light in the yard of the house in the distance. Pushing against the wind, the children chatted happily about the game.

Glancing up in the direction of their home, Pen noticed a dark shape that seemed to be crouching on the side of the road. He picked up his pace a little, encouraging the girls to do the same. "There seems to be someone there," Pen whispered to the two girls. "Let's just pass by him as quickly as possible and get home for supper."

As they neared the spot where they had seen the figure squatting, Pen breathed a sigh of relief. No one was there. "It was probably just my imagination," said Pen, chuckling. "I must be seeing things."

The words had no sooner left Pen's lips when three tall boys stepped out from behind the bushes. Pen immediately recognized them from his classroom. They were the three boys who were forever tormenting him at school: Brutus, Butch, and Thane. Slowly and menacingly, they walked toward the three children. Turning to run, another group of both girls and boys approached Pen, Sheila, and Snapper from behind. With his heart pounding wildly, Pen stepped in front of his sisters.

"We're almost home," Pen said to the quickly approaching gang of kids that was beginning to surround them. "Our mom and dad are waiting for us, and my sisters are tired. If you need to talk to me, just let them go home, and I will join them later." Brutus approached Pen with a smirk on his face. "Why do you need to go home, Pen?" he asked, with a mocking sneer on his face. "After all, you eat so much lunch every day at school. Surely you're not hungry again!"

The other two boys in front of Pen snickered.

"We found out, Pen, that your mom visited our school today to protect her little baby boy!" Brutus continued. "Do you need to go home and hide behind your mommy's skirt tonight?" Pen had no idea of what they were talking about. He wondered if Tameka had really gone to the school. He couldn't be sure. Maybe they were just trying to upset him again.

"My mom didn't go to our school today," replied Pen. "She's been at home all day."

"Oh no, but she has been to our school today, guys," continued Brutus, the leader of the bullies. "And it looks like you asked her to talk to the principal to tell on us so that we could get a little detention at school today and so that he could call our moms and dads at home. You are going to be sorry for that, pretty boy," the gang leader laughed.

"Hey, Brutus!" Thane called out. "What should we do to them?"

"I haven't decided yet," Brutus replied. "But I think that we should teach them a lesson that they will never forget. After all, they should learn that tattling is a really *not cool* thing to do on your classmates."

Pen froze in horror as the words seemed to leave Brutus's mouth slowly, one at a time, as if he wanted Pen to understand every syllable before he took action. Pen immediately thought about his sisters. He had to save them. He had to protect them.

Once again, Pen spoke to the bullies, pleading with them this time, to let his sisters go. "They don't know anything about this," Pen explained to them. "Please let them go home. They are tired and have had a long day. I can stay here as long as you need me to."

"Hey, Brutus!" shouted Butch. "I know what he's doing! He's sending his sisters home so that they can tell his parents to come and save him!"

"Hmmm ..." replied Brutus, mockingly. "I never thought of that. A smart little brat, hey! Well, guys, we should teach all three of them a lesson then. That way, they'll learn to never tattle again!"

Pen grabbed Snapper and Sheila's hands and stepped back from the group, in horror. His heart was racing. He had never been so afraid in his life—not for himself—but for his sisters. What if he couldn't protect them? He quickly looked around. There were at least ten to twelve bullies that were surrounding them. He recognized some of the others from Sheila and Snapper's class as well. Tommy was there too, standing beside a group of bullies behind them.

Pen started to sweat, and he pleaded with them once more. "Please, I give you my word that they're not going home to tell my parents. We promise that we won't tell them. Just please let my sisters go home. They've had a tough day."

Snapper and Sheila stared at the approaching gang, trembling. Neither of them was able to move or to scream. Sheila dug her nails into Pen's arm, scarcely able to breathe. Pen was so terrified that he didn't even feel the pain.

Taking a quick step back, Pen pushed the girls suddenly toward the house. "Run, girls! Run!" he screamed.

Snapper and Sheila, who had been frozen in fear, now suddenly snapped back into reality. Whirling around, they flew toward the house as fast as their legs could carry them.

"After them!" yelled Brutus. "If they get away, we'll be in even more trouble!"

Tommy and two of the girls lunged at Snapper. Grabbing her hair from behind, they threw her to the ground, with Snapper flailing her arms frantically. Two other girls caught Sheila's hand and yanked her backward. Pen watched in horror as Tommy, Prisa, and Vivian grabbed Sheila by the collar and slammed her body against a nearby oak tree. Sheila screamed as her head hit the tree, the impact almost knocking her unconscious.

As Pen rushed to try to get to the girls, Brutus grabbed his arm and pulled him back. Thane and Butch came over and punched Pen in the stomach. Pen didn't even feel the pain. All he thought about was his sisters in trouble.

"Please! Please!" yelled Pen, now screaming. "Let them go!"

"Shut his mouth before he calls the whole neighborhood," Brutus yelled. Thane pulled off his scarf and wrapped it around Pen's mouth. "Okay, baby boy. Let's see you call your mommy. She can't save you now!" Pen struggled to get away, but the three boys held him with a tight grip.

A few pieces of binder twine lay on the ground. The farmer must have dropped them on his way home from the field. Grabbing the thin ropes, Brutus threw them to the boys. "Tie him up against the tree until we've finished teaching him his lesson," Brutus called out, pointing to a large maple tree close by. Thane and Butch quickly did as they were told and tied his arms up securely.

Glancing to see where his sisters were, Pen watched Prisa stride over to Sheila, still pinned against the tree, and slap her violently across the cheek. "That will teach you not to tell on any of us to the principal," the girl sneered. The smack was so violent that Sheila's head smashed against the tree again. Blood trickled down Sheila's face. The smack was enough to knock her unconscious for a few minutes.

Snapper, who had managed to get to her feet, screamed out Sheila's name, but got no response. Snapper tried to rush to her side, but she was once again grabbed by the other two girls. Snickers and sneering laughter exploded from the group of bullies as they watched tears welling up in Snapper's eyes. Snapper looked frantically at Sheila. She was not moving. She lay limply against the tree.

At that moment, Snapper realized that Sheila was not just her friend—she was not just a sibling in her new family. Sheila had become her sister, her sister who—at that very moment—was hanging limp and seemingly lifeless against the tree, with drops of blood running down her cheek.

Once again, Snapper struggled to break free from the cruel grip holding her back. Opening her mouth to scream for help, Tommy pulled a thick woolen sock from his backpack. Unraveling it, he wrapped it quickly around Snapper's mouth. Echoes of laughter exploded through the gang as he gagged Snapper's mouth shut.

"Sorry, what were you going to say?" Tommy mocked. "What's the matter? Cat got your tongue?"

The group once again exploded into laughter.

It was at that moment that a low growl emerged. Whirling around, Brutus looked to see where the sound was coming from. He stared at Pen, mouth open. "They're weirder than we thought" he sneered. "They're freaks! They're all freaks!"

Snapper tried to shake her head frantically at Pen, with the hope of getting Pen's attention, but without success. Awaking suddenly from her short unconscious state, Sheila raised her head. Her head throbbed uncontrollably. Raising her hand to her cheek, she felt something wet and sticky. Bringing her hand to her face, she gasped when she saw that it was blood.

Grabbing Sheila violently by the hair, Prisa yanked her up. Sheila screamed. "We will see you tomorrow, freak!" the girl mocked. "Breathe a word of this evening, and you'll wish you were never born."

A shudder of fear crept up Sheila's back, and she suddenly felt tears rolling down her cheeks. She so badly wanted Hamza there at that moment. Her silent tears turned into sporadic sobs that produced hiccupping sounds when she tried to breathe. "I want my brother. Please, I just want to go home," Sheila cried. "I just want to go home. Please let me go home with my brother and sister. Please."

Pen could no longer control the rage he was feeling inside. His arms were red from his constant tugging at the rope tied snuggly around his wrists. Sheila had called him her brother. An emotion that Pen had never felt before—no, not since his father had died— washed over him. An emotion of deep love—deep love and rage mixed into one. These were his sisters . . . his clan . . . his responsibility when Hamza was not there. His eyes flashed with anger.

Brutus let go of Pen and walked nonchalantly to a rotting piece of dead wood lying on the ground beside Sheila. Picking it up mockingly, he raised it above his head. "Do you want to know what happens to kids who tell on other students at school?" Terror filled Sheila's eyes, as she looked from him to the piece of wood. A sly smile crept across his face. "I'm going to show you. I'm going to hit you hard enough so that you will never forget. Actually, so that all three of you will never forget."

Pulling the wooden weapon backward into position, he held it mockingly, ready to strike. Taking a deep breath, he swung the piece of wood hard at Sheila.

A deafening roar shattered the terrifying silence. Ropes snapped in all directions as the outline of a black panther sprang with lightning speed at the gang leader. The piece of wood never made it to Sheila's arm. Shattered splinters of wood cracked and fell everywhere as the enormous panther seized the weapon with his bone-crushing jaws. His massive paws hurled Brutus through the air. It happened in slow motion that it seemed almost surreal. The muscular and massive cat ripped the club from Brutus's grasp, as if it had been a toothpick.

He flew through the air with Brutus until they both landed with a deafening thud on to the ground. Speechless, the other bullies watched in horror as the angry panther shook Brutus violently in the air like a rag doll. Screaming in fear, Prisa, who had been holding on to Sheila's hair, now turned to run. With one leap and just one swipe of Pen's paw, she was hurled into the air. She crashed on to the ground. Before she could move to attempt an escape, the giant panther was on top of her. Screaming in fear, she watched in horror as the panther's jaws closed on her shoulder. She shrieked as her body was raised effortlessly from the ground, and she felt herself being shaken as if she were weightless.

By this time, Snapper attempted to raise her temperature and finally managed to get away from the girls holding her back. Although she did not allow her body to burst into flames of fire, her arms became so hot that the bullies let go, yelling. She pulled the sock out of her mouth and was screaming frantically at Pen to stop. Sheila, who had been frozen in mute fear, suddenly snapped back into reality. Rushing to each other, Snapper and Sheila grabbed for each other's hands and began to shriek out Pen's name.

"Pen! Pen! Pen!" screamed Sheila as loud as she could. "You've got to stop! Please!"

With Brutus's arms still in his mouth, Pen suddenly stopped and stared at Sheila. Opening his mouth, Brutus dropped limply to the ground.

Pen slowly morphed back into his normal self. Pen stared in disbelief at the gruesome sight around them. Brutus, the leader of the bullies, lay in a heap, with his leg bent in an unnatural way. Butch and Tommy lay on the other side of the street, with rips in their clothing. Prisa's shoulder was bleeding. Her torn shirt revealed ugly teeth marks and cuts that were bleeding profusely. Thane lay in a heap at Pen's feet, his arm broken.

"Oh no! What have I done?" Pen gasped. Sheila reached for his hand to reassure him. All three children stared, mouths open, shuddering at the devastating sight. Only three of the bullies had managed to get away. The rest were seriously injured. Painful groans emerged all around them. Butch was whimpering softly. Thane was crying. Brutus was sobbing like a baby, clutching his arm. All three children stared at him.

The groans and cries of pain were suddenly broken by the loud piercing sound of sirens. Blinding lights pierced the dusk. Men and women dressed in black uniforms spilled out from the vehicles. Moving toward the three of them quickly, one of the policemen shouted to Pen to move away from Sheila and Snapper. Large black machine guns were pointed straight at Pen, and the policemen quickly surrounded him. Pen froze and then obediently followed them into a sinister black van.

CHAPTER EIGHT

Lab Tests

Dr. Callist, the lab specialist, entered Pen's cell. He wore a white lab coat and white sneakers that squeaked when he walked on the concrete floor. His black hair was shiny and gelled back. It looked like some sort of plastic helmet. Outlining the edges of his chin was a thin, well-groomed goatee. His cold, blue eyes looked intensely at Pen as he lay on the small cot. Pen's new room was made up of white concrete walls, a white concrete floor, and a heavy steel door. Just above the cot was a tiny window encased in thick iron bars. It looked out on to a courtyard monitored by many video cameras and enclosed by barbed wire and electric fencing.

"Pen, it's time for your scheduled tests," Dr. Callist announced coldly, not looking up from his notebook.

Pen barely moved. His skin was gray. Bags around his eyes showed he hadn't slept in days. Finally looking down from his notebook, Dr. Callist narrowed his eyes in Pen's direction.

"Pen," Dr. Callist repeated slowly and methodically, "you can either get up on your own or you will be given a needle as a sedative to make you more compliant."

Reluctantly, Pen weakly rose from his bed and followed the doctor. By his thin arms and legs, it was obvious that he hadn't eaten in days. Every day for the past four days, he had refused to eat the bowl of grey slop that was placed in his cell on a metal tray. Suspecting that there were drugs in his food, Pen would leave it untouched.

When Pen first arrived, he thought it was a mental hospital. Dr. Callist assured him that this was no such place. "This is not a place where we are trying to make you better," he had told him. "This is a government lab that the public does not know about. Our purpose is to study strange anomalies like you, which are a threat to our world. Here, our main concern is our safety, not yours.

You can either participate willingly in our tests, x-rays, MRI's and CAT scans, or we can and will force you against your will. If you fight us, we will make your stay with us even more unpleasant than it already is."

Pen longed to be home, or to at least see his family. Pen had never felt so lonely before, no, not since the passing of his father a few years ago. He wondered if he would ever see his family again.

Dr. Callist led Pen through a set of large metal doors marked *top secret*. Pen shook involuntarily. He had never been in this room before. The room was mostly dark, except for a bright lamp that lit up a large, silver chair in the center of the room. Covering the chair were wires, leather straps, electrodes, and flashing lights. Toward the top of the room, Pen noticed a small window from an observatory room.

"Sit!" commanded Dr. Callist curtly. Pen was terrified and did not budge. Grabbing Pen by his thin arm, Dr. Callist dragged him like an animal and forced Pen into the chair.

Shaking, Pen felt the cold, smooth leather straps of the chair being tightened and locked around his arms, legs, waist, and forehead. Dr. Callist was never one to waste words. He was always succinct. "The government has me conducting these tests to probe what causes your transformation . . . pain, fear or anger? Let's start with pain first, shall we? I will ask you a series of questions about your family and you will answer me truthfully. If your reply does not satisfy me entirely, then you will receive an electric shock. If I am deeply dissatisfied, then the electric shocks will become increasingly longer and more painful. I do hope that you cooperate for your sake. I am a scientist and will discover the truth, one way or another."

All of a sudden, bright red lights came on throughout the room. One, not more than four feet away from his face, blared into his eyes. Pen could feel the heat from the lamp. He was immediately irritated. An intercom light flickered on in the room.

Dr. Callist's voice rung out into the chamber and seemed to bounce off the walls. "Pen! This is Dr. Callist. I will be waiting in the observation room. This will only last for thirty minutes. I will not be able to release you from the procedure until after the time has passed. If you feel that you cannot endure the tests, please feel free to call out and scream. Once again, however, I will not be able to release you from the test until after the thirty minutes has passed. We will be monitoring you from the cameras inside the room. Unless your condition becomes life-threatening, we will not allow you to leave—even if you become unconscious. Good luck, Pen. I'm sure that you will do just fine!"

"Question one . . ." boomed Dr. Callist's voice through the intercom. "Are you the only member of your family that can change into an animal?"

Closing his eyes, Pen responded. "Yes."

"Very disappointing, Pen," retorted Dr. Callist.

Just as Pen heard the stale echo of the doctor's voice, he opened his eyes. Two red lights attached to wires and his leather straps flashed. Pen cried out in pain as he felt a jolt of stinging electric shock passing through his arms.

"Very well," said Dr. Callist in a clinical-sounding voice. "Question two. Did the hurricane that occur in your sisters' class have anything to do with their having supernatural powers?" Pen grit his teeth. He had to protect his family no matter what!

"No!" he hollered angrily at the cameras.

"Doubly disappointing, which means double the shock for you, Pen," announced the voice robotically. Pen screamed as this time the electric shocks shot through his arms and legs. Pen's body was convulsing now as he felt the sensation of hot fire crawling over his skin. Gasping for air now, he finally felt the pain subside.

"Third question," stated Dr. Callist, clearly unperturbed by Pen's reaction. "Did you or did you not use your ability to turn into a panther against some schoolchildren? Think carefully about your answer now. It is difficult for me to conduct this test if you lose consciousness due to the stress on your body."

Pen's thoughts were now frenzied. He knew that his secret was out as he had exposed himself to protect his sister. What harm could it do to admit it now?

"Yes," groaned Pen weakly.

"See how easy this can be when you cooperate?" echoed the voice. "Well my scientific findings show that pain does not initiate the change. We will have to proceed and test your fear responses now."

Assistants were ordered to help Pen out of the chair, as he was too weak to even walk. Men in white lab coats resembling alien-like drones rushed in to usher Pen's almost limp body to the fear chamber. The fear chamber's title alone made Pen panic. Upon entering, Pen understood the reason for the title. Instead of a chair, there was a hospital bed in the center of the room with a thin white mattress supported by a silver frame. Similarly to the chair, it had straps, but no wires, electrodes, or flashing lights.

Around the bed, there were padded walls. Pen looked confused. "Why are the walls like that?" asked Pen. One of the assistants, a short man with black-rimmed glasses, leaned over to answer Pen quietly. "The walls were made like that because some of our test subjects were so afraid that they had managed to break free of the straps and run screaming blindly into the walls. We can't investigate what happened in their fear session if they get a concussion, fall unconscious, or die, can we?" He, too, spoke with a mechanical voice, but there was a whisper of humanity in it that Pen detected. It was as though he was trying to be cold and calculated because of the others around.

Soon, Pen was strapped onto the bed and breathing hard. "Calm down and control your breathing!" Pen repeated over and over to himself out loud.

"It's no use," recited Dr. Callist, as he read from the procedural manual. "Let yourself feel the fear and don't fight it. Administer the injection," ordered Dr. Callist to one of the assistants.

Opening a black briefcase, one of the assistants revealed a set of seven sharp syringes and five fluorescent vials of liquid. "Let's start with the blue one," began Dr. Callist. "It should be the one that will cause our test subject to associate fear with a memory from his past. Men, please have your tranquilizer guns at the ready, in case this is the test that causes Pen to become a panther. Our own safety comes first!"

Pen watched helplessly as he saw Dr. Callist suck the bright blue liquid into the needle by pulling back the syringe. Bringing it close to his face, he gently pushed the back end of it in. A small, thin spray of blue liquid spurted out of the sharp needle. Satisfied that it was ready, Dr. Callist ripped open a sanitizing wipe package and swiped the cold, wet, white cloth over the skin of Pen's forearm. Pen tensed. He hated needles. Closing his eyes tightly, he felt the prick of the sharp needle entering his skin. Then he felt the cold liquid shooting up his arm and entering into his bloodstream.

Pen stirred. He felt cool, wet, beach sand against his face. "Where am I now?" Pen thought gloomily. Sounds of soft waves lapping up on the shore filled his ears. Squinting in the gray misty light, Pen finally opened his eyes. Pen was engulfed in gray. Gray shore, gray water, gray sky, and gray fog. Gazing ahead, he saw a lighthouse and a vague pile of sharp rocks through the smoky haze. Standing, he shivered from the damp chill in the air and headed toward the lighthouse. Pen needed to find someone to help him.

There was something creepy about this place. Had he been here before? The memory was foggy, and it unnerved him. As Pen strained to make out the lighthouse, he noticed there was a shape that was moving in the water. Was it a shark, a stranded person, a fish? He couldn't tell. Pen began to run toward the figure. The damp, cold beach sand stung his bare feet. Panting wildly, he finally reached the pile of rocks in front of the lighthouse where he saw the shape stir in the still water.

Climbing the rocks was challenging. They were slippery. Finally, Pen reached a good vantage point to look at where he saw something move from the shore. The water barely moved. It was almost impossible to see much below its cloudy surface. There was nothing but a few slight ripples. After waiting a few minutes, Pen decided to make for the lighthouse.

In the eerie gloom, Pen heard a sound behind him. It was slight at first, barely audible, but then it grew. There was definitely something in the water. Turning around slowly, Pen stared in horror at the ghostly figure of a man rising out of the ocean. Pen let out an ear-piercing scream of fright. The man looked like a ghost and was terrifying! Grayish, pale skin stood out in contrast to his sunken, black eyes. Pen shook as he stared in terror at the man who looked more like a monster than a man.

There were large weblike dark cracks running down the creature's forehead. Black lips opened to reveal black and rotten teeth. What little flesh he had was thinly stretched over his nearly skeletal body. Water dripped from his stringy, black dreadlocks. It dripped from his chin. Water poured down from his fingertips and from the tip of his nose.

Drip, drip, drip . . . the sound was haunting as each drop hit the still, murky water.

A torn, gray shirt blended in almost exactly with the misty water from where he rose out of its depths. The skin over his hands was covered with gruesome open sores. Without warning, the creature waded through the water, moving closer and closer to Pen. Pen recoiled in fear, inching away from the creature.

All of a sudden, a voice that Pen recognized called out his name. "Pen, where are you going? I'm your father." Pen froze. "That night that you saw me drown, you did nothing. You are the reason I've become like this!"

"But, Dad," Pen cried, "I couldn't swim. I tried my best to get to you from a boat, but a wave knocked you unconscious, and then you were gone!"

"I never raised my son to be a coward!" his father bellowed.

Pen always remembered his father as a kind and gentle man. There was something wrong. This memory was not right. Just maybe this was not real. Suddenly, before Pen could reason it out anymore, his father leapt out from the ocean and onto the rock. Pinning Pen's hands down, he laughed out eerily. Just the sound sent shivers down Pen's spine. Like a low rumble, it echoed through the air. "Now you shall feel what it is to drown helplessly, my son," his father snarled.

Dragging Pen by his wrists, his father pulled him into the water. Pen thrashed in the water, but he was no match for his dad who was easily three times his size. Pen was in a frenzy of panic now. His head was forced beneath the waves. Struggling to hold his breath, Pen knew that if he did not think clearly, he would die. His heart was racing, and fear was coursing through his veins. He needed to fight to live!

Water was Pen's element and even though he was drowning, flooding into his head was his knowledge of water, reminding him that he had to slow his heartbeat down. If he didn't, he would lose oxygen faster. Forcing himself to calm down, Pen stopped moving and willed himself to relax. The instant his body became limp, his mind became clear. It just occurred to him that he was in a science lab. Even though everything seemed real, this was not his father. If this was not his father, then this was not real. If this was in his mind, then he could control everything with his mind.

When Pen had stopped moving, he felt the man let go of his hands. Waiting a few moments, with his hands free, he summoned the waves to disperse with an awesome display of power. Obediently, a mighty wave catapulted Pen through the air and on to the shore. Pen watched as the creature that resembled his father was hurled by a tsunami, a tidal wave, far into the distance. Gasping for air, Pen finally collapsed and passed out on the sand.

Pen heard a high-pitched buzzing noise in the distance. It became louder and louder as it screeched in the room. Pen instantly tried to bring his hands up to his ears to block out the noise but remembered that they were tied down. Pen could feel bright, stinging light shining down on his face. He squeezed his eyes tightly shut. He needed time to adjust to the brightness, and his eyes were burning.

"Dim the lights," announced Dr. Callist's clinical voice. "Our subject has obviously not responded in fear the way we had hoped. There were no animal transformations taking place on his body.

"But Doctor," Pen heard one of the scientists remark, "he did scream out and shake."

"Yes, he did," answered Dr. Callist's voice coldly. "But Pen found some type of coping mechanism to control his fear and work his way out of it. Most disappointing!" the doctor added callously. "Get him out of my sight and into his cell!" Dr. Callist ordered the scientists curtly.

The moon hung in the sky. Pen was grateful to have a small window of rest. In the back of his mind, he knew he had one more test to go: anger. He was relieved that the day was over. Seeing his father again was painful, but the thing that saved him was that he knew that his real father would never hurt him. Now that the fear test was over, good memories of his dad began to flood his mind.

In the darkness of his cell, Pen closed his eyes and remembered what his father looked like. His warm smile. His bright eyes that always had a twinkle. His strong hands and his tall, muscular frame. His warm eyes, full of love as they look into his. "Pen," he would hear his father say, "I love you son. I am so proud of you, and I'll always be proud of you. Whatever you decide to do in life, remember that I am always behind you." Pen smiled at the memory of his father. His dad loved him more than anything else in the world. Pen knew that.

CHAPTER NINE

Brutus

Brutus lay quietly in his hospital bed, his eyes closed. The steady sound of morphine dripped through his intravenous tube, and into his arm. He was thankful for the painkiller running through his body. It made him drowsy and numbed the pain. Every now and then, he drifted into a deep, gentle sleep. Opening his eyes, he looked up at the white hospital ceiling. Cards from his buddies had been taped up there. Just yesterday, his mom and dad had stood on chairs and somehow attached the cards to the panels on the ceiling so that he could see them.

A slight rustle of wind moved against the window. Brutus tried to move his head to look outside but remembered abruptly that his head was locked firmly in a vice. Right. He remembered. The terrible fight. That crazy and creepy guy that had turned from a weak, lanky boy into a gigantic, massive panther. Was he crazy? Had he imagined it all? No, he had jaw marks of a panther all over his body to prove it.

His collarbone had been cracked in two. He shuddered at the thought of Pen's massive jaws cracking that bone like it was a piece of candy in his mouth. He had heard the sound of something breaking—it sounded like a piece of wood—and then he had felt terrible pain. That's when he knew that the breaking sound came from his own neck. Brutus closed his eyes shut again, trying to get rid of the terrifying memory. He had tried to plead with Pen to stop, but it was too late. Pen was in a rage and didn't hear his screams.

Brutus lifted his right hand and ran it over his left arm. He could feel the rough edges of the newly sewn stitches that kept his huge gaping wounds closed. The surgeon had carefully sewn the edges of the bite marks together.

"I'm sorry, son," the surgeon had told him, "I'm doing the best that I can. You will have many scars because of the attack. We will send you to a plastic surgeon to see if they can cover up some of the ugly teeth marks. Unfortunately, though, I do have some good news and some bad news."

Brutus looked into the surgeon's eyes, nervous of what he was about to hear.

"The good news is that we have saved both of your arms. The bad news is that your left arm will never fully heal. The panther's jaws tore the tendons in your arm, as well as a lot of muscle tissues in your neck and leg. You will never be able to play competitively in sports again, and you will likely always have a handicap even with physiotherapy." Fortunately, you are not paralyzed, and in a few months, you will be able to walk with a crutch."

Brutus looked at the surgeon. Clenching his teeth together, he tried to stop the small tear that was threatening to escape down his cheek. Unable to hold back the grief any longer, tears ran down his face. He lifted his hands over the large white contraption that was holding his neck in place and covered his face. Brutus sobbed uncontrollably. One moment in his life had destroyed everything. Pen had stolen the most important thing from him: his pride.

Brutus was the captain of both the lacrosse and the rugby team. He was the pride of his school. He loved the sound of his fans cheering and calling out his name when he entered a field. He loved the feeling of running on to a field full of fans, with his team keeping up the pace behind him. He was a tough competitor, showing no mercy to the opposing team.

For the last three years, his school had won the gold medal in both rugby and lacrosse. Although Brutus knew that they had won because of the incredible team players, he was always given the credit. And he loved it. He loved the sound of his name on the cheerleaders' lips when they cheered him on before and during every game. He proudly waved the school flag in the air as he ran through the field at every tournament.

His parents, Dr. and Mrs. Callist, were his strongest supporters. Dr. Callist was a lab scientist who worked in a compound not far from

Brutus's school. He had never missed a game. "Life is tough, so you always have to be tougher," he taught his boys as they were growing up.

Brutus had a younger brother who had never been interested in sports. His name was Jeff. Jeff loved to cook. He had always stayed home and helped his mom in the kitchen. Dr. Callist would shake his head in disgust at his youngest son. But he was deeply proud of Brutus. "Brutus is turning out to be exactly the type of son I have taught him to be," he would say proudly. "He's tough, strong, and doesn't back down on anything or from anybody."

And Sherrie. Sherrie was the most beautiful girl that he had ever seen in his life. Her big brown eyes, long brown hair, and stunning figure made her the most popular girl in school. She was a cheerleader. Just last week, after a big win, she had run up to him on the field. Throwing her arms around him, she had given him a quick kiss on his cheek. For Brutus, time had stood still at that moment. He could hardly breathe. "I'm going to win the next game just for you, Sherrie!" Brutus announced to her. Sherrie blushed, turned, and had run back to the rest of the cheerleaders.

A sharp pain in Brutus's left arm brought him back to reality. Wincing in pain, he reached for the red button on the side of his hospital bed. Shortly after pressing it, a nurse who had been just outside his door rushed in. She quickly removed the empty morphine bag and replaced it with a new one. After a few seconds, the agonizing pain in his arm began to subside as the new bag of morphine took effect. No, he was never going to play lacrosse again. No, he was never going to win the next game for Sherrie.

As he drifted into another deep sleep induced by the painkillers entering his body, his last thought was: "Pen, I will get even with you. You will pay for what you have done." With that, he drifted completely into a deep, comatose-like sleep.

A soft stirring roused Brutus from his deep, morphine-induced sleep. Rubbing his eyes gently, he opened them slightly. A soft knock on his door startled him, and he turned his eyes as far as he could to the side without moving his neck. A middle-aged woman with short blond hair stepped into his room.

The sound of her high heels echoed loudly on the cold, tiled floor as she approached. She was well dressed. Clutching a green, snakeskin purse, she strode toward him. She wore an elegant purple and gold paisley, silk blouse, a knee-length black skirt, and purple pumps. Blood red lipstick stood out starkly against her white-powdered face and black eyeliner. Brutus was puzzled because of the dark sunglasses pushed back to the top of her head. It was such a cloudy day. Why did she need sunglasses?

"Brutus," the mysterious lady began, as she approached his bed. "You don't know me, but I'm a friend of your father. I wanted to drop in to see how you are doing."

Brutus looked at her, a bit irritated. How dare his father invite people to come and see him without his permission?

"I will leave if you'd rather that I go," continued the woman. "I just thought that it would be better for me to come and visit you while your story is still somewhat fresh in your mind."

Brutus looked at her puzzled. "Who are you?" Brutus asked, even more irritated now. "Are you some kind of reporter coming to tell me once again how crazy I am."

"Oh—no, no, no!" replied the stranger soothingly. "On the contrary, I wanted to hear your story, because I have seen Pen and his family change into animals before. I mean—I think that they're a danger to our society. I am doing everything in my power to have Pen locked away forever. My name is Marcella"

Brutus's eyes widened. Now very interested, he smiled.

"Oh well, in that case, pull up a chair!" invited Brutus. "You obviously know then that my dad works in the lab where Pen has been imprisoned."

"Yes, of course, I know that," answered Marcella with a grin. "Together, we will put Pen away for good. However, I have a better plan for Pen—one that does not involve prison."

Brutus frowned. "I want him to pay for what he did to me!" He replied. "If you don't want him to go into prison, why are you wasting my time when I could be sleeping and recuperating?"

"Hmmm . . ." answered Marcella with a twisted, evil grin. "I think that you might want to know what my plan is, Brutus. When we get finished with him, he will wish that he was in prison."

Brutus looked up at her again. She was a strange woman, he thought.

"What do you have against Pen?" asked Brutus curiously.

"Well let's just say that he has something that I want," answered Marcella quietly. "You want revenge—I want something that he has— we would make a fabulous team."

"Yah. Well, I don't think that I would make a great team player," stated Brutus miserably. "It looks like I'll never be able to walk again. So in case you weren't paying attention, I can barely move. I'm out. Besides . . ."

"Hmmm . . ." interrupted Marcella. "That's where you're wrong. You see, Pen isn't the only person in the world who has powers, and he's not the only person in the world who can change form."

Once again, Brutus stared at Marcella.

She reached up suddenly and pulled the curtains closed. Tapping her brooch, Marcella coaxed the green amulet to come out of his hiding place. The tiny green snake slid noiselessly off the brooch, slipped on to the floor, and, within seconds, had doubled then tripled in size and was expanding rapidly into a full-sized green anaconda.

Brutus opened his mouth to scream. Rushing over, Marcella put her hand over his mouth. Beckoning to the snake, she commanded him to shrink and retake his shape. Picking up the shrunken reptile again, she placed him into her brooch.

Brutus's eyes were wide now. "H-h-h-ow did you d-d-d-o that?" he stammered.

"That, my child," began Marcella, "is the easiest trick in the book. "I could change into any creature at will. Name anything."

"Okay," said Brutus, deciding that this lady was kind of cool after all. "Turn into a hydra—a three-headed hydra!"

Standing, Marcella raised her hands in the air. Instantly, her two hands became snake heads, and her arms turned into the snakes' long necks. Then her two legs joined to form one long snake body, and her head transformed into the remaining head of the hydra. The three heads hissed and rose high into the air. Brutus laughed, partly in excitement and partly in fear. The hydra was terrifying. Within seconds, however, Marcella had changed back into her normal self and was sitting on the chair beside his bed with her legs crossed.

Using such powerful magic drained her momentarily. Inky blackness leaked out through her pupils and began to pool at the corners of her eyes. Feeling the change come on, Marcella quickly slipped on her sunglasses. Brutus was still so amazed that he took no notice of Marcella's eyes.

"That was awesome!" belted out Brutus. "That was unbelievable!"

"Why, thank you." replied Marcella, dryly. "If you're impressed with something so small, I'll have to show you spells that are truly impressive at another time. However, there's no time for that right now. Now, Brutus, do you want to get revenge or not?"

"Well, yah!" replied Brutus, trying his best to lift his head to look at her. "But remember, I'm kind of paralyzed. Unless you can change me into a guy with healed bones, I'm kind of out of luck."

Marcella shook her head. "Humans," she muttered. "Why is it so hard to get through to you guys sometimes?"

Brutus looked at her again.

"Of course, I can heal you, Brutus," she said, a bit irritated now. "But are you in or not? Do you want to join my team against Pen or not? You choose."

"You can heal me!" Brutus blurted out. "Well, in that case, it's a no-brainer! Of course, I'm in! I can't wait to kick Pen's butt!"

Marcella smiled. "Now that's what I'm talking about, Brutus!"

Lifting her hands in the air once more, she placed them gently on Brutus's legs, his arm, and then on his neck. Brutus closed his eyes in excitement, afraid to breathe. He didn't want this to be all a dream.

Suddenly, Marcella snapped her fingers. Brutus felt his bandages, and collar brace begin to get loose. Brutus reached up and touched his neck. The neck brace was gone. The pain was gone. He could move his head from side to side!

Sitting up carefully, Brutus stared at his bare legs. The casts were gone. The only things that remained were the ugly scars from stitches from Pen's bite marks.

"I left the scar marks, Brutus, so that you could remember what Pen tried to do to you. You won't have any pain, though. Just memories from the marks."

Brutus looked down at the ugly teeth marks that zigzagged across his legs. An evil smile crept over his face.

"Let's do this!" hissed Brutus. "I'll kill him!"

"Now we're talking," Marcella replied. "Oh, by the way—one more thing—I'm also Sheila's stepmother." Her face turned into a twisted grin. "Let's say, her evil stepmother."

Taken aback, Brutus stared at her in amazement. Soon his shock turned into grim satisfaction at the irony. "I want to take them all down," smiled Marcella.

She reached out her hand to him. Brutus took it and leaped gingerly out of bed like any athlete would do. She then handed him a bag with some clothes in it.

"Now, Brutus, get dressed and walk out of the hospital with me like you are a visitor. No one is ever going to suspect that you're Brutus. After all, the Brutus that they're supposed to be taking care of will never walk again."

Brutus chuckled. He quickly got dressed, and together, they left the hospital room. No one noticed that his hospital bed was empty. In fact, it was only when a nurse brought him dinner three hours later that anyone realized that Brutus had left for good. Even his bandages were gone. Brutus wished that he could have been there to see the look on the doctors" faces.

CHAPTER TEN

A Union of Evil

Night began to fall on the three apprentices as they followed Marcella into the conservation walkway. There was an eerie glow on the uneven grass. It lit up their shoes as they stepped onto the mysterious path. Marcella was walking a few meters ahead of them.

"What if she is just leading us here to kill us?" whispered Thane, wiping his long shaggy blond hair out of his eyes.

"Why would she heal us and take us out of the hospital if she wanted to harm us?" replied Brutus. "That's just stupid, Thane."

Butch followed behind the two of them. "Well," Butch shrugged, "if she tries to attack us, then we're just going to have to kill her. We can totally defend ourselves."

"That's stupid," replied Thane. "How can you kill a witch? You can't! Besides, I think that Brutus is right. She probably wouldn't have healed us if she wanted to destroy us later."

Brutus shook his head. "You guys worry too much! We're going to follow her, and she's going to give us what we need to defeat Pen. Don't you guys want to get some revenge on the freaks?"

"Yah!" whispered Thane, ready now for anything.

The three boys followed Marcella through the trees in the park and into a clearing in the woods. The moon shone brightly and seemed to illuminate that one spot more than it did its surroundings.

Marcella walked into the center of the clearing and stopped. The boys followed her. Closing her eyes, Marcella began to chant some words. Then she pointed to the ground. Wisps of purple smoke smoldered and rose just an inch or two from the grass, forming a pentagram. "Each of you boys need to stand on a tip of the pentagram," she ordered them. "My sister will be joining us," Marcella suddenly announced. "Her name is Kalik. She is coming from quite a distance away, so she might be a bit late. She will stand on the fifth side of this pentagram."

Brutus, Butch, and Thane did as they were told. Each of them stood on the tip of a triangle that extended out of the pentagram. Marcella stood on one of the tips as well.

The boys looked around, expecting another woman to show up at any moment. Brutus noticed, though, that Marcella wasn't looking around. She was looking up. Peering up into the sky, Brutus suddenly noticed a blurred shape flying toward them. The figure seemed to be floating in the wind. For one split second, the flying image seemed to become a perfect silhouette of the moon. Then it made a beeline toward them.

"Thane and Butch!" whispered Brutus, trying to get their attention. They were still looking around them, waiting for a woman to step out from behind the trees. "Look up!"

Staring up in amazement, all three boys watched as the mysterious woman glided down from the sky and landed gracefully on the fifth tip of the pentagram. She was dressed in a gray cloak. She didn't resemble her sister at all. While Marcella looked like she could run for town mayor with her well-coiffed hair, made-up face and expensive burgundy business suit, her sister Kalik suited the medieval sorceress persona. Her long blond hair hung un-brushed and unkempt limply around her pale face. The tombstone color of her misty cloak brought out her cold gray eyes. Compared to her sister, Kalik was thin and skeletal.

"Where were you?" hissed Marcella at her sister, impatiently pointing a long, red fingernail at her. "Don't you know that I'm busy and have work to do?"

"Don't you dare talk to me that way, you fool!" hissed Kalik. "You're lucky that I came at all. Besides, you should have just called the hag instead. She would have loved to be here and meet the three boys!"

"You know full well that she could harm them," Marcella hissed back.

"And how do you know that I won't?" quarreled Kalik. "What can I possibly do with three stupid little boys?"

Brutus, Butch, and Thane looked at one another. This wasn't the type of meeting that they were expecting.

"Should we make a run for it?" whispered Thane.

"What good would that do, you stupid human?" answered Kalik, sneering at him.

All three boys jumped. They were sure that they had talked softly enough so that the witches couldn't hear them.

"I'm s-s-sorry," stammered Brutus. He was the leader of the gang, and he felt responsible for them right now. "We didn't mean to upset you. We just want to help you to destroy Pen and his sisters."

"Don't worry about my sister, Kalik," interjected Marcella. "She won't hurt you—not while I'm here. She just doesn't have any manners. It's no use even trying to teach her basic etiquette."

"How dare you insult me, you miserable old wretch!" hissed Kalik to her sister, Marcella, again. "We should have a witches' duel right now. The only problem is that I'll win before you even get started."

"Oh, shut up!" exclaimed Marcella. "Just help me to perform this ritual and then get back to your ridiculous world. I'm so glad that we don't live close to each other. I can't stand being near you."

"And I hate you too, Marcella!" retorted Kalik menacingly. "I would have destroyed you years ago if Mom and Dad hadn't put that curse on us."

"Ahhh! Don't talk about Mom and Dad to me!" shouted out Marcella. "One day, I'll find a way to break the curse!"

"What curse?" blurted out Brutus. He put his hands over his mouth, shocked that he had spoken. "I-I-I-I'm sorry," he stammered. "I didn't mean to interrupt."

"Well you just did," said Kalik. "I wish that I could turn you all into frogs. Then at least I could have frog legs for supper!"

"Oh, shut up!" exclaimed Marcella again. "Don't you ever get tired of hearing yourself talk?"

The two of them just glared at each other again.

"My mom and dad put a curse on us," explained Marcella. "They knew that we hated each other. So to stop all the quarrelling and violence among us, they used the binding spell. We can't kill each other. If we try to do it, we will all die together. If I try to cast a spell so that Kalik's hand falls off, then mine will too. So whatever we do to one of us will happen to all of us."

Marcella shook her head and sighed. "The spell unfortunately does not affect anyone else harming us. If someone else were successful in injuring me, my two sisters would be unharmed. However, the exception is that if I die or am near death by someone else's means, my sisters are weakened. Our parents arranged it this way so that we could revive the other sister and that we would be forever dependent on one another to survive."

"What a stupid, useless spell!" sputtered Kalik. "The moment that we figure out how to break that curse, I will take great pleasure in destroying you and watching your body melt into the ground, Marcella."

Once again, the two women glared at each other. Brutus, Butch, and Thane looked at one another nervously. There was certainly not any sisterly love present. The only thing that was keeping them from killing each other was the curse that their parents had put on them.

"Okay, shall we begin, Kalik—or should I say, onion face?"

"You're the one to talk!" shouted Kalik. "You look like a catfish turned upside down. I don't know if your face is your butt, or if your butt is your face!"

The three boys managed to keep their urge to laugh well hidden. They were way too scared to upset these two strange creatures in the slightest way.

Marcella looked at Kalik disdainfully. There was no point. They hated each other, and they always would. But right now, she needed Kalik's help. If Kalik left to spite her, she would be in big trouble.

"Okay, okay," Marcella began, trying to be tactful. "I'm sorry that I called you onion face. I really need you to just help me do this ritual. Then we can both go on with our lives until we need each other again."

Kalik grunted a sarcastic laugh. "What makes you think that I want to help you now, you ridiculous piece of nothing."

Marcella sighed. Standing a little straighter now, she pulled a wand out of her black cloak. "Okay, let's just begin this ritual. Kalik, I need these boys to spy on Sheila, Pen, and Snapper. Then I need them to trap them for us. They're willing to do both of these things."

Although Marcella had never mentioned the spying part to Brutus and the boys, none of them dared to correct her. They all agreed quickly and wholeheartedly.

"Now boys," began Marcella, "part of this ritual is to ensure that once we have given you powers, you won't use these gifts for yourselves and forget about our plan."

Brutus and the boys nodded.

"So first of all, we are going to sign a contract with you. However, the ink that we use is probably not the kind that you're used to."

Brutus looked at Marcella. Butch and Thane shifted their weight from one foot to the other, feeling a bit uncomfortable now.

"We're going to use our blood to sign this contract."

"Okay, I'm out of here," announced Butch. Brutus sprung over to Butch and pushed him back over to his spot.

"Stop being such a wimp, Butch!" insisted Brutus. "You're embarrassing me."

Kalik and Marcella looked over at Butch and Brutus and smiled, clearly amused. It was the first time that they had agreed on anything since they had seen each other again. They both obviously thought that this interaction between the bullies was somewhat comical.

Taking their places again on the pentacle, Butch, Brutus and Thane looked over at Marcella and Kalik.

"I will begin the process," announced Marcella. She reached back into her long, black cloak, and produced a small but very sharp knife. Plunging the tip of it deep into her wrist, she began to pull back the knife. It sliced a neat, deep cut into her arm. Blood quickly oozed from the open wound and began to run down her arm.

"You idiot! Did you have to make it so deep?" insisted Kalik angrily. The boys looked over at her, shocked. Blood had begun to run down her arm as well. In fact, it appeared as if the very same cut was on her arm too. Brutus suddenly remembered that Marcella had said that whatever one sister did to herself or one of her sisters happened to all of them. That was part of the curse.

"Well, if I'm going to make you hurt, I might as well do it properly!" replied Marcella, smiling. She was pleased with the fact that Kalik was in terrible pain at that instant.

"Well, if you didn't want our third sister to find you and the boys, you probably shouldn't have done that to her as well!" sneered Kalik.

Marcella remembered that her other sister would have the same cut, and that she would be furious. That was definitely not the state she wanted to meet her third sister in again.

"Bloody hell! I'd better heal myself a bit, so that she doesn't come looking for us!" Marcella said, a bit nervous now. Raising her wand, she chanted a few words under her breath and pointed it at the wound. Three quarters of the deep cut miraculously healed, as if it had never been there.

Stroking her arm carefully, Kalik seemed to be less angry now. "That's better," she said.

"Now it's your turn, boys," announced Marcella. "You can either cut yourselves, or I can do it for you."

Butch shuddered with the thought of Marcella plunging that knife into his flesh. "Oh, I think that we're alright," he said, taking a small knife out of his own pocket. Brutus and Thane agreed with him. They quickly produced their own small knives from their pockets.

"Apparently bullies make sure to have their own weapons handy," said Kalik sarcastically, as she watched the boys opening their knives.

Brutus looked up and nodded. He quickly plunged the sharp tip into his hand and made a clean, quick slice through his palm. Butch and Thane followed his example and did the same thing.

"Now I'm going to give each of you a pen," Marcella said. "Each one of you is going to dip the writing end into your blood. Then you are going to write your name at the bottom of the contract."

Pulling out a long silvery piece of thick cloth paper, Marcella held up the contract. This is what it said:

> *This contract is a binding contract between Party A and Party B. Party A consists of the following people: Marcella, Kalik, and the Blue Hag. Party B consists of the following people: Brutus, Butch, and Thane.*
>
> *This contract is signed in blood and will therefore be forever binding. Party A will give Party B certain abilities and powers. All powers and/or gifts that come from Party A must be used by Party B against the individuals that Party A will name. If Party B attempts to use these gifts or powers for their own benefit, or any intention other than what Party A has set out for them, Party B will be immediately destroyed. Party B will be subject to do the bidding of Party A forever. If Party A is divided on their instructions or intentions, then the bidding of Marcella will be followed from Party A.*
>
> *This contract is forever binding once signed by both parties with their blood.*

Brutus gulped as he read the contract. "Brutus, it means that we have to do whatever the witches tell us to do forever, or we'll be killed!" Butch whispered nervously.

"I don't know if we can enter into a contract like this one!" added Thane. "What if Party A tells us something crazy, like to destroy our family or something like that?"

"Relax, boys," said Marcella in her most charming voice again with a laugh. "You know that we would never ask you to do anything that would be harmful to yourselves or to your families. The only reason that we're going into this contract together is because we all want Pen, Sheila, and Snapper to be destroyed. Isn't that right?"

"Right!" answered Brutus, who was beginning to fall under Marcella's charm again. "Come on, boys! We can trust Marcella! After all, didn't she heal us? I would never have been able to walk again, and now I can not only walk but also run."

Butch and Thane nodded in agreement. Marcella had the most charming way about her at times.

"Yes, my sister is right!" chimed in Kalik suddenly. "Why would any of us ever want to hurt you?"

Joined by the will to gain Sheila, Snapper, and Pen's powers, the two sisters were suddenly united.

Brutus stepped up toward the contract. Taking the pen from Marcella, he plunged the tip of it into the blood that was still running down and dripping off his fingertips. He then signed his name in big bold letters on the bottom of the contract: BRUTUS.

"There!" said Brutus. "I've signed my name. Now how about you guys get moving and do the same."

Butch and Thane were a bit more hesitant.

"I'm not dead yet, right guys!" announced Brutus, confidently. "I'm looking as healthy as ever. If you don't want to help me beat the crap out of Pen, then don't sign the contract."

That was exactly the motivation that Butch and Thane needed. They hated Pen and couldn't wait to fight against him again—but this time—with powers. They both rushed to the contract. Butch was first. He took the pen that was dripping with Brutus's blood, and stuck it into his own hand. Pulling it out of the cut in his palm, he wrote down his name beside Brutus's, in big block letters as well: BUTCH. Finally, Thane took the pen from Butch's hand and dipped it gingerly into his own blood. Beside Brutus's and Butch's names, he scribbled down his name: THANE.

A big, slightly eerie smile crept over Marcella's face. "Great, boys!" she said, delighted to see their signatures. "Sign it now, Kalik," she said, handing her the pen and contract.

"Don't order me around, Marcella," she said, gritting her teeth together. "I can still back out of this and leave you high and dry, you know."

Marcella pretended that she was remorseful. "I'm sorry, dear sister," she lied. "I am so thankful for you here today, and I wish that you could stay with me a little longer—like a whole year."

Kalik glared at her. Snatching the pen from Marcella, Kalik quickly signed her name on the page, eager to go home, and to forget temporarily that she had a sister.

Holding up the contract, Marcella smiled happily. "It's my turn now!" she announced.

Pushing the pen deep into the cut in her wrist, she began to twist it violently. The pain was unbearable for her, but it was worth it to see the agony on her sister Kalik's face. Kalik's face turned red and then purple.

"You'll pay for that one, you idiot!" growled Kalik.

Smiling spitefully at Kalik, Marcella wrote down her name in stylish calligraphy: MARCELLA.

"Show off!" said Kalik angrily.

Now that the blood contract had been successfully completed, Marcella rolled it up tightly. Taking her wand with one hand, she threw the contract into the air with the other hand. She then pointed the wand at the contract, said a few words under her breath, and the contract disappeared in a puff of purple smoke.

"Now the last step of this contract is to join hands. Then your part to play in this ritual will be over, and you can go home, Kalik."

Kalik quickly reached over and grabbed on to Marcella's hand. Then they leaned across and took the boys' hands. As soon as all ten hands had met, a cloud of red smoke rose from the ground and engulfed them. The smoke circled up from around them and disappeared into the sky.

"Well, that's it!" exclaimed Marcella. "Now you can go home, Kalik. I hope that I don't need to see you for a very long time."

"Actually," replied Kalik, "I hope that I never see you again. I am going to work harder than ever on breaking Mom and Dad's curse so that I can destroy you, a little bit at a time."

"Ha ha ha!" laughed Marcella. "Considering that you're the dumb one in the family, I don't think that you'll quickly find the spell to break it!"

"Well, I know one thing!" yelled Kalik, even angrier now. "You're the ugly one! I never know what side I'm looking at when I see your face!"

"Well, your nose looks like the end of a rotting turnip!" shouted Marcella, forgetting that Brutus and his gang were still there, staring at the two sisters with mouths wide open.

"Well, your face looks like a pig's butt after he's sat down in thick, black mud and rotten oats!" retorted Kalik.

Grabbing for their wands, they both cast a spell on each other, letting white fire blaze from the tips. The next moment, the two sisters began screaming in pain. They had once again forgotten about the curse that their parents had put on them before they died. Doubled over in pain now, both sisters collapsed on the ground.

"Just get out of here, you imbecile!" shouted Marcella.

Grabbing her wand and shoving it back into her black cloak, Kalik jumped into the sky. "Don't call me again, you fool!" she yelled back at her sister. "I won't come anyway—unless it's to take the children's powers! And I hope that our other sister, The Blue Hag, comes and visits you and the boys today!"

Marcella's face went pale at the thought of it. In her anger, she had forgotten that her other sister would have felt all of her and Kalik's attacks as well. Stepping off the pentagram, she hurried off the field, beckoning for the boys to follow her. They had no idea who or where The Blue Hag was right now, but they had a feeling that they shouldn't be in a hurry to meet her. Looking over their shoulders, they quickly followed Marcella out of the park.

"I will meet all three of you here tomorrow, at 8:00 p.m. sharp," Marcella said as she turned to leave. "Go home. Your parents will be worried about you when they learn that you're no longer in the hospital."

Brutus, Thane, and Butch nodded. They had almost forgotten that they had left the hospital that very day.

"You are free to tell your parents whatever you wish. It won't matter. They will be so happy to see you completely healed that they won't care how it happened."

"What about our hands?" asked Thane, pointing to where they had cut their palms.

"Good point," muttered Marcella. "We don't need to draw further suspicion. With a swift touch of her wand, their cuts magically disappeared.

Giving one another a high-five, they headed for their homes.

"See you at 8:00 p.m. tomorrow, guys!" called out Brutus.

Butch and Thane waved back, and then all three disappeared into the night.

CHAPTER ELEVEN

Water and Fury

Pen woke up with a start. Nightmares of drowning flooded his mind. "Where am I?" He thought, trembling. Looking around him, he saw that everything was unfamiliar. Everything was shrouded in darkness. "What am I doing in a prison?" Pen involuntarily shook in the cold cell. He guessed that it was still in the very early hours of the morning.

It took him a few minutes to adjust. His memories were hazy. They were like sand slipping through an hourglass, and slowly, he began to remember. Instinctively, Pen knew that some of the thoughts floating through his mind were poison from the injections and were not real.

One memory, he knew, was real. Over and over, the memory kept playing in his head like a persistent nightmare. When he saw the rotten piece of wood being swung almost in slow motion at his sister's hand, he remembered the pain. The stinging pain of hot rage welling up and spreading like fire inside his chest. After that, almost everything else went blank.

It was as if the animal side of him took over. Once unleashed, his animal nature, the pure ferocity of the beast, controlled his body and his mind. Only the sound of Sheila's and Snapper's yelling voices woke him from his trance of fury. He remembered the horror of looking down and seeing Butch's body hanging limply by the mangled arm Pen clutched in his jaws.

What was scary for Pen was that he didn't remember how it all happened . . . just a faint memory of his fierce instinct to protect his family. Why was he not able to control it? Had he killed anyone? How could he live with the fact that he could be responsible for their deaths or even for their suffering? Had he put his family into even more danger by exposing their secret? Maybe that's why his family had not come to rescue him. Maybe they were in danger too. Pen couldn't stop the thoughts of guilt from squirming and pricking him, like scorpions inside his brain.

Pen was almost relieved to hear distant, echoing footsteps, for they interrupted his thoughts. A low buzzing sound, like that of a swarm of bees, filled the air, as the low hanging ceiling lamps were switched on one by one, with light edging closer and closer to his cell. Shortly after, the metal door to Pen's room swung open. Occupying the narrow entrance was the lab assistant that Pen recognized from the day before.

This man was a little nicer than the others, he remembered. His starched, white lab coat billowed around him. Nervously, he fidgeted, rubbing his bright blue, latex-gloved fingers together. Squeak, squeak, squeak . . . the noise echoed and bounced off the walls of the concrete prison. Startled by the noise, the lab assistant quickly clasped his hands tightly together in front of him. Clearing his throat awkwardly, he finally spoke. "I'm Mr. Moe, and I'll be escorting you to your final test today."

His voice was high-pitched for a man, and it matched his rather mousy appearance. Black-framed spectacles wobbled on the edge of a rather thin, sharp nose that jutted out from a small and round face. Even though you could tell by the lines on his face and the short brown stubble on his chin that he was a man, he was remarkably short. Mr. Moe looked like a boy playing dress-up, wearing a scientist's costume.

Pen stood to his feet. He was eager to get this retarded test over and get back to his family. In his mind, he resolved not to change into a panther. If he could get through the final test, maybe they would just let him go.

"I'm sorry that we have not given you any breakfast, Pen," apologized Mr. Moe sympathetically then continued. "It's just that . . . there could be a chance that the anger test might be more effective on an empty stomach. These orders came from Dr. Callist," said Mr. Moe, shaking his head disapprovingly. "I will make sure you are fed right after."

Pen had forgotten that this was an anger test. The very emotion that had made him change in front of the bullies. He surmised that one of

the bullies who managed to escape called the police from a cell. He just
had to control it. He had no choice. What Pen didn't know was that Mr.
Moe had a son exactly the same age. Even though he knew what he had
to do, he felt that he wanted to make this as easy as he possibly could
on this boy. Inside, he didn't feel right about what they were doing. Pen
was just a kid, like his son. When Pen looked into his face, Mr. Moe's
expression said it all.

Pen felt the cold leather straps being tightened around his wrists.
A bright light shone down on his face. Dr. Callist towered above him,
expressionless and cold as ice. One of his assistants unlocked a leather
case filled with bright fluorescent vials and a sharp syringe. This time,
Dr. Callist took the blood red vial. He inserted the needle into the end
and sucked the liquid into the transparent syringe. Pen shivered.

Dressed in a blue hospital gown, he felt exposed. He could feel the
cold air, the cold hospital bed, and the cold leather straps binding him
to his bed. Closing his eyes, he waited for this ordeal to begin and finish
quickly. Wincing, he felt the sharp needle prick his skin and the toxic
venom enter into his blood stream. Although he fought against the
poison, it was no use. Pen could feel his mind spinning.

When the mist in his mind finally abated, he found himself in the
corridor of prison cells. His cell was the only one that was vacant. The
others were filled with monsters barely resembling humans. Skeletal,
gray faces gnashed with pointed teeth. The creatures growled and hissed
like animals, banging their bodies wildly against the confines of the
barred doors of their cells. Blackish gray veins ran down their faces and
spilled down their necks.

Standing in the walkway, Pen shuddered as he saw their milky
eyes cloud over. These creatures were nearly devoid of humanity and
were hungry for violence. He sensed imminent danger. Backing away
instinctively, he felt the sharp prod of a tranquilizer gun at his back
nudging him to move forward. Turning around, he stared into the cruel
smiling face of Brutus. "How did you get here?" gasped Pen.

"I came back to finish the job I started!" Brutus growled. "I said I
would teach you and your freak family a lesson! Bring out his sisters,"
he called out to the other lab assistants.

"No, don't!" yelled Pen. "You have me. Let me pay for what I've
done and leave them out of this."

Dr. Callist rested his hand on Brutus's shoulder. "Family is important, isn't it, Pen? Looks like you had no regard for mine. My son got the best medical treatment money could pay for and look how quickly he's recovered. I hope your sisters do as well as my son did," Dr. Callist said, curling his mouth into a twisted grin.

At the end of the long corridor, Pen's sharp hearing picked up the sound of chains dragging and footsteps nearing the door. Slowly, the metal door creaked open. Sheila and Snapper stepped out, held by two lab assistants. Methodically, they gagged and chained the two girls to the back wall. "Let them go now!" screamed Pen. Pen felt the barrel of the gun jab painfully into his shoulder blade.

"Shut up!" Brutus hissed. "Next time, it will be a tranquilizer bullet you feel. I'll be the one giving the orders now."

A shrill alarm filled the air and flashing red lights spilled out onto the floor.

Before Pen had time to scream out their names, the doors to the cells all swung open. Zombies with gray skin, sharp protruding teeth, and foaming mouths lumbered out. The sound of growling and hissing was bone chilling. Their sight was fixed on their prey. Pen yelled to get their attention, but they ignored him and continued to advance closer to their target victims—his sisters.

"Leave them alone. It's me you want!" Pen yelled hysterically. The scientists laughed. "Why don't you do something about it, Pen?"

Dangling from Dr. Callist's lab coat, Pen detected the glint of a chain with a silver key. Adrenaline pumping through his veins, Pen spun around and knocked the gun out of Brutus's hands. Madly dashing toward the doctor, he scooped up the key before Dr. Callist could even react. Within seconds, Pen had sprung past the zombie hoard and was unlocking the handcuffs on his sisters.

Grabbing Snapper's and Sheila's hands, Pen growled menacingly at the zombies edging forward. The lab coats pushed past the crowd of zombies and pointed their tranquilizer rifles at Pen. "Let your sisters go, and we will let you live. We want to see how the effect of a zombie bite affects your sisters," announced the scientists. Pen could feel his blood boil. He did not fear death. His sister's safety meant more to him than his own life.

The instant he saw the scientists grab his sisters' hands, leading them into the mob of monsters, he lost control. Pen could feel his fangs grow inside of his mouth. He could feel the sensation of hair cover his skin and his nails growing into razor, canine claws. Withdrawing the syringes from their pockets, the scientists gripped Sheila and Snapper by their necks, preparing them for the injection. Hot anger took over Pen.

Unfortunately for the scientists, Pen was not only a lethal panther but could also control water. Any form of water, even if mixed with other substances, was under his control. Pen raised his claws. Instantly, the needles, as if with a mind of their own, leapt out of the scientist's hands and flew, injecting the substance into the scientist's necks. Groaning under the sedation of the drug, they collapsed to the ground, unconscious.

Dr. Callist, who still stood by the door, turned to run. There was no stopping Pen now. Like a wave of fury, the animal inside of him had taken over. He was out for vengeance! In full-blown panther form, Pen felt himself strapped down to his hospital bed. Somehow the drugs that were poured into his veins had worn off. But his anger and rage to protect his family had not. Somewhere between reality and illusion, Pen was still in fight mode. He needed to get to his sisters.

Opening his fanged jaws wide, Pen let out a deafening roar that shook the room. His muscles rippled beneath black waves of fur. Extending his needle-like claws, Pen tore through the leather straps as if they were made of butter. His eyes were on fire. No one threatened his family! They were all he had left. The fur on his back stood on end as he crouched into striking position on the hospital bed, back arched.

Even though Pen was heavily sedated by the drugs, his mind had controlled the water-based vials. With his power over water, he controlled them and injected them into his enemies. The scientists all lay convulsing and unconscious on the ground. Scanning the room and ready to pounce, Pen searched for Dr. Callist. Although still drunk with rage, he was slowly coming into reality. The zombies were not real. His sisters were not in danger . . . but where were Brutus and Dr. Callist?

Suddenly, Pen heard the shot of a gun behind him. Lunging to the ground, he spun around to see where it came from. Pen's vision began to blur and the room began to spin. Pain from the arrow stung at the base of his back. He knew he had been shot. Before he finally collapsed, he made out the faint shape of Dr. Callist holding a tranquilizer gun aimed sharply at him, with his son Brutus standing at his side.

CHAPTER TWELVE

Transformation of New Enemies

Brutus, Butch, and Thane arrived promptly at eight o'clock the next evening. They knew exactly where the open field was by now and had no trouble finding it. As they entered the clearing, Marcella was already there.

The three boys stood together, side by side, waiting for their first gift of power. They were so excited.

"Now," began Marcella, "you know that Pen can change into a panther. Sheila, his sister, can change into a raven, and Snapper can change into a deer. Both of Pen's adopted parents can change into panthers. Only Pen, Sheila, and Snapper, though, have powers—beyond changing into animals, that is. I am going to give each of you a chance to pick one animal that you think will be a formidable force against each of them. In a few seconds, I will begin a powerful incantation that will allow you to transform into an animal of your choice. You will only get one chance. The spell allows you to choose only one animal. You can't choose a different animal later. Do you understand?"

"Yes!" answered all three of them together.

"When I call your names, each of you will close your eyes and think of one animal. You will then transform into that form, and that will be the one and only form that you will ever be able to transform into."

"Brutus, I will start with you." Brutus stepped up to Marcella. He already knew exactly what he wanted to be. Marcella began to speak out the words of incantation over him in a guttural tone and language that he had never heard. Raising her hand, she beckoned for him to think of an animal. Closing his eyes, Brutus envisioned a strong and powerful cougar, with massive wings that stretched out on either side of him. Instantly, Brutus transformed into a cougar, with muscles that rippled down his arms and legs. His wings were folded on either side of him. Pushing them, they stretched out magnificently. Leaping into the air, he flapped against the wind as hard as he could. Soaring into the air, he let out a thunderous roar that shook the trees around him.

"A very good choice, Brutus!" Marcella applauded him. "Okay, now Thane, it's your turn." Brutus quickly landed beside them, so that he could see what forms his friends would take.

Thane was tall, thin, and lanky, but tough. He stepped forward, holding his head high. When Thane stood tall, he appeared to be even taller than he really was. That was maybe the most intimidating part of him to other kids at school. Marcella looked him up and down. "Choose well, Thane," she said. "You want the animal that you morph into to be even more intimidating than your human self, and that will take some thought on your part."

Thane grinned slightly and then closed his eyes. Marcella began chanting again. Thane knew already what he wanted to be. When he was six years old, his mom and dad had taken him to the city zoo. Thane was excited to see the animals in the outside enclosures. He saw the lions basking in the sun, the cheetahs sleeping under a tree, the Bengal tigers lying lazily over large rocks. But when they had reached the grizzly bears, Thane saw something that he would never forget. The large, male grizzly bear sat with his back to Thane and the other onlookers. He seemed to be uninterested in their presence and pawed at some leaves near the door of his man-made cave. A few boys beside Thane started to shout at the bear. Nothing happened. He didn't even turn his head to look in their direction.

Just before Thane and his family could leave to go to the next enclosure, a slight rustling of leaves caught Thane's attention. Thane asked his dad to carry him up so that he could see what was making that sound. Through the strong wire cage, and over the cement enclosure, Thane made out the shape of a jack rabbit. Thane wondered how he had managed to get into the enclosure. "He must have dug his way under the wire cage and the cement," he thought. Thane's dad was just about to put him back down on the ground when they heard a deafening roar. Thane got such a fright that he wet his pants. His dad was so shocked that he didn't even notice that the warm pee from Thane was running down his arm. The grizzly bear lunged across the yard toward the poor jack rabbit. He never had a chance. In what seemed to be two leaps, the bear was on top of him and had closed his massive jaws on the rabbit's head. Within moments, the grizzly bear was back at the wall, with a lifeless rabbit lying under his paw.

Thane didn't sleep for nights after that encounter. He had never seen an animal move so fast in his life. He remembered the roar, the speed, the strength. Thane knew that that was exactly what he wanted to be: a grizzly bear. A large, male, fearless grizzly bear.

As Marcella continued to chant, Thane's long lanky arms stretched and expanded. Long thick brownish-black hair replaced his blond hair. Gigantic paws emerged where his hands had once been.

"Yah!" shouted Brutus, a bit scared of his friend beside him now. Thane's shirt split at the seams and tore into shreds as a shape of a grizzly bear emerged.

"Way to go, Thane!" shouted Butch, impressed at the sheer size of Thane. He was at least eight to nine feet tall. Marcella smiled in evil delight at what Thane had become. Thane looked down at himself. Yup, that's what he remembered seeing in the cage that day.

Thane lifted his paws and let out a deep rumbling roar. Birds flew from the trees in all directions. Squirrels and mice sped out of sight.

"Wow! Now that's cool, Thane!" said Butch. "Wait until you see what I'm going to become, though. I'm going to blow you both away with my sheer greatness!"

Both Thane and Brutus, still in their animal forms, turned to Butch. Marcella began the incantation again. Butch closed his eyes and stepped forward. He lifted his arms, flexing his muscles. He was quiet, but tough. He took great pride in bullying other kids at school. The sight of watching his classmates squirm and beg for mercy was always very satisfying to Butch.

Brutus and Thane waited in anticipation to see what Butch would become. They were sure that he would choose a terrifying animal. Would it be a crocodile? Or better yet, a fire-breathing crocodile? Would he change into a flying cobra? One could only guess.

Within seconds, Butch began to transform. Brutus could hardly wait to see what formidable, powerful animal Butch would become. He cheered with excitement as Butch's brown, curly hair gave way to sleek, shiny black hair. "This is so awesome!" he whispered to Thane. "Now we'll be the three fearless predators!" Butch's muscular arms shrunk in size into tiny, slender, rather spindly legs. "He's going to be a fast animal, Thane!" yelled out Brutus once more. "Go, Butch, go!"

Butch, the strong, fearless bully that he was, seemed to mysteriously shrink in size. A thick, bushy tail protruded from his backside, and fanned out from side to side. Brutus and Thane stopped. Puzzled, they watched the final few transformations. A tiny snout grew from his face. Two beady eyes peered out over a little button nose. Finally, a bright and distinct white line appeared on his head, near his nose, and an invisible paint brush painted the line down his back, all the way to his tail.

Brutus and Thane stared at Butch in disbelief. Butch had just morphed into a skunk. Yes, a skunk. And not just a skunk—a farting skunk—because as Butch peered back at his friends nervously, he began to fart, just like skunks do. His stink juice, near his backside, was ready to explode at any moment, and the more nervous he became.

"You idiot!" they both yelled together, covering their noses. "You could have chosen any animal in the world, and you chose to be a skunk!"

"It was an accident," Butch moaned. "I heard a sound in the bushes as soon as I closed my eyes and remembered that I saw a skunk yesterday."

Marcella glared at Butch. "You are a waste of time to me and my powers," she hissed at him.

"How could you be so stupid!" shouted Brutus.

"I-I-I-I'm sorry!" answered Butch. Giggling nervously, he let out another series of popping farts. Butch always farted when he was nervous. Except, this time, it was going to be a problem for his friends.

"Oh my god!" yelled Brutus. "He's going to kill us with his stench."

The more Butch farted, the more the odor wafted around him and over to his friends.

Finally, unable to keep in his stink juice any longer, Butch let out the worst fart of them all. Spray exploded from his backside and into the air. Marcella, Brutus, and Thane dove for cover. Leaping into the air, Brutus flapped his wings, escaping to the nearest tree to take cover from the stink storm. Hurling himself into the bushes, Thane let his strong arms launch him as far away as possible. Marcella shook her head once more and disappeared into thin air, muttering to herself something about how dumb humans are.

All alone, Butch hung his head. The smell was unmanageable, even for him.

"What the hell are you going to do?" yelled Thane. "Throw stink balls at Pen and his sisters?"

When the smell finally died down, Brutus and Thane ventured back into the clearing and sat down. Butch, who had managed to morph back into his human self, sat down beside them.

"I'm sorry that I messed up, guys," Butch began, feeling embarrassed.

"Well, we can't do anything about it now, can we?" replied Brutus, still feeling a bit agitated. "Hopefully, when we get our second set of instructions from Marcella, you won't choose to turn into a tooth fairy or anything like that."

Thane started to chuckle and shook his head. "That was just crazy, Butch. Just crazy! I thought you'd choose a dragon or something, and you chose a skunk!"

Butch hung his head again. "It was pretty stupid!" he muttered under his breath. "One chance, and I blew it—royally!"

"Well," said Brutus, ready for the next lesson from Marcella, "let's just forget about it. How about you just stay in your human form when we fight. At least you're pretty intimidating as a guy. Just don't morph—ever—unless we need to use farts for weapons."

As soon as he had said the last comment, Brutus and the others started laughing.

"It was pretty funny to see Butch change!" laughed Thane. "You should have seen how small your arms got! It was hilarious!"

"The best part was when we saw this tiny little nose grow on to your face!" exclaimed Brutus. "You went from being the almighty Butch to the stinky little skunk!"

Again, the three boys starting snorting with laughter. Brutus threw himself backward onto the grass and started howling.

"It's not that funny, you guys!" exclaimed Butch, who was relieved that he was still part of the gang.

"Ha ha ha ha! Butch the skunk!" snorted Thane between fits of laughter.

With that, Butch clenched his fist and punched Thane in the arm.

Hitting him across the head, Thane jumped on Butch and pretended to pound him on the chest. Brutus jumped up, and diving on Thane, wrestled him to the ground. Before long, the three boys were play fighting in the grass and wrestling with one another as if nothing had ever happened.

Everything was going to be okay. "Even if we have a gang member that's really a girl in disguise—a little dainty black and white skunk queen," Brutus said laughing. "I don't even think that the skunk is a male skunk. I think that it's a little girl skunk!"

With that, the boys began play wrestling again.

Finally, exhausted, they lay on their backs in the grass and looked up at the clouds. "It's okay, Butch!" laughed Brutus again, but somewhat comforting this time. "You're still part of our gang, buddy. You give a mean punch in your human form."

"Thanks, guys," said Butch, still feeling sheepish.

Getting up from the grass, they began to head for home again. "I'll let you know as soon as I hear from Marcella," Brutus instructed the boys. "And then we'll meet and continue our training."

It was really happening. They were really going to be able to beat Pen. With that, the boys grunted at each other and made their way home.

CHAPTER THIRTEEN

An Unexpected Guest

News reporters and photographers from various magazines and television shows surrounded Hamza and Tameka's house. Sheila pulled back the curtain from her bedroom window, just enough to peer at the conglomeration of video cameras and flashes going off constantly. Snapper walked into Sheila's room, still rubbing the sleep from her eyes. Without a word, she bent down beside Sheila to peer out the window. "Oh my gosh," she muttered. "They're everywhere. They're like flies. We can't even go to the store without being mobbed and have cameras flashing in our faces."

Sheila sighed. "I wonder how Pen is today," she said, looking into space. "It's just not fair."

Snapper nodded slowly, unable to say a word. The girls were really missing their brother. Since the day that they had left on their journey from Sheila's hospital room, they had never been apart and had stuck together like glue. The house seemed quiet, like the very breath had been taken out of it. Looking out the window once more, Sheila felt a barrage of lights and flashes meet her eyes.

She quickly stepped back from the curtain and pulled it firmly shut. "It feels like we're in a prison too, Sheila. Boy, I miss Pen."

Hamza put his arms around his two girls. Tameka put her hand on her husband's shoulder.

"He could have easily killed all of those kids in the gang. You and I both know this, Tameka. He chose not to. With or without Snapper calling his name to stop. Tameka, he chose not to use his full strength.

That's why Brutus is in the hospital with only a broken arm and a few teeth marks."

Tameka nodded again, hesitantly at first and then with more passion as she saw what Hamza was trying to say.

"We are not at a morgue right now with eight or nine dead children. They all survived the attack. Pen wasn't trying to badly harm them. He was just trying to deliver the message that they have to stay away from his sisters."

From the distance, no one saw, or even suspected, an approaching small dot in the sky. If anyone had taken the time to notice, he would have not only spotted the raven flying toward the house but have been in awe of its size and magnificence. The bird glided effortlessly over the heads of the reporters and photographers with their eyes glued to the home, cameras pointed in anticipation for the slightest movement from the house.

The raven flew to the top of the chimney, threw back its head, and gave a loud shrill caw. It hopped along the roof of the house and disappeared into a small opening, just below the eaves trough where a small family of swallows had nested that spring. Climbing past the empty nest, the raven made his way through to the attic. Once in the attic, the raven morphed into a tall, majestic, handsome man. Bending down, he lifted the latch of the door leading from the attic into the house. Carefully, he lowered himself through the hole and dropped to the floor.

Tameka was the first one downstairs as usual. Rubbing the sleep from her eyes, she walked into the kitchen. Eggs were on the menu this morning. As she cracked the eggs open and let each one gently slip into the simmering pan of hot butter, tears moistened her eyes. She would have made twice the number of eggs if Pen were home. Pen had a hearty appetite and could eat as much as all the members of the family, including Hamza, put together. The eggs cooked noisily over the fire. Carefully turning them over, Tameka checked the dough that she had made and let rise the night before. It had filled the large bowl and was spilling over the sides. She punched it down with both hands, shaping it into three loaves. This was Pen's favorite type of bread.

She was going to attempt once more to visit him in the compound. She had been turned away only yesterday. Pen wasn't allowed any visitors. She had pleaded with the security at the door that she just wanted to see her son, but she was denied the privilege. She had once more returned home with a heavy heart. But she was going to try again today. And if she couldn't get in, hopefully a security guard would at least take the bread up to her son. Hopefully Pen would know that his mom loved him and was trying to get to him. Once again, her eyes filled with tears, and a tear dropped into the dough. She wiped her eyes. Somehow, she had to stay strong for her family.

Her thoughts were interrupted as quiet footsteps approached her from behind. "Did you sleep at all last night, honey?" she asked, turning to kiss Hamza. To her surprise, it was not Hamza at all. She gave a gasp as she recognized the tall man standing majestically before her. "Raven!" she gasped in disbelief. "How in the world did you get in here? How did you get past the myriad of cameras? Oh my, do we ever need your help right now!" she exclaimed. "Pen is in trouble. We've got to save him. We just don't have any idea how." With that, Tameka broke down in tears. Raven gently put his hand on her shoulder.

She suddenly remembered that Hamza was still upstairs, washing up. "Hamza, girls!" she shouted. "Hurry, come down right away!" Startled, Hamza and the girls bolted downstairs.

"Raven!" cried Sheila and Snapper, rushing over to him and throwing their arms around him.

Hamza grabbed Raven's hand and shook it. "Boy, we're glad to see you right now, Raven. I think that we could use a little help," Hamza said, his voice shaking slightly. Raven smiled at Hamza and the family and suddenly shifted his shape into the most radiant, motherly woman. Black, thick, braided hair streamed in waves of curls around her now. Her eyes grew gentler, and her lips fuller. Her figure lost its rugged edges and gradually flowed into gentle curves, like that of a mother goddess.

"Yes. I'm aware of Pen and his situation," replied Raven. The girls felt the warmth of her voice. It seemed to echo through the air like the sound of songbirds.

"I have come to help you. But there is a second reason as to why I am here."

Tameka and Hamza looked quizzically at Raven. Everyone's eyes were fixed on her with silent anticipation.

"I have received word from an unlikely source. Last night, one of the eagles brought me a message that they just received. Pleading cries for help were carried to their ever-keen ears as they glided across the horizon during the spring moon of the equinox. Souls have been said to appear there during season-changing moons. Following the direction of the cries, they were led to the opening of a very peculiar burial site that has long been forgotten by many. It is an old and ancient stone chamber, built at least three thousand years ago.

"Glandor, the eagle, called out to his son, Nassor, who joined him at the foot of the cave. The two of them carefully and soundlessly entered the tomb site. As they passed one of the enclosed tombs, they noticed that a strange and eerie glow was seeping through the cracks of the room. Approaching it carefully and peering inside, Glandor and Nassor saw something that is difficult for even me to believe. He saw what seemed to be the figures of a young man and woman chained to the stone wall. They seemed to be neither dead nor alive. The woman's long hair was matted and hung down one side of her face. They seemed to know that he was there, and the lady whispered, 'Help us, please, please help us.'

"Whispering quietly to his son to help him, the two men attempted to open the huge stone door. As strong as they are, it wouldn't budge. Glandor sent Nassor to find a pick axe or a heavy tool so that they could break down the door.

"When footsteps once more returned to the cave, Glandor turned around, expecting to see Nassor. Instead, he saw the approaching shadow of someone else. He slipped quickly into an empty chamber and hid behind the door. Peering through a crack, Glandor caught a glimpse of a figure well-known to all of us. Glandor swears on his life that he saw the outline of none other but the wicked Kalik. How this is possible, I do not know. However, Glandor does not lightly or idly speak. As soon as the person he believes to be Kalik turned the corner, Glandor quickly and quietly left the burial chamber and intercepted Nassor in the sky.

"They came straight to me to bring me this unfortunate news. Now here is the most shocking and horrifying news of all."

Hamza, Tameka, and the girls stared into her face, hardly able to breathe.

"Glandor described the facial features of both the man and woman, who appear to be husband and wife, chained in the first room that he saw. Snapper, I don't know how to tell you this . . . but there is a slight possibility that they are your mom and dad."

Snapper, who had been very still the entire time, gasped, and stifled a scream behind her hands. "No! No! It can't be!" she cried out horrified.

"We're not sure," answered Raven. "We could be entirely mistaken because the report said that your parents died in a car crash. However, it would definitely explain a mysterious disappearance of a coven of white witches to the south of Ireland. Your mom and dad were part of that coven, Snapper."

Looking at Snapper, Raven continued. "Every year, a group of good-hearted and conscientious white witches from around the world come together to join hands and offer up chants for the betterment of the world. They bless the trees and the animals and call forth rain. This year, however, they mysteriously disappeared. I have been to the Stonehenge myself, where they were, and studied the site for any clues. The only evidence that they had been there were a few misplaced stones on the ground. Also, one of them had left a page with Wiccan spells on the ground. They would never have left that behind. But those were the only clues that I found that they had been there."

"If my parents are in trouble, I need to go and save them!" Snapper exclaimed, with tears running down her face now.

"That is exactly why I am here," Raven replied tenderly. "You will need to have Pen with you for this task."

"But how?" Tameka questioned Raven. "I have done everything to get into that compound. There are at least fifty guards between him and me. Hamza and I have sat up every night, trying to strategize a plan to get to him, and every one of them so far has failed." Hamza nodded sadly in agreement.

"There is only one way to get into the compound," Raven offered wisely.

"Hamza," Raven began, "has Sheila earned the privilege to regain her powers?" Hamza looked into Sheila's eyes. "What do you think, Tameka?" he asked. "I agree if you agree."

"Well Sheila," Tameka began, "Are you ready to use your powers as Raven has intended?" She paused dramatically.

Sheila lowered her eyes. She knew how important this was. Her brother's life lies at stake.

"Yes," answered Sheila.

"Last question," Tameka continued, "are you willing to use your powers to help your family and to protect those in need? And in a way that shows respect and dignity?"

Sheila nodded eagerly.

"Then I think," concluded Tameka, "that Hamza, myself, and Raven can grant you permission to once more take the form of a raven and control the wind." Sheila beamed in gratitude.

Gently, Raven bent over, took Sheila's hands, and blew from her mouth a cool wind that engulfed her. She could feel the surge of power, wind, and magic flowing through her veins once more.

"You don't need to morph into a panther to use your panther instincts," Raven said to Tameka and Hamza. "After all, a panther can get into almost any corner of the woods without being detected in the slightest. You can travel with them in your bird form, Sheila. As for you, Snapper, you also have very sharp instincts, and you are light on your feet. Between the four of you, you will know what to do once you are there."

Beckoning for the girls to follow her, Raven whispered, "Think about the gifts that the druid gave the three of you. You have Pen's backpack here, with all of those pens. Choose the ones that will help you to get in, and to rescue Pen safely."

Sheila and Snapper looked up at Raven. "Of course!" Sheila laughed. "We have all kinds of gifts from the druid that we can use!"

Without another word, Raven suddenly morphed into a mighty raven and flew up through the opening in the attic. Squeezing through the opening in the wall, she was once again swooping over the heads of the reporters, and soon, all they could see of her was a tiny dot in the horizon.

"I think that I have a great idea!" announced Sheila suddenly. "I think that I know just what to do!"

Before Snapper or Hamza and Tameka could question her, she had morphed into a raven. Flying up to the attic, she squeezed through the same hole that Raven had come through. Within seconds, she had left the house and was flying toward the compound.

CHAPTER FOURTEEN

Pen Gets a Special Guest

Thursday morning came quickly. The red and yellow hues of the early sun's rays tinted the edges of the horizon. As the sun continued to rise, the colors of the sun's beams reached out and drenched the entire sky, leaving splatters of red, orange, and yellow here and there. Mr. Moe arrived at the prison gates at promptly seven o'clock. He turned the large key in the heavy iron gate and pushed it open. After a few steps, he arrived at the great steel door. The air was cool this morning. As he breathed, a small cloud of vapor formed in front of his face. The door handle felt cold to the touch as he opened the door.

Before he could close the door behind him, a beautiful, bluish-black raven glided effortlessly and landed at the entrance of the doorway. If Ed Vice, the other guard, had been there, he would have simply raised his large gun to his shoulder, and fired a shot at the bird. Mr. Vice had a good eye and had killed many birds that way. Mr. Moe just didn't have the heart to harm animals. A little innocent bird, such as the one standing peacefully a few steps in front of him, posed no threat.

Cocking her head coyly to the side, the raven raised one of its wing feathers and groomed it from back to tip with its beak. Then it raised its head and looked right at Mr. Moe.

"Dumb bird." He chuckled. "You're lucky that Ed's not here, or he would have killed you by now."

The little bird gave a soft caw and turned its head once more to look at him. Mr. Moe could have almost sworn that it had nodded its head.

Remembering the ham and cheese sandwich his wife had packed for him for dinner, an idea occurred to him. Reaching into his lunch bag, he pulled it out and peeled back a small corner of the wax paper exposing the crust of the bread. Breaking off a small piece, he crumbled it between his fingers. Gently he tossed the few crumbs at the black bird. Sheila flew back a few paces, pretending to be startled. Bending down, Mr. Moe picked up the bread crumbs and held them invitingly with an open hand. Whistling softly, Mr. Moe called out to the bird. Shyly, Sheila inched forward cautiously. "It's okay, little guy," said Mr. Moe beckoning the raven. "I'm not going to hurt you." The scientist loved nature and enjoyed going camping with his family every summer to get a rest from the sterilized, clinical nature of the lab. Never before was he able to get that close to a bird. The thought of petting its wings excited him like he was a small boy again.

She hesitated for a few seconds. Cocking her head again to the side, Sheila studied Mr. Moe. Hiding her eagerness, she turned her head away. "Aren't you hungry?" Mr. Moe said trying to entice the bird. Careful not to scare the bird away, he slowly edged an open palm forward, so that it was just below Sheila's beak. Slowly the raven lowered her head into his open hand and pecked at the breadcrumbs.

Mr. Moe smiled. Very carefully, Mr. Moe brought his other hand around and softly petted Sheila's feathers. Her feathers were so glossy and soft that it made Mr. Moe's heart skip a beat. Exhilarated now, Mr. Moe wished there was someone there who could take his picture. What a story he would have to tell his son later when he saw him. No sooner had that thought crossed his mind when, all of a sudden, Sheila threw her head back cawing loudly and extending her wings. Beating her wings hard, Sheila soared up with tremendous speed and flew through the open doorway.

"I'll have to find a way later to coax you back outside!" Mr. Moe called out to the bird. "I'm afraid you've made me late for work," he said smiling. With that, Mr. Moe continued on his way to his station.

A few minutes later, he arrived at Pen's cell, with a platter of food on the breakfast tray. Turning the key in the lock, he entered, balancing the serving plate in one hand and pushing the door open with the other. The glass of orange juice threatened to tip over on to the bowl of oatmeal. Using his foot to hold the door open, he quickly steadied the tray with both hands.

"Whew!" Mr. Moe exclaimed. "You almost had to eat your breakfast off the floor, just like a panther!" Although he had just meant it as a harmless joke, he sighed when Pen didn't respond. "I'm sorry. That was just a joke, Pen," he whispered. "I didn't mean any harm by it. I'm sorry that all this has happened to you, son."

Pen didn't look up. Sadly, Mr. Moe placed the platter beside Pen on the small wooden table. He hadn't wanted to add to Pen's pain. Turning to leave, he pulled back the big medal door. As it opened, he suddenly heard the slight whoosh of flapping wings. Looking up, he saw the small black raven slip through the top of the door and land on a small gap between the top of a steel post and the ceiling.

"There's that raven. I'd wondered where you flew. You are going to get me in trouble, handsome fellow," Mr. Moe joked. "Don't worry, Pen! I'm going to find a net to catch it with."

This time, Pen looked up. His eyes darted up to the ceiling.

"Don't worry, son. Don't scare it. I'll be back in a minute. I just need to find a net in the basement."

Pen jumped to his feet and rushed to the wall. The bird gently descended in flight, landing on the small bench where he had been sitting.

"Sheila!" whispered Pen eagerly. "Is it you?"

"It's me, Pen," answered Sheila quietly. "I don't have much time to speak to you, as Mr. Moe is obviously coming to try to catch me. I can't dare to change into my human self, or someone may notice me."

Pen shook with excitement at the soft echo of Sheila's voice in his cell. It was the most beautiful sound that he had heard in days.

"Mom and Dad are worried sick about you as is, Snapper," Sheila continued. "We're going to try to get you out of here tomorrow. Have you noticed any entrances or passageways that could help us get in?"

Pen shook his head. "It's too risky," he said. "If you're caught, who knows what they'll do to you and Snapper and Mom and Dad."

"Do you have even one suggestion, Pen?" asked Sheila.

The two siblings sat nervously together, barely daring to move their mouths too much as they spoke for fear that they would be caught.

"Raven came and visited us today, Pen," Sheila continued. "He has big news for us. Snapper's parents have been found. They were trapped by Kalik. We need your help to free them."

Pen swung his head and looked at Sheila, his mouth open. "You can't be serious, Sheila," he sputtered. "But how am I ever going to get out of here? And the last thing that I want is to put you and the family in danger!"

"Pen . . . just think! Is there any hidden or secret passageway?"

"No," Pen replied, heaving a sigh. "You'll have to go and save Snapper's parents on your own. This place is guarded at all times, and there are no ways to escape." Pen sighed again.

"Well, just be ready to attempt an escape with us tomorrow night," Sheila whispered emphatically. "I think that I have an idea that I'm going to share with Mom and Dad tonight. Here's the strategy that I have in mind . . ."

Suddenly, the sound of the key turning in the lock startled both of the children. Before either of the children could react, Mr. Moe walked in. "Now where is that bird, Pen?" he asked, looking around the room, searching for a sign of its black wings. He lifted the long brown pole with the brownish-gray net attached to the end of it. With a mischievous gleam in Sheila's eye, she suddenly flew into the air and landed on Mr. Moe's shoulder.

"Why, you crazy little bird!" he exclaimed.

Dropping the net, he quickly reached up and grabbed the small raven. Admiring her beautiful feathers, he gently cradled her in his huge hands.

"Well, that was easy!" he remarked to Pen. "I'm going to take her outside and set her free. What a beautiful creature!"

Sheila winked at Pen. She had already figured out that this was the safest way to leave the prison. After all, Mr. Moe had no intention of hurting her, and it was apparent that he loved birds and animals. Pen and Sheila's eyes locked as she was carried away. He watched Mr. Moe carry her down the hallway and then turn to the right.

Sitting back down on the hard, wooden bench, Pen's mind raced wildly. Snapper's parents were alive. Kalik was alive. How could that be? "I need to get out of here," Pen mused to himself. But how? There are no unguarded exits. There are no passageways that are not monitored day and night by the watchful eyes of the security cameras. All he could do was wait and hope that Sheila's idea would be a successful one.

CHAPTER FIFTEEN

Brutus Meets the Third Sister

Brutus lay awake in bed. The reunion with his parents had been exciting, but they had a lot of questions that he just couldn't answer. Like how he was healed so quickly and who Marcella was. Brutus found out very quickly that Marcella had not told him the truth, that his father had no idea who she was. He couldn't understand how he could be so trustful after that. But bullying and lying went together—I mean, he and the boys lied all the time. That's why the teachers never knew that they were such bullies outside of school. And Marcella and Kalik were definitely bullies, so what else could he expect.

Lying awake in bed, Brutus tried to collect his thoughts. So much had happened in such a short time. He closed his eyes, trying to go to sleep. He just couldn't seem to doze off. Where had Marcella come from? Why did he trust her so quickly? Did he hate Pen so much that he was willing to make such a rash deal with a stranger? Pausing for a second to think, he grit his teeth in determination. Yes, he did hate Pen enough to sign a contract in blood with two witches.

Brutus shuddered when he thought about Kalik. She was definitely the most terrifying person that he had ever met in his life. He hoped that he would never have to see her again.

As Brutus's mind raced through the events of the day, he suddenly had the feeling that someone else was in his room. Opening his eyes, Brutus looked up. There was nobody there.

"I must just be really tired," he thought yawning. *"Everyone in their right mind is fast asleep at this hour of the morning.*

"He turned over on to his side. Reaching for his alarm clock, he tilted it so that he could see the time. It was 3:00 a.m. Laying his head back down, Brutus thought that he saw a shadow again.

"Who's there?" whispered Brutus, a bit nervous now. Nobody answered.

Sitting up straight in bed, Brutus reached for the light switch just above his bed. He switched it on. There was nobody there. Satisfied that it must have been his imagination, Brutus turned it off again and settled back into bed to try to get some sleep.

Before he could close his eyes, he thought he heard something again. Straining to hear, the sound grew louder. Scratching sounds scraped the walls, edging closer and closer to his bed. Just mice scurrying inside the walls, thought Brutus, trying to talk himself out of his fear. And then he heard it—the sound of heavy breathing looming over his pillow.

Opening his mouth to yell out, Brutus felt a bony hand with sharp nails close over it before he could make a sound. With all his strength, he used both of his hands to try to pry the hand away. It was no good. Whatever was holding his mouth shut was too strong. Then he felt a thick rag being shoved inside his mouth. Roughly, the creature pulled his head forward and bound strips of linen around his head until the gag in his mouth was held firmly in place. Brutus shook with fright. Beads of sweat dripped down his forehead.

Again, Brutus felt a bony hand that, as strong as iron, wrapped its claws around his wrist, first one wrist and then the other. Helplessly, he felt his hands being tied painfully tight to his bedposts. Although he kicked as hard as he could, he was no match for the iron grip that pulled and tied his ankles to the foot of the bed. Why would Marcella and Kalik do this to him?

Brutus tried to reason in his head . . . unless this was the third sister that they didn't want him to meet. A cold shiver ran down his spine. Could it be her? How did she find him? Hearing the sound of his lamp switch on, he watched as the dim light flickered.

Standing before him was the most horrific monster he had ever seen. Vaguely resembling a woman, the tall creature hunched with abnormally long arms hovering over him. Sharp nails grew from her thin, knotted hands. Blue skin was thinly stretched over her nearly skeletal skin. Matted, black hair hung over most of her face.

Glaring down at him with a milky eye, the hag opened her mouth to reveal a set of razor sharp teeth. "I must say," The Blue Hag hissed, "I never expected my sisters to leave me such a ripe delicacy when they lured me here." Brutus tried to yell for help, but only soft moans escaped from the gag that felt as though it were choking him. "The funny thing about that gag," snarled the blue witch "is that the more you try to make noise, the deeper it sinks into your throat."

Looking away from the hag's face, he stared down at her waist. His eyes widened in terror as he noticed what she was wearing. Dried and hollow skins of children were sewn together as a sash around her waist. Seeing Brutus's face, the hag cackled and drew her black mouth into an evil grin. "Sing for the new boy, my children," she crooned, "He will join you soon in your misery." All at once, it seemed as if a wind blew into the room. The rags of human children swayed in the breeze. It was the most bone-chilling sound to hear. Soft sounds of sobbing, like tortured souls, wailed from her hideous sash.

Brutus shook hysterically. He wished his parents could come to his aid, but he knew there was no way that they could hear him. He had a bedroom on the main floor and there were two floors separating him from his parents and sister.

Bound and helpless, Brutus watched in the flickering light as the witch extended her sharp claws. With a single finger, she traced a red line over his arm, gently breaking the surface of the skin. Brutus winced at the pain as he felt his blood begin to spill out of his arm. Smacking her lips hungrily like she was savoring every bit, she leaned in closer to Brutus. Brutus's body shuddered as he felt her long black tongue run over his arm, greedily lapping the trickling flow of his blood.

Again and again, Brutus cringed as he felt scratch after scratch of her claws grazing his stinging skin. It felt like the sensation of hot fire burning and ripping. Angrily he fought back the tears. He wouldn't cry. He had to be tough. But how much more could he take? Was he going to be eaten alive by this hideous crone? At last, the bedroom lamp burnt out. He was all alone. Left in the darkness to the mercy of a monster.

A puff of bright purple smoke suddenly appeared in the darkness. "What are you doing here?" a familiar voice called out. It was Marcella's voice.

"What do you mean, what am I doing here?" the voice beside Brutus answered in a low cackling voice. The very sound of the creature's voice sent shivers up and down Brutus's spine. "You called me here, didn't you, Marcella? You and Kalik seemed to have lots of fun last night, and you forgot to invite me."

"That boy belongs to me," Marcella's voice rang out again. "He is untouchable. He has signed a contract in his own blood, promising to help me catch the three children. He is off limits, even for you!"

"Can't you just find another kid?" the voice asked. Pure evil seemed to drip from every word. "He is so delicious!"

"No. I can't just find another boy," answered Marcella curtly. "He is passionate about destroying Pen, Sheila, and Snapper, and that is something that I can't just create in someone. I am warning you. Get away from him. If you eat him, you will need to face me afterward, and I am not afraid to cut myself to the bone to make you hurt."

Hissing and leaping from the side of his bed, The Blue Hag crawled backward like a spider up the side of the wall, and shuffled out of the open bedroom window.

There was silence. Brutus heard the sound Marcella casting a spell. The throbbing of his slashed arms subsided. Then suddenly, as quickly as it had come over him, the terrible pain left him. All the blood-chilling memories faded as quickly as they had come. The marks that were cut into his arms vanished, the gag was removed, and Brutus's hands and feet were untied.

Looking around him, Brutus saw Marcella standing at the corner of his room near his door. He sighed a sigh of relief. She looked exhausted, and somewhat gray and pale, paler than usual if that was possible.

"Who was that?" exclaimed Brutus, still shaking from fear.

"That—" said Marcella, "that is my sister."

Brutus stared at Marcella, his eyes wide with fear now.

"You and your friends are no longer safe here," Marcella continued. "I have plans for you anyway—just not this soon—but that's okay. I need you and your two friends to meet me at the clearing at ten o'clock sharp tonight. This is an extremely important meeting. Don't be late."

With that, Marcella waved her wand and disappeared in a cloud of purple smoke.

Reaching his hands up to his face, Brutus rubbed his eyes. *Wow. What a nightmare*, he thought. It was only four o'clock in the morning, but there was no way that Brutus was going to fall asleep now. Getting out of bed, he pulled on a pair of torn old blue jeans and a black top.

Grabbing his cell phone, Brutus texted Butch and Thane. It would be hours before they woke up, but at least he would hear from them the moment they got out of bed— hopefully.

Opening his door, Brutus sauntered down the stairs to the kitchen. Pulling out a loaf of bread, he began to make himself a roast beef sandwich.

Tiny flashlights could be seen from a distance as the light shone between the trees in the conservation park. Brutus, Butch, and Thane made their way quietly through the trees and to the clearing that they knew well. None of them said a word. They were all too nervous after hearing about Brutus's experience.

Stepping into the clearing, they sat down behind bushes—out of sight. The moonlight shone down, eerily, and seemed to illuminate their meeting place. They shut off their flashlights and waited. They were a few minutes early. They were all terrified that the third sister might appear in the clearing before Marcella could get a chance to arrive there.

"Good! You're on time!" announced a voice behind them. Almost jumping out of their skins, the three boys turned and sprang to their feet. Marcella had a way of appearing out of nowhere.

"Now step out into the clearing," she commanded.

Brutus, Butch, and Thane did as they were told. They had a newfound respect for her, especially now that they knew that she was their only defense against that other witch—or creature—whatever she was.

"Now, boys . . . it appears that Pen, Snapper, and Sheila have made a connection with a certain druid." Marcella informed them. "I just got news that they have been enrolled to learn about witchcraft through them. I am going to send the three of you to that school early. It will be the safest place for you right now because I am not available to babysit you 24/7." Brutus, Butch, and Thane looked at one another.

"What?" sputtered Brutus. "We can't just leave our homes and begin in some new school. Our parents would be furious!"

"Yes!" added Butch. "My mom and dad would kill me!"

"Just one minute boys—" Marcella said, "need I remind you that you signed a contract in your blood to do whatever I say, whenever I decide?" With that, she reached up and pulled the contract out of thin air.

"Do you know what happens if you disobey me?" she asked dryly. "I give you over to my sister, the third one that you haven't officially met yet. And trust me, you don't want to meet her on your own, as I'm sure Brutus has informed you."

Gulping, Brutus, Butch, and Thane shook their heads in agreement.

"I am sending you for your own good," said Marcella. "You won't last until next week if you stay here. I can only hold off my sister for so long."

The boys looked at each other terrified. Again, they simply nodded.

"Now the first thing that I will need to do is give you new identities. Nobody will ever suspect you. I will put a cloaking spell on you so that not even your parents will recognize you. I will even change your voice and the way you walk."

"Can we ever turn back into our old selves?" asked Brutus, a bit nervous now. "I kind of like the way I look."

"Of course, you can!" exclaimed Marcella. "I will teach you how to disable the spell and how to enable it when you need it. It is best, however, that you never disable it when you are with the druids. Even though they won't be able to see through it, they are very smart. They are always watching and could easily catch you changing back and forth."

"Okay," agreed the three boys again.

"You will need to say goodbye to your parents tonight and get ready to live with the druids."

"How long will we be there?" inquired Thane, already starting to miss his family.

"I don't know," answered Marcella. "I am hoping that as the bullies of your school, you aren't really little girls inside. I assumed that school bullies are tough!"

"Of course, we are!" blurted out Brutus.

"We are tough inside and out!" chimed in Butch and Thane.

"Good then," said Marcella. "We will begin the process tomorrow morning, and you will be on your way to live with them. You will be arriving quite early, so that will be a good thing."

Butch looked at Marcella confused.

"What I mean," continued Marcella, "is that you will get a lot of training before Pen, Sheila, and Snapper arrive, and that will hopefully be to your advantage. When the time comes for you to fight against them, you will hopefully be more powerful than them with your wands."

"That makes sense," said Brutus, smiling. "If it means it will help us take Pen out, I'm all for it!"

"Me too!" agreed both Butch and Thane, suddenly finding their courage. "We'll do anything to be able to give Pen a good beating."

"Now that's what I'm talking about!" said Marcella. "I think that I found my three school bullies again. Hopefully the three little girls that came out in you earlier are gone for good!"

Brutus, Thane, and Butch went a bit red. They were starting to be a bit excited now about their new adventure. Leaving the clearing, the boys chatted as they walked down the path and on to the main road.

"What are you going to tell your mom and dad?" Butch inquired, looking directly at Brutus.

"I think that I'm going to tell them that I was accepted into a prestigious prep school and that I have to leave in the morning. I can tell them my teacher recommended me for a scholarship because of my rugby skills."

"That's lame," said Butch, laughing. "Do you think that they'll buy such a bizarre story?"

"Yah, of course," answered Brutus. "Especially if I tell them that I received the letter late because of my time in the hospital. They didn't open any of my mail while I was away, so they don't know. I'm pretty sure that I can type up a pretty good acceptance letter to show them."

"Hmmm . . ." mused Butch, "not a bad idea. Maybe I'll tell my folks that I got accepted there too."

"But they're going to ask where we're going to get the money for the plane ticket," argued Thane. "Even if we all type up acceptance letters and convince them, we still have to come up with a ticket."

"And what if they tell us that they're going to take us to the airport?" asked Butch, worried now.

"Relax, boys," laughed Brutus. "I know the perfect way for Butch to leave his house—as a skunk! His parents would be pushing him out of the house!"

Thane started to laugh. Butch turned and punched Brutus as hard as he could in the arm. Brutus was so tough that he hardly felt it. It just made him laugh harder.

"You, jerk," said Butch, angrily.

"Okay, okay, you two," interjected Thane. "We still have to figure out how to get out of our houses unnoticed, with our suitcases."

"What if we sneak out of our houses super early in the morning?" suggested Butch. "We could leave a note on our beds, saying that we made a mistake on the flight and that we had to be at the airport earlier. We could say the airfare was covered by our scholarships."

"Hmmm . . . that would work," answered Brutus. "But they would know for sure that we were lying because how could we get there?"

"Well, we could say that Butch and his family picked us up," Thane said.

"That's dumb!" exclaimed Butch. "Then your mom and dad would ask my mom and dad, and I'd be found out!"

"That's actually not a bad idea," said Brutus suddenly, scratching his head. "But instead of saying that Butch picked us up, we could just say that a friend picked us up. Then they wouldn't know who to ask."

"I'm going with that idea," announced Thane, "because it's the best idea yet. I'll just sneak out of my house at 4:00 a.m. with my suitcases and wait for you guys in the clearing."

"Me too," added Butch, "I'll leave a note saying that I got the times mixed up, and I had to be at the airport at 5:00 a.m. and that a friend who was also accepted picked me up."

"Now we're talking," smiled Brutus. "I'll tell my folks that I'll write to them from the prep school. I'll also tell them that I'd prefer to go alone because I want to feel responsible and independent. They'll like that." All three boys gave one another high-fives in the air.

"Well, see you tomorrow at 4:00 a.m. then or shortly after," said Thane, already heading for home. "I've got to come up with a mock acceptance letter ASAP."

"Me too!" called out Brutus. "If you want, I'll make one up really quickly and just email it to you guys!"

"Sounds good!" the boys called out to each other. With that, the three boys disappeared into the night.

CHAPTER SIXTEEN

Brutus, Thane, and Butch Go
Through the Porthole

Brutus, Butch, and Thane stood side by side once again in the familiar clearing in the forest. Butch tried to be brave as he stood beside Brutus. He didn't want to let the guys know how much he already missed his family. He had left that morning with a lump in his throat. He swallowed hard at the tears that wanted to make their way to his eyes. Where were they going? Had they made the right decision? Would they ever see their families again?

Brutus stood tall in between the two boys. Although he remained tough on the outside, he too was fighting his emotions. He had left the note on his bed and carefully picked up his suitcase and gone downstairs. As he was quietly passing through the living room, on the way to the front door, he had glanced at the family photo on the wall. In the photo, his mom was sitting in a chair. He, his brother, and his dad were standing behind her, each with a hand on her shoulder. His little sister, who was six years old, was sitting on her mother's lap. Even though you couldn't see it in the picture, his dad had his hand on Brutus's shoulder. That was a very rare moment for Brutus because his dad had hardly spent any time with him growing up. He was a very withdrawn man and preferred to spend his free time alone.

Brutus had pleaded with him to take him with him to work, or even to play catch—anything—even to take out the garbage with him. Brutus knew that his dad loved him, but his dad often retreated into his own world and sometimes seemed oblivious to the fact that Brutus even existed.

And his little sister. Brutus loved his little sister and would have killed anyone who even dared to hurt her. Her name was Maria, and she adored her big brother. Her dark brown curls always seemed to be in her face. She had dark brown eyes and was tall for her age like her brother. Every now and then, she would push the curls out of her face and look at the world around her. Even though there was a big gap in age between them, Brutus enjoyed her company when he was home. He loved to see her play with her dolls and have fun in her own little world. Brutus wasn't as close to Jeff, his younger brother, but he would miss him too. Brutus looked at the picture one last time as he was leaving the house. He wished that he could run upstairs and tell them that he was leaving. "I'll be back soon," he thought, not sure whether or not to believe himself.

Thane stood on the other side of Brutus. "I'm going to miss my parents," he said, blurting it out.

"Oh, don't be such a little girl!" Brutus exclaimed, pretending that it didn't bother him to leave his family.

"Yah!" chimed in Butch. "Haven't you ever been away from home?"

Thane nodded. "No, I'm good. I just didn't get a chance to say goodbye."

"We'll be back before you know it, Thane," said Brutus, punching him in the arm.

Before long, Marcella had appeared magically beside them and was ready to start the cloaking spell.

"She doesn't even seem to care that we have just left our families behind," thought Butch miserably. "But then again . . ." thought Butch, "she doesn't exactly want to be with her own family. She hates her sisters, and she's glad that her parents are dead. So what do you expect?"

"Brutus, I'm going to start with you," announced Marcella sharply. "Come over here and stand in front of me." Brutus did as he was told.

"Remember at all times that your mission is to bring down Pen and his sisters," she began.

"Gladly!" said Brutus, happy now that he remembered why they were leaving. It was suddenly worth all the pain of lying to his family and leaving home.

"I am going to choose a look for you, Brutus. You may not be pleased with the face and body that I pick, but your mission is to be a spy and then eventually to be their undoing."

"All right," said Brutus, a little nervous now. "You're not going to make me into a little girl or anything like that though, right?"

"I don't think that you understood me!" repeated Marcella, a bit agitated now. "You will be completely different, even your voice will be masked."

"Okay." Brutus sighed.

Lifting her wand, Marcella chanted over him. He made out the words "mutatio, mutatio, mitigationem"' It sounded a bit like Latin, but he couldn't be sure. A rushing wind suddenly blew up from underneath him. A strange sensation came over him. He felt an unusual vibration and shaking throughout his entire body.

As soon as Marcella had finished the chanting, Brutus stepped back. He looked down at his hands and his feet. He let out a gasp. Turning to Butch and Thane, he saw a shocked look on their faces.

"Can I please see what I look like?" asked Brutus, wide-eyed.

Marcella quickly waved her wand, and a full-sized mirror appeared beside her. Brutus looked into the mirror and gasped. Before he could say a word, Marcella had already beckoned for Butch to come.

"Okay, Butch!" called out Marcella. "It's your turn!"

Butch stepped out and stood in front of her. She repeated the ritual with him. When the wind had died down, Butch reached up and touched his face.

"Everything about my face seems to be entirely different!" exclaimed Butch.

Butch looked at Brutus and Thane. They were both trying not to laugh.

"What's so funny?" he shouted. "Do I look that bad?"

Looking into the mirror, he gulped. Speechless, he stared at his reflection.

"No! No!" Butch cried out. "Please change me into another form!"

Marcella pretended as if she had not heard him. Brutus could hardly speak. He was holding his stomach. "Oh my god . . . you look . . . well, you look . . . really, really interesting, Butch!"

Butch scowled.

Thane quickly stopped laughing when he realized that it was his turn next. He stepped up to Marcella before she could call him. "Can you make me kind of handsome at least?" he asked, hoping that she would favor his request.

Marcella raised her wand as if she hadn't heard him at all. Waving it and chanting the same spell, Marcella pronounced the same words over him. Thane felt himself getting smaller. He didn't like this feeling. He liked the idea of being tall. When the transformation had finally ended, Thane reached up and touched his face and neck. Then he looked into the mirror.

"What the heck!" he screamed out. "No! You can't do this to me! Marcella, please change me!"

Marcella hissed at Thane. "No! That's the face and body that you're going to have, Thane!" With a flick of her finger, the mirror disappeared into thin air. Horrified, Thane turned and looked at Butch and Brutus. Butch had a look on his face that said "okay, maybe I don't look too bad after all. I could have turned out to be a lot worse!"

"Now!" announced Marcella, unconcerned that Thane was so upset with his new look. "I am now going to send you to your teachers."

"Looking like this?" Thane said, pleading with Marcella one last time.

Marcella lifted her wand and began to wave it in a spiraling motion, raising it toward the sky. Then she began chanting "porta ad mundum" over and over.

A tiny, red whirlwind appeared at the end of her wand. It became bigger and bigger until it was the size of a house. As Marcella continued to chant and wave her wand, a doorway appeared in the whirlwind.

"Now go!" screamed Marcella in the wind. "The door will only remain open for a short while."

The three boys stared, terrified, into the red hole. Violent winds tore around and around the doorway and seemed to suck everything into the hole. Brutus was the first to approach the door. After all, he was the leader of the gang. He had to be brave for his boys.

"Follow after me!" he bellowed out to the other two. "That's an order!"

With that, Brutus dove through the doorway and disappeared. Butch and Thane hesitantly stepped forward.

"I don't know about this," whispered Butch to Thane. "Where does this lead anyway?"

Before either of them had a chance to say another word, Marcella had reached over and pushed them through the doorway.

Raising her wand once more, she called to the whirlwind. "Claudite ostium!" The whirlwind immediately stopped turning and then disappeared out of sight as if it had never been there.

Looking over the clearing in the woods one last time, Marcella raised her wand. As she disappeared in a cloud of purple smoke, she uttered, "I hope you boys get along with the druids." And then she was gone.

CHAPTER SEVENTEEN

Poo!

"I have a great idea of how to rescue Pen that I'm sure will work!" announced Sheila excitedly.

Tameka noticed a twinkle in Sheila's eyes and right away touched Hamza on his shoulder. "I think that Sheila has an idea!" she said, motioning for him to look at Sheila.

"Mom and Dad! I know exactly what to do! I can poo on the video cameras! Birds have thick, white, sometimes grayish, pasty feces. I can cover every single video camera completely!"

Tameka stared at Sheila, her mouth slightly open in shock. Snapper looked at her, eyes wide with disbelief. "Sheila, are you all right?" she began. Tameka walked over to Sheila with a concerned look on her face and touched her forehead.

Sheila giggled, especially at the expressions of Tameka and Snapper. She tried to continue between her farting sounds of laughter.

"No! I'm fine! But I think that if I pooped all over the cameras, the view would be completely blocked!"

Snapper rolled her eyes. "And to think that we're supposed to be sisters! What are you thinking?"

"Honey," began Tameka, who had finally found her voice, "I am sure that we can think of a better way! Just save your poo for other places—such as the toilet, my dear!"

At this, Sheila went into another fit of giggles. Snapper was standing beside her, staring at her. Her mouth was open and her hands were on her hips in disgust.

"You are more disgusting than Pen when he's trying to gross me out with disgusting farts and burps, Sheila! Get a grip!"

All of a sudden, Hamza cleared his throat. "Actually, Sheila," he began, "that's not a bad idea."

"What?" screamed Tameka, shocked that her husband would even entertain the thought. "Can you imagine our daughter flying from camera to camera, taking a dump in public, from pole to pole?"

Again, Sheila began to laugh hysterically at the thought of Tameka's watching her poo in plain view for everyone to see.

"No, no!" continued Hamza. "Nobody would suspect her. And by the time the cameras would be clear again, we would have already gone inside, rescued Pen, and left for the reserve without anyone knowing."

Tameka walked over to Hamza this time and rested her hand on his forehead. "I think that both of you are ill!" she exclaimed.

"Tameka," Hamza said, more seriously this time, "it's our only chance. I have been thinking about this for quite some time, and I haven't been able to come up with any kind of solution. This is the best idea that I've heard so far." Hamza continued. "And, honey, just think of it this way: you've always encouraged bowel regularity and healthy eating," he said with a smirk.

Tameka rolled her eyes, and Snapper shrugged her shoulders. "Well, I guess it can't hurt."

"Oh, one more thing, Dad!" Sheila announced. "Can you please cook the bean dish that you love to make?"

Hamza looked at Sheila, puzzled. Nobody in the family liked his cooking. In fact, every time it was his turn to cook, the children always found an excuse to be away for supper that evening.

Pen was the least subtle of the three children. As soon as he came home from school and smelled his dad's food cooking, he would let out a groan. He would cup his hands over his nose and face. Then miraculously, he would always be invited out to one of his friends' homes for supper in the neighborhood.

"Okay!" said Hamza, quite pleased with himself. He thought that he was a rather good cook. He just couldn't understand why everyone had such a problem with his cuisine.

Turning at once, he slipped into the kitchen to begin his famous dish.

Looking at her daughter again, somewhat puzzled, Tameka raised an eyebrow at Sheila.

"It will be easier for me to have diarrhea if Dad cooks!" Sheila explained in a low whisper.

Tameka cupped her mouth and suppressed a giggle before it escaped. Snapper folded over in laughter.

From the kitchen, the girls giggled as Hamza whistled his favorite tune. He was delighted that Sheila had asked him to cook.

Sheila entered the kitchen, overjoyed to see a pile of slop on her plate. Tameka walked into the kitchen and took one look at Sheila's plate. She looked like she was going to gag. Snapper followed close behind. She held her nose and groaned at the odor that was wafting through the room. "I'm going to be sick just looking at it," she moaned.

Sheila sat down in front of the thick brownish goop that was sliding down the side of her plate in lumps and gobs. She stuck her fork into the lumpy mass of squashed beans and lifted it to her mouth. Slimy strings of mucus-looking gel dripped from her fork back on to the plate.

Snapper gagged and rushed to the washroom. She slammed the door behind her.

Tameka stared in horror at the gruesome sight.

Hamza, however, stood proudly beside Sheila. He had a hand towel slung over one shoulder. His arms were crossed in great delight. He beamed, highly satisfied with his efforts. He wore an apron that said "The Chef Is In!"

Hamza watched with great pride as Sheila maneuvered the dripping, slippery, brown chunks of bean sauce into her mouth. From the kitchen, everyone could hear Snapper gagging and heaving into the toilet in the bathroom.

Walking over to the stove, Tameka stopped in alarm. There was a large pot full of this revolting mass of bean goop.

"Oh, Hamza. Honey," Tameka started, "why in the world did you make so much?"

"Sheila wanted me to make enough for her friends!" Hamza exclaimed.

He beamed with pride at the slimy gunk that was slowly dripping back into the pot. The lumpy bean mixture was so thick and brown and sticky that it rolled down the side of the pot in little balls that resembled balls of snot.

Tameka's eyes widened as she stared at Sheila again. "Sheila! Are you trying to embarrass us? How could you do this to me?"

Hamza, clearly offended, stepped forward. "My dear Tameka, you are not the only one who can cook around here! Finally, someone recognizes my culinary skills! This is a highly desired dish in some parts!"

"Where?" demanded Tameka, with her hands on her hips. "Where, Hamza, where?"

Hamza looked at Tameka blankly.

"Even Volsan the vulture back home wouldn't eat that when you made it for him one time!" exclaimed Tameka. "He ran out of the house screaming and clutching his stomach. And Hamza, just in case you have forgotten, Volsan feeds on dead animals! He preferred to feed on death before even tasting your food, Hamza!"

Turning to Sheila, Tameka put her hands on her hips. "Okay, this wonderful joke has gone far enough, Sheila! What in the world are you doing?"

"Oh!" exclaimed Sheila, pretending to look shocked and wounded at the thought that someone might question her intentions. "It's just that all of my raven friends (the kind that can't change into humans, but are really ravens), would like to taste some tonight and tomorrow morning as well. I thought that I'd just leave it outside so that they could all sample it."

All of a sudden, Tameka understood what Sheila was up to, and a twinkle in her eyes appeared. The twinkle grew into a giggle and then became lost in full-out laughter that she was no longer able to control. The picture of a flock of birds all suffering from uncontrollable diarrhea was more than she could bear.

Snapper came out of the bathroom, just long enough to find out why Tameka was laughing. Her face was green. She took one look, however, at the slimy mixture still rolling down the sides of the pot, and quickly rushed back into the bathroom.

The next morning, at the crack of dawn, Snapper heard a strange pecking sound at her window. Rolling over lazily in bed, she peered through the glass. What she saw next was a truly shocking sight. Hundreds, no, thousands of ravens lined the railing of the home. They gobbled the brownish gunk of slime that had been put out the night before. The only difference now, though, was that the bean food from last night had begun to rot. So it not only looked disgusting, but the odor was also revolting. Tiny maggots had already begun to crawl around the oozing concoction and were ravenously devouring the meal. Their yellow stomachs grew with each bite.

The ravens didn't seem to mind, however. They understood that they had a special task that day. Their mission was to poo! They gobbled up the bean mush as well as the yellow, plump maggots that wiggled and squirmed relentlessly around the guck.

Snapper quickly shut the curtains, resisting the urge to run to the bathroom once more. Sheila stood on the railing, perched in her raven form, triumphant and ready for battle. She could already feel her stomach begin to gurgle and churn from last night's dinner. Her stomach made rumbling sounds, as if in strong protest against what she had fed it.

"Okay, pooper troopers!" Sheila yelled in a language that only ravens could understand, "let's show them what we've got . . . or in this case, what we've got to lose!" Taking a jump off the ledge, Sheila flew into the air, straight for the compound where Pen was being held.

Deep, rumbling sounds echoed and filled the skies as the birds struggled to fly to the compound. Hamza's bean food had hit the spot for every one of these birds. Sheila tried to close her nose as she flew. Daphne, Rachel, and Purdy, the elderly ravens who flew just in front of her, were letting out terrible and smelly farts of gas into the sky as they flew. The odor was putrefying. The problem was that there were so many birds crowded together that Sheila had nowhere else to go but straight into the wind that smelled like the rottenest of rotten eggs.

Every time Sheila heard another fart come from one of the bums that was flying close to her face, just inches in front of her, she shut her eyes tight. She tried to ignore the wafting odor of a stinking stench of old beans mixed with rotting maggots.

Suddenly, Daphne, one of the elderly ravens, who was flying a few meters ahead of her, let out a deafening fart. It began as a low-sounding rumble. Then it bubbled and gurgled out from behind her. Finally, it exploded into the air in an ear-piercing elephant's trumpet-sounding fart.

Bob, Jeremy, and Tyler had been the brave young ravens following closely behind her. They took their last breath of air, froze, stiffened up . . . then fell from the sky.

Sally, their sister, having fainted from shock at the offensive trigger, catapulted from the sky as well. She fell face first into a pile of hay.

As the fart continued, all of the ravens behind Daphne, including Sheila, let out blood-curdling screams!

"Can't you just wait to let it out at the compound?" yelled Stanley, her husband, who had almost fainted from the stench. "What is your mission, anyway?" he shouted angrily.

"They're the enemy—look—they are the enemy, not us! We're your friends, or at least, we used to be."

"Oh dear, oh dear," stammered poor Daphne. "I was trying to hold it in until we reached the enemy!"

"Until you reached the enemy?" shouted Stanley angrily. "Wow! If they're the enemy, and you just killed a third of us with your fart, look out! You don't need a flock of us with you. We should have just sent you. You could save Pen single-handedly. Heck, you don't even need to poo anywhere. Just fart and they'll all die!"

Sheila giggled as she heard the old couple quarrel in front of her. She had to admit that poor old Daphne had almost killed them all. Peering below, Sheila spied the camera lenses.

It was a beautiful sunny day in the compound. The bright yellow sun hung lazily in the sky like a big golden ball. Brosto and Strupis, the maintenance crew, were busy methodically cleaning the tiny camera lenses. The cameras stared with unblinking eyes above the wire fences that surrounded the laboratories. Brosto was a rather muscular fellow.

Although he wore his maintenance attire, he never really had need for a shirt or pants for that matter. The reason is that every inch of his body was covered in tattoos. On his left arm he had a brimming bouquet of roses etched with the words, "I love you, mama." Sheila mused how comical it looked. It was surrounded by a vast array of skulls, snakes, and dragons. His thin, brown hair was greasy. Parted in the middle, it hung in a mass of tangled curls at the back. Brosto reminded Sheila of a headbanger rocker from the eighties. Instead of a bright metallic red electric guitar, he clutched a rickety rake in his left hand and a walkie-talkie in his right.

His coworker, Strupis, was thin and lanky. His hair, too, was curly, except that he had bright red hair. It curled around his balding head like a catcher's mitt clutching a round baseball. His eyes were black and beady. His nose was thin and hook-like. Every few seconds, he wiped his nose, as streams of snot incessantly escaped. Occasionally when he missed stopping its escape, the strings of snot would spray into the wind. They would ride the currents of wind and attach themselves to whatever unsuspecting host was nearby.

If Strupis was not trying to catch his snot with his long bony finger, then he was constantly trying to sniff it back. Sometimes the streams would only make it halfway down his nose, and then he would sniff as strongly as he could, and they would run their way back into his wide hairy nostrils.

Brosto took great pride in spraying tiny drops of cleaning solution into the middle of the camera lens and then rubbing it vigorously, making it shine and glisten. He would then peer into each lens, delighted to see his large, dark brown eye and big black pupil fill the entire glass. Then delighted to see himself, he would flutter his eyes, laughing in glee at the size of the reflection of his pupil in the camera lens.

Back inside the surveillance room, Strupis the security guard had dozed off as usual, with his feet up on the desk in front of him. A mosquito buzzed passed his ear, causing him to stir from his lovely nap. Reaching for his coffee, he opened one eye slightly, just long enough to pick up his mug, and looked lazily up into the video screen. A massive eye stared back at him from the video camera. Spilling his coffee all over his security uniform, he dropped his favorite mug and it crashed noisily to the ground, shattering into a thousand little tiny pieces.

Jumping to his feet, he ran screaming from the surveillance room down the hall, snot trailing behind. Regaining courage, however, he inched his way back to the surveillance room. Peering around the corner, he watched, with great irritation, as Brosto, the maintenance worker made funny faces in the lens.

Strupis was furious. "Idiot!" he muttered under his breath. "What in the world was he trying to do—give me a heart attack?" he said, sniffing because of his perpetual cold.

Strupis rushed out to confront Brosto, who was happily whistling and dancing in circles around the lenses. Looking up and seeing Strupis running toward him, he waved, with the biggest smile that his face would allow.

Suddenly, Strupis stopped dead in his tracks and pointed up at the sky with a look of shocked horror on his face. White, grayish globs of liquidy goop began to fall from the sky toward them. Brosto lifted his head and peered up at the strange, chalky white flakes.

"It's snowing!" Brosto called out gleefully. "It's snowing!" he chimed opening his mouth wide and extending out his tongue. "I'm gonna catch me a snowflake! A big fluffy one!"

"It's not snowing, you moron!" shouted Strupis, who had already begun to run for the compound. "That's poo! It's a poo storm!"

As the ravens took aim with their bums, white bird poop exploded, sprayed, and gobbled over the immaculate, newly-cleaned lenses of the cameras. Everything else that surrounded them, including Brosto's tongue, was covered. He had not retracted it quickly enough!

"We've got this covered . . . and even more!" shouted Sheila triumphantly to the conspiracy of ravens.

Strupis and Brosto unfortunately, were not fast enough. They were unable to make it to the compound in time before the poo wave hit! Not just the cameras, but almost every inch of the ground was sprayed, including Strupis and Brosto.

Strupis and Brosto looked like beautiful and magical evergreen Christmas trees in the snow of poo! The only movement from one of the branches was the sound of "sniff, sniff" and streams of white snot.

Finally, the Christmas trees wiped the chalky sewage out of their eyes and off their faces. It dripped in smelly globs from their heads. Brosto was spitting out the not-so-pleasant taste of poo from off his tongue. Walking through the mounds of bird feces, they finally made their way into the compound.

CHAPTER EIGHTEEN

A Rescue Mission

Sheila swooped down from the sky at the sight of Pen's backpack hovering precariously just a few inches off the ground. A backpack suspended in the air, held by nothing, would be a scary thing to see if Sheila didn't know better. Changing into her human form, she spoke to who she suspected was Snapper carrying Pen's backpack.

"Wow! Mission accomplished!" Sheila exclaimed, pointing to the poo lying everywhere.

Snapper rolled her eyes. Reaching down, she laid Pen's backpack on the ground in front of Sheila. "I brought Pen's case of pens because we thought that it would be a good idea to make ourselves invisible before going into the compound," Snapper said.

Sheila nodded. "That's a good idea," she said.

"Did it work?" Snapper asked worried. Looking down at her hands, she gasped. There was nothing in front of her.

Sheila chuckled. "Don't worry, Snapper. If you can't see you, no one else can."

Opening and fumbling around in Pen's backpack, Sheila finally found the right pen. Remembering it was the pen with the silver tip, she pulled it out of a cluster of smelly and ripe gym socks. "Gross!" Sheila said, revolted.

"And that's less appetizing than your pooping spree?" jibed Snapper dryly.

Sheila stuck out her tongue, knowing full well that Snapper's back was turned, and she couldn't see her. Quickly she performed the spell on herself, the way the druid had showed them. Sheila was careful, making sure that she was holding the backpack while casting the spell so that it would disappear too. As much as Sheila thought that Snapper was brilliant, she seemed to not have a brain for common sense stuff. A floating backpack was helpful for Sheila to locate her family, but maybe a little suspicious to bring into a well-armed and monitored government lab.

"Hey, Dad!" Snapper called out. "Are you here?"

"Of course!" rumbled a deep voice right behind her. Snapper just about jumped right out of her skin.

"You almost gave me a heart attack!" Snapper muttered, clutching her chest.

Tameka giggled. "Well guys, we'd better start making our way toward the door," she announced. It was so much fun being invisible that she was afraid that they'd forget why they were there.

The four of them walked toward the door, bumping into one another as they moved forward.

"Hey, watch my feet, Sheila!" grumbled Snapper. Sheila was enjoying the fact that she could bump into Snapper and get away with it. "Hey, Mom and Dad! Sheila's hitting me on purpose."

"Oh, Snapper, I would never do such a thing," responded Sheila, pretending that her feelings were hurt. Then before Snapper could take another step, Sheila swung her hand in her direction again, hitting Snapper in the behind.

"That's it!" sputtered Snapper. "You knew that I was there, Sheila. You are just purposely hitting me on the bum now."

Hamza was glad that he was invisible, so that he could hide his wide grin. Snapper was kind of funny when she was annoyed. Her voice became more and more high pitched. No wonder Pen was always trying to bug her. It was so easy to get a reaction from her.

Finally, they made it to the front door of the compound. It was locked.

"Now what?" Tameka sighed.

"We can use Pen's seventh pen to create a doorway and get in through it," Snapper suggested.

"Yes, we could," mused, Hamza, "but then we would really draw attention to ourselves."

"Well then," said Tameka, "why don't we just knock. I mean, they can't see us anyway, and maybe we can slip by them."

"Well it's worth a try!" agreed Hamza.

Tameka knocked on the large door. Everyone stood, hardly daring to breathe.

Suddenly, the sound of the lock turned, and Brosto and Strupis opened the front door. They peered out in disgust over the chalky white poo that was all over the ground and cameras.

"Those dumb birds," muttered Strupis, as he sniffed noisily. They probably are pecking on the door to finish the job in here!" Strupis grabbed his shotgun that he used for duck hunting on the weekends. Sheila almost gagged at the sound of his snot being sniffed back. He opened the door and stepped outside, with Brosto close behind him.

"I'll get you for this!" Stupis yelled, pointing his clenched fist to the sky. Sheila's cheeks went purple from trying to hold her breath and not laugh.

The men were so busy surveying the area that they didn't notice that the door took longer than usual to close behind them.

In Sheila's rush to get through the door, she forgot that Snapper and her parents were invisible. She smashed right into Snapper's back.

"Be careful, you idiot!" hissed Snapper. "Don't you know there are four of us that are invisible now?"

"Sorry," responded Sheila sheepishly, trying not to giggle. Snapper was furious that Sheila had run into her yet again. Every time Snapper let out an angry sigh, Sheila just struggled harder to suppress her nervous giggles.

Making their way down the corridor, the family searched past the guards for Pen. Thankfully, Sheila had already been to his cell and knew exactly where he was. It was tricky trying to follow Sheila, though, because, of course, no one could see her. They finally decided to hang on to each other's shirts from behind and to make their way single file.

It wasn't always easy doing this, though, as guards, lab technicians, chefs, and all sorts of people raced back and forth through the corridor. Sheila did her best to avoid whoever was rushing her way. It didn't always work, though. Just as they were turning a corner, one of the staff came rushing out of a door to their right. He was balancing two trays, one with turkey sandwiches, and the other with sausages and cupcakes. Sheila didn't see him until it was too late. She ran right into him, knocking the wind right out of his stomach. The turkey sandwiches and sausages went flying, and the cupcakes landed all over the floor.

Scrambling to his feet, he looked around wildly, clutching his stomach. He looked terrified, as if he had seen a ghost. Getting up, he ran for his life down the hallway, leaving the food in the middle of the floor. Sheila and Snapper giggled at his horrified expression.

Sheila continued to lead her family toward Pen's cell. As they neared his cell, Tameka gasped. Through the glass, they could see him. His face was tired and pale. His expression was gaunt.

Running to the prison cell, Tameka took out the pen with no inscription. This pen was the passage-opening pen. Knowing she would need it, she had slipped it into her pocket the night before. Quickly she drew a door on the large metal bars of Pen's cell. Immediately, an opening appeared. The four of them hurried through the doorway, hoping that no one had seen them. The doorway disappeared behind them.

Looking up, Pen watched as a doorway emerged through his cell wall and then disappeared from sight. He opened his mouth to shout out in surprise, but Hamza closed his hand over Pen's mouth in time. Snapper whisked out the wand and quickly reversed the spell, making them visible once more.

"It's us, Pen!" Hamza whispered. "We're going to get you out of here."

"I thought I was hallucinating!" Pen said, relieved to see his father again.

A noise at the cell door startled all of them. It opened, and Dr. Callist walked in briskly.

"Well, well, Pen!" he said, smiling coldly. "This must be your family. And here I thought that I would need to make an elaborate plan to bring them in. Thank you for making my job easier."

Pen stared at Dr. Callist. He was looking at his two sisters. "Hmmm . . . I wonder how you two girls will do in the fear chamber this afternoon. Glancing in Tameka's direction, he continued callously. "I think that we'll make an appointment for you, Madam, in the anger research room." Reaching for his intercom, Dr. Callist clicked the side of it to call for back up, and to make the necessary appointments. Dr. Callist never had the chance to say the first word.

Water pipes all around the cell, and from down the hall, shattered in perfect unison, as Pen's eyes turned from yellow to a deep red. Water gushed through the open door and picked up Dr. Callist. It twirled him around like a spinning top and then smashed him mercilessly against the glass wall. Again and again, the stream of water bashed him onto the glass, until Dr. Callist finally fell to the ground, unconscious.

Hamza watched Pen viciously control the water without even attempting to stop him. How dare this monster threaten to hurt his family? Hamza held Tameka and the girls back until Pen was done.

Hamza's and Pen's eyes met. They nodded at each other. They understood each other. Pen understood that if Hamza had had the gift of controlling the waves, he would have done the very same thing.

Officials raced up and down the hallways, out of the water's way.

Looking at the open door, Pen's eyes suddenly lit up.

"Let's get out of here!" shouted Pen excitedly. Several long plastic sheets floated past Pen in the water. Grabbing a hold of one of them, Pen jumped on top of it. "Here's to leaving in style!" Pen steadied himself on the narrow board. Raising his hands, he called for the water to rise and form a wave. "Grab a hold of one of these plastic boards," called Pen out to his sisters and parents. Sheila grabbed a long, white plastic sheet floating past her. Pen waited until Snapper and his parents floated safely toward the door and were probably outside. Then bending his legs, Pen started to surf on the tip of the wave. Sheila climbed onto her plastic board as well and began to surf on the rushing water.

Leaning his body from one side to the other, Pen surfed around the corners. The spray from his makeshift surfboard hit the side of the wall as his board sliced through the water. Sheila caught up with him on her board. She swerved right in front of him, twisting so that the spray hit Pen's face. The two of them raced toward the door on their wave. The force of the water smashed through the door and the wall. Pen and Sheila surfed right through the opening, ducking as they left the compound.

Pen surfed for another twenty feet or so before his water began to run out. Jumping from his surf board, Pen somersaulted into the air, morphed into a panther in mid-flight, and then landed on all fours on the ground. Sheila also jumped off her surf board at the water's edge, but in mid-air, she commanded the wind to catch her. Twirling around in the wind, like a figure skater, Sheila gracefully landed on the ground.

Hamza, Tameka, and Snapper stared in disbelief at the acrobatics in front of them.

"Show offs!" shouted Snapper, feeling a bit left out. Pen and Sheila looked at each other and gave each other a high-five.

"Nice surfing there, sis!" commented Pen, clearly impressed.

"You're not too bad yourself!" laughed Sheila. "Wow, that was fun. When we're close to water, we totally have to try it out again!"

"You bet!" said Pen, his adrenaline still rushing.

Hamza, Tameka, and Snapper caught up with Pen and Sheila. "Okay, that was fun, but we've got to get to the wildlife reserve as quickly as possible," Hamza said. "The authorities will be back on their feet before long. We don't know how much enforcement will be dispatched." Tameka and the kids nodded. "Let's all change into our animal forms and start running. We're only a few hundred yards away."

The five humans quickly morphed into their animal forms. Hamza led the way, at a full stride toward the wildlife reserve. The other two panthers and deer followed close behind him. Sheila flew just above them, keeping as close to them as possible.

A sudden spark of light shot through the air like a lightning bolt. Looking above him, Hamza saw that it was a spray of ammunition from guns lighting up the sky.

"Run!" yelled Hamza. "They're after us!"

The sound of many approaching helicopters vibrated and shook the ground as they ran. "Return to the lab immediately, Pen!" the voice in the loudspeaker rang out. "If you disobey us, the consequences will be grave!" Pen rushed faster, extending his legs as far as they would go. A crack of noise and light exploded around them.

Pen, Sheila, and Snapper looked up and around them. "Should we use our powers?" yelled Sheila.

"No!" answered Pen, running. "We'll end up killing hundreds of innocent men and women. Let's just try to outrun them."

"But why don't we just attack them all with our powers!" insisted Sheila. "They deserve it, Pen! They're barbarians!"

"No!" shouted Pen and Snapper in unison this time. "Let's only fight back if we're cornered." Sheila looked over her shoulder. She wished that she could just hurl them all into oblivion with a myriad of tornados. But she decided to just comply for now and run with the others.

"Run!" yelled Hamza, barely glancing behind him. The five animals, now filled with adrenaline rush, darted toward the wildlife reserve. Police cars, with sirens blaring, sped down the long driveway, threatening to smash into them from behind.

Hamza darted over the stone barrier that separated the road from the grassy ditches. Pen and the girls followed close behind him, barely breaking their stride as they leapt over the high wall.

A helicopter swooped down from overhead, and a loudspeaker resounded into the night.

"Stop where you are, or we'll shoot. Again, one more warning—stop where you are!"

Hamza rushed faster and faster through the long grass. His black paws barely touched the ground as he flew through the air. Pen and the girls hurtled behind him, Sheila not daring to leave their side, even though she could fly.

"This is your last warning!" the military from the helicopters bellowed out once more.

"Take aim!" Guns emerged from the sides of the air craft. They focused on the small family of animals, running for their lives.

"Fire!" a voice yelled from the helicopter.

Hamza shut his eyes for a split second. Was he doing the right thing? If he stopped now, he and his family could be captured.

Gritting his teeth, he allowed the surging adrenaline to pulse through his veins. Gathering every minute bit of strength that he had left in his body, he forced his legs to gain even more speed than before. His muscles bulged and stretched as he forced his body to exceed its very limit.

"Run!" he yelled once more to his panic-stricken family, running close behind him and desperate to keep up the pace.

A gunshot from the helicopter shattered through the night sky and splintered a large rock beside Hamza as he ran. The pieces of rock exploded, smashing to smithereens in front of him. They sliced deep into his face and neck. Ignoring the piercing pain and the warm blood trickling down his thick, furry forehead, Hamza darted around the rock blast. He rushed at a ferocious speed.

"That was just a warning!" the voice in the loudspeaker roared out. "The next shot will be at your daughter's head, Hamza!"

In a frenzy, Hamza shouted out to Snapper, running close behind him, "Zigzag, Snapper! You're a deer! Zigzag! Make them miss, but don't slow down."

Without questioning, Snapper immediately began to zigzag. In the distance, she could see the horizon of trees emerging. As eloquently as only a deer can prance, Snapper began to dance her crisscrossing fancy steps. Shots rang out in the darkness, aimed at Snapper. They grazed her side, her legs, and passed close by to her feet, but Snapper escaped, missing each and every one of them. From the helicopter, she seemed to be almost mocking them with her zigzag patterns. She seemed to be jumping and avoiding each shot as eloquently as if she were performing a highly sophisticated dance routine in a ballet competition.

Clearly enraged now, the voice from the loudspeaker rang out once more in a deafening roar. "There will be no more games, folks. Junior!" he yelled to his partner in the helicopter. "Blast them all."

Hamza's heart pounded in his chest as he heard the warning from the loud speaker ring out once more, vociferously. They were still hundreds of feet away from the edge of the wildlife reserve. "We can make it, kids! We can make it! Don't stop now."

Mustering every ounce of strength that he had left in his entire body, Hamza roared into the night, with the most deafening rumble that Tameka or the kids had ever heard "Run! Run with everything that's in you! This is it! It is our only chance!"

The kids felt the desperation from his voice course through their very veins. With a force within them that they had never before experienced, they dove toward the reserve. Their adrenaline caused them to speed to limits that are beyond the velocity of the fastest panther or deer ever recorded in all of history.

The blast from the helicopter was deafening as the ground vibrated and shook from the force of the gun shot. Rocks shattered. Branches splintered. Trees split from the tremendous force.

Two hundred feet to go. Trees zoomed past the valiant companions as they ran faster and faster, dreading the next blast that was certain to come within seconds.

One hundred feet. Fifty feet. Dashing past the jagged rocks and thorns that threatened to tear them into pieces, Hamza leaped over them. They grazed his paws and side. Pen dashed close behind him. Snapper sailed high above not only the thorns and rocks, but far above

Hamza and Pen as well. As she sailed through the air, Sheila flew beneath her, her heart beating wildly.

Twenty feet to go. Ten feet. The trees seemed to reach out, desperate to embrace the tiny group in their arms.

A thunderous blast from the helicopter sounded out once more. The shot rang out, deafening the family and exploding into the first line of trees. Flames of fire immediately leapt into the air. They exploded into a furious and thunderous roar.

For one split second, Hamza slowed his pace, horrified at the raging fire in front of him. Then without another moment's thought, he plunged into the flames, scarcely feeling the fire burn his fur. Pen and Snapper dashed into the blazing inferno behind him, hardly noticing its scorching wave of heat on their faces. Snapper quickly morphed for a split second into a human. Just long enough to extinguish the fire that was destroying the helpless trees. She then changed back into a deer, and darted after Pen and the others.

Nobody noticed Sheila stop and turn around at the edge of the forest. Glaring up at the approaching helicopters, she raised her hands to the sky.

"How dare you try to hurt my brother!" she hissed at them under her breath.

Ferocious churning winds suddenly appeared out of nowhere. They hurled four of the helicopters into one another. They exploded into flames and shattered into pieces in the sky. Soldiers with parachutes floated away from the destruction.

Waving her hand at the approaching ground troops, rushing wind swept the soldiers high into the air. Screaming with terror, they spun furiously through the air. Clapping her hands, the wind lifted and smashed two of the approaching army vehicles together. Clapping once more, three more tanks rose in the wind. The men's and women's eyes widened in terror as they looked into Sheila's face from their vehicles. She was sneering back at them.

The tanks crashed into each other in mid-air with such a powerful force that they blew up and burst into flames. Sheila smiled as she watched the petrified looks on the soldiers' faces that were still running toward her. They hesitated for a second. Hundreds of bodies lay motionless and wounded between them and her. Waving at them mockingly, Sheila turned and vanished into the woods. Before her family could suspect anything, she morphed back into a raven and glided high above the treetops and to where they were.

Deeper and deeper, they plunged into the forest. They did not slow down, even when the vines and ferns became thicker and the trees stood closer together. Onward and forward they sprinted around trees, over thorns, between vines, and under branches.

Finally, deep in the thicket, with the thick brush and undergrowth surrounding them, and the canopy of dense leaves and foliage hiding them, they collapsed on to the ground. The children sprawled out on either side of them, panting and wheezing, exhausted.

Finally, regaining enough of his breath to speak, Hamza began, "We can't stay here. They will search these woods for us. However, this temporary home will buy us some time. It will be much more difficult to locate us among the wildlife here." Tameka and the kids nodded.

All of a sudden, before Hamza could continue, Snapper's ears perked up. "Oh no!" cried Snapper. "It's the helicopter! It's coming this way!"

Hamza sprang to his feet. "Snapper, are you sure?" he cried out.

"Yes!" shouted Snapper.

"It's over!" Pen sighed despondently. "They've found us. They'll just burn down this whole forest to find us."

Snapper shook. She shut her eyes. Was this the way it was going to end? Was this to be the end of her family that she had wanted for so long?

Hamza, straining to hear the sound of the aircraft, finally picked up a faint roar in the distance. Slowly it approached their hiding place. The voice in the loudspeaker, seemingly louder than ever, bellowed over the treetops.

"We have found you, you alien freaks. You won't get away this time. We will make sure of it!"

Pen lowered himself to the ground beside Hamza. Tameka wrapped her arms around her terrified family.

"You will be sorry that you ever tried to resist arrest, Hamza!" the voice in the loudspeaker continued. "You and your precious family will be locked up forever. You or your wife and children will never see sunlight again!"

Hamza shook with fear and rage. The bright light from the helicopter combed the forest, and shone down intensely through the trees, about two hundred feet from where they were hiding.

"That's strange," queried Sheila. "Why is the light shining so far away from us?" Without warning, she leaped into the air, and flew through the trees before Hamza could catch her. She glided over the forest to where the beam of the aircraft was pointed. As Sheila neared the location of the helicopter, she gasped at what she saw next.

Military men were descending from the airplane via ropes, and were surrounding a small group of terrified panthers. Somehow, they had also located a deer that was grazing close by, and had dragged it to the scene.

Yelling at the animals, the sergeant bellowed out at the largest panther, "Okay, Hamza, put your hands up immediately!" The panther growled at the sergeant, menacingly, yet terrified. Sheila perched on a nearby branch, mouth open at the hilarious scene.

"You will never outwit us again!" yelled the sergeant, aiming his machine gun at the largest panther's head. "Now morph into a human being immediately, before we shoot!"

The panther bared his teeth at the soldier, ready to tear him apart at any moment. "Okay, this is your last chance, you lowlife!" threatened the team.

All of a sudden, one of the soldiers tapped the head sergeant on the shoulder.

"Sir!" he called out. "That panther has a tag on his ear, sir!" Looking closer, the sergeant noticed that all of the animals had research tags on their bodies. His face turned beet red with embarrassment. "These are ordinary wild animals," continued the soldier.

"I know!" answered the sergeant perturbed.

"Back to the helicopter!" yelled the team, terrified now of the angry group of panthers. As the men raced for the ropes leading to the air craft, the small raging team of panthers attacked them. Knowing that it was a crime to shoot wildlife, the soldiers ran for their lives. Diving for the trees, the men scurried up the branches. The panthers followed close behind them, snapping at their behinds.

Sheila laughed uncontrollably at the hilarious sight. Remembering that her family was still waiting for her news, she flew back to their hiding place.

CHAPTER NINETEEN

The Emerald Country

Iridescent colors shimmered though the tunnellike portal, sucking the family into its wake. Just when they thought there was no hope left, Raven had appeared to them in the forest in her female form. Her raven black hair flowing and cascading around her stately shoulders made her look like a wood nymph. Her indigo silk gown shimmered in the moonlight. Her strong eyes gave them courage.

As she raised her hand, a large spinning portal of spiraling water emerged out of thin air. Nodding at the family, she silently signaled to them that this was their way of escape. A few seconds longer and they would have been done for, thought Pen. Just knowing that this was Raven's doing was of some comfort to everyone despite the overwhelming feeling of helplessness. It was still strange for Pen that Raven could appear to them as a man or as a woman.

"But women are so weak!" Pen had retorted to Snapper and Sheila one day. That was the last time he made that comment. Raising her hands, gusts of ice cold, wintery wind scooped Pen up and took him for a little trip. Sheila had decidedly felt that this was the most opportune moment to teach him how to fly. Sheila acted very confused when Hamza demanded why her brother had mysteriously been found shivering and dangling from the top of the tallest cedar tree in their backyard.

"Pen's hair looks like dreadsicles, the way they are frozen," Hamza said. "Care to explain, Sheila?"

"I guess the art of flying isn't for everyone," Sheila had replied bashfully.

Out of all of them, Pen was the most calm to be floating around in a spinning portal. He was just relieved to be out of prison and with the ones he loved again. He remembered the first time he and the two girls were sucked into a portal. At least this one was a choice. He remembered how the fear and overwhelming shock of being pulled into a strange mat and then coming up out of the grass into a foreign land gave him back his voice.

Tumbling lazily through the portal, Pen looked around him and saw the dust and colors in the wind around him. It spiraled toward a distant, bright blue light.

Pen was a great observer and loved to watch other people's expressions. Snapper's expression was a little difficult to see, as she had grabbed Sheila's feet and had buried her face into them. Sheila had a determined expression on her face and looked like she was swimming furiously in the air with Snapper hanging from her feet. What was really comical to Pen about the whole thing was neither of them had any control over where they went.

This was no ordinary wind. It was a magical portal, concluded Pen. When he looked over to his other side, he saw Hamza and Tameka running as fast as they could to reach them. However, gravity was not present, so while their paws moved at lightning speeds, their body didn't move an inch closer to the children. One thing Pen had learned by his power over water was that sometimes you just had to go with the flow.

Just as Pen was beginning to settle into his trip through the tunnel, his keen eye caught something moving toward them from the blue dot that was steadily growing bigger and bigger. Pen's eyes widened with wonder when he saw what it was. Rushing waves of water were spilling through the tunnel of wind toward them.

Brimming with excitement, Pen shouted out to the girls, "Hang on! This time, I've got your back." Gleaming with pride, he lifted his hands, and instantly, the water cradled around all five of them and drew them out of the portal into the sea.

Feeling the water against his skin reminded Pen of home. Like a dolphin, he dove deep beneath its blue waves, arms at his sides, his legs synchronized and pumping hard. Pen swam like a merman and was the embodiment of a young Poseidon, the Greek god of the ocean. On his way up, he noticed Tameka and Hamza struggling to swim to shore. He had forgotten that panthers hated water and were not strong in swimming any great distance.

Before he could think to help them, a monstrous wave overtook Tameka and Hamza and smashed them against a big, sharp rock very near the shoreline. Instantly, Pen commanded the ocean away from his mom and dad. Obediently the waves withdrew, exposing Tameka clutching at a gaping wound in her side. Blood trickled out from between her fingers as she tried desperately to clamp it shut with her hand. Tameka took the worse of the blow, even though Hamza's legs were scraped up badly by the impact of the rocks.

Soon Sheila and Snapper had joined their parents. Their hearts sunk at the sight of Tameka wincing in pain. The whole family could tell that the only thing stopping her from crying out from the agony was the need to protect her family from worrying over her.

"Are you okay, Mom?" cried all three children at once. Tameka weakly nodded and tried her best to feign a smile, but they could all tell she was far from okay.

By now Hamza had taken off his shirt, ripped it into strips, and was wrapping it tightly around Tameka's wound. Whimpering, Sheila knelt down beside her mother and took her hand in hers.

"We need to get help fast," announced Snapper, always the practical one. Pen surveyed their surroundings. They were on the shore now. Tall cliffs rose from the beach on either side for miles. From where they were, they could not see beyond that.

"Sheila!" snapped Snapper curtly. "We don't have time for tears! You are the only one here who can fly! Change into a raven and fly above the cliffs and find someone who can help us. We need to get her to a hospital as fast as possible. Maybe there is a village nearby. It will take the rest of us way too long to get up over those cliffs."

"Yah," interjected Pen, "those cliffs are way too steep." Pen shivered thinking about how his father had died and tried his best to block it out. "Go now, Sheila, we will take care of Mom until you get back."

Still a little dazed from the ordeal, Sheila wiped her tears with the back of her hand and flew as quickly as she could into the air. It was a long way up from the beach and Sheila couldn't imagine climbing it by foot. Even for a bird, it took some time before she reached the top. When she finally did, the sight that filled her eyes was breathtaking!

Where had Raven sent them? Unfolding, beneath her beating wings, were the most spectacular, emerald green hills she had ever laid eyes on. A tall stone tower stood regally, surrounded by lush, rolling hills, a relic, no doubt, of a time long ago. Further over the green hills and peaks, she flew past stone castles that looked like they came out of story books or from the medieval times. The intricate stone masonry of the castles spun her imagination into a whirlwind of wonder and excitement.

Suddenly, she was jolted back into reality. She needed to find a village of people fast, and these buildings were all abandoned, and though magnificent to behold, would not save her mother. Peering into the distance as she flew, Sheila noticed a few wisps of smoke delicately swirling just above the trees. "At least there's a sign of life," she thought. It can't be a very large village, but perhaps whoever is making the fire can help us.

Sure enough, amid the trees in a green clearing, she saw four figures dancing in a circle around a fire. They were all dressed in flowing, white cloaks. The two women wore wreaths woven with small dainty red and white flowers. The two men covered their heads with the white hoods from their cloaks. Their music was sung in a hauntingly beautiful language. To her surprise, the minute the four people saw her, they froze and became silent. "Why are they suspicious of me?" pondered Sheila. "After all, to anyone else I'm just a raven. Do they not have birds like this in this strange land?" Nervous as she was, she knew she had no choice but to blow her cover to these strangers.

First, Sheila let her face, neck, legs, and feet morph into its human form, leaving her feathers untouched. She knew that if the shock was too great for the people, she still had a chance for a quick getaway. To her amazement, as she gradually descended, the four figures did not seem at all shocked or frightened by what they had seen. Despite their hesitant acceptance of her arrival, Sheila still kept her feathers on her arms.

"Don't be afraid," Sheila said softly to one of the women who had silky, chestnut hair.

"We're not," replied the woman. "We knew who you were the minute you stared down at us from the sky. You see, we have a cloaking spell over our homes and sacred grounds for where we perform rituals. No animal or human can see us unless they are meant to," replied the woman with the chestnut hair.

"You must be the girl that Raven said he would send to us," greeted the other woman stepping forward to meet her guest. She had long red hair, a freckled face, and shining green eyes. "Where are your other companions?" she inquired.

"My mom is hurt badly and I need help quickly," said Sheila. "My family is with her. Can you help us or call a doctor?"

"Let's find her first!" said one of the men, taking off his hood to reveal a crop of red curly hair and a thick beard. "My name is Grian, and we can help. We are druids, which you may know in your language as priests or witches of high magic."

"Let's not waste too much time on stories," interjected the other man, taking off his hood to reveal his gray hair. Sheila lit up as she recognized him. He was the druid who had given them their gifts. He winked at her. "We can do introductions later," he added. "We need to leave now. Time is of the essence!"

The four adults joined hands and began to levitate off the ground. Sheila watched in wonderment as the four druids, as she now knew they were called, spun in unison. They circled round and round in the air only a few feet higher than where she stood. Minutes later, the white cloaks they had worn were now replaced by lizard-like bodies with gleaming golden scales. Expanding out from between each druid's shoulders was a golden pair of bat-like wings. "They are dragons!" exclaimed Sheila out loud. With no time to gaze at the awesome sight, Sheila leapt off the ground and joined her new companions in the sky, leading them to where her family was.

From the shoreline, Sheila could make out her brother and sister waving frantically to alert her to their location. All at once, Sheila felt her heart skip a beat when she saw Hamza carrying the limp, seemingly lifeless body of her mother. With a greater sense of urgency, Sheila raced toward her mother, barely breathing. The four dragons arrived first, swooping down with leathery, golden wings. They snatched them up with ease in their talons.

When they arrived at their huts, they speedily transformed back into humans and gently placed Tameka on one of their beds. "We need to take her to a hospital immediately!" insisted Snapper.

"Trust me," reassured the green-eyed woman with the long red hair. "There is no time, and we can help her more here." She put her hand on Snapper's shoulder as Snapper's eyes welled up with tears. The two druids sprang into action, grabbing glass jars of herbs and strange plants off the shelves to form a medicinal paste. The woman with the chestnut hair dashed out the door, seemingly on a mission to fetch something of great importance. The druid with the red beard had lit some incense and was waving the smoking stick over Tameka, chanting in some foreign-sounding tongue.

"It's Gaelic!" Snapper deduced with tremendous satisfaction. She had finally put all the puzzle pieces together from the scenery, language, and the customs. They were in a round thatched home of a druid family in the highlands of Ireland. She remembered from what she had read that the druids were the high priests or witches of the Celtic peoples and possessed potent healing powers and great magic. They had the power to transform themselves into animals, make themselves invisible, and cast spells. They were respected healers.

Hamza ran his hands tenderly over Tameka's forehead and through her long, black hair. "You are going to be fine," Hamza said, trying to steady his trembling voice. "Just hold on a little longer. We are right here, my love."

Rushing through the doors, the woman with the chestnut hair entered with a red, hot iron rod. She hurried to get to Tameka's side but was abruptly stopped by Pen. "What are you going to do with that?" demanded Pen angrily.

"Please Pen," she pleaded. "I don't have time to wait. I have to use the burning iron rod to cauterize your mother's open wound. If I don't do it now, your mother will die of infection long before she opens her eyes. I promise she won't feel a thing. She is unconscious." Pen grimaced, still distrustful, but he stepped aside.

Carefully the druid lowered the glowing, red-tipped iron rod onto the gaping wound. Snapper and Sheila screamed and dove into Pen's arms as they heard the sound of searing flesh.

Brushing past Hamza and the children, the red-haired woman stood beside Tameka with a needle and thread. For a split second, Snapper turned her head away from Pen's chest just to see the druid penetrate Tameka's skin with the needle and see blood gushing everywhere. Snapper almost fainted at the gruesome scene. Undaunted by the amount of blood lapping around her hands, the druid continued to pierce the flesh. With the needle, she pulled and joined the gaping sides of the wound, drawing them together.

Finally she was finished. Her hands were bright red, soaked with Tameka's blood. "Don't worry," she said to the children. "Your mom will be fine. It's almost over."

Finally the gray-haired druid came forward with the paste that they had made from their store of herbs and plants. Gingerly he dipped his fingers into the green paste and applied it liberally over the wound. Everyone waited, barely breathing. They all stared at Tameka, studying her for any sign of recovery. Suddenly, her eyes flickered slightly. Everyone gasped with excitement! But to their dismay, the movement of her eyes and her rapid breathing slowed down. Right before their eyes, Tameka began to turn a grayish color as if the life was being sucked right out of her.

Tameka's breaths became more and more labored until she finally became still. Unable to contain his pain, Hamza dropped to his knees. Finally he let out a bloodcurdling roar. Unashamed, he wept violently, his whole huge muscular frame shaking uncontrollably.

The children were utterly grief-stricken. There was nothing left to do. Their mother was dead. Blue-tinged skin and lifeless, Tameka lay before her grieving family.

Sheila stood to take her mother's hands to arrange them respectfully across her chest. When her hand touched her mother's hand, she heard a slight gasp for air. Placing her ear closer to her mother's body, she could hear her mother's breath, though soft and rattled at first, slowly become stronger. Rushing to her father's side, she grabbed him by the arm to alert him. Sure enough, Tameka's color had flushed back into her cheeks and she was now breathing steadily, as if in a peaceful slumber.

A quiet smile of relief spread across Hamza's face as he tenderly took his wife's hand and pressed it against his lips. Pen and Snapper wrapped their arms around their father. They were going to make it together as a family, just as they always did.

CHAPTER TWENTY

Fairies Among Us

The sound of fluttering wings against the window shutters startled Snapper out of a deep sleep. Snapper stirred. She detested insects. Judging from the rustic nature of the hut, there was probably no glass on the windows to keep out the creepy crawlies. Rustle, rustle, rustle. Snapper heard the same sound again. This time, the sound ventured closer to her pillow. Managing to stifle a high-pitched squeal, Snapper leapt from her bed.

Careful not to cause any more noise than she had already made, she lit her pinky finger with a flame no bigger than a candle. In the corner, perched on Snapper's bed post was a dragonfly. Snapper shivered at the thought of the wretched insect crawling all over her while she slept. She didn't want to wake up her family with any more of her racket.

Summoning her courage, Snapper grabbed the small garbage pail that was beside her bed and stealthily moved toward the winged menace. Snapper lifted the pail, and hovering just above the winged creature, got ready to capture it.

Suddenly, she froze at the sound of another strange noise creeping behind her door. "Boooooo!" wailed the unseen voice, sending Snapper yelping in fright. Pen, who had heard Snapper's frightened voice, had decided to try to scare her. Pen loved scaring Snapper. She always gave him the best reactions!

Snapper dropped the pail and began bouncing frantically all around the room, hollering, "I'm not afraid of you, I'm not afraid of you. You will be sorry if you ever come near me!" The insect jumped too and buzzed all around the room looking for the safest place to land. In all the commotion, it found that the safest place to land was on top of Snapper's shoulder.

That very instant, light and laugher lit up Snapper's room. Pen was bent over with laughter after he'd managed to light his gas lamp. "Gotcha," he managed to wheeze between snorts of laughter.

"Pen, you idiot, get it off me. Now's not the time for your ridiculous pranks! If I am bitten by this dragonfly, and I die, I will play endless pranks on you as a ghost. Pen, you listen to me! I swear I will haunt you and your children and your grandchildren after you! Now stop laughing and get this thing off me, you immature imbecile!"

Finally catching his breath, Pen sauntered over to Snapper to see what species of harmless insect this could be.

"You are too funny, Snapper," Pen chuckled. "I think you had a brain freeze from when you got startled. I may not be as smart as you, but I do know that there are no seriously poisonous animal or insect species in Ireland."

Snapper couldn't argue with Pen's logic, but she was eager to get whatever it was off her shoulder. "Wow, would you look at those wings!" exclaimed Pen, clearly mesmerized. "I've never seen anything like them! I mean, look at the transparent rainbow colors and look at the way they glow. I don't think that it's a lightning bug. Too big for that . . . but too small for a dragonfly either." Pen was back in his role as a detective. "I've never seen or read about this species before," Pen remarked.

Fluttering its wings again, the mysterious insect flew off Snapper's shoulder. Much to her relief, it rested on Pen's outstretched fingertip. Snapper recoiled to the back of the room, close to the door in case the strange insect decided to make any more sudden moves toward her. Trembling with excitement at discovering a new species, Pen took out his trusty magnifying glass from his pants pocket.

"Snapper, come over here and look at this!" called out Pen. "This is a totally cool bug! In fact, it almost looks like it has hair on the back of its head!"

"What do you mean?" inquired Snapper from halfway across the room.

"Stop being a scared little girl, and take a look," insisted Pen, knowing full well that what he said would infuriate Snapper enough to prove she was not afraid.

"I was merely being cautious," Snapper replied indignantly. It was just the reaction Pen was looking for, and he smiled mischievously.

The strange-looking bug suddenly raised its two arms in the air and stood up on its legs.

"Oh my god!" said Snapper, suddenly peering closer at the creature. "It looks like a faerie or faie."

"What the hell is a faie?" exclaimed Pen, a bit agitated at the walking dictionary beside him, who was clearly excited now.

"That's the original term for what we know as 'fairy' today, Pen! It's a fairy!"

Sure enough, as the two siblings gazed through the looking glass, they realized that the sight before them was dazzling. She was a fairy, all right. Now that they could see her properly, she was so beautiful. Her blue skin shone, as if it were lit up by stardust from the inside. Eyes like sparkling sapphires stared inquisitively back at them. She had delicate pointed ears, a small dainty mouth, and her blue silky hair billowed around her, waving in the wind of her fluttering wings. Clothed in what looked like an array of woven feathers and leaves, she blended in perfectly with a forest.

Opening her mouth to speak, the fairy sounded exactly like a song bird.

"Her voice reminds me of a skylark," announced Sheila loudly, who had crept into the room noiselessly. Pen almost jumped out of his skin and let a high-pitched squeal.

"Why Pen," teased Snapper, "you sound remarkably like a frightened little girl".

Red in the face now, Pen muttered, "You shouldn't sneak up on us like that, Sheila, you could have woken Dad!"

"Really," replied Snapper sarcastically. "I say it serves you right for trying to scare me earlier!"

"Man, it sucks to be the only boy right now," grumbled Pen. "I'm always outvoted by two girls!"

"Well you may be quite grateful for my help right now even though I'm a girl," remarked Sheila, smiling. "I am the only person here who can interpret the fairy. Not only am I a raven, but I can also understand every bird dialect that there is."

Lowering herself to her knees so she was on eye-level with the fairy, Sheila and the fairy began talking in bird talk. Pen and Snapper stared, speechless. There were times that Sheila would break out into giggles mid-chirp, and there would be times that the fairy would cover her mouth and snicker too. It was the oddest sight. Finally Sheila rose to her feet.

"Her name is Daphnaie, and which one of you was trying to kill her?" Sheila demanded dryly.

Sheepishly Snapper raised her hand. "Tell her I'm so sorry. I mistook her for a dragonfly."

"I think I'll just tell her the 'I'm sorry' part. You know, her job is to protect the forest animals and nature, so she may not be too thrilled with the last part," added Sheila half-laughing.

"Yes, oh my goodness, yes—don't relay that last part. Did I mention I'm sorry . . . so sorry." Sheila rolled her eyes and conveyed Snapper's apologies in chirps.

"Okay, guys, grab your coats and shoes," announced Sheila abruptly.

"Where are we going at this time of the night?" asked Pen, bewildered.

"We are going to go join our hosts the druids in the forest," replied Sheila. "They sent this fairy to tell us to come and follow her."

"I guess they were counting on you as an interpreter," piped up Snapper who was acting doubly friendly after her not-so-favorable encounter with the fairy. The fairy just gave Snapper dirty looks and chirped incessantly with Sheila.

"Hurry, guys, we've already wasted enough time, and we're late!" insisted Sheila.

Leaving the cream, clay-colored hut with the sloping, grass-thatched roof, the three travelers made their way toward the forest. Only a few feet away from the hut and the cobblestone walk lay about fifty feet of lush, green grass that was tightly surrounded by dense forest.

"Snapper," whispered Pen. "Give us some light."

Snapper pulled out her open hand, palm faced up. She clenched her fingers tightly together, forming a fist. She closed her eyes and slowly withdrew her fingers. A small ball of light hovered over her palm. As it spun, it grew larger until it had become the size of a nectarine. A small amount of light that would be just enough to guide their way, but not enough light to draw attention, reasoned Snapper.

Reaching the border of the forest, the blue fairy began to glow even brighter, bathing the trees in a brilliant blue light. Snapper extinguished her light and silently, they followed the fairy. Magically the forest seemed to respond to the fairy's presence. Bramble, thorn bushes and trees creaked as they bent over to the side, making a clear path for the children to follow. Above them, the moonlight spilled out over the treetops, and the stars sparkled like shining dust in the night sky. This forest reminded them of Raven's world. The air felt rich with old and strong magic.

"Do you hear the sound of singing and a drum?" asked Snapper, turning to the other two. Sheila and Pen shook their heads, but they didn't question her. Snapper's hearing as a mule deer was stronger than theirs put together. Up ahead, the children saw a tight wall of tall oak trees. The trees were so densely grown together, that they almost looked like one tree stretching out for miles in both directions.

"This must be where the druids are!" Snapper announced ecstatically. Rushing forward, Snapper ignored the frantic warning calls of Daphnaie, the blue fairy. "Come on!" Snapper called out to the others. "What are you waiting for?" The instant Snapper stepped too close to the wall of oak trees, a thunder rumbled through the forest. Green lightning crackled in the oak trees' branches and a mighty torrent of wind surrounded Snapper. It took her and hurled her helplessly into the air.

Realizing the danger her sister was in, Sheila transformed only her arms into raven's wings so she would be large enough to fly Snapper out of harm's way.

Unfortunately, the girls didn't just have the wind to escape but also bolts of green lightning shooting out from the branches straight for them. Managing to get to Snapper, Sheila lowered herself in place so that Snapper could grab a hold of her back. Together they darted through the steam of lightning bolts and met Pen who was anxiously watching them from the ground.

"Are you guys okay?" asked Pen, staring rather stunned at Snapper.

"Yes, of course, I'm okay," said Snapper, trying her best to keep herself calm. Looking up, Snapper saw the blue fairy giggling merrily with a slightly devilish glint in her eye.

"You see, I told you guys we couldn't trust her. Just like an insect, she's sneaky."

Snapper looked at Sheila and Pen. They were both staring at her, wide-eyed, holding their breath.

"Why are you two holding your breath?" Snapper blurted out. "My gosh, your faces will turn blue!"

Unable to hold it in anymore, Sheila and Pen let out the air, almost blowing each other away, and then erupted into an exploding fit of laughter.

"Snnnnnapper," wheezed Pen, almost unable to speak, "Your hair!"

Slowly, Snapper lifted her hands to her head. To her surprise, she felt her hair standing straight up on end and stiff like a broom on top of her head.

"Very funny, you two!" grunted Snapper angrily.

"I think the lightning must have just caught the end of your hair," said Sheila, trying to sound comforting while still recovering from her fits of giggles.

Snapper grabbed a hold of her hair and yanked it down to her shoulders. However, the frizz from the lightning hadn't worn off, and as soon as she let go, back up it bounced as straight as an arrow.

"Don't worry," said Pen, seeing Snapper getting more and more infuriated. "I'll fix it." With that, he sent a shower of water on top of poor Snapper's head.

"Ahhhhhh! What are you trying to do to me, Pen?" Snapper screamed, hearing the sound of crackling in her hair.

"Trust me," said Pen smiling nervously, "maybe it will work."

"Maybe?" snapped Snapper, getting more agitated by the second. When the cloud of smoke cleared and the sound of crackling faded, Sheila and Pen looked up at Snapper's hair, hoping for the best. Snapper's hair was now vibrating with electric energy but had managed to make its way halfway down.

"It looks great," said Sheila, trying to comfort her frazzled sister.

Sheila and Pen looked at each other. They thought it best not to mention that while Snapper's hair once looked like it was jumping off her head, it now looked like it was running away behind her head.

Chirping from the blue fairy signaled that it was safe to come out of hiding. "Daphnaie is telling us," interpreted Sheila, "that only a fairy is capable of opening up the oak tree barrier. Shut up everyone, and she will summon the guardian of the sacred druid grove. She said that we must promise to never speak to anyone of anything or any person that we have seen in this secret place." The blue fairy stopped chirping and looked directly at Snapper and Pen, awaiting their answer.

"We swear to keep it secret," they answered together. Sheila chirped the interpretation for the blue fairy.

Suddenly, the blue fairy began to sing a song that pierced sharply through the night air. So enchanting was her voice that they didn't even notice there were no words—just hauntingly beautiful sounds, like the music of a flute. Blue, glistening light radiated from her lips as she sang. They streamed like thin waves into the sky. Snapper, Pen, and Sheila stood with their mouths open, mesmerized by the music. The sound of violently loud and massive wings arose from the distance. Before their very eyes, a magnificent creature emerged. Its head and wings were in the form of a mighty eagle, but its muscular body, claws, and tail were that of a lion.

"It's a griffin!" said Pen pointing up to the sky. "Wow!" remarked Sheila. "Look at the sheer size of it! I sure am glad it's on our side!"

"You hope," said Snapper cynically, still not having recovered completely from her ordeal. She decided to wait and see what was going to happen before she made any more assumptions.

As soon as the gigantic griffin landed, it began to flap its enormous wings toward the oak trees. The blue fairy began to chirp once more at the children.

"Daphnaie is telling us to come quickly!" shouted Sheila to her brother and sister.

"How are we going to get past that thing without being blown or knocked over?" asked Pen, terrified.

"Go through the griffin's legs, the blue fairy is saying," said Sheila struggling to listen and interpret at the same time. "Hurry, the door will only stay open for a few more seconds."

"What door?" retorted Snapper. "There is no door."

"That door," said Sheila. Sheila's sharp eyesight had detected a tiny hole expanding out from the knot near the base of the oak tree.

"It's too small!" insisted Snapper, panicking. "It's only a keyhole."

"Okay, hold my hand Snapper, I'll get us through." Somehow Sheila felt connected to the blue fairy and trusted her. Without thinking too much, she stuck her hand through the knot that was only a few inches wide. Instantly, it sucked Sheila's hand in. The miraculous part was that as it sucked Sheila in, the opening adjusted, streamlining its width and height exactly to the proportions of her body as each part entered. Holding on to Sheila in front and Pen behind, Snapper was relieved to discover that the hole pulled each of them in easily. Obviously a test of faith, thought Sheila to herself as she pulled Snapper behind her.

Tumbling on to the soft grass, Snapper, Pen, and Sheila looked up into the faces of the four druids who had helped them.

"Well, you guys finally made it!" said the druid with the red beard. "I'm Grian, this is Eridanus," he said, pointing to druid standing beside him with a long gray beard.

"My name is Lyra," said the female druid with the long curly red hair, "and this is my sister Delphinus."

The woman standing next to Lyra had dark chestnut hair that she had braided into two braids. She was obviously the least talkative of the bunch. She gave the children a shy smile.

"I'm sorry we didn't have time to give proper introductions," Lyra continued, "but things were a little hectic and busier than expected when we met you."

Thinking back, Sheila could just remember bits and pieces, as everything happened so fast. "We would have loved to tell you where we were meeting you, but just like you, we made a pact with the blue fairy to not speak of this place outside of its walls."

"Everyone has been so eager to meet you," announced Lyra proudly. "They all have heard that Raven sent you to us personally! He enrolled you into our school!"

Suddenly, Sheila, Snapper, and Pen became aware of many more eyes staring at them. Stepping out from the grass-thatched huts, hundreds of children appeared around them.

"Sorry, I forgot to mention," Lyra apologized, "this secret, unmentionable place . . . is a school for young apprentice druids. Druid is a word used by us Celtic people for wizard or witch. We are going to be your teachers, and tomorrow, your training begins!"

CHAPTER TWENTY-ONE

Speaking to the Stars!

"Come, students, let the welcoming celebrations commence!" boomed Grian's deep voice. It echoed as it tumbled through the air.

"I thought classes will only start tomorrow," said Sheila, sounding a little bewildered. Before she met Snapper and Pen, she was a bit of a loner. Mostly she kept to herself. All this undue attention was making her really uncomfortable.

"Your lessons start tomorrow, yes, dear child. But we have planned something very special for all three of you. Call it the druid ritual of initiation if you will," replied Grian, slightly bowing.

"Oh, I think I know a little something about that," added Snapper eagerly. "Sheila, you are in for a treat! These rituals are ones I've only read about, but I've never seen any in person."

"Any human sacrificing involved in this ritual, namely us?" Sheila whispered to Snapper nervously. The druids chuckled, as obviously Sheila hadn't whispered quietly enough.

"No, silly," giggled Snapper, "they are going to give us a complimentary fortune telling."

"Now Snapper," teased Lyra, "I've heard tales of your book smarts but don't ruin the surprise just yet."

As usual, Pen left all the talking to the girls while he investigated the situation for himself. All of the druids were dressed in these weird, white robes—even the boys and men. Around their waists, their gowns were tied with a silver cord. Along with the two druid women, all the girls had garlands of flowers woven through their hair. Lyra and Delphinus carried mistletoe branches. Grian and Eridanus held wooden staffs carved and wrapped in places with thin strips of leather.

"Sheila, Snapper, Pen, please join us," beckoned Eridanus.

Arranging the three children to hold hands, he asked them to form a triangle. Turning to the rest of the students, he motioned for them with his hands to sit down.

Pointing his staff at a fire pit surrounded by large, smooth stones, Eridanus chanted a few words in Gaelic. Moments later, an orange flame sprang from the ground and curled around the dry logs. A drum sounded. Pen spied a young boy effortlessly moving his hands over the stretched animal hide of the drum. The beat of the drum was spine chilling and made Snapper's body shiver with excitement.

"What are they doing now?" asked Sheila nervously.

"They are going to speak to the stars," announced Snapper confidently. "According to legend, it is said that druids are known for their ability to foretell future events by reading the stars."

"Is that even possible?" asked Pen.

"Well, we'll soon find out," replied Snapper.

"Maybe the stars will show us how to get to a great burger joint in the very near future," remarked Pen. "I'm starved!"

"It's not a map, you moron," snapped Snapper. "How can you be thinking about food at a time like this?"

"Look, you two clowns, look up in the sky! It's happening!" shouted Sheila with excitement. Sheila's loud voice brought Pen back into reality. As Lyra and Delphinus sang and danced, waving their branches of mistletoe, the stars began to shine brighter and brighter. Soon all the children were chanting together in Gaelic. To Snapper, Pen, and Sheila, it seemed as if the whole forest and field were painted over in a silvery light that spilled out from the stars.

"Look at those five stars up there," gestured Sheila. "If you draw an imaginary line connecting them, it almost looks like a 'w.' They're getting brighter and brighter like they're coming closer."

Snapper looked up smiling proudly to herself. "Well my astronomy studies sure paid off! That constellation of stars, Sheila and Pen, is Cassiopeia. Or in layman's terms . . . the vain queen."

"And looks like the vain queen is headed our way," interrupted Pen, grabbing his two starstruck sisters by their hands and pulling them.

"Look, there are more constellations that are getting bigger!" exclaimed Snapper ecstatically. "The one below Cassiopeia is Andromeda, or the chained woman, as she's called. See the stars that, when connected together, look like a sideways L? That's Andromeda."

Sheila didn't care much about their names as much as the fact that these stars were nearing Earth at an alarming speed. "Can you please stop this?" Sheila pleaded with the druids. "It's okay, we really don't need a reading of our future."

"At this rate," Pen grumbled, "none of us will have any future to tell if those stars collide with the Earth."

"Did you know?" continued Snapper, happy to be the authority on the matter. "Did you know that most stars are much larger than our Earth and are made up of mostly exploding gas like hydrogen and helium?"

"That's great!" answered Sheila dryly. "If you somehow survive this then you can write that description in our obituaries."

"Have some faith." Eridanus chuckled.

Lifting his wooden staff, he whispered another spell. Instantly, the stars froze. Breathing a sigh of relief, Snapper, Pen, and Sheila stared up at the utterly spectacular sight. For the students watching, this event seemed absolutely normal. They smiled at the new students' reactions. But to the three children, seeing massive stars hanging suspended just a few yards from the ground was unbelievable. Even though the druids still had to shrink them a little to bring them that close, they were still gigantic, white flaming spheres to the children. Grian raised his staff. Magically the stars began to fuse together to form two shining figures of pure white fire.

The light became so bright and so hot that all the students had to cover their eyes and move back a few feet. When the light dimmed to a steady glow, they opened their eyes. What towered above them was equally as terrifying as it was beautiful. Cassiopeia, the vain queen, rose from her starlit throne. At about fifty feet high, everyone else was just an ant to her. Her long hair tumbled in curls down the sides of her long sparkling tunic.

Only her eyes, cold as ice, gave away the cruelty of her nature. Her smile twisted into an evil grin when she saw the chained woman fall to her feet. Her nails began to grow long and sharp. Leaping forward, she wrapped her hands tightly around the chained woman's neck. The chained woman cried out in agony. Again the vain queen grinned as she sunk her sharp nails deep into Andromeda's neck. Suddenly, a violent crash rang through the air. Stars in the shape of a raven sped toward the queen. As he flew through the air, flashes of lightning trailed behind him. Screeching in rage, the queen flung her mirror at the bird.

Sheila closed her eyes at the gruesome sight of the glass shattering and slicing through the bird's chest. Silvery rivers of blood spilled down its thick neck. Something just occurred to Sheila. Maybe this confluence of events was foretelling another encounter with Kalik. Another encounter right here in Ireland. Turning quickly to tell her brother and sister what she had discovered, she soon realized from their expressions that they were all thinking the same thing. Knowing either or both of his sisters was about to speak, Pen gently closed his hands over their mouths. Snapper huffed. Sheila just took the hint.

Without warning, the raven spread open its wings, and a blinding light poured out on to the ground. The second it touched the queen's skin, she let out a bloodcurdling scream. Recoiling her nails from inside Andromeda's neck, the queen's body began to dissolve into stardust. All that remained of the queen was her mute and severed head. Now free of the queen, Andromeda's body, limp and weak, loftily floated into the night sky. The only figure left standing was the raven hovering over the decapitated head of the evil queen.

No one made a sound. Even Snapper was silent. Lyra and Delphinus stepped forward. The drum sounded again, low and pulsing like a heartbeat. The two women's voices mingled like wind and water, sending the stars spinning back up into the sky. Grian looked worried. Drawing his fingers down his bright red beard, he exhaled slowly.

"Do not be alarmed, my new friends," he said looking down at Sheila, Pen, and Snapper's panic-stricken faces. "That was only a story told by the stars by our request. No one was harmed. The stars just acted it out for us to see plainly."

"Ummmm, excuse me, Mr. Grian. Sir?" piped up Sheila raising her hand. "I'm not so worried about the stars as I am about us! If that's our future, then why are we here? I mean, clearly, dangerous things are about to happen to us. We came to Ireland to escape the danger that was happening to us at home and now we're in trouble again?"

Grian paused and looked knowingly at Snapper. A silent tear fell down Snapper's cheek. Slowly she spoke, "Sheila, that chained woman could represent my mom."

"Or it could represent you or me," interrupted Sheila.

"Either way, Raven sent us here for a reason, and if there is a possibility that we could save your parents . . . wouldn't you take that risk, Sheila?"

"We're here to help you" announced a tall, strapping boy from the back. He stood, raising his fist high into air. "We are powerful druids, aren't we guys?"

"Druids in training, Rocco," Lyra reminded him grinning. "Well who's with me?" Rocco roared. As hundreds of students jumped to the feet, the ground shook from the mighty roar of their warrior chant.

Grian beamed. "Well my fearless travelers, you haven't even began your classes and you look like you have an army of supporters."

Sheila smiled. For once, she didn't feel like a freak. She didn't even have to try to keep her family's secret. They were finally among friends.

CHAPTER TWENTY-TWO

Druid School

"Hurry up, Pen, or we'll be late for class," warned Snapper curtly, rushing ahead of the two them.

"Where are we going? You don't even know which class we have first," panted Pen, finally catching up to Snapper.

Still running, Snapper turned to Pen and produced a schedule. "This was posted up in our dorms if you took the time to notice. Classes start promptly at eight o'clock, and we are part of group 3C, which means . . .," continued Snapper, refusing to break her stride to explain, "our first class is Spells and Potions."

"Who's the teacher for that class?" wheezed Pen, trying desperately to keep up with Snapper's fast pace.

"Professor Lyra," replied Snapper.

Out of the corner of her eye, she saw Pen's cheeks flush a little red. He must be having trouble with my fast speed, Snapper thought to herself proudly.

"Where is Sheila?" asked Snapper, finally noticing they were missing one sibling.

"You know, Sheila," muttered Pen, "she's probably dawdling and picking flowers or she's gone back to bed. You know how many late slips she would have gotten at school if Mom hadn't forced us out of the door early."

"Well, I hope she's not too late. I'd hate to make a bad impression on our very first day." Snapper sighed disapprovingly.

Much to Pen's and Snapper's surprise, Sheila was already seated and browsing the text book. "No need to be out of breath, you two, there is one whole minute before class begins," called out Professor Lyra, grinning from the back of the room. "Why don't the two of you make yourself comfortable and take your seats. Your sister Sheila was my first student to arrive. I was very impressed by her studiousness. She was here so early that she is a quarter of the way through the textbook. Look, she saved you two seats next to her at the front of the classroom."

Beaming, Sheila looked up from her text book. "My pleasure, Professor Lyra! I can't wait to begin my first class on spells and potions. I took the liberty of reading a few chapters from several of the books that you had suggested from the syllabus outline of the course!" Pen and Snapper stared at each other in disbelief.

"What gives?" whispered Pen to Sheila, finally taking his seat. "Really, Sheila, how did you get here so fast? You didn't even manage on the way here to keep up with us," demanded Snapper suspiciously.

"I don't know what you two are talking about," replied Sheila innocently.

"Please open up your textbooks to page three," began Professor Lyra sweetly. As she walked up to the front of the class, Pen blushed. She was exquisite, the way she held her head and the way her long, curly, red hair seemed to bounce as she walked. Her porcelain skin was delicately splashed with tiny freckles, and her green eyes dazzled like emeralds.

Pen had never seen anything so divine. He couldn't stop staring at her, barely hearing a word she said. She moved so gracefully, like jelly, he thought. Hmmmm, jelly, he again thought to himself. Soon he was thinking about food again and had forgotten about his beautiful teacher. Breakfast, he remembered, was really good. Well to him it was. He couldn't understand why his mostly vegetarian sisters barely touched anything on their plates. After all they did eat eggs and fish every once in a while.

Pen was delighted to try a traditional Irish breakfast. Blood pudding, rashers, potatoes, and baked beans were heaped in great quantities on his plate. Now only a few hours later, Pen could feel his belly rumbling. A sharp slap to the back of the head woke Pen up. "What did you do that for?" groaned Pen, rubbing his aching head. Refusing to interrupt her teacher, Snapper showed Pen the wet drool on the page of her textbook.

"Sorry," mouthed Pen to Snapper, who had begun to form an ugly snarl on her face.

"Now make sure that when you wave your wand, make the movement flow from your wrist not your arm," explained Professor Lyra. "If there is any jerky motion to your swish, the spell will backfire, producing less than favorable results."

Kicking the already agitated Snapper under the desk, Pen tried to get her attention. "Which wand is she talking about?" exclaimed Pen nervously.

"If you were paying attention like the rest of us instead of drooling all over my textbook dreaming about lunch," lectured Snapper, "then you might have noticed the entire class storming up to the front to get their pick of wands first."

Pen looked to the front of the class. There on the desk beside his statuesque teacher was the last wand, which looked like a bruised banana. It was clumsily taped up in at least a dozen different places. The rest of the students were practicing the perfect swishing motion with their wands and chatting merrily as Professor Lyra circulated to help her students. "Sucks to be you!" said Snapper, grinning from ear to ear.

"Sorry to disappoint," snickered Pen, "but I may have something just as good."

"What's that?" asked Snapper quizzically. Reaching into his knapsack, Pen pulled out his silver tipped pen from a tangled mess of cheesy and overripe smelling gym socks. "Gross!" wailed Snapper, covering her nose. Thrusting it forward, it instantly became a thin silver wand. Pen beamed, quite pleased with himself.

"Attention, everyone!" cried Professor Lyra enthusiastically. "Now that we've practiced the wand swish, we are going to put it into practical application! By that, I mean . . ." paused Professor Lyra dramatically, "We are going to fly!" Snapper's hand shot up like a firecracker.

"Yes, Snapper," said the professor, "you seem very perplexed about this flying spell."

"It's just that we have no brooms, unless you mean to turn us all into birds, which makes me slightly nervous," replied Snapper.

"Not to worry, dear Snapper," chuckled Professor Lyra sympathetically. "For our first go . . . just baby steps. Today we will just float a few inches off the ground. Our wands require no accessories," joked the professor with a playful grin. "You'll see just how powerful a druid wand really is."

Pen looked at his wand, remembering that his didn't come from the class set. Just then he recalled that his wand was given to him by a druid. It will probably work just as well, mused Pen to himself.

"So who would like to go first?" called out Professor Lyra to the class.

"I would, I would, I would!" chimed Sheila, like a peppy ring tone.

"Of course, she would go first," muttered Pen to Snapper. "She doesn't even need a wand to fly and she practically does it every day!"

"Raise your wand," beckoned the Professor. Jumping to her feet with a grin so wide it could crack her face, she shot out her wand like a bullet straight in front of her. Professor Lyra's eyes nearly popped out of her head from Sheila's exuberance. "Okay, Sheila, relax your arm, so you don't impale your fellow classmates," instructed the professor nervously. "It's a graceful swishing motion side to side with your wand, while chanting the spell: 'snámh san aer'."

Everyone watched as Sheila began to slowly levitate up from the ground about a foot or so. "Well done, Sheila!" congratulated her professor. "Now to descend, point your wand down and say 'sios'. Be aware," cautioned Professor Lyra "that the slightest mispronunciation or error in the wrist motion can direct the wand in ways that you may not have intended." As soon as Sheila spoke the Gaelic word for down, she lightly descended back to the ground, to the sound of thundering applause.

Grinning again a little too heartily, she bounded to the front of the classroom. Throwing her arms around the professor's waist, she began thanking her over and over for the delightful opportunity to learn how to fly.

"Sheila, what in the world are you talking about?" blurted out Pen. "You know how to fly!"

Gasping for air, the almost asphyxiated professor managed to unwrap Sheila's arms from their death grip from around her.

"Okay, Sheila!" she wheezed, still trying to catch her breath. "Why don't you take a breather?"

"Now that we've seen it done, boys and girls, why don't you all give it a shot?"

"Snámh san aer," chanted Snapper mystically, whooshing her wand high into the air.

"No, Snapper!" yelled Pen, who saw what Snapper was doing a little too late. "You're supposed to swish your wand from side to side."

Before Snapper could hear the rest of Pen's sentence, she had shot up like an arrow and burst through the thatched roof of the classroom. Higher and higher she flew, seeing the school become increasingly smaller.

"Stop this instant!" she screamed at the wand furiously.

"The wand only speaks Gaelic," hollered a voice trailing from below the busted roof. Snapper's heart began to pound. She didn't want to look. She was scared to think of how high she was now. Scrambling for facts to keep her calm, she tried to think about what altitude a person would begin to suffer from lack of oxygen. "Maybe I better start conserving my air now and slow my heartbeat down," reasoned Snapper, still afraid to look.

Suddenly, she felt a hand wrap around her wand and aim it to the ground. "Sios," the voice called out firmly.

Instantly, the wand responded, and Snapper began to gradually float down to the school. Plucking up her courage, she opened up her eyes. Staring back at her with concern in his bright blue eyes was a tall boy around her age with dirty blond hair. With one hand holding her wand and the other holding his, the boy helped the shaken Snapper make it down safely.

"Are you okay?" cried Pen, rushing over to his sister.

"Yes, I'll live," quivered Snapper, "thanks to his heroics. By the way, I didn't catch your name . . ." said Snapper extending out her hand shyly. Remembering she was still clutching her wand, she dropped it, squealing slightly.

"Don't worry, Snapper," said the tall boy smiling, "Remember, the wand doesn't respond to English."

"Oh right," said Snapper, reflecting on the fact that she'd learned that the hard way.

Grinning warmly, the tall boy introduced himself, "I'm Todd, nice to meet you."

"I'm Snapper," replied Snapper, blushing.

"I think he knows your name by now," interjected Pen. "Thanks, man, for getting to her. I would have but I was a little busy."

"I can see that," laughed Snapper grabbing the banana peel off the top of Pen's head.

"Well yah I ended up landing in the garbage can head first a couple of times, but I was luckier than some," Pen muttered, looking up at the ceiling.

Several students hung awkwardly in the rafters and some were suspended upside down. While a small handful of students were able to hover just above the ground, the majority was either tangled in the grass-thatched roof or was bouncing like a ball in a pinball machine from wall to wall. A rather plump, pear-shaped boy was doing repeated somersaults until his face turned into the color of a giant blueberry. Sheila was running after the teacher, reciting everything that she had memorized from the textbook.

Finally, Professor Lyra had had enough. "Stad! That means stop." Instantly, students from every corner of the classroom began to plop back into their seats. "My young apprentice druids," Professor Lyra said with a smirk, "I suppose you have now discovered that practicing magic is no laughing matter. It is a discipline of precision and belief. Now talking about laughing matters, it brings me to my next lesson: laughing gas."

"Ha, ha, ha, ha!" howled Sheila hysterically. "That is the funniest thing I've ever heard!" Snapper and Pen spun around and stared at Sheila with blank expressions.

"With your permission, Professor," implored Sheila, shaking with excitement, "I would love to share with the class all the ingredients, in alphabetical order, which are used for the laughing potion."

"It's quite all right, Sheila," insisted Professor Lyra, feeling a little overwhelmed by Sheila's abundance of energy.

"Boy, Sheila's acting strange," whispered Pen to Snapper "and she's getting really annoying."

"Since when did she become a teacher's pet?" grumbled Snapper, feeling threatened.

Once again, Sheila's hand shot up like a volcanic explosion into the air, followed by a chorus of desperate grunts. "Yes, Sheila?" sighed Professor Lyra, weakly.

"Could I possibly be excused to go and use the restroom, Professor?"

"But of course," replied the professor eagerly, "and Sheila, please and I do mean please, take your time. Don't feel any pressure to come back quickly. In fact, if you want to have a snack or a nap before your next class, by all means do so!"

Some of the children giggled. Pen buried his face in his hands.

"Turn to page four of your textbook and there you will find the ingredients for your next potion recipe," instructed Professor Lyra. Flipping the page over, Snapper's voice joined a series of disgusted groans. Beneath the description of laughing gas potion was the most revolting concoction of ingredients.

"Toad's fart!" gagged Snapper. "What the hell kind of an ingredient is that?" Pen laughed out loud. The list nauseated him too, but seeing Snapper's reaction and her face turn purple was hilarious.

"Hey guys," burst in Sheila, rather winded. "Did I miss much?"

"Okay, Miss Suck-Up, I never knew you had it in you," teased Pen.

"Really Sheila, you should get your temperature checked because you gave *weird* a whole new definition today," stammered Snapper. "You were only gone for about a minute to go to the washroom."

"Shhhhhh!" hushed Sheila, leaning in closer to her sister and brother. "I told my clone with my mind that she needed to go to the washroom so that we could switch spots," she whispered. "Do you think anyone noticed?"

"Are you for real?" exclaimed Snapper, a little louder than she'd intended.

A few students spun around at the sound of Snapper's voice. "Oh no, the know-it-all teacher's pet is back from her washroom break," Sheila heard a spiky-haired blonde mutter to her friend.

"Maybe that will answer your question," replied Snapper dryly.

"Oh no," moaned Sheila, "I might have told my clone to behave like a really good student."

"Oh she sure did!" piped up Pen, "in alphabetical order and everything. You better work hard to change your rep soon," warned Pen, "because the class sees you as the new suck-up brainer. Not a good label to have in any school, normal or not."

"I knew something was up when you didn't use your power to rescue me when I was propelled almost up into space by my wand," concluded Snapper.

Sheila looked down sheepishly. "Sorry guys, I just thought it was a waste of my time to come to the beginners' flying lesson."

"No problem at all, Sheila!" lied Pen, rubbing his hands together and scheming a plan of how to get even with his tardy sister. "You can make it up to us by collecting the stuff for the potion."

They're at the front of the classroom. "Snapper, you get the hot plate and I'll go get the cauldron."

Returning back to her seat, Sheila gingerly opened the black leather case by unsnapping its metal hinges. "What's the big deal about . . ." stopping halfway through her sentences, she stared speechlessly down at the contents of the box.

"As you were saying," nudged Snapper, smiling. "You had just arrived a little late and missed reading the potion recipe from the textbook." Snapper grinned at Sheila.

"Why don't you do the honor of reading the list, Pen?" suggested Snapper.

"But of course, I'd be happy to!" chimed in Pen eagerly. "The laughing potion calls for a toad's fart, olive oil, lungwort leaves, slugs, newt's eye juice, and black pepper."

"Oh my god, I think I'm gonna be sick," gagged Sheila, covering her mouth.

Clapping her hands, Professor Lyra got the students to stop what they were doing and look her way. "Right, boys and girls, I suspect that I will have most of your undivided attention after our first little experimental spell. If you were surprised at how finicky casting spells were, that was child's play compared to creating and executing potions properly. Let me demonstrate," she said opening her black leather case. "This plumb, warty toad is the key component to your spell," the professor explained. "You want to encourage him to release flatulence for a sensible amount of time, with a sensible amount of smell, and a potent amount of sound. Too short of a flatulence added to the potion will cause a short and stunted laugh. A high-pitched flatulence may effect a whine, a cry, or a squeal, while too low a pitch might cause erratic sounds. And by no means underestimate the smell. You want to capture a full-bodied, wet, and murky odor. As soon as it escapes his posterior, catch it in the glass vial provided and cap it immediately! Any questions?"

A scrawny, shaggy-haired boy raised his hand. "Yes, William, you had a question?" invited the professor warmly. "Ummmmm," stuttered William, "can yoooou exxplain the word flllatulence and posssterior. I have mmmmany allergies," he spluttered, "and I want to know if they are tttthings that I'mmmm allergic to."

"Where's my class star who has memorized the textbook and no doubt the glossary of terms found on the back page?" called out Professor Lyra. Sheila gulped and slunk down into her seat and then under her desk. "Please don't call me, please don't call me," prayed Sheila closing her eyes tightly and hoping to go unnoticed.

"There you are, Sheila!" rang out the professor's voice. "Back from the washroom just in time to help your fellow classmates."

"Stupid, useless clone!" Sheila murmured under her breath as she crawled out from under her desk.

"What was that you said?" asked Professor Lyra.

"Oh I said spells and potions are stupendous!" replied Sheila quickly.

"Okay, Sheila lets have it, the definitions of flatulence and posterior."

Panicking, Sheila answered with the first thing that came into her head. "Flatulence is how to make things flat. Like maybe using a rolling pin to flatten the toad. Posterior is how to sit up straight and pay attention." Just by looking at the professor's wide gaping mouth, Sheila knew she'd blown her clone's cover.

Finally recovering from her shock, the professor explained the terms, trying very hard to stifle her laughter. "I think you mistakenly thought I said posture," she said politely. "Posterior refers to a person's or animal's behind. Flatulence means . . ." Snapper raised her hand, glad to be the brain of the class again. "It means to pass gas."

"You mean fart," replied a few boys, snickering from the back of the class.

Professor Lyra pretended not to hear the boys' comment and proceeded with the demonstration.

The students watched as their teacher took the bottle of gelatinous and milky newt's eyeball juice and then pour it liberally into the cauldron. Then she peeled about six slugs that were stuck to the lungwort plant and placed them into an empty glass jar. Scraping the slime trails they left on the leaves, she stirred it into the mixture. Setting aside the lungwort leaves, she proceeded to pour olive oil and sprinkle pepper all over the slithering slugs. They glistened and shone in their new peppery, oily coats. Several students were squirming uncomfortably in their seats. Sheila glanced back at the allergic boy. He was rocking back and forth, green in the face, and looking like he was going to hurl any second.

Taking the lungwort leaves again, she lit the end with a match and let them smolder slightly in a small petri dish. Finally she picked up the lumpy toad. With her other hand, she rubbed him just under his chin gently with her forefinger.

"You're such a hungry boy," she cooed to him softly. "Are you going to eat lots of slugs for these boys and girls?"

Raising her eyebrows, Sheila looked over to Pen and mouthed the word "creepy." Pen didn't pay attention to Sheila. Eager to see what was going to happen next, he was sitting on the edge of his seat.

Setting the toad on the desk, Professor Lyra emptied the slugs all around him. Already slimy, the oil made the slugs even slicker. As they slipped and slid all around the toad, they left long, stringy trails of oily slime. The allergic boy couldn't hold it in anymore. Desperately, he crawled on all fours to the garbage pail and threw up. Undeterred by the vomiting sounds, the toad hungrily lapped up each and every slug with its long, sticky tongue. Placing the smoking plant in front of the toad's nose, the toad began to sneeze. Suddenly, the toad's eyes began to bulge.

The combination of peppery slugs and smoke gave his stomach terrible gas, just like baked beans would to a human. Grabbing the glass vial quickly, anticipating a giant fart, the professor held it ready just below the toad's bottom. It was a small sound at first, but slowly, it grew louder and louder. The smell that wafted through the classroom was like sweat mixed with moldy, old cheese that been floating on a marsh. Almost everyone had their shirts hiked up over their noses to block the smell. Satisfied that she'd trapped enough of the fart in the vial, the professor capped it.

Inside the glass tube, the toad fart looked like moss green smoke. Reaching over for the hot plate, Professor Lyra turned it on high and then placed the cauldron on top. Once the goopy liquid boiled, she added the toad fart and stirred it into the potion.

"All done!" she announced proudly. "Any volunteers to give my potion a try?"

No one dared raise their hands. In fact, some students were so terrified of being selected that they sat on their hand. "Now I know I can surely count on Sheila!" remarked the professor confidently. Sheila was curled up in a tight ball underneath her desk, vowing never to send another clone in her place to school ever again. Taking the hint, the professor continued to implore the disgusted class.

"My goodness, you scaredy cats! You don't have to drink it, just smell it." Still no volunteers. Unfortunately for the poor allergic boy, his head was still spinning from dizziness, and he hadn't quite heard the professor clearly. Raising his hand high, he hoped to get her to repeat the question.

"Now there's a brave lad!" cried the professor exuberantly. Striding with potion in hand over to the boy crouched beside the garbage can, she placed the potion just under his nose so he could take a whiff. Helplessly he took in the rotten smell. He wrinkled his nose. His eyes watered furiously and his face turned purple. Everyone stared, barely breathing, waiting to see what would happen.

The allergic boy took his asthma puffer from his pouch. Panting wildly, he took a few desperate puffs from his inhaler to get some clean air into his lungs. Then instead of coughing, he fell over backward.

"Is he dead?" yelled Pen.

They all waited. Suddenly, out of the blue, William began flailing his arms and legs. Spellbound, the class watched as the allergic boy started to hoot, holler, and hiccup with laughter. He laughed and snorted almost non-stop for a full five minutes.

"Your turn!" said the professor, gleaming proudly at her students.

Luckily for Pen and Sheila, Snapper followed the directions perfectly. Sheila was nominated by her sister and brother to be the test subject for the potion. Eager to make it up to them for being late for class and embarrassing them with her clone, she conceded. While their potion worked, the same could not be said for some of their classmates. Some reacted to a badly made potion by wailing, crying, singing, whistling, barking, and even quacking. One boy reacted to a botched-up potion by burping out the entire Irish national anthem on key. Relieved to have made it through the first day of school, Snapper, Sheila, and Pen made their way to the dining hall. "You know . . ." said Pen, to the surprise of his sisters, "I think I may have lost my appetite."

CHAPTER TWENTY-THREE

Powers on Display

When Pen got back to his dorm, he found a crowd of boys waiting for him.

"Dude, what took you so long?" asked a tall, strong boy, pointing his fist at Pen. Instantly, Pen recognized him as Rocco, the boy that rallied everyone their first night at druid school.

"Listen, I don't want to fight. I don't want any trouble," replied Pen, stiffening.

"Yah, really? Well that's not going to happen," grinned Rocco, pulling his chestnut hair back out of his face. The rest of the boys circled Pen with stone-cold expressions. Rocco was obviously the leader of this gang, thought Pen angrily to himself. He had just traded one group of bullies for another.

"Man, that's how we greet each other around here," Rocco chuckled playfully, bumping fists with another boy in the crowd.

Recognizing the boy from class, he remembered his name was Todd. He was the one that had saved his air-launched sister earlier that day.

"Sorry, man. I thought you were trying to start a fight," Pen apologized to Rocco.

"Nah, man, that's just how we roll!" laughed Rocco. "We're all freaks. That's why the druids found us. But you'll learn to love it at this school. My buddies and I already practiced flying from Spells and Potions class. We used our flying skills when we were playing rugby a few hours ago."

"Yah, you should join us for our next game," suggested Todd.

"Sure, I'm up for it," said Pen confidently.

"We heard so much from our professors about you! They told us that Raven himself gave you powers. We'd like to see the powers you have," invited Rocco. Pen hesitated. It seemed that every time he exposed his powers to anyone outside of the family, he regretted it.

Seeing Pen's nervous expression, Todd interrupted. "Why don't we go sit in the common area where the couches are, and we'll all show our powers? I can go first. I don't mind."

Once again thankful for avoiding being in the spotlight, Pen followed the guys and took a seat on a leather couch. Raising his hand, Todd closed his eyes and muttered a few incantations in a low voice. Nothing happened at first. "Didn't work this time for you," joked a short, Mexican-looking boy with straight, black, mushroom-cut hair. "But your voice sounded so pretty when you sang that little rhyme." "Really, Frankie?" smirked Todd. Before he knew what was happening, the couch's cushions bent toward him and locked him into place. "What are you doing to me?" "Oh, nothing much," jeered Todd, grinning from ear to ear.

Suddenly, the couch began to bounce up and down.

"Get me outta here!" Frankie hollered.

"Hold your horses!" Rocco chuckled. "I thought you said that Todd here had a power shortage?"

"Horses are a great idea," mused Todd.

Instantly, the couch jumped into the air and began to gallop on all fours around the common room.

"Okay, okay!" cried Frankie. "I got it, I got it! You have a really cool power, and it works!"

Todd raised his hands, and slowly, the couch trotted over to its resting place and retracted its arms.

"That is so cool!" exclaimed Pen. "So how does your power actually work?"

"It works on inanimate objects or objects that are not alive. I can control them with my mind and make them move the way I want," answered Todd.

"Awesome, isn't it, Pen? But you haven't seen anything until you see what I can do," bragged Rocco. The boys cheered, waiting for the show.

Sauntering over to the wall, Rocco pressed his palm face down on to its surface. A chill came over the room. To Pen's amazement, a ripple of ice crawled out from under his hand and spread like a wave over the wall. Within seconds, the walls were glistening with a thin layer of ice. Now the ice continued to flow until it coated the floor, furniture, and all the fixtures in the room. Pen's mouth dropped.

"Now that's a cool power!" commented Frankie, "but don't underestimate the short guy." Rocco laughed and banged the wall with his hand. Magically the ice began to retract under Rocco's hand until there wasn't a trace left.

"You show 'em Frankie boy," Rocco teased.

Frankie's feet couldn't reach the floor from the couch, so he had to shuffle off awkwardly to get to the ground. "I can't really show you much here," muttered Frankie, "because I don't want the professors hearing the sound."

"Just give 'em a small show, Frankie," insisted Rocco.

"Okay, but for the real thing, check me out on the rugby field." Bending down, Frankie gently tapped the floor with his fists. A low rumbling sound filled the room and the ground began to tremble. Bookcases, beds, and cupboards rattled. It lasted for only a few seconds and then gradually subsided.

"Holy cow!" said Pen. "Was that an earthquake?"

"Nah, Pen," chuckled Frankie, "just a mild earth tremor. Don't want to wake the old guys up. If you want to see the real thing, I can make the ground outside shake like you've never seen!"

"Yah, it's true!" chorused the crowd of boys.

In the corner, Pen noticed a huge boy that looked almost like a young man. He was kind of quiet and seemed a little shy. Despite his enormous muscles, he wasn't cocky at all. Pen was curious about him. He came across as a gentle giant. "What's your power?" Pen asked, looking his way. At first he didn't answer, thinking Pen was talking to someone else.

"Yo, Blake!" Rocco called out. "You asleep?"

Jolting a little, Blake raised his head and answered. "Oh I didn't know anyone was talking to me."

"This oughta be rich," snickered Rocco under his breath.

Blake answered slowly, "My power is psychic, so I can get small visions or vibes of things that will happen in the future."

"Wow, that's a macho power," jeered Rocco to the other boys. "So, like, if you were in a fight, you could tell the other guy to pause while you get a vision of the future, and then you could see him punching you a few seconds before he pounds your lights out!"

The rest of the boys roared with laughter. The large boy looked down. Pen felt bad for Blake. Even though he was popular for the moment here, he knew what it felt like to be bullied.

"Okay, guys, that's enough," interrupted Pen. "My sister Sheila can get premonitions of stuff that can happen in the future and that's saved our butts more than once. What else are you good at?"

"Well I'm really good with the skateboard," Blake said, looking up shyly.

"Cool! What kind of tricks can you do?" said Pen, really interested now.

"I can control my skateboard so that it will come to me from anywhere," answered Blake. "So far I can do a San Francisco flip, a casper, a 360 spin, a frog stand, and I'm working on the nosehook impossible."

"Wow!" gasped Pen. "I'd love for you to show me your moves sometime. I love to surf, which is kinda like skateboarding, but on water. I'll bet we could teach each other."

"Talk about water interrupted," said Rocco, feeling bored, "let's see if your powers are all the professors cracked them up to be."

"No problem," responded Pen. Closing his eyes, Pen clenched his hands tightly into fists. A rushing sound filled the air. The taps in the bathroom burst open, sending an explosion of water rushing toward them. Just as the wall of water threatened to engulf the boys frozen to their seats in fright, Pen opened his hands. Instantly, the water stopped.

As Pen thrust his hands backward, the water obeyed. It receded and was sucked back into the bathroom faucets. The sheer force of the water gushing down the pipes twisted the taps tightly shut behind it. Silence filled the room. After a few seconds, one of them and then two and then everyone began to applaud.

"That was spectacular!" cheered Todd. "But I hear that's only one of two tricks that you can do."

"Yah. Show us the panther, Pen!" egged Frankie.

"William, you may want to use your special power now," snickered Todd.

"Yyyyess," stuttered William, "I am alllllergic to ccccat hair. Are you sure that this is sanitary, guys?" pleaded William.

"Ahhh William," groaned the boys, "do your thing already."

Feeling his allergies already coming on, William began sneezing. Before long, his nose began to run. As he continued to sniff and sneeze, a bubble began to form on the end of his nostril. Pen tried to be polite and hide the expression of repulsion on his face. Pen shivered as he watched the tiny bubble popping in and out of William's nose each time he sneezed.

Finally, the allergic boy did one super sneeze. The small bubble that was jiggling on the end of his nose began to expand. It got bigger and bigger until at last it surrounded his whole body. At last William was safe inside his protective bubble shield. "Well that's allergy boy's trick, or bubble boy," chuckled Frankie, "whichever you prefer!"

Trying to get the nasty sight of the snot bubble out of his mind, Pen concentrated on morphing. A low thundering growl emanated from deep inside his throat. The boys watched in awe as Pen's smooth black skin and clothes grew into a thick, black coat of fur. Needle-sharp, white claws replaced his fingers and toenails. Pointed, fanged incisors extended out of his black mouth. Even Pen's bright yellow eyes darted around the room as he took in many of the boys who dove behind the couches, trembling in fright.

Striding confidently over to the huge cat, Rocco ran his large hand over his back. "It's just Pen, boys. Nothing's gonna happen!"

Slinking across the room, Pen lunged and landed effortlessly on the ledge of the couch. Allergy boy couldn't take his heart pounding one moment longer. Both he and his protective snot bubble bounced safely out of the room, through the doorway, and disappeared down the hall. It was a good thing that his allergy bubble muted his sound, or he would have woken everyone up in the dorm with his wailing.

"You're going to love transmogrification class," whispered Blake from across the room. "Looks like you are already an expert at it."

The next morning, Professor Eridanus rallied his bustling students together. As usual, Snapper's hand was the first to shoot up in the air. "Professor Eridanus, where are our textbooks and why are we not in a classroom?"

Smoothing down his fuzzy, gray beard so that his voice would not be muffled from the furry obstruction, he spoke. His voice was very soft and gentle, so much so that the students had to stop what they were doing to strain to hear. "Good morning, class." he whispered.

"As Snapper has astutely pointed out, we are not in a classroom, nor do we have a textbook. Transmogrification is a delicate art not to be encumbered by paper or the stagnant indoors. Every class that I instruct shall be held outdoors come rain, cold, snow, or shine." Groans emerged from the crowd.

Professor Eridanus raised his hand and smiled. Once again, there was silence. "You are expected, however, to have your wands ever ready. Today I will make an exception, but only today. There is a bag of wands with me if you forgot yours."

Pen pulled out his silver-tipped pen from the box in his backpack. He held it up and said the incantation under his breath. Thrusting it forward into the air, it extended into a wand, springing into its full size.

Sheila and Snapper picked up their wands as well. Snapper turned her wand over in her hand. It was unbelievably light.

"You know, I've never believed in magic," she began slowly. "Not until now."

Pen and Sheila nodded their heads.

"I know," Pen said, still looking at his wand. "If anyone had told me that magic really exists, I would have thought that they were crazy."

"Now, children," Professor Eridanus interrupted. "We don't have a moment to lose. If you're going to learn how to use those wands, we have to start right now. After all, there's a battle to win!" he added, grabbing his wand tightly.

"Now the first spell that we're going to learn is called Creidim. This is the Celtic word for 'believe.' If you don't believe in yourselves and in your own power, it will never matter what spell you choose to do—it will never work. Magic comes from within you. If you look for magic outside of yourselves, you will never find it. We are all energy and, therefore, are all connected. If you can see beyond what things appear to be and connect with the energy it is made up of, you can transform almost anything."

Pen, Sheila, and Snapper looked intently at Professor Eridanus. He had such a kind and patient way about him. Smiling gently, he motioned for them to look at the tree that was standing just behind him. The tree, although standing erect, was old and knotted.

"Do you see this poor tree behind me?" Professor Eridanus asked again.

"Yes," replied all the children in unison.

"These branches once sprouted beautiful, green leaves, and its pink blossoms were the beginnings of bright, juicy apples long ago," Professor Eridanus continued. "Do you believe that this tree can ever live again?" He watched their faces carefully.

Snapper went over to the tree and examined it. "No," she said, shaking her head. "It's dead. Magic can never bring anything back to life."

Pen and Sheila reached out and touched its branches.

"There is not even the slightest sign of life," said Pen, running his hand down the tree's rough bark.

"Then you will never be able to bring life to this tree," Eridanus replied. "If you do not believe in what you are trying to create, it will never happen."

"Now here is your first spell, children," Eridanus continued. "The words of the spell are 'Creidim—beo arís.'"

Reaching for his wand, Pen was the first to try. He thrust his wand forward and said, "Creidim—beo arís," in a commanding voice. Nothing happened.

"Wow!" Sheila giggled. "What an incredible transformation, Pen! The leaves are springing up everywhere!"

"Oh, shut up!" muttered Pen. "You try it if you're so good, Sheila!"

Before Sheila could begin, however, Snapper had pointed her wand at the tree and was pronouncing the spell. To everyone's surprise, the tree began to wither and dry up even more.

"What happened?" cried out Snapper. "The tree looks even worse now!"

The students burst out laughing. The professor rested his large hand comfortingly on Snapper's shoulder. He looked at Snapper, who was still clearly devastated.

"What a dumb spell!" she sputtered, angrily. "It's supposed to bring back life to the tree, but instead, it killed it even more!"

"Snapper," said Professor Eridanus. "What were you thinking about when you cast that spell? Were you thinking about how dead it was?"

"I guess so," muttered Snapper, a little embarrassed.

"Try to think of the miracle of life when you cast the spell again. Focus on what you want—not on what you don't want! Magic can't distinguish between the two. It will just give you what you think about."

"Can I give it a shot?" asked Blake quietly. Everyone spun around. Blake never spoke. Sheila rolled her eyes. "I can imagine how well this football star is going to do at the delicate art of making a tree grow," Sheila whispered to Pen.

"Actually," replied Pen, raising his eyebrow, "I think he just may surprise you. It's like our professor said, appearances aren't always what they seem."

"You are welcome to try, dear boy, by all means," invited the professor warmly.

Rocco, Frankie, and Todd were already beginning to snicker at the sight of this huge boy lumbering over to the withered stick of a tree.

Tenderly Blake bent down and lifted its drooping branches with his large hands. Then the oddest thing happened. He looked up just above the tree with bright blue eyes and the biggest grin on his face. Reaching up, Blake looked as though he were picking an apple from thin air.

"Is he crazy?" muttered Sheila. "There's nothing there."

"Just wait," hushed Pen, anxious to see what would happen next.

"Creidim—beo arís," he said simply. Like a whirlwind, the seemingly dead tree began to viciously twist and turn in the ground. Its thin, fragile branches began to shake. Then like an explosion, branches sprouted madly from its stem, catapulting in every which way.

Before the students' wide-eyed expressions, green leaves and pink blossoms budded all over the now sturdy branches. Seconds later the pink blossoms fell to the grass and small apples took their place. Swelling second by second, the apples ripened into plump, juicy fruit. Plucking a large apple from the tree, Blake took a huge bite and winked at Sheila.

"Maybe you shouldn't underestimate his hearing either," remarked Pen, grinning.

CHAPTER TWENTY-FOUR

Prepare for Battle

Gray mist still clung in thin cobwebs to the dewy grass. Even though Sheila was wearing her blue jeans and sneakers, both her shoes and pants were soaked almost to her calves. Morning air here was dense and smelled rich. Professor Grian led the way to a clearing in the field surrounded by smooth stones. Pulling back the white hood from his cloak, he revealed a mop of curly, red hair and a long, furry, red beard. He seemed more like a bulky and well-built Viking from the north than a professor. His deep, rumbling voice seemed to echo whenever he spoke and would vibrate through a listener's whole body. The professor had a rough and rugged look to him. A stern look in his eye told everyone he didn't put up with any nonsense.

"Right!" he boomed, almost knocking the allergic boy off his feet and jolting awake a few of the half-asleep students. "Combat and self-defense is what I'm here to teach you today. I don't expect to receive gym notes excusing you from this class because you have a toothache. Evil does not take a vacation or care if you are ready for it or not. I don't care if you are the shortest, weakest boy, or the strongest, tallest girl, or if you have one leg or three."

"Who has three legs?" mouthed Snapper to Pen, looking around her curiously. Pen shrugged his shoulders.

"I will teach you all to be strong and tough," continued the professor. "Even those who think that this class is pointless and wish to speak at the same time as me!"

"Snapper!" barked Professor Grian.

"Who, me?" whimpered Snapper, extremely humiliated at being singled out.

"Yes, you, unless there are any other Snappers present. Would you prefer to be called by your given name, Molly Green? Clearly you don't seem to recognize your nickname."

Embarrassed, Snapper shook her head. "Snapper's fine," she said meekly, hoping not to draw even more attention.

"Follow me, class," ordered the burly professor. "You, Snapper, will have the honor of being my first volunteer!" Silently the students trudged behind Professor Grian, barely daring to make a sound. No one wanted to be the next volunteer after Snapper. Striding at a quick pace, the professor led them to the edge of the forest. Sheila shivered with anticipation. Large, sweeping branches from yew trees were arched and joined to form a tunnel. Stepping on to the grassy path and staring at the sunlight spilling out from the end of the tunnel felt exactly like a magical adventure for Sheila.

Thick boughs towered over the children like giant pillar guardians to a secret passage. When they finally reached the end of the archway, they came to a solitary yew tree. "Wow!" gasped Pen, unable to contain his amazement. Surrounded by radiant beams of sunlight, the massive tree stood about forty feet tall and about thirty feet wide. Dark green, spiky leaves covered its branches, and it was speckled with delicate, red berries. At the tree's center is a silver door glowing with blue light and carved with ancient Celtic symbols.

Reaching into his pocket, Professor Grian produced a pan flute. Bringing the musical instrument to his lips, he blew into it. A haunting airy melody escaped and floated loftily into the tree. A murder of crows cawed out loudly from the branches above. They flocked and swarmed in a black cloud in tighter and tighter circles around the tree.

From the center of the black cloud, a brilliant blue light emerged. Most of the children mistook it for a bug. Sheila knew better. She would know that distinct chirp anywhere. She knew it was Daphnaie, the blue fairy. Steadily the insect-like creature grew taller and taller until she was the size of a human. Her blue gown shimmered like dewdrops clinging to cobwebs in the morning light. With barely a slight flutter of her thin, transparent wings, she floated over to the gigantic yew. At the touch of her fingers, the door creaked and opened a sliver.

Once again, the black cloud of crows descended noisily and surrounded the blue fairy. Engulfing her completely, she disappeared in a noisy cluster of black, beating wings. The students still stood in silence with their mouths gaping.

"Those who are ready to train for magical warfare, step this way," commanded the professor briskly. There was an edge in his voice that said that this was not really a choice.

Snapper was the first to push open the silver door. Outstretched before her was the most bizarre sight. There were ropes hanging from trees, ladders, cannons, mud, water, and even snake pits. A large rotating circular contraption was made up of spinning wheels and swinging metal hammers attached to pulleys and all sorts of other harsh, mechanical-looking devices arranged in a row.

"This training apparatus," announced Professor Grian proudly, "is one of my more brilliant inventions. The goal is quite simple: Make it in one piece to the other side and then retrieve the emerald jewel."

"The one hanging from the pendant around your neck?" inquired a short cinnamon-skinned girl with beaded black hair.

"I don't recall seeing any student raising her hand, asking me to grant her permission to speak," snapped the professor. "What is your name, my talkative friend?"

"Ummmmmm . . .," she hesitated timidly.

"My word, that's an interesting name," remarked Professor Grian. "Your parents must be complete idiots for giving you such a ridiculous name like 'Ummmmmm.'"

"No, it's Hansika," the girl finally sputtered out nervously.

"Well boys and girls, Hansika has graciously volunteered to go second. Please give her a round of applause." The claps were forced and awkward sounding, as if the students were part of an army training camp. Hansika crossed her arms over her chest in silent protest but didn't dare to speak again.

"Well, now that I've got everyone's undivided attention," Professor Grian continued abruptly, "I will give you some strategies to try to pass this test. I will warn you that no one has ever succeeded in making it through the first time. We do have some gnomes known for their healing abilities on site ready to assist you in the highly likely case you need their assistance."

"Doesn't exactly inspire confidence, does he?" whispered Pen to Sheila, sure that the professor's back was turned.

"Did I hear someone say confident?" barked the professor, spinning around. Narrowing his eyes at Pen, he pointed at him followed by an unnerving, bellowing laugh. "You must be the confident lad who is eager to volunteer to go third," he bellowed.

Pen's eyes bulged wide as he looked at Sheila. She could tell what he was thinking. How in the world was his hearing that good?

"Three words that are crucial for you all to learn," emphasized Professor Grian. "'Scoir,' 'reoite,' and 'sciath.' You may be wondering what these three words mean, as Gaelic may not be your mother tongue. No one dared to raise his hands, still unsure if his question was rhetorical or not.

"Scoir is word to strip someone of their magic," explained professor Grian. "The spell usually only lasts temporarily, as magic among druids is inherent and can be rejuvenated upon command. The length of time that a druid is magically incapacitated depends on the delivery of the spell and where the target is hit. For instance, if the spell grazes their toe, it probably will last a second or two. Now if the spell lands on their heart from which all magic originates, that is an entirely different story."

Unable to stop from asking a question, Snapper's hand shot up. "Well," commented the professor, smiling, "I guess we have learned our lesson, haven't we? You will still go first but I did like how you raised your hand."

Eager to get an answer, Snapper ignored the professor's sarcasm. "Professor Grian," Snapper addressed the professor politely, "A well-aimed spell like that one . . . how long would it last?"

"Hmmmm," said the professor, scratching his beard thoughtfully, "I've heard of it lasting several days," warned the professor solemnly, "but I wouldn't get my hopes up, as only the most powerful sorcerers or druids have ever been known to accomplish this spell that efficiently."

The same rules apply to the other two spells. "Reoite is a freezing spell and sciath is a shielding spell for protection. Given that most of you are just beginners, I would highly recommend the third spell sciath."

Another student raised his hand. "Yes, Rocco," replied the professor. Professor Grian respected Rocco because he was tough.

"Professor, why don't we learn offensive spells that can really do damage to someone attacking us. I mean—disarming them from magic or freezing them seems kind of lame."

"I see your point, Rocco," assured the Professor, "but we don't wish to create killers in our students. That's what distinguishes good magic from evil magic. As you may have already guessed, magical battles are not won by strength but rather by wisdom and speed.

Learning to dodge a well-aimed spell for your heart or to jump and kick a wand out of your opponent's hand can mean the difference between life and death. These tests are designed to test your reactions and reflexes. Hesitation and poor reflexes will also lead to a speedy failure in battle. Remember, evil sorcerers don't play by good magic's rule. We have to trust that the power of love is of a stronger energy than hate."

Pen grimaced and Sheila snickered. Pen didn't have to talk, she knew what he meant. His expression told her . . . Gosh, if the professor is demonstrating warm, fluffy love, I'd hate to see his version of hate!

"I will give you a run-through of this training apparatus," explained Professor Grian. "You are free to use any natural spells or magical abilities you have to get through this training course. You can only use one spell at a time, however," he added chuckling. "In this obstacle course, one spell will cancel out the previous one. If you are lucky enough to pass all of the obstacles successfully, then you will need to use cunning and skill to get the green emerald. Oh by the way, I didn't want to make it too easy, so the green jewel is being guarded by a fire-breathing dragon. Good luck to you!"

With that, Professor Grian dashed up the giant staircase. At the top of the staircase were two large metal poles joined by another pole lying horizontally at the top. Attached to that pole was another long metal bar with a series of metal rings hanging across it. Below the ringed monkey bars was a pit of tangled, writhing, and hissing snakes. Often one or two would untangle from the squirming knot of vipers and lunge, fangs bared at the swinging rings up overhead.

"He's not going to make it," wheezed Snapper, panicking beyond what she thought was possible. "Well the positive thing in all of this," chimed in Sheila, "is that if he can't make it, we won't have to do it either. I mean, really Snapper, does Professor Grian look like he's in optimal shape to be a stream-lined gymnast? Please, he couldn't carry his own weight with agility and finesse even if he tried." Sheila giggled at the thought of this huge hulk of a man doing twists and acrobatic leaps in the air.

Looking over to Sheila, Professor Grian winked and swung himself from the bar to the first hoop. "That man has the ears of a hawk," whispered Sheila.

Below the hanging Professor, the snakes sensed there was fresh meat close by. Straining their necks, six snakes managed to unravel themselves from the slithering heap. As the professor swung from hoop to hoop across the snake pit, one snake managed to wrap around his hairy leg. Just as the snake opened its mouth to expose its poison-tipped fangs, Professor Grian let go of the hoop with one hand and pointed his wand at the snake. "Reoite," he cried. Immediately the snake froze. Seeing the frozen snake, the other five lowered their heads and hissed at the professor from a safe distance.

Finally making it across the snake pit monkey bars, the professor landed with great precision on a wooden walkway no wider than a balance beam. In fact, the beam was so thin that it was too narrow for two feet to be side by side. In order not to fall, one had to place one foot strategically in front of the other. Unfortunately, the catch was that while you were trying to balance on a thin wooden beam, huge metal hammers suspended from above were swinging back and forth across the beam. There was only a few feet of space in between each one. Calculating the distance between the swinging hammers and their speed, the professor jumped, flipped, and somersaulted across the balance beam without so much as one even grazing his toe.

"Dddddid youuu sseee thattt?" stuttered the allergic boy, quivering.

"Sorry, no doctor's notes," said Todd, putting his hand playfully on William's shoulder.

Passing the swinging hammers and the balance beam, Professor Grian lunged and landed like a cat on all fours on the spinning wheel of death.

"That doesn't look so hard," observed Pen. "I mean, it's just a spinning wheel. All you have to do is hold on."

"Trust me," retorted Snapper, "I know that it's going to be harder than it looks."

Sure enough, just as the words escaped Snapper's lips, four black cannons tilted back, raising their aim at the spinning wheel. Staring in disbelief, the students watched the professor bouncing nimbly like a spider from one end of the spinning wheel to the other. Each time, he narrowly avoided the fiery cannon balls shooting his way. Diving once again into the air, he clasped a rope dangling from the branch of a tree. Swinging back and forth, he gathered enough momentum to latch onto a rugged stone wall. Using pure upper body strength, he pulled himself to the top, stone by stone.

Another long rope awaited him. A few of the girls let out shrieks of fear when they saw the next task. Not Sheila though. She would never admit to fear. She just clenched her teeth. A few feet from the rope stood a giant metal circle about six feet in diameter.

Once the professor had grabbed the rope, the circle erupted with fire all around its edges. Undaunted by the flames, he swung through the fiery circle without a burn.

Grabbing the next rope, he swung past a mud pit, a spike pit, and then a pit of water swarming with bloodsucking leeches. Passing all three pits, the professor latched on to a rope ladder and grabbed a hold.

"Look, he's almost finished!" yelled the spiky-haired blonde Sheila recognized from class.

Hansika shook her head dismally. "No, Kim, see those tree sprites camouflaged in the trees?"

"No, I can't," Kim said, squinting to try to spot them.

"Okay, Kim, to be fair, they are hard to see," admitted Hansika. "The tree sprites are wearing leaves and have green faces, but you may notice the bows and arrows that they are holding." The metal glint of the tip of the arrow was the only hint of their presence.

Overhearing the conversation was the only way that Sheila, Snapper, or Pen would have even paid attention to the slight movement. They weren't the only ones. The professor hadn't seen them either until it was too late. All of a sudden, arrows came whizzing out of the trees. Caught off guard, Professor Grian spun around on the rope ladder only to get an arrow planted firmly in his behind. Aiming his wand at the winged menace, he yelled, "Sciath, sciath." A shield of yellow light formed around him. Struggling now to maintain his balance and hold his wand firmly in the direction of the mischievous tree sprites, he finally made it to the ground. Within a few seconds, the spell faded. Unfortunately, he needed to keep moving and couldn't keep his arm steady enough to maintain the shield.

Luckily he came at last to a red metal tube. Quickly he dove inside it to avoid the spray of arrows. Once inside, he removed the arrow from his bum. The arrow was more of a nuisance and annoyance than a real injury. After all, tree sprites were really tiny and so were their arrows. Removing one felt like removing a small splinter from your finger.

Crawling on all fours, the professor made his way through the tunnel. Emerging successfully on the other side, he was welcomed by a huge applause. Professor Grian smiled, bowed, and then unlatched the emerald amulet from around his neck.

Before their eyes, Professor Grian's body began to grow to an enormous height. Slowly his arms elongated, transforming themselves into red, leathery, bat-like wings. Reddish golden scales covered him from head to toe. Reptilian eyes replaced human ones and a long, spiky tail swished back and forth behind him. Smoke curled in wisps from his black, snorting nostrils.

"Professor Grian has turned into a fire-breathing dragon!" cried spiky-haired Kim moments before she collapsed, fainting from fright.

CHAPTER TWENTY-FIVE

Either You Want It or You Have It

Snapper stared half-dazed at the treacherous path ahead of her. Her knees were weak, and her stomach was in knots. Examining every element of the obstacles, she tried to calculate the math and science of it all. A voice rang out, breaking through her mind cloud.

"Snapper! Snap out of it! I know what you're doing." Startled, Snapper opened her eyes, just to see Sheila's eyes staring into hers. "Don't use your brain this time!" said Sheila. "Use your instinct. Think about it," continued Sheila. "You have amazing speed, flexibility, and agility." Snapper grinned modestly.

"Not to mention," reminded Sheila, "most of these obstacles have to do with fire, including the grand finale of the fire-breathing dragon. Snapper, you control fire!"

"Yah!" interrupted Pen. "You have a better chance of winning this than any of us."

"You're right!" said Snapper, feeling a lot more confident now.

"Go show 'em, sister!" cheered Pen.

An instant hush swept over the crowd of students as Snapper leapt up in a fury of speed. You could barely make out her shape. She was just a blur blazing through each obstacle. With lightning speed, she soared, flipped, and somersaulted past the pit of snakes that didn't have time to react to the whirlwind of smoke that swung past them. A roar of cheers rang out.

Not slowing down for a second, she mounted the spinning wheel of death. Morphing suddenly into a deer, Snapper effortlessly danced her way out of range of the firing cannons. The crowd went wild. Changing back into a human, she came to the ring of fire. Up until now, no one but Sheila and Pen knew that Snapper wielded power over fire. Looking back over her shoulder, Snapper caught her sister and brother beaming. They knew she was about to give everyone a show they would never forget.

Clasping the rope tightly, Snapper swung toward the ring. Instead of swinging through it, she grabbed the top of the ring with both hands and hung.

"Get off it!" hollered Todd boisterously. "Snapper, it's going to catch on fire any second!"

"Looks like you're going to have to save her again, Sir Lancelot," sneered Kim.

Suddenly, the ring burst into flames. Instantly, the gnomes sprang into action. Sprinting at full speed, they aimed streams of water with their hoses at the fire. The students shrieked. Some of them fainted.

Without thinking, Todd bolted off the sidelines, with Pen and Sheila following close behind. Finally catching up to him, Pen grabbed Todd by the shoulder and held him back. "What are you doing?" Todd demanded whirling around to see who was stopping him. "She's going to die if someone doesn't stop it!"

"It's okay," panted Sheila, winded from running. "Snapper's got this one under control."

No matter how much water the gnomes sprayed on the ring, the fire just wouldn't go out. "You're just going to stand there and watch your sister die?" shouted Todd angrily.

Before anyone could say anything else, Todd stared in disbelief at what he saw next. Snapper had become on fire, only she wasn't burning at all. Snapper was the fire. Her eyes, once radiant blue, had transformed into red, hot, burning coals. Her hair rose and floated above her shoulders in smoldering flames. From her fingertips, wisps of fire curled and spiraled. Swinging back and forth, Snapper gathered momentum and speed. To a chorus of gasps, she blazed into three backward swings, two one-handed swings and finally finished off with a pristine handstand. Slowly Snapper extinguished the flames that coiled in her hair and swept out from her body.

"That girl was smoking!" exclaimed Todd, signaling a thundering applause from the audience.

Armed with her sharp instincts and reflexes, Snapper blazed through every obstacle with the finesse of a mule deer. Crawling through the tunnel, she emerged. Grian, now a dragon, raised his scaled head and roared a fierce roar that made the ground shake. Undeterred by its fiery breath, Snapper searched for the green jewel. Spotting it close to its underbelly, Snapper sprinted across the grass. Nimbly she dodged the dragon's sharp claws and razor sharp fangs. Seeing that his fire had no effect on Snapper, the dragon clasped the glowing green amulet with its long claws. Unfurling its leathery wings, it beat them furiously against the air. The sound was deafening and almost blew Snapper off her feet. Gradually the colossal reptile started rising into the air.

Snapper paced anxiously. What could she do?

Spying the dragon's tail, last to rise from ground, she frantically lunged for it. Careful to avoid the spikes on the bottom, she clutched it tightly and crawled her way up. Maybe I can maneuver myself up its tail enough so that I can leap and pry the jewel away from inside its claws, reasoned Snapper.

Everyone watched Snapper speechlessly as the dragon soared higher and higher, with Snapper clinging desperately to the dragon's swishing tail. Below, Snapper saw the forest becoming smaller and smaller. Her chest began to ache. Snapper hated heights. Last time she tried flying, she needed someone to save her. Could she do it? Chills ran up and down her legs and nerves knotted her stomach once again. Shaking uncontrollably, she tried to calm herself. "I can do this," she murmured weakly. Blinded by her fear, everything in front of her became blurry.

A shining object caught her attention. Spying something glistening from the corner of her eye, Snapper saw the green amulet. It was clutched in the grasp of Grian's enormous claws. It was so close that she could almost touch it. She reached for it. It was still too far. There was only one thing left to do, Snapper decided. She had to try to dive for it as soon as Grian slowed down.

It was almost as if Grian read her thoughts because he immediately stopped flapping his wings. He slowed down almost completely in the sky.

Now's my chance! thought Snapper. Digging her feet into the dragon's tail, Snapper crouched into position, like a jockey on a horse—ready to jump over the next hurdle. Taking a deep breath, she swallowed hard. Then taking one last look at where the green jewel was, Snapper jumped. Her fingers touched the green amulet, but before she could grasp it, Grian took off again at full speed, turning swiftly in the air. Snapper screamed.

When Snapper's vision became clear again, she was aware of the sensation of falling at a terrific speed.

"Snapper's in trouble!" Sheila cried.

Running to help her sister, Sheila spread her arms out and transformed them into wings.

"Reoite!" commanded an unfamiliar voice.

Sheila's wings suddenly transformed back into arms. "Hey!" cried Sheila. "Who did that?"

A chubby, rosy-cheeked gnome waddled his way toward her. "No interference allowed," he ordered in a high-pitched squeal, while waving a chubby finger in her face. Pen whipped out his wand, ignoring the doll-like little men.

"Snámh san aer," Pen commanded his wand. Suddenly, the wand pulled him up into the air. Pen only made it a few feet before he heard the word "Scoir." Instantly, a blinding yellow light engulfed him, and he fell back on to the grass.

"Why is my wand not working?" he demanded angrily.

"Because you didn't duck." The brightly dressed, little man cackled.

Meanwhile, Snapper plummeted faster and faster toward the ground before the eyes of the horrified crowd. Moments before she smashed into the ground, the gnomes raised their wands and began chanting. Snapper froze in mid-air. As lightly as a balloon, her body wafted safely on to the soft grass.

Eyes still firmly shut, Snapper had to be prodded by the gnomes' wands to open them. When she finally opened her eyes, Snapper saw the strangest sight. Seven little men dressed like Christmas were poking her with their wands. Each of them wore bright red, pointed felt caps and green blazers with shiny gold buttons. Their long white beards hung down to their middles, which were wrapped around by a wide, black belt and fastened by a golden buckle. Sticking out from beneath their plump, round stomachs were two polished black boots.

Satisfied that she'd come to, they shoved a red pill in her mouth and ushered her toward the crowd of noisy onlookers.

To Snapper's surprise, she was one of the most successful candidates.

After her, Hansika was next. Hansika didn't quite make it halfway through the course. Though she dazzled everyone with her use of electric, shocking powers, she was beaten by the formidable spinning wheel. Unable to control her balance when a cannon blasted her way, she slipped and tumbled off.

Pen made it up to the pool of leeches. Unfortunately when he looked down, he fell right into the muddy pool of bloodsuckers. Pen managed to stop panicking and holler out "sciath," the shielding spell, but by then, he had five or so latched on to him. Luckily, the well-prepared gnomes had their salt shakers at the ready to disarm the black blood-sucking worms.

Pen squirmed uncomfortably. "Get them off me!" he spluttered.

The gnomes smiled jovially and went to work on them quickly. He hated spiders, and for him, leeches were a close second. One by one, the leeches let go of their victim at the liberal spray of salt. Then the gnomes lathered a smelly green paste over the red bite marks.

Rocco thought he was smart when he tried to use his wand to help him soar high above the obstacle course. Unfortunately, he forgot that the wand in this challenge was only allowed to cast one spell at a time. Hearing the roar of cannons roar below him Rocco aimed his wand and cast the shielding spell. Luckily for Rocco he shielded himself from the fiery canons. Not-so-luckily for him, his new spell cancelled out his flying spell. Spiraling downward, like an out-of-control spinning top, Rocco finally landed onto a tangle of messy branches.

Even more unlucky for him was that this was the same tree that was home to the arrow-happy tree sprites. Yelping and jumping like an injured puppy, the once proud Rocco now looked like a hedgehog. Thankfully, when removed, the arrows felt more like burrs or pinpricks. However, to the amused onlookers, the tough, burly, Rocco made a gigantic fuss like a big baby.

One by one, Sheila watched the students in front of her in the line tackle the insurmountable obstacle course. One by one, Sheila saw them tumble, trip, slip, fail. As she neared the front of the line, her heart pounded wildly inside her chest. How could she pass this test? What did she have that was so special? Doubt crept into her stomach and tied it firmly in aching knots.

Suddenly, out of nowhere, Sheila felt a gust of wind engulf her body. Giant black, feathered wings wrapped around her and drew her into shadow. Although afraid, she felt comforted to be taken away from the others. When the wings unfurled, she saw the most amazing but terrifying sight. A giant raven, wings outstretched, loomed about twenty feet high above her. Suddenly, she was aware that she was alone with this giant bird. The students and the training course had disappeared. The raven cawed out with a sharp and piercing cry into the echoing forest. Sheila stood frozen.

Gradually the massive, black bird shrunk until it was the size of a tall eight-foot, dark-haired man. Tribal tattoos covered his muscular arms. Around his waist, he wore a long, black cloth. Instantly, she recognized him as Raven. Bowing before him, she waited patiently for him to speak to her. His presence announced majesty.

"Sheila!" His voice sounded as if it had rumbled out of gathering storm clouds. Sheila trembled but didn't answer. She was too afraid. "Your fear is crippling you! Do not forget all that was taught to you. I have sent you here for a purpose. Do you think that the strongest or the fastest or the wisest of you has a better chance of completing this task?" Sheila hesitated. Somehow she knew this was a trick question. She didn't know which attribute to choose.

"I don't know," she sputtered.

"Yes, you do," insisted Raven. "Think about what you've been taught."

Closing her eyes, Sheila desperately tried to think about everything that she had learned from the druids. Only one image came into her mind—the dying tree.

When Sheila opened her eyes, she saw a radiant woman standing before her dressed in a shimmering blue gown. Her raven hair spilled around her like waves. A soft voice replaced the rumbling one. "Your victory depends on your faith."

As though she were reading Sheila's mind, Raven interpreted. "You see the tree in your mind's eye that professor Eridanus illustrated as an example. If you can see the tree as full of fruit even though it's dead—if you can envision the emerald in your hand even if it is out of reach—then you can change your destiny."

Muddled by the riddles, and Raven changing body from man into woman, she had only one question. "How, Raven?"

"You don't need to know the how, your path will be revealed to you as you believe," instructed Raven tenderly.

"No, I meant . . . how do you change so effortlessly from man to woman and yet I still get the sense that nothing has really changed and that you are still you?" asked Sheila inquisitively.

Raven smiled with the most loving and warmest smile that Sheila had ever seen. It was as if starlight had lit up her face from the inside out.

"My transformation appears that way to you and only you because just like me there are two spirits living inside of you. Two spirits that, although different, are living in harmony: Woman, the nurturer and healer. Man, the protector and warrior."

Although Sheila didn't understand what Raven meant, it made her feel peaceful and whole. Raven's voice now resembled the musical trickle of water running over the rocks of a riverbed. "Close your eyes again, Sheila, and this time see the green amulet in your hand. Feel how smooth it is. Imagine how it reflects the sunlight and sparkles." Sheila did as she was instructed. Slowly she began to imagine the green jewel as if it were actually in her hands.

"Sheila, Sheila, Sheila! Stop daydreaming," nagged a nasal-sounding voice. Opening her eyes, she stared straight into the not-so-friendly beady eyes of spiky-haired Kim. "Get going," she nagged. "We don't want to wait here all day!"

Feeling a rush of wind, blowing away all the self-doubt and fear inside of her, Sheila lunged into the clear blue sky. Her strong, black wings, like thunder, grew out on either side of her human body and beat the air.

The sheer power of her wings swept the students off their feet and scattered them into an open path on either side of her. Higher and higher, she soared. Wind and flight was hers to control. Still having the free use of her wand she bellowed out "sciath!" A protective dome of brilliant yellow light instantly shielded her from the onslaught of fiery cannons and prickly arrows.

Looming menacingly in the distance, she saw the colossal fire-breathing dragon clutching the emerald and heading her way. Undaunted, she heard Raven's powerful voice reverberating in her head "see what you want to see and believe!"

A mischievous smile came over Sheila's face as she flew toward the dragon. She imagined that the green jewel that Professor Grian was carrying was really a vicious, electric eel that was desperate to get out of the dragon's claws.

On leathery wings, Professor Grian swooped down toward Sheila, hurling and bellowing clouds of smoke and fire at her from his gaping, fanged jaws. Undeterred by the dragon, Sheila advanced. Holding her wand firmly, the shield thwarted the fire and it bounced harmlessly off in all directions. The crowd cheered but half expected Sheila to fall at any second.

Still, the glowing jewel remained guarded in the sharp talons of the dragon. Seconds before Sheila and Grian were about to collide in the sky, Sheila focused one last time with all of her might. In an instant, the jewel transformed into an electric eel! Sparks exploded in the dragon's claws and traveled in electric jolts over his entire body. Vibrating uncontrollably from the shock, the dragon dropped the eel. Spotting the eel, Sheila dove and rocketed after it. Focusing again, Sheila imagined that it was once again a green amulet. She didn't see the eel. She saw the green gem. By the time her hands clutched it, the eel had transformed back into a shiny emerald.

Grian reached the ground first. Coughing, shaking, and sputtering, he morphed back into a Viking-looking druid with the bright red beard. However, after his electrifying experience, his red hair looked like a red bush, frizzing out into a massive fuzz ball. His once stately, long, hanging beard looked as if it were so frightened from shock that it tumbled straight out in front of his face. If that wasn't enough to tempt his students into hysterical laughter, the electric shock had changed his voice too. Instead of the intimidating low grow that shook everyone to attention, his voice now sounded like that of a young, shy girl.

"Boys and girls, please give a round of applause to our first victor of the combat and defense challenge!" sounded his very raspy and feminine voice. Unable to hold it in any longer, the entire class rolled on the ground from laughter. "I mean it, students!" cooed the professor, trying his best to sound authoritative. "I want your undivided attention!" pleaded the professor with a feminine, high-pitched voice. No matter how hard the class tried not to, they were now crying from laughter.

Luckily for the flustered Professor Grian, Professor Lyra was there to rescue both him and the class. With a swish of her wand and a few words, she cast a seriousness spell on the children. The children, who had been laughing hysterically, suddenly all began to cry. Everyone looked very solemn and unhappy.

"There now!" exclaimed professor Lyra. "That spell should do the trick, Professor Grian."

"Thank you!" the burly professor chirped gratefully to her in an airy, girly, high-pitched voice.

Feeling that she was about to explode into giggles as well, Professor Lyra quickly cast the same seriousness spell on herself!

CHAPTER TWENTY-SIX

Astral Projection

Drifting off into sleep, Sheila felt someone's breath brush against her cheek. Someone was staring at her. Opening her eyes, she made out a blurry face hovering just inches away from her own. "Who are you?" she yelped.

"Keep it down over there!" groaned Kim's disgruntled voice. "Some of us are trying to sleep," grumbled a few other girls from across the dorm.

Startled, the giant face moved back and shrunk to a regular size. As Sheila's eyes adjusted to the dark, she drew a sigh of relief when she recognized it was Snapper.

"What are you trying to do to me?" whispered Sheila gruffly, "Give me a heart attack?"

"Sorry, Sheila," apologized Snapper, "I just wanted to see if you were awake."

"A piece of advice . . ." Sheila muttered, "when someone is awake, he generally has his eyes open!" retorted Sheila.

"But are you awake now?" asked Snapper.

"I am now," mumbled Sheila, yawning.

"Good!" said Snapper. "After all, you never know, do you? Did you know that some people have been known to talk and even answer questions in their sleep?"

"You are the most unique sister in the world," said Sheila. "You think there's a chance I might be awake when my eyes are closed, and

then you think there's a chance that I may be sleeping when I'm talking
to you."

Satisfied that her sister was awake, Snapper hopped up beside Sheila
onto her bed. "I was just wondering how Mom is doing."

"Do you mean Tameka or your real mom?" asked Sheila.

"Well, both, I guess," answered Snapper.

"Shhhhhhhhh!" chorused their roommates.

Lowering her voice as much as she could, Snapper continued. "I
mean the whole reason we are here is because Raven said that my real
parents may possibly be here. But how do we find them? How do we
know that Glandor even saw my parents?"

"Honestly I don't know," Sheila answered, trying to keep her voice
quiet. "All I know is that when the time is right, we will know where to
look and what to do. We have things to learn."

"But what if my parents really are here?" interrupted Snapper
impatiently.

Taking her sister in her arms, Sheila spoke as softly as she could,
"We will find a way. Trust me. We are getting stronger and stronger.
Raven believes in us. We just have to believe in us too."

It was a good thing that Snapper was so prepared with her map and
punctuality. Professor Delphinus's class was hard to find. Following
obscure twists and turns through the forest, the girls finally found
the rustic, wooden cabin. Tall, leafy, green trees almost shrouded it
completely from the pathway. No one was in the class when the two
girls opened the creaky door. Cautiously they entered. If Sheila wasn't
completely awake before, she was definitely awake now. A chill ran up
her spine. Instead of an ordinary classroom with desks, a blackboard,
and books, it was filled with floating candles, and large mirrors adorned
the walls. Satin, indigo pillows hovered mysteriously just above the
ground, arranged in a wide circle.

"How are the candles floating in the air?" queried Snapper
inquisitively.

"Beats me," said Sheila, reaching for one just a few inches above
her. Pulling it toward her, she inspected it. "Seems just like an ordinary,
white candle," she said. When Sheila let go, the candle mystically floated
back to its former position in the air.

Exploring the room, Snapper came across glowing pink, blue, and
white crystals on a table, suspended just a few feet above the floor. She

was mesmerized by their beauty and the way they shone. While Snapper examined the crystals, a large bowl of red water on a round table caught Sheila's attention out of the corner of her eye. She felt as though it was drawing her to touch it.

"Look at the red bowl of water!" Sheila called to Snapper.

"Don't touch that!" Sheila heard a woman's voice from behind her yell out. It was too late. The minute she touched it, a pale woman's face appeared in the pool of water.

Black hair draped around the round, ghostly face. Empty, lidless, socket-less eyes took up the place where normal eyes belonged. Her serpentine hair was laced with hundreds of eyes, black as coal, staring up at Sheila. Slowly the mouth gaped open, wider and wider, until it took up the whole face. Rows of sharklike teeth emerged from the woman's black lips. Sheila screamed out in pain and panic. Professor Delphinus and Snapper grabbed Sheila and tried desperately to shake her back into reality. It was no use.

Suddenly, Sheila tilted her head back like she was in a trance. Her brown eyes turned black. The black shadow seeped like ink and spread over her entire eye.

"What's happening to her?" demanded Snapper, shaking.

"Your sister has been taken over by an evil spirit. Stay with her," ordered the professor sternly. I may have something that can un-possess her.

"Stupid druid! You are no match for me," spat out Sheila in an unfamiliar deep guttural voice.

"That's not your sister talking!" warned professor Delphinus, still rummaging through her wooden chest.

"I'm coming for you, I'm watching you every day and I'm here all around you," the strange voice coming out of Sheila's mouth hissed.

"Sheila, if you're still in there, fight it!" commanded Snapper.

Pushing past Snapper, the professor tied a green amulet around Sheila's neck. Professor Delphinus screeched out in fury: "By the ancient line of druids, I order you to leave this girl! Sheila is under our protection! Be gone!" Snapper watched her sister, barely able to breathe.

Gradually the blackness in her eyes began to fade and the earthy brown color in Sheila's eyes shone through once again. With a loud clunk, the red pool of water dropped from Sheila's hands and spilled on to the ground.

"Are you okay, Sheila?" asked the professor with deep concern in her eyes.

"Yes, I'm fine," responded Sheila weakly.

Quickly professor Delphinus looped an identical amulet over Snapper's head. "Who was that?" said Snapper, trying to control her quivering voice.

"My guess," replied the professor grimly, "is that it is some kind of evil witch who is after the two of you. My questions are why was Sheila most drawn to the seeing pool and was it telling the truth when it said that it was here and watching you? I'm not sure how that is even possible. Our borders are heavily protected from dark magic. These questions are worth investigating, for sure. For now, those amulets will protect you from whatever is haunting you within these walls." With that, Sheila and Snapper heard the sounds of voices and laughter as the group of students approached.

Maintaining her composure, Professor Delphinus conducted the class. "Boys and girls, please take a pillow and have a seat," she instructed the students.

Looking around her, Snapper could see looks of anticipation on all of the students' faces. They were staring at the classroom—at all the floating objects—in wonderment. Satisfied that she had their attention, Professor Delphinus commenced the class.

"Boys and girls, today I know you are expecting me to give you a lesson on astral projection. Instead, I'm going to surprise you. Today's lesson is on energy. If you don't understand energy, then you won't understand astral projection."

Kim's hand shot up. "Professor Delphinus, what does energy have to do with transporting yourself somewhere else? I thought there would be broomsticks, not a lecture about energy!"

Professor Delphinus paused and shot a mischievous look over in Kim's direction.

Suddenly, Kim, while staring at Professor Delphinus' face at the front of the classroom, felt the creepy sensation of someone touching her shoulder behind her. Screeching in fright, she whirled around to see who it was. Grinning from ear to ear was a glimmering, ghostly reflection of her professor.

"But how did you . . . ?" sputtered Kim.

Instantly vanishing and reappearing in front of her, her professor floated with a pen in her outstretched hand.

"I think this pen," suggested the professor, "is a far more useful tool to you than any broomstick." Pausing dramatically, she winked in Sheila's direction and then turned to Kim. "Maybe it will be useful to you, young lady, to take a few notes and leave your broomstick behind."

Professor Delphinus closed her eyes and then opened them once more, standing at the front of the classroom before her students. All the other duplicates of herself had vanished.

"Case in point," she concluded. "Energy is the most important component to achieve astral projection. By definition, astral projection is transporting oneself with one's mind or energy to another place and time. It takes a higher degree of discipline, skill, and concentration," she explained.

"Now we will continue this lesson tomorrow," the professor said, ending the class. "You all need a good night's rest because tomorrow you will need a lot of concentration if you are going to succeed in astral projecting at all. The majority of you won't be able to do it on your first try. Just the same, sleep always aids concentration."

With that, the students were dismissed. A chilly breeze blew through the yard as Sheila, Pen, and Snapper left their classroom.

"It looks like there's going to be a storm tonight," observed Snapper, pulling her jacket tightly around her neck. Sheila and Pen nodded, anxious to get into the dining hall. Drops of rain began to fall as they finally entered into dorms for the night.

At 9:00 p.m. sharp, the lights were out at the request of Professor Lyra. It wasn't long before all they could hear were the sounds of heavy breathing and snoring.

CHAPTER TWENTY-SEVEN

An Unnatural Storm

Lightning streaked through the clouds. Thunder rumbled from a distance. Growing louder, it sounded loudly overhead then growled across the sky. Rain pounded against the windowpane. It sounded like sharp nails beating against the glass, threatening to break it. It was as if the mighty Zeus, the Greek god of Thunder, was waging war in the heavens with his bolts of lightning. They illuminated the trees just outside of the dorm windows in frenzied flashes.

Snapper sat up in bed and looked around her. She barely slept at all. All she could think of were her parents. When she did manage to fall asleep, she fell into nightmares of her parents being trapped in Shadow Land. She rubbed her eyes and yawned. Turning to see the lightning through the window, she caught a glimpse of her reflection. Her cream-colored skin shone almost silvery in the flashes of electric light. Still sleepy, Snapper pulled her blankets over her and rested her head back on her pillow.

Closing her eyes, she heard a rustling sound that caught her attention. Pulling herself back up to a sitting position, she tried to listen. It was almost impossible to hear anything above the storm and the sound of the heavy breathing of the other girls. Rolling thunder drowned out whatever noise she had heard. When it died down, she strained to see where the noise had come from.

Suddenly, something moved in the shadows in the far corner of the room. *It must be that stupid mouse again*, thought Snapper irritated. *I'll have to ask Pen to help me set a new trap tomorrow.*

Reaching for her small night light, Snapper knocked her lamp over. It fell noisily on the ground before she could turn it on. She froze, expecting the other girls to wake up and complain. Nobody woke up. "How strange," she thought.

She was just about to reach for her flashlight when the same shadow moved again.

"That's no mouse," thought Snapper. "Maybe it's just the reflection of something tall from outside."

Pulling out her flashlight from her night table, Snapper turned it on. Nothing happened. "The batteries are dead again," thought Snapper, shaking it up and down. "Looks like I need new batteries and a new lamp." Snapper tried to light a fire in her hand, but every time she did, a gust of wind mysteriously blew it out.

Pushing back her covers, Snapper swung her legs over her bed. "Hopefully the ceiling light is working at least," she thought, grumbling. "The girls are going to kill me, but I've got to figure out what is making that noise!"

Snapper leaned over, ready to stand, when the shadow of a face appeared in the darkness. Shocked, Snapper opened up her mouth to scream, but no sound came out.

"Is something wrong, Snapper?" a voice asked.

Snapper jolted.

"Who are you?" Snapper demanded, starting to feel nervous.

No answer.

"Who are you?" Snapper asked again, starting to feel more panicky now.

Again—no answer.

The figure standing in the corner moved again. The face stared back at her with an unblinking eye.

"I can see you, Snapper," the voice whispered in the darkness. "I can see you, and I'm coming for you."

Snapper went cold. "I know that voice," she thought. She just couldn't remember where she had heard it. Unable to move, Snapper continued to stare into the shadows. A black hooded figure, shrouded in mist, draped in a black cloak slowly rose to its feet. Though its face was half concealed with a shroud of inky blackness, Snapper could make out the faint outlines of its face. Its complexion was gray. A lifeless cold gray eye peered out menacingly and was staring in Snapper's direction. The nose was sharp. The blond hair fell lifeless, draped like straw around the pale face. As her mouth twisted into a warped smile, yellow, rotted teeth protruded. The mysterious figure raised its clawlike hand. And out of the gray mist, a thin, white wand emerged from its bony hand.

Snapper sat motionlessly. Her mind raced. Although she could not see the face completely, it seemed hauntingly familiar.

"How had this figure entered into the dorm room?" Snapper wondered. She stared in disbelief.

Slowly and menacingly, the black, hooded figure moved toward her, laughing a low and eerie laugh. "Are you glad to see me, Snapper? I'm glad to see you. I have come to finish the job that I once started. I've come to destroy you."

Snapper could feel her heart racing. Before she could yell for help, the wind screamed and smashed in rage against the fragile glass pane. The window shook violently and opened, knocking against the wall loudly. The curtains blew frantically in the gusts. Snapper glanced at the open window and then quickly back to the shadows.

The black-hooded figure was gone.

"I must be hallucinating," thought Snapper. "This is crazy. Maybe I was just dreaming. It's not the first time that I have walked in my sleep."

Mustering up what little courage she had left, Snapper stood up. She walked over to the window. Reaching up, she bolted it closed. Lightning crackled again in bright streaks and lit up her face.

Suddenly, a bolt of lightning burst from the sky and headed straight for the window. Reaching out her hands toward it, she ordered it to vanish. It kept coming.

Staring at the approaching fire bolt in horror, Snapper gasped and dove for the floor. It wasn't going to stop. "Get down, everybody!" she screamed. No one stirred in their beds.

Hot flames exploded against the windowpane. Giving way, the glass shattered. It spilled out on to the floor in a million sharp shards. Reacting solely on instinct, Snapper immediately crouched into a fetal position. She had to protect her face and chest. Her hands and arms were cut and bleeding from the explosion of glass. The pain from the sharp shards penetrating her skin felt like needles and stung bitterly. Hot blood ran down her hands and legs.

"Sheila!" yelled Snapper. "Wake up! Help me!"

Reaching out for Sheila's bed that was only a few feet away from her, Snapper shook Sheila's foot. No response. Desperately, Snapper reached for Kim's foot. She hit it as hard as she could. Nothing happened. No response.

"Did you think that you could stop my storm, Snapper?" the same mocking voice asked. Whirling around, Snapper looked back in the direction of the voice.

"Snapper—you are all alone, and you are all mine," it echoed eerily. "I am going to destroy you."

Snapper screamed. "Help! Help! Please, somebody help me!" Snores from all direction seemed to muffle her voice. "Grian!" screamed Snapper louder. "Pen! Sheila! Anyone!"

"Oh, they can't hear you, dear child," the same voice hissed. "Do you think that I could risk them coming and helping you? Of course, I put a sleeping spell over everyone in the school, including the druids. But go ahead and scream some more. Scream as loudly as you wish."

Snapper's heart beat wildly. She glanced at Sheila. She was sleeping peacefully with a smile across her face, obviously dreaming about something very pleasant.

"And don't worry, this special storm is under my control, so every time that you scream, the thunder will just roar louder! How's that for an ingenious plan! That's why I always win in the end—because I'm smart—smarter than you, Snapper!"

"This must just be a dream," cried Snapper, trying desperately to calm herself down. "This is just a hallucination! I've got to get up and run for the door!"

Jumping to her feet, Snapper made a wild dash to escape the room.

Just before her hand could reach the doorknob, the figure appeared from thin air in front of her, blocking her way.

"Going somewhere, Snapper?" the voice asked.

Staring wildly at the same hooded creature, Snapper's mind spun. The ghastly creature raised her hand and pointed a wand at Snapper. Snapper tried to duck to avoid it. She couldn't move.

"Wait!" cried Snapper's voice, screaming in her head. "Something is paralyzing my body."

There was an unnatural feeling crawling up her skin, sparking the hairs on her neck to stand on edge. "I'm under some kind of a spell!" Snapper thought, panicking.

Slowly the figure removed her hood and lifted her head. Lightning lit up the stranger's face. Snapper gasped. She was fighting for air now when she saw who it was.

It was Kalik—the witch Kalik.

The look of pure malevolence on her face was enough to make anyone's color drain completely from his complexion and turn his hot blood cold!

When Snapper finally found her voice, she stammered weakly to the witch, "Bbbbbut we destroyed you, how can you possibly still be alive?"

The witch's face turned into a grim, twisted smile and her eyes stared right through Snapper as if they were piercing her skin.

"You merely vanquished me, foolish child," Kalik sneered. "I have voices and a presence in many worlds, including this one. Besides, did you not know that your old enemies, Butch, Brutus, and Thane are living here among you? They are getting to know all three of you quite well—in their hidden forms, of course. They were so kind to show me how to get in tonight."

Snapper looked back at the witch, her mind racing wildly. Brutus, Butch, and Thane were somewhere in the dorm? She had to warn the others! Once again, she tried to move. She was completely paralyzed.

Kalik opened her cloak slightly at the neck. As she did this, Snapper noticed a green, glowing amulet brooch pinned to her collar. It was in the shape of a snake. The tiny snake seemed to move slightly at first. Then it trembled. Little by little, it started to move on the brooch. It began to writhe and hiss at Snapper.

In horror, Snapper watched as the jewel pendant doubled—and then tripled—in size. It slid off the golden pin that was around the witch's collar. Its fangs flashed. Swelling uncontrollably now, the snake raised its head. Springing at her, it wrapped itself tightly around her throat. Within seconds, Snapper was helplessly engulfed in its coils.

"I'm going to die!" despaired Snapper, "I don't even have the strength to make a flame."

The snake maneuvered its head so that it could see Snapper's face. Large, yellow unblinking eyes stared into her own. Swaying slowly from side to side, it kept her in its gaze. Then it opened wide its gigantic mouth. Two sharp, white fangs extended out. Venom dripped down from the tips. The smell of its breath was musty and reeked of death.

As she felt the life slowly draining from her limp body, all she could think was: "I didn't even get to say goodbye to my family."

A tear fell silently from her red eyes as the room began to grow dim. The gleam of the snake's green scales was the last image that Snapper remembered. She vaguely heard the voice of Kalik ringing out into the night. "Don't eat her, you fool! I want her as my prisoner!"

Snapper finally succumbed to the darkness. All hope of survival began to fade. She closed her eyes. Snapper let herself be carried away into the blackness.

CHAPTER TWENTY-EIGHT

The Hydra

All was dark. Snapper felt her body being carried away. She felt like the wind, moving . . . light . . . lifeless. She drifted into space. She wondered where she was going. Was she dead? She couldn't tell.

Something was holding her up by the arms as she flew through space. She looked up to see what or who it was.

Two large demons flew, floating on either side of her. They were draped in smoky gray cloaks hanging like cobwebs from nearly fleshless bodies. Skeletal faces looked down on her with red glowing eyes. Sharp, white claws extending from gnarled, gray hands gripped her body tightly as they floated through the air.

"Let go of me!" screamed Snapper, trying to squirm out of their grip.

The demons didn't answer her. They simply looked back into her eyes and held more tightly on to her. Freakish wide smiles came over their faces.

"Where are you taking me?" Snapper called out again, pleading with the terrifying creatures.

"You will see, child. You will see," answered one of the demons. His voice hissed slowly at the end of each word.

Snapper shuddered.

She tried to move her hands and feet. It was no use. She felt like a lifeless doll being carried into the night. Snapper felt a small tear run down her cheek. At least she could feel her face.

On and on, Snapper drifted. It seemed like an eternity, but it was only a few seconds.

"We have a special surprise for you," the second demon said in a low, creepy voice.

When the demons spoke, Snapper could hear the sound of their breath being sucked in and pushed out through their long, exposed teeth.

Shuddering, Sheila peered back into the dark, black tunnel. She looked down. She was floating at least ten feet up in the air.

"At least, if I can get away from these beasts, I can fly to safety with my wand," she thought.

A small light in the distance caught her attention. Snapper wondered where these creatures were taking her. Snapper wished that her brother and sister, Pen and Sheila, were there. They would know what to do.

As they grew closer to the light, Snapper could hear angry voices. She was still unable to see clearly. All that she could make out were shadows. They looked ghostly in the darkness.

The demons flew over to where the sounds were coming from. They hovered in the air just above two figures.

"Take a good look, child," one of the demons said slowly. "I'm sure that our guests will welcome you."

Before Snapper could say a thing, a terrible scream abruptly pierced the night. It was the voice of a woman. She was crying in agony. A low, evil laugh sounded out beside her. Snapper peered below her into the shadows. Two tiny candles flickered uneasily on either side of the figures below her.

One of the figures was definitely a woman, and the other was a man. They were chained to the floor of the tunnel. The ground underneath them looked like hardened mud that had never seen rain. Long, winding cracks penetrated the earth in all sorts of directions. The woman had long blond hair that was matted in knots. It hung partly over her face and down her shoulders and back. The man's head was down, and he looked like he was unconscious.

Trying harder to get a good look, Snapper gasped at what she saw next. Instantly, she recognized the creature. This was most definitely the hydra—a dreaded, fearsome, three-headed snake that was all but a legend from ancient Greece. Three heads lashed in malice against any imminent foes in three different directions. It hissed. It struck. It lunged. It rose seemingly out of hell. Slime from its mouth dropped on to the ground beside the woman and the man. Its breath reeked of rotting flesh.

Thick, green, pasty snot from the snake's nose ran down its face in gobs. Tiny worms, covered in green, sticky goo hungrily licked up the mucus from his nose. They hung from his nostrils in tiny, green strings. Every now and then, the snake stuck out his long, slimy tongue and licked up all of the strings that hung from his nose and all of the worms that were hanging from them.

Thinking that she was going to be sick and throw up, Snapper squeezed her eyes shut. The second she did that, the terrible scream rang out again.

"I know that voice," thought Snapper. Opening her eyes again, Snapper looked below her at the woman.

Crying out in terrified groans, the woman pleaded with the snake. "Let me go, you beast. I will kill you. When the other witches come, we will defeat you, and you will wish that you were never born."

The snake laughed, hissing. "No one will ever find you," the snake sneered in a spine-chilling voice. "I will destroy you, a little bit at a time." Laughing again, the snake snorted in her face. Dripping in gruesome gobs, green snot spilled and splattered into the woman's hair.

"You beast!" the woman screamed at the snake. Calling out in a language that Snapper could not understand, she cast a spell on the snake.

Before she could finish her sentence, however, the snake hit her mouth hard with the end of his gigantic, spiked tail. Blood trickled down from the woman's lip and cheek.

Gasping in horror, Snapper tried to muffle her voice, but it was too late. The hydra had heard a sound above him and had turned his heads to see who was there.

"Well, well, look who's here!" two of the heads sneered as they looked up at Snapper. "Have you brought me another prisoner?"

"Yesssss," hissed the demons.

The woman raised her weak head and looked up at Snapper.

A cold shiver went over Snapper as she looked at the woman.

Staring back at Snapper, with chains tied around her feet and legs, the woman opened her mouth in horror as well.

It was Snapper's parents.

"No!" screamed Snapper. "How can this be? This has got to be a dream. Please, please, somebody, help me wake up! Pen, Sheila, someone help me!"

"Molly!" her mom cried out. "What are you doing here?"

The snake raised one head and looked into Snapper's eyes, and with the two other heads, looked at Snapper's mom.

"Well, well, what a fabulous reunion," he snickered. "Wouldn't it be wonderful if you could both die together? After all, isn't that what family is for?"

"You have got to get out of here!" shouted Snapper's mom.

"I can't move," cried Snapper. "They are way too strong for me!"

The demons glared at Snapper's mom.

"Do you honestly think that your daughter can escape us?" laughed one of the hydra's heads.

"Exactly!" answered a second snake head. "You're no match for our Master Kalik!" sneered the first head again.

"Shut up. I was going to say that!" said the second snake head.

"No! You shut up!" exclaimed the first head again. "You always interrupt me when I'm trying to say something!"

"Will you two focus and stop this useless fighting?" exclaimed the third snake head.

"Yah, you're a useless fighter!" sneered the first head to the second head. You're so stupid, you wouldn't know stupid if you saw it!"

"Oh yah?" retorted the second head. "Well, yo mamma's so dumb that when the news reporters told her they wanted to shoot her for the paper, she raised her tail and cried, 'Dear Lord, I'm too young to die!'"

Lunging at the first head, the second snake head yelled at him, "We have the same mamma, you idiot," and then bit him in the neck.

"Stop that foolishness this instant!" yelled the third snake head. "Focus! We have a job to do! If you don't stop fighting, I will summon Kalik immediately!" Stopping in mid-air, the two snake heads whirled around and looked at the third head.

"Okay! Okay!" muttered the first two heads. "We were just settling our differences!"

"Now is not the time!" demanded the third snake head.

Snapper stared in disbelief at the hydra.

Turning to look at both Snapper and her mother again at the same time, the three snakes sneered at them in unison now.

With all of the strength that Snapper's mother could summon, she began chanting. Furiously the snake hit her face again with his spiky tail. Blood ran down her forehead, but she did not stop this time. This was her daughter.

Chanting louder and louder, Snapper's mom began to cast a spell. The hydra suddenly froze in mid-air. The demons came to a halt as well, as if they had been immobilized.

"There!" shouted Snapper's mom. "The demons and the hydra have a time-freezing spell cast over them, but it won't last for very long! I would leave with your father, but our chains are enchanted. My magic isn't strong enough to break through them. Now go back and fight. It is not your time to die."

"I can't, Mom!" cried out Snapper. "The witch Kalik has sent her snake to strangle me. If I'm not dead yet, I will be soon!"

"You must go back!" insisted her mother, louder now. "You are the descendant of a powerful line of witches. You are more powerful than Kalik. But she will defeat you if you do not believe in yourself. You have the power!"

"But I can't even get free from these demons!" argued Snapper. "Their grip is too strong!"

"Close your eyes, Snapper, and envision yourself back in the room with Kalik," said Snapper's mom.

"I have the gift to control fire but it's not working against Kalik," argued Snapper.

"Your powers won't work when you're afraid!" explained Snapper's mom. "Fear disables them. You need to believe in yourself. All magic comes from faith. When you are back, see in your mind the fire burning and tearing the snake from off your neck. Fire is your gift. You can control it. And it is just one of your gifts. Go now, or you will die!"

"I want to stay and save you, Mom!" Snapper cried out. "I can use my powers on this monster."

"No!" Snapper's mom shouted at her firmly. "Close your eyes now, and do what I said. If you do not fight against Kalik, I will die. She is keeping me captive here. She has plans to destroy all of the witches everywhere so that she can have the ultimate power. You are my only hope, Snapper!"

Between violent sobs, Snapper did as she was told and closed her eyes. She envisioned herself back in her room. Focusing on herself, she slowly felt herself becoming heavier and heavier. An agonizing pain crushed her neck, as once again Snapper felt the grip of Kalik's snake wrapped around her.

Trying not to succumb to the throbbing pain, Snapper focused on the fire. She could feel a slight crackle of heat circulating around her. Focusing all of her strength on that fire, she summoned it to her and willed the flames to grow.

Once again, with all of her concentration, Snapper envisioned the fire becoming stronger and stronger until it was a mighty whirlwind of fire. Blazing now, the fire began to turn and vibrate in circles. Gradually it gathered speed and force, churning and roaring.

From her mind, Snapper commanded the fire to reach out and burn the snake from her neck. The fire howled in rage and reached for the snake. In the shape of a gigantic hand, it tore the snake from her neck and whipped it into the air. Screaming with rage now, the witch held up her arms and projected a shield of green light, protecting her from the flames.

Snapper opened her eyes. Her eyes looked like they were on fire. Pointing at the witch, Sheila called for the fire:

"I command you, fire. Gather from the center of the earth. Come to me out of the air. Burn through her shield of magic! Take Kalik and her snake and cast them through the window! Capture them with the speed of a hurricane of flames and send them into the ocean!"

The fire obediently shattered Kalik's mystical barrier of magic. It lifted Kalik and her snake from the ground. In a torrent of mighty, blowing flames, it hurtled them through the window.

Snapper watched, exhausted, as the two of them flew through the air, burning and screeching. As the witch and her snake vanished, so too did the sleeping spell that was cast over her roommates.

Collapsing on to the ground, Snapper cried out into the darkness. "Pen, Sheila, Kim, someone!" she screamed. "Help me!"

The door swung open violently as Pen, Blake, and Professor Grian clamored in to rescue her. Sheila, Kim, and the girls bolted out of bed and dashed to her side.

With hands covering her tear-stained face, Snapper sat crouched on the wooden floor, sobbing and shaking like a leaf. Sheila reached for her sister and rubbed her back gently.

"Snapper! What's wrong? What happened?" Professor Grian asked her, his voice filled with concern. At that moment, Professor Delphinus and Professor Lyra came into the room as well. "What in the world is going on?" they asked, loudly. "I thought that I had asked everyone to get a good night's sleep! This isn't what I had in mind!" Professor Delphinus announced, a bit annoyed at the fact that all of her students were wide awake in the middle of the night.

After a few moments when her sobs finally subsided, Snapper looked into the eyes of her everyone around her. There were looks of concern on all of their faces, especially Pen and Sheila's. Snapper wanted to tell them everything, but she was confused. She examined her hands and arms and there wasn't a scratch to be found. She didn't know what to say. Would they think she had lost her mind?

Finally Snapper told everyone what had happened to her. Nobody said a word. The professors looked puzzled.

"I'll go get us some hot tea," Professor Grian offered. Professor Grian felt awkward when he couldn't do anything to help a situation. His motto was take action and do something until it's better. There was nothing to do but listen. "Tea," he thought. "Tea will help them feel better."

For Professor Grian, it was hard for him to see Snapper upset and there was nothing else that he could think of doing. He also thought of the students as his own children. Although he was gruff on the outside, he was soft and caring on the inside.

While Professor Grian scurried downstairs to the kitchen in search of a kettle and chamomile tea, known for calming nerves—including his own right now—the others worked hard to comfort Snapper.

Snapper's usually neat, straight hair was half in her face and half in knots. Her bright, blue eyes were wide and darting, giving her nickname true merit. Snapper looked snapped.

Pen looked half asleep but worried. His afro was lopsided, leaning with great preference to the side of the pillow on which he had very recently and peacefully been soundly sleeping. He smacked his lips together and yawned, forcing his eyes open to no more than a sliver.

As the girls chatted, they didn't notice that Pen had begun scouring the room for clues. Still half asleep, he searched the room for any evidence that Kalik had been there.

All at once, Pen spoke up. "Look over here, guys!" he said quietly. Everyone, including the professors, looked up. While Sheila had been trying to figure out the dream, he had been scouring the room for clues. Pen had a unique talent for discovering the most minute detail or piece of evidence that would be overlooked by anyone else. Be it a hair, a speck of dust . . . or even a misplaced fingerprint. You could always count on the highly refined detective skills of Pen. Maybe all those years of not talking had helped him to tune out any distractions and follow his hunches.

Looking up at Pen, everyone went deathly quiet. From Pen's fingers dangled a piece of bright green snakeskin. From his other hand, he gingerly held a small piece of black material. "It must have come from her cloak," whispered Pen, his voice shaking. "And the tiny piece of the snake's scales must have been torn off in the fight."

Walking over to the window, he ran his hand over the glass. There were no scratches. Staring quietly, nobody said a word.

"I was hoping that Snapper had just had a bad dream," groaned Sheila. A cold shiver ran up everyone's spine.

"So Kalik must be alive and well then . . .," Pen said, his voice trailing off.

The three children looked at one another.

"That means that all three of us are in danger," whispered Sheila, trembling.

"Nonsense!" interrupted Professor Lyra. "Kalik could never come into our school! Our institution is well hidden from the outside world."

Some of the girls began to cry. "Who is Kalik?" asked Kim, trembling.

"She is a witch from another world, students!" answered Professor Lyra. "But that is no concern of yours. Snapper just had a very bad dream. In fact, she probably doesn't exist anymore. As far as I know, Kalik was defeated a while ago—by Sheila, Pen, and Snapper, might I add!" Professor Lyra said smiling. "Now back to bed everyone!"

"I'm sorry about your mom . . .," Pen began again as he was leaving their room.

"We'll help you rescue her, Snapper," added Sheila. "We'll find a way."

"We defeated Kalik once before," Pen said, trying to comfort Snapper. "We can do it again."

Snapper nodded, trying to be strong.

"You'll have to write down all the details about the place where the demons took you," Sheila said. "Then at least, we have someplace to start. She can't be that far."

"I will help you find your mother," Sheila said, rubbing Snapper's back. "Pen and I will figure out a way to get to her."

"I wish that Raven were here," Snapper said suddenly. "He would know what to do."

"I'm sure that he will come and help us at the right time," answered Pen once again, trying to be strong for Snapper.

Snapper nodded. The painful thought that her mom and dad were out there somewhere was almost too much to bear.

"Yes. I will find my mom," Snapper said. "I will find her and I will defeat that hydra! I will make him pay for what he is doing to her!"

"And we are both with you!" chimed in Pen and Sheila.

"Kalik will be sorry that she ever messed with us!" said Pen. His eyes turned from dark brown to a deep yellow. They flashed with anger. Although Pen did not morph into his panther self completely, his panther eyes told everyone that he was livid with rage.

Professor Lyra stepped over to him. "We will get to the bottom of this, kids," she reassured the three children. "We should all try to get some rest. We can't defeat anyone or anything if we're exhausted."

"I don't know about anyone else here," Pen suddenly interjected out of the blue, "but it is two o'clock in the morning, and I'm really hungry. I always think better on a full stomach."

He looked sheepishly over at Professor Lyra with big, brown, puppy-dog eyes.

Professor Lyra rolled her eyes. Pen was always hungry. He used any excuse to be fed. Sheila wondered if Pen was really a cow disguised as a panther in that he could very well have two stomachs. The only problem was that it seemed like both stomachs were always empty!

Giggling and with the mood a little lighter now, the girls and Pen got up quietly and headed downstairs with Professor Lyra in search of the infamous tea that was never brewed. Before long, all of the children were huddled together in the dining area. They found poor Professor Grian fast asleep with his head on the table. His one hand was around the handle of the copper teapot that never quite made its journey to the stove, and his other hand loosely held a bag of chamomile tea.

"Well," said Professor Lyra, gently tapping Sheila on her shoulder, "At least we know now that Professor Grian has discovered where the tea is kept."

CHAPTER TWENTY-NINE

Land Between the Living and the Dead

"Please put your arms out in front of you," Professor Lyra instructed the class. Without question, the class obeyed.

"If you see only muscle, skin, and bone, you are irrefutably shortsighted," said the professor. "We are all made up of energy. Knowing this, your mind can transport your body to wherever you choose."

"Now students," the professor instructed, "please dismount your pillows and step over to one of the many looking glasses around the room. If you are nervous to try this on your own, you are welcome to tackle this as a team effort. Focus with all of your concentration on a certain place or person. Then imagine your energy going there. You probably won't be successful on your first try. It takes years of practice. However, If you do succeed, which you won't, imagine yourself in your body again, feel your surroundings, and you will be back immediately."

Without a word, Snapper, Sheila, and Pen stood in front of the same mirror. Snapper turned to her brother and sister and gripped their hands tightly. She knew, beyond doubt, that they wanted to join her on her quest to find her mom. Standing before the mirror, Pen looked at her and said, "We're here for you, and we're going to help you. Let's do this."

Closing their eyes, they envisioned the crumpled, worn-out photograph of Snapper's mom. She kept it on her at all times. Even though it was slightly foxed around the edges, she cherished it. Seeing Snapper's mom clearly in their minds' eyes, they closed their eyes and astral projected into the unknown.

Snapper opened her eyes. She put her hands out in front of her. They were transparent, like she was made up of smoke.

"Snapper, what's happened to us?" demanded Sheila frantically.

"I think that we are separate from our bodies right now," Snapper answered.

"What do you mean?" asked Pen.

"Remember, the professor said that we are transporting our energy?" answered Sheila slowly as though she was figuring it out at the same time she spoke. "Well, we have projected our thoughts and sent them in a different form to find Snapper's mom and dad, Pen."

Looking around, the children found themselves in a gray, barren wasteland. Rolling hills of nothingness stretched out for miles. Mist clung like cobwebs to the sand dunes and hung in billowing sheets from the air above them. "This feels really weird," said Pen. "Whenever I move, it's like walking through water, like I'm floating over the ground."

"Maybe we are in a different world, like Raven's world," suggested Sheila suddenly. "It feels like a limbo sort of place that I heard of. Somewhere between the land of living and the land of the dead."

A small light in the distance caught their attention. Mysteriously it glowed in the gray mist. "What's that over there, Snapper?" asked Pen, squinting to see. "Let's follow it, but we have to move as quietly as possible," insisted Sheila. "We don't know what else could be lurking." Snapper and Pen nodded in agreement and silently moved in the direction of the light. The sensation here of walking felt as if they were walking on the moon with very little gravity. As they grew closer to the light, Sheila could hear a voice echoing in the fog. She was still unable to see clearly. "Molly, is that you?" a distant voice rang out. Snapper almost jumped out of her skin.

"That's my mom!" exclaimed Snapper. "We found her!"

"I don't see her anywhere," said Sheila, looking around her.

"No, it's her, I know it is!" cried Snapper. "I recognize her voice".

"Where are you, Mom?" Snapper pleaded. "I know it's you!"

A moaning wind pulled back the curtain of mist. Like two ghostly shadows, gray and transparent stood Snapper's mom and dad. Just like Snapper, her mom's hair was long and blond. Her father was tall. His red curly hair was unkempt and his long beard was overgrown. Running as fast as she could despite the lack of gravity, Snapper rushed toward her mom with open arms. When she reached her mom, her heart dropped. All she felt was air.

"What's happened to you?" Snapper cried out.

"Snapper, she must have astral projected like we did," reasoned Pen out loud.

"The boy's right," said Snapper's dad gently. "I can't touch you in this form. We are so happy to see you, Molly! We always knew that one day you would gain your powers as a witch. It's in your blood. You come from a long line of witches and wizards."

Snapper's father ran his transparent hand over the top of her head. "We are so proud of you!" beamed her father.

"Where are your real bodies?" asked Sheila, who had been quietly watching up until now.

Snapper's mother sighed, with so much sadness filling her breath. "We are trapped in a world between the living and the dead. Kalik has trapped us here."

"Then we will free you!" announced Snapper eagerly.

"You can't," whispered Snapper's mother. "Your powers are useless in this place. In your astral form they won't work. That is why Kalik has trapped us here. She is using us as bait to lure the three of you in to obtain your powers. We overheard her plan. If she knew that we felt your presence and astral projected here to meet you, then you all would be in a lot of danger. You need to go," pleaded Snapper's mother. "You need to go now before she finds you!"

"But we can't leave you here. There must be something that we can do!" cried Snapper.

"There is," reassured Snapper's father. "Once a year, we can appear in the burial chamber in the land of the living on the high moon of the summer solstice. There you can use your powers. The ancient druids built this chamber thousands of years ago to commune with spirits departed from their world. This magic is strong and even Kalik cannot stop you from summoning us to the burial chamber on that night."

"But we want to help you now," insisted Snapper.

"Please, Molly," pleaded her mother. "If she captures you now, then you will be helpless, and we will have to watch you die."

A loud hiss sounded from a distance. The children could hear it approaching faster and faster.

"It's coming for you!" warned Snapper's father.

"Snapper, we have to go!" pleaded Sheila and Pen.

"We will rescue them at the burial chamber. But we need our powers and a plan. Kalik won't kill your parents as long as she thinks that she can use them to get to us," explained Pen, trying to stay as calm as he could while the threatening hiss seemed to come closer and closer. Reluctantly Snapper closed her eyes and the three children transported themselves back to their bodies.

CHAPTER THIRTY

Wolves in Sheep's Clothing

"We've got to figure out how to get back to your mom, Snapper," said Pen. The three children were making their way across the yard to their class.

"I think that we should talk to Professor Grian about what happened," said Sheila. "We need his help if we're going to save your mom, Snapper. Also, he needs to know that Kalik is definitely alive."

"What if he doesn't believe us?" asked Pen. "I know that you had that dream and all, Snapper, but what if he thinks that we're all crazy?"

"We just have to take a chance on it," said Sheila, answering before Snapper could say a thing.

The three children nodded.

Professor Grian had arranged a dueling match that day. All of the students had been placed in teams. He insisted that it was time for the students to try out their new found powers and spells.

"There are very specific rules for this duel!" Professor Grian had instructed them. "There will be no force, no violence. No usage of any power that could harm one of your colleagues. The aim of this duel is to be able to use your spells and powers wisely so that you are able to tap your opponent on an exposed part of his body. Once a team has been able to tap the opposite team three times, that team wins. The winning teams will then compete to see who the finalists are."

"This is not a real competition," Professor Delphinus added. "This is just a chance to experiment with what you have learned."

"Yes!" Professor Lyra had added emphatically. "If any of you can astral project, that would be wonderful to see in the arena!"

"The arena?" many of the students had yelled out at once. Everyone was excited with the thought that they would be able to try out their spells in the dueling ring. That was a special place where only the most experienced witches, wizards, and druids go to compete with one another.

Pen looked at the schedule. There were five teams of fifteen students that were going to duel before him and his sisters. Pen had decided to stick with his sisters for this duel. Even though he would have enjoyed pairing up with Blake, he decided against it at the last moment. He was going to have to fight with his sisters against Kalik and her sisters at some point, and so they needed all the practice working together that they could get.

The first few teams competed against each other quickly. It didn't take long for a team to gain three points.

"I hope that our turn isn't over in just three minutes!" Pen said wistfully. "I hope that our competing team is a good one."

Sheila and Snapper agreed. They were pretty good at warfare, and they knew it!

Finally, the team before them finished. From the beginning of their match to the end—it had taken all of four minutes. The losing team groaned.

Pen, Snapper, and Sheila stood outside the arena, waiting for their turn in the ring. "I'm really excited that we finally have a chance to try out our new skills," said Pen.

"Yah!" agreed Snapper. "It's a safe place to experiment with what we've learned!"

Sheila didn't say anything. She reluctantly followed Pen and Snapper to the door leading out to the arena. Something didn't quite feel right to Sheila, though. She couldn't shake the nagging feeling that something was wrong. But she couldn't put her finger on it.

"Why are you so nervous, Sheila?" laughed Snapper. "Remember, nobody's going to get hurt today! The point of the exercise is just to tap an opponent on an exposed part of their body. That's how easy it will be to get a point!"

"I don't know . . ." began Sheila. "I just am not looking forward to this duel!"

"We'll be fine, Sheila!" said Pen cheerfully.

Giving one another high-fives, the three children pushed open the large iron doors. Stepping through the doors, they found themselves on the far south end of the ring.

Looking across the arena, Pen, Sheila, and Snapper saw their opponents.

"Hmmm . . .," wondered Sheila aloud. "Who are they? I thought that we knew everybody at the campus now!"

"I don't know," mused Pen, "but they had better get ready because we're going to take them down today! We're the strongest, fastest, most skilled team here!" Pen put up his fists and bent his legs slightly, ready for battle.

Snapper nodded eagerly in agreement. She normally didn't like conflict, but this wasn't a real fight. It was just basically a game of tag, she thought to herself.

Sheila continued to stare at the three opponents on the other side of the arena. There was something strangely familiar about the three students standing there. They kept their faces down.

"Hey, guys!" shouted Pen at the opposing team of three boys. "Don't worry, we're not going to hurt you . . . not today, at least," he joked, trying to make the mood lighter.

Still, the three tall boys facing them did not raise their heads. They did not move a muscle.

"This does not feel right," whispered Sheila again. "Something's wrong."

Professor Grian blew the whistle, signaling for the duel to begin. Pen, Sheila, and Snapper watched the three boys in front of them. With their heads still down, they clenched their hands into tight fists. Slowly and purposefully, the boy in the middle began to raise his head. The two boys on either side of him kept their heads down and their fists clenched. The boy raised his head until his eyes met Pen's.

Shocked, Pen gasped. Sheila and Snapper froze.

"What the . . ." Pen began, unable to finish his sentence. "It can't be . . ."

"Oh, but it is!" called out the boy staring back at him. "Do you remember me, Pen?" the boy asked him.

The second boy to the left lifted his head. He sneered at Pen.

"Just in case you don't remember his name," he began, "his name is Brutus."

Brutus didn't take his eyes off Pen. It was Brutus all right. His eyes were filled with the deepest hate and revenge that Pen had ever seen in his life. Pen shuddered as he looked into his eyes. The dark hatred was deep. The third boy raised his head. Pen, Sheila, and Snapper stood motionless as they stared into the eyes of their old foes: Brutus, Butch, and Thane.

"Surprised to see us, freaks?" asked Brutus slowly, callously. "We started the job once, but now we're here to finish it."

"How d-d-d-did you get here?" stammered Pen, when he finally found his voice. "I wanted to tell you how sorry I was that I hurt you. I didn't mean to hurt you so badly. I was only trying to protect my sisters."

"Sorry!" sputtered Brutus. "You're sorry, and you really thought that that would cut it, Pen?" He turned and looked at Butch and Thane. "He's sorry, boys. That makes everything all right now, doesn't it?"

Butch grunted a sarcastic laugh. "Sure. How about we say sorry now, Brutus, for what we're about to do."

Brutus laughed. "Good one, Butch. We're sorry, Pen, that we're going to kill you and leave your remains all over these hills." Thane sneered at Pen, Sheila, and Snapper. "And we're sorry that we're going to beat the crap out of your sisters, Pen—and guess what—there's not a lot that you can do about it."

Professors Grian, Eridanus, Lyra, and Delphinus, who had been stuck to their seats, trying to figure out what had just happened to their students, finally got up together.

"I'm afraid that this duel is over, kids," Professor Grian announced. "Besides, these challenges are only for our own students. I don't know who you are or where you've come from."

"Well, old man," scoffed Brutus, "we *are* your students! We sit in your classes every day and eat in the lunch room with all of your students at every meal time! We've even had tea together, old man, like a lot of students here. But here's the problem for you—a very powerful witch has put a cloaking spell on us. We look completely different when we sit in your classes every day. And guess what? We even have different names. We are part of this school! We have been enrolled into your classes, just like the other kids here. The unfortunate part—for you, that is—is that you have no idea who we are! We could be anyone!"

Professor Grian stared back, bewildered at the three boys standing in front of him. Grabbing his wand, Professor Eridanus and the other druids pointed at the three boys. "Detego detectum," called out all the druids together. Nothing happened.

"It's an uncovering spell," whispered Snapper to Pen and Sheila. I saw it in the book of spells. It means "uncover." Pen and Sheila waited, not taking their eyes off the three boys.

Again, the druids pointed their wands at the three boys and called out loudly, "Detego detectum!" Again, nothing happened.

"Too bad that you're not smart enough to see through our cloaking spells, guys!" called out Brutus. We had you fooled from day one. We're going to kick their butts, and there's nothing that you can do about it." Butch and Thane starting laughing.

Pen, Sheila, and Snapper looked at one another horrified. Brutus, Butch, and Thane could be anyone in the school. And there was no way to go through hundreds of students to find out which three were missing.

"Now here, you listen to me, you young, foolish wizard!" shouted Professor Grian. "You are going to stop or else . . ."

"Or else what?" retorted Brutus, provoking the old wizard.

"Or else I'm going to turn the three of you into statues until we can get to the bottom of this."

"Hmmm . . . that might be a bit difficult, seeing that you may have a battle of your own to face, old man!" snorted Butch. "We brought you some company. It looks like they're strong enough to intercept your spells."

With that, three dark figures from the back of the audience rose to their feet.

Sheila, Pen, and Snapper watched in horror as three very familiar faces emerged from the crowd.

"Remember me, Grian?" a voice rang out from the crowd.

Grian didn't need to look over to know that voice. "Kalik," Grian answered. "My old enemy. You have no right to be here. You know that you are no match for Raven. All I need to do is call him, and you will be instantly defeated!"

"Oh, but my sister was hungry. How could I deny her a feast like the one that you've just provided for her?"

"She won't touch my students!" yelled Grian. Professor Eridanus and the other professors raised their wands, ready for battle.

"Now, now!" called out Kalik. "Don't be hasty, Grian. You see, there's a little problem. Every few thousand years, the Raven, who is the ruler of our kingdom, dies. He is absorbed back into the universe. We have been watching the stars and seasons for the last few months. We knew that it was just a matter of time before his strength would wane. Well, Grian . . ." smiled Kalik, with a twisted grin, "it looks like Raven's time has come! We just left him on a mountain top—almost dead! We have defeated Raven! As the second most powerful beings in the universe, we have automatically become your new leaders!"

"That's impossible, Kalik!" retorted Professor Grian. "You have always been the liar of all liars!"

"Oh, but it's true!" smiled Marcella. "We will be taking over your school, old man! I mean—that is, if there are any students left to teach!"

The Blue Hag, who had not said a word up until now, just grunted. With one of her crooked fingers, she began to count the students. Then with the other hand, she lifted her fork and knife, and the sash of dried children's skin wrapped around her waist. As she did this, wails from the souls of the children that she had destroyed echoed in the wind.

The students, petrified now, scrambled to their feet. Screams of terror rose from all corners of the campus, as children tried to run for their lives. Their screams just excited The Blue Hag. Their fear just incited her primal instincts and appetite. Reaching forward to try to run after them, Kalik and Marcella grabbed her shoulders and pulled her back.

"Not yet, dear sister!" croaked Kalik. "Your time will come, and we will even help you catch every last student. Before you begin feasting on their flesh, however, we want to sort out the strong leaders from the weaker students. We may want to raise leaders under us to help us rule our people."

The Blue Hag grunted angrily. She growled menacingly at her sisters.

"Just a few more minutes, sister!" said Marcella sharply. "You will do as I command you to do, or I will see to it that you have no children at all to eat!"

The Blue Hag sat back down in her seat. She glared with her one milky eye at the children running frantically for their lives.

The four professors had already begun their ritualistic chant to call for Raven. Calling for him, in their druid tongue, they waited patiently for him to answer.

A worried look came over Professor Grian. "He's not answering," he whispered to Professor Lyra.

"Try again," she replied under her breath.

Looking over the empty stadium, Sheila looked across the ring again at the three boys. Brutus, Butch, and Thane were enjoying the scene before them. They loved to see fear and pain on the faces of their fellow students. That's why they had been the bullies at their previous school. It had been so difficult not to bully their peers at this new school. They had to remain hidden. They had been warned by Marcella that their job here was to spy on the three children and to blend in. They could not cause any trouble. It killed them that they had to try to be nice to the other students here. Brutus beamed that they could finally step into their real bodies again and be the bullies that they really were.

Brutus lunged into the air. Morphing into a lion, he spread out his gigantic wings. Flapping hard and fast, Brutus rose in the air until he was high above Pen. Then swooping down, he dove full force toward Pen. His enormous claws were aimed straight at Pen's face.

Shape shifting immediately into a panther, Pen sprang into the air to meet him. The two massive bodies collided in mid-air. A deafening thud resounded in the arena as Brutus smashed the black panther on to the ground. Still on top of Pen, Brutus swiped Pen through the face with his razor-sharp claws. Brutus bit down hard on to Pen's neck. Screaming with pain, Pen slashed the lion's face with his claws and sunk his teeth into Brutus's ear. Brutus let go and leaped into the air again. Thane, who had already morphed into a grizzly bear, raced with Pen at a tremendous speed. Swiping him with one of his claws, Thane knocked Pen through the air. Pen crashed against the side of the ring. Before he could get up again, both Brutus and Thane were on top of him, biting at his neck and back.

Sheila and Snapper screamed in rage. As they raced toward Pen to save him, Butch grabbed his wand. Butch, who had decided against turning into his infamous animal self—the skunk—decided to stay in his human form. Grabbing his wand, he pointed it at Sheila. A white fire bolt streamed from the end of it and knocked Sheila to the ground before she could fight back.

Snapper, however, was ready. Wand in hand, she aimed her wand in Butch's direction. A stream of white magic met Butch's. Snapper and Butch, eyes fixed on each other, continued to stream their fire as sparks exploded on either side of them.

Brutus and Thane clawed and bit at Pen relentlessly. Pen tried to fight back. But each time he succeeded in biting one of them, they became even angrier. There was no hope. There were two of them. Brutus and Thane were too powerful for Pen. Again and again they struck him, until Pen could no longer move. His body felt weak and lifeless. He called for water to save him. But he was too weak to summon it.

"How does it feel to have every bone broken in your body, Pen?" taunted Brutus, before slashing him again in his face. "Come on, tough boy," said Thane, smashing his giant paw down on Pen's chest. Pen felt his life's force seeping out from him. He could hardly breathe. It felt like every part of him was broken. He couldn't even move his face to see if his sisters were all right.

Changing back into their human forms, Brutus and Thane grabbed their wands and rushed over to Butch's side. He and Snapper were still locked in a battle, where no one was winning. Brutus and Thane aimed their wands at Snapper at the same time and fired at her. The force was too much. Dropping to her knees, Snapper tried to fight back against the stream of fire hitting her chest, arms, and body. Sheila, who had finally recovered from the first bolt that had come from Butch's wand, jumped to her feet. She was barely up when all three wands were aimed at her. She fell to the ground beside Snapper. A line of smoke rose from Sheila's body. Snapper tried again to get up. This time, the power from the wands increased. Her body shook and vibrated with the relentless force, and she fell to the ground, unconscious.

Running to the girls, Brutus kicked Sheila hard in her side. She didn't move. Thane and Butch soon joined him. They kicked Snapper as hard as they could, jumping on her legs. Snapper didn't move. She lay on the ground, motionless.

Smiling, Brutus, Butch, and Thane let their wands drop to their sides. "Well boys, I guess we got our revenge!" Brutus chuckled. "I don't think that any one of them will ever walk again."

"Or even get up again, for that matter," added Thane, laughing sarcastically.

"I hope that you didn't kill the three children," a voice suddenly echoed from the side of the ring. Freezing in their tracks, the three boys looked up at Marcella. The three witches stood side by side. They had successfully immobilized the professors. Raven had not come to save them.

"Yes," agreed Kalik. "Because if you did, your contract with us is null and void because you did not obey us. If that is the case, we will just hand you over to our sister."

The Blue Hag ran her forked, black tongue over her hungry lips. She nodded her head rapidly and grunted what appeared to be consent to what was happening.

Trembling in his shoes, Brutus ran over to where Pen was lying. Putting his hand on his chest, he tried to feel for any sign of life. Nothing. Pen didn't even seem to be breathing.

Brutus' eyes grew wide. Now they were in trouble.

"Oh, Pen's just knocked out—that's all," he lied to the witches. Butch and Thane, who were already beside Sheila and Snapper, knelt down beside the girls. Butch tried to find a pulse from Sheila. There was nothing. Thane did not have any luck either from Snapper. They looked at each other terrified.

"They're fine too, right?" called out Brutus.

The boys looked up at him. They gave him the thumbs up reluctantly. "Yup. They're going to be just fine," lied Thane.

"Good news for you," replied Marcella. "We still need to extract their powers from their bodies."

"And besides that, a little bit of torturing when they wake up wouldn't hurt either!" sneered Kalik.

"We will need to transport them to the prison cells," said Marcella. "Let's come back for them, though. We need to round up as many children as we can, so that our sister can have her fill. Otherwise, she is going to be in a very bad mood today. Just try to keep the stronger children alive, and to one side. We'll deal with them later."

Brutus, Thane, and Butch did as they were told. Following the witches, they left Pen, Snapper, and Sheila alone in the arena behind them. They were desperate to do a good job of rounding up the children. They feared that they had gone too far with Pen and his sisters. Bullying other students was what they loved to do best. Running into the buildings, Brutus, Butch, and Thane began locating students everywhere—under the beds, behind doors, in cupboards. Grabbing students by their hair, Brutus started pulling kids from under the beds.

Morphing into a lion and grizzly bear, Brutus and Butch began pushing students toward the doors. Frightened screams broke out again. Butch, who remained in his human form, joined in the fight.

In the arena, Pen lay motionless. Gaping wounds and broken bones protruded throughout his body. Sheila and Snapper lay beside each other, with smoke rising from their arms and legs. None of them moved a muscle.

As far as the frozen druids were concerned, all was lost. They watched helplessly as their students were rounded up by a lion and a grizzly bear. Many students tried to retaliate with spells. It was no use. Kalik and Marcella intercepted any spells from the students. They waited outside with their sister.

With all of the commotion, and plans to divide and conquer the captive students, no one noticed a slight rustling in the tree just beside the arena. A small, insignificant-seeming black raven jumped soundlessly from branch to branch. It swooped down effortlessly and landed on the ground beside Sheila and Snapper.

The witches and Brutus and his gang were so busy rounding up the students that they didn't notice the small bird perch itself on Sheila's arm. It pecked on her cheek. No response. It pecked on her arm. No response. Shuffling over to her hand, the raven moved one of her fingers with his beak. No response still. Sheila and Snapper lay side by side— lifeless. Pen was so badly hurt that his body lay in an abnormal position. He, too, didn't move.

The raven hopped nimbly over to Sheila's ear. Once again, if anyone had been paying attention, they would have seen the raven whisper something quietly into her ear.

"Sheila!" the raven whispered softly. "Sheila, this is Raven speaking. It is the last time that you will ever hear my voice. My days as Raven are finished. My time is drawing to a close. From this day forward, you will be the new Raven. I am passing my spirit into you, as the Great Raven before me did. Right now, you are a young girl—destined to become a wonderful girl. But once you become Raven, you will be neither male nor female. You will be neither man nor woman. You will become both.

You can appear to others in the form of a strong, strapping young boy, or you can choose to show yourself as a graceful, beautiful woman, who you already are. The choice will be yours. When I transfer my spirit into you, you will automatically take the form of a boy. Use my powers well. Do not use these great powers for your own gain.

Remember that you are the Great Raven now. You will learn with time how to use your powers. And above all else, Sheila, believe in yourself. From this day forward, you will no longer call yourself Sheila because you are no longer a young woman. You will not call yourself by a young man's name either, because you are not trapped in only a man's body. You will call yourself "Raven."

With that, the raven morphed into a tall and handsome man. As he stood tall, he morphed once more into a beautiful woman, with her black hair streaming over her shoulders. Walking over to where Pen was lying, she reached out and gently touched Pen. Healing power seeped into him, as bone reconnected with bone. Gaping cuts closed perfectly, leaving no scars.

Within seconds, Pen was completely healed and looked as if he was sleeping peacefully. Walking back over to Snapper, she touched her cheek. Color returned to Snapper, and a smile came over Snapper's face as she lay with her eyes still closed.

As Raven remained standing, she morphed between both the muscular, strapping young man and the beautiful, graceful woman. As he continued to morph, Raven's body became more and more transparent, until all that was left was the outline of a shape, blowing in the wind.

Then, softly and gently, the outline of Raven's shape flowed effortlessly into Sheila's body. First, Sheila's face lit up and began to shine. She gasped as air once more filled her lungs. Then little by little, her whole body shone brightly. Bright flashes of light shone through her fingertips, in streams. Rays of light pierced through her feet and surrounded her body in a blinding white aura. It was so intense that it lit up the entire dueling ring and surrounding stadium.

Startled by the sudden glare coming from the ring, Brutus, Thane, and Butch turned to see what was happening. Kalik and Marcella flew back to the arena, with The Blue Hag close behind. The rays of light were so powerful that they were not able to approach. The light was hot and blinding.

Shielding their eyes, they tried to peer through their fingers. As quickly as the light had appeared, it suddenly vanished.

Brutus, Thane, and Butch rushed into the stadium and down into the arena. Kalik, Marcella, and The Blue Hag sped through the sky and landed beside Pen. Out of breath, Brutus was the first of the boys to arrive at the scene. He looked closely at Pen and kicked his leg. No response.

"It doesn't look like he's going to move anytime soon," said Butch, huffing and puffing.

"No," agreed Thane. "He's out cold, man!"

Kalik and the two witches didn't say anything. They examined Pen a bit closer. "Well, sis," said Kalik to The Blue Hag, "it looks like you can add three children to your banquet—after we have extracted their powers from them."

Rubbing her hands together with glee, The Blue Hag grinned. It was worth the long fast.

"I first need to draw out their powers, and then they are all yours," Marcella reminded her sisters.

"Where should we take the bodies?" Brutus asked, walking over to Sheila and Snapper.

He bent down, ready to pick up Sheila. Suddenly, Brutus let out a scream.

"What the hell?" shouted Butch and Thane whirling around.

"W-w-w-here is Sheila?" Brutus stammered. "She's gone!"

"What do you mean, she's gone?" asked Butch and Thane. "Isn't she right there in front of you?"

"No! No! She's gone! This is a guy! He looks like Sheila a bit—but he's definitely a guy!"

Running over, Butch and Thane and the three witches peered down at the strange boy lying on the ground in front of them.

"Is there something wrong?" a deep voice suddenly asked them. Jumping back in alarm, the six onlookers stared at the strapping young boy who had mysteriously appeared, lying beside Snapper. He opened his eyes, sat up, and then rose to his feet.

His eyes were bold. His voice was deep. His arms rippled with muscles. His thick, black hair hung loosely over his broad shoulders.

"You look confused," the boy said to the witches. "Maybe this will jog your memory."

With that, the boy's face suddenly softened. His thick bulging arms straightened into slender, muscular ones and the rest of his body transformed into the body of the young girl who they all knew—Sheila!

"I-i-i-it can't be!" stammered Marcella, grabbing for her wand.

Sheila once again morphed into her male self. Large black wings appeared on either side of his body. Raising his hands to the sky, wind exploded in torrents toward the witches and Brutus and his gang. Grabbing her two sisters, Marcella disappeared in a puff of pink smoke.

The sound of the rushing wind woke up both Pen and Snapper. They had been completely healed and were in a deep sleep. Standing, Pen and Snapper stood beside Raven. They both stared at him. They had no idea who he was.

Brutus, Thane, and Butch, realizing that they had been abandoned, rushed for the exit and slammed the door behind them. Pen dashed after them. Tearing it open wildly, Pen looked in horror. Hundreds of students were running panic-stricken through the hallway. It was too late. In those few seconds, Brutus and the boys had dived behind a ledge and spoken over themselves the veiling spell again. Now they were running through the building with the other students, completely hidden and disguised.

Walking back to the arena, Pen called out. "Hey dude! I'm Pen. I don't think that we've met before. Thanks for helping us out."

"No problem!" the boy replied. "Glad I could help."

Looking around, Snapper tried to spot Sheila. "And where's Sheila?" Snapper asked, worried.

"Did you see our sister when you came in to help us?" Pen asked, trying to remain calm.

"Pen and Snapper, I'm Sheila," the young boy began. "I just look a little different right now!"

"Hahaha! Yah, okay, whatever!" exclaimed Pen. "Seriously, dude. Just answer the question."

A smile came over the young man's face. "Wow, this is going to be fun, Pen!" the boy retorted. Morphing slowly, Raven transformed into the "Sheila" form and then, within seconds, changed back into the strapping young boy.

"Whoa!" shouted Pen, staring at Sheila. "What the . . ."

Snapper was so shocked that she stood staring speechlessly at Sheila.

"Okay, guys!" said Sheila. "Fight now—catch up later! For now, just know that I'm the new Raven. We've got to find the three witches."

"But what about Brutus and his gang?" asked Pen, staring uncomfortably at his new brother—or at least he thought—he wasn't quite sure.

"We can't find them. They've changed back into their 'other' selves. They could be anyone in the school. And we've got to free the druids."

"Oh, they're already free!" exclaimed Snapper, pointing up to where the druids were standing. "The witches are not strong enough to hold them under a spell like that. Now that they've left, the spell has automatically broken from over them."

The professors were already trying to reassure the students and clean up the mess that the witches had left. Their safe haven had obviously been breached. The unnerving thing for them was that Brutus, Butch, and Thane were three of their students. However, they had no idea which students they were. Each time that they comforted a student, they wondered if that student was Brutus.

Leaving the arena, the three children walked into the yard behind the school. Finding a quiet place, they sat down. None of them said a word. They all knew what they had to do.

CHAPTER THIRTY-ONE

The Final Battle

The pale gray stones of the burial chamber shaped like a shallow dome stood aloft on a soft bed of green grass. The Boyne River flowed to the north. The moon marking the summer solstice hung suspended in the night sky. It was hard for Snapper and Pen to get used to calling their sister Raven. Every time they said Raven's name, Sheila was on the tip of their tongue. Somehow she was different, yet the same. She had chosen her male form today. Raven's black hair was pulled back into a braid. His chiseled jaw line, high cheek bones and muscular frame resembled nothing female. Only Raven's brown eyes shining through reminded them of Sheila.

As the moonlight spilled through the open doorways of the burial chamber, it seemed to light it up from the inside out. "Do you think that my parents are there?" whispered Snapper to Raven.

"They said they would be," he answered calmly.

"I don't think the three sister witches are going to make it that easy for us," interjected Pen cautiously.

"We have our gifts," said Raven placing his hand on his brother's shoulder.

"And we have Raven with us!" added Snapper beaming with pride.

Sure enough, the closer they got to the entrance, the clearer they saw three dark shadows approach. Drawing back the hoods from their dark cloaks, the three children saw the familiar faces of Marcella, Kalik, and The Blue Hag.

"Come to retrieve your poor defenseless parents, Snapper?" sneered Marcella. "Well you have to get through the three of us first." Before the witch could finish her sentence, Snapper was already racing off in full speed toward them.

Snapper's face turned red with rage. "How dare you hurt my mom and dad, you murderer! How dare you touch my family!"

Kalik quickly grabbed at her wand. She saw the anger in Snapper's face and knew that she had to act fast.

"Black spell of despair, black spell of despair, sink your claws into this girl here!"

Black, heavy mists, thick like engine oil, floated toward Snapper. It wrapped itself around her body and propelled itself toward her nose, trying to get into her body.

Unfortunately for Kalik, Snapper had just slipped on her nothingness ring moments before and the lethal spell passed through her like she was made of air.

"You've forgotten who you're dealing with, you stupid witch!" barked Snapper, shaking with fury. Her cheeks were hot with rage and her eyes were wild with frenzy. "Did you forget that I am the one that greets with fire?"

In a moment of fear, Kalik stepped back. Snapper opened up her palms. Flames of fire leaped up into the air, burning ferociously. Flames exploded around Snapper. You could barely see her face through the blazing furnace that roared around her.

Reaching for her broom, Kalik took off into the air. She hadn't anticipated an attack like that from Snapper. Flying up at about thirty feet, Kalik turned to look down at the children. "You may have broken the spell this time, but you won't next time! You just got lucky this time, you miserable creatures!"

Witnessing Kalik's failed spell, Marcella unleashed their secret weapon.

"We're tired of playing nice," Marcella yelled. "My other sister isn't one for words, and we've been holding her back. Let's see how you manage against The Blue Hag."

Whipping off her cloak, The Blue Hag got on to all fours and scampered toward them, her claws and fangs long and outstretched.

Grabbing Raven, Pen took out his silver-tipped pen and immediately transformed it into a wand. Chanting loudly, he said, "like smoke into dust, like fire unseen, take my essence, as though I've never been." Both Raven and Pen vanished from sight. Snarling, the Blue Hag stopped and began to sniff the air. Pen shuddered.

This creature looked more like a monster than a woman. Her milky eye looked around, and her head tilted back as if she was catching the scent of the children on the breeze. She ran her long, forked tongue over her sharp fangs. Without another sound, she lunged like a tarantula, grabbing the unseen. Her sense of smell was well rewarded. Even though she couldn't see the children, she could smell the sweet scent of their blood.

Tackling them to the ground, she sunk her fangs deep inside Pen's leg. Pen screamed out in pain. Snapper was too busy sending bolts of fire toward Kalik to notice the commotion behind her. If she had, she would have been at their side.

Raising his hands, Pen summoned the flowing river. It overflowed its banks and rushed toward them. Despite the water pooling around them and the waves lashing at their backs, The Blue Hag stubbornly held onto Pen's leg. It was clenched in her locked jaw, like a crocodile relentlessly gripping its prey. She slashed at his body cruelly with her sharp nails and sunk her teeth more deeply into his body. The more pain that Pen was in, the weaker his control became over the water.

Raven groped around for Pen's wand that he clutched in his hand and said the words for him: "Let what is unseen be seen."

Suddenly, the gruesome scene was unveiled. From The Blue Hag's mouth spilled Pen's blood, and while she gnawed at his leg, her long, black tongue licked up the blood.

Raven heard voices in her head. "Stand up and be the guardian. You have the power! Do not be afraid to fulfill your destiny!"

Raven opened her large, black wings. She felt a surge of power swelling around her. The more she embraced it, the taller she grew. She began to grow so tall that she now stood twenty feet above the ground. A white, blinding light exploded out from her wings and engulfed The Blue Hag. Screeching from the radiant light, as though its brightness was stinging her very skin, The Blue Hag let go of Pen, in fits of screeches and hisses.

Seeing her sister crumpled in a ball, writhing in pain, Marcella rushed to her side. She stretched out her wand to attack Raven, but she was weakened by the very fact that The Blue Hag was dying. Kalik was also weakened by The Blue Hag's injury, and her shield shattered, leaving her unprotected against Snapper's fire bolts.

Raven spoke, "I am no longer Sheila. I am Raven. Raven gave his powers to me. Your sister, The Blue Hag, is dying. The white light that I cast over her is love. Darkness is destroyed through love. She has so much darkness inside of her that it is eating her alive."

Marcella, realizing that she was going to lose one of her sisters, did the only thing that she could think of doing. She knew that she had to save her and hope that Kalik was strong enough to defend herself. If The Blue Hag died, they would be so weakened that instead of one defeated witch, there would be three.

In that moment, Marcella grabbed The Blue Hag and disappeared in a puff of pink smoke.

Reaching down, Raven placed his hand on Pen's mangled leg. The same blinding, white light that engulfed The Blue Hag seeped into the wound. "Pen," Raven said, "this is the same force—this is love in its purest form. There was no love inside The Blue Hag, but there's love inside of you. And love has the power to heal."

Pen's body began to respond. Pen felt the light's heat like a warm blanket pulling his skin back together and comforting him. He felt its power coursing through his veins. And he felt strong.

Raven and Pen, both having regained their strength, stood up. Neither of them had the gift of fire, but if they did, they would have been engulfed in flames right about then. They were livid with anger.

Kalik eyed them mockingly. "Why don't you all run home and tell your mom and dad about it. You are just kids, you know! Stupid, insignificant kids that like to play with water, wind, and matches!" Kalik felt safer from a distance now.

"Did you ask your mom and dad to buy you a wading pool so that you can play with water, Pen?"

Pen glared back at Kalik, reeling in rage now. "And what about you, Sheila? Did you get yourself a fan so that you could try to move some air around?"

"How dare you insult my powers!" Raven screamed out.

"Come, come now, children. You know that your gifts are just like play toys in comparison to my real power and spells!"

"Ahhhhh!" roared Raven, glaring at Kalik, hovering above them in the sky. "I'm going to kill you, you beast!"

Kalik laughed. "I'm no match for you, you brats! Be careful who you decide to mess with!"

Before Kalik could finish her laugh, Raven bellowed a command to the wind. "Four winds of the earth, come immediately, and do whatever I bid you to do!" A rushing sound of roaring wind emerged in front of Raven. "Carry me into the skies!" she ordered.

Leaping up into the air, Raven flew through the skies, the wind gathering in massive force around her and lifting her. A thunderous hurricane rumbled and shook violently behind her, blotting out the sun's light momentarily. Raven flew higher and higher in her human form until she was at the same height as Kalik. Raising her hands, she pointed at Kalik.

Right behind Raven, Snapper pointed her fingers at the ground. Explosive bolts of fire hit the ground as Snapper soared into the sky. Riding on the massive flames of fire that were at least thirty feet in the air now, Snapper stood on a gigantic fireball beside Raven. Fire sprung from her palms. She took aim at Kalik, who was still sneering at the three children mockingly, but was feeling somewhat nervous now.

Pen, who had decided to morph into his panther form, beckoned with his paw for water to come. A mighty wave from the Boyne River rose high above the water into the air. It froze, suspended above the rest of the water in space and time.

"Waters of the earth, come to me, I command you!" Pen called out in a bellowing roar. It flew in a tidal wave across the forest and to where Pen was standing. As the water approached him, he sprinted at full speed to meet it. Springing into the air on all fours, he landed on top of the water. Rising in the air to meet his two sisters, Pen stood tall in his black panther form. His fangs flashed as he bared his teeth. Throwing back his head, Pen let out a deafening growl that would have paralyzed the most formidable prey. The water rose until Pen was standing between Snapper and Sheila.

All three children stared across the sky at Kalik.

"If it's a war that you want, then it's a war that you will have," growled Pen, menacingly. "Remember this day that you chose to mess with us. We did not choose to mess with you!"

Kalik sneered at Pen. "Do you honestly think that you can hurt me, you stupid little boy?" scoffed Kalik. She adjusted her broom to be able to begin war. Peering across the skies, Kalik immediately withdrew her hand and beckoned for her wand to appear. Grasping tightly on to her wand, she pointed at the three siblings. "How dare you confront me, you miserable wretches! I will show you what true power is today, and you will never forget it!"

Kalik began to chant an incantation. Slowly and menacingly she glared at the three children. "Black spell of despair, black spell of despair, destroy all you find over there!"

Snapper, who was still wearing her nothingness ring, grabbed her two siblings by the hands. Kalik was not aware that not only could the ring protect Snapper, but anyone that she decided to touch. The spell fell to the ground and dissipated under their feet. There was a toad hopping by, however, far below, where the spell hit, who began to croak in fits of distress and sorrow at the sogginess of his life.

At that moment, Pen threw back his head once more. Letting out a deafening panther roar, that only the water could have possibly understood, water sprung up in front of Pen and gushed at Kalik.

Both Raven and Snapper immediately followed with their own weapons in unison.

Raven called in her commanding voice: "Wind of the earth, I beseech you! Shatter Kalik into a million pieces, to the four corners of the Earth."

Snapper opened her hands, conjuring up raging balls of fire, and whipped them at Kalik. "Let's see how awesome you are now, Kalik!" shouted Snapper. "What are you going to do against wind, water, and fire coming at you at once!"

"Yah! Let's see what you do with this!" growled Pen, still in his panther form.

"Let's give her a dose of her own medicine!" yelled Raven, who was having a bit of fun now. "Let's hike up the storm, guys!"

Kalik tried to say something nasty back to the children, but she never had a chance. Water, wind, and fire ripped at her body in steady streams, spinning her around and around. Screaming with rage, she tried desperately to reach for her wand, but it was shattered into a million pieces by the fury of the elements. The wind, fire, and water intensified. The fire grew to a heat that Snapper could never have imagined. The water beat with a violence that Pen had never been able to conjure before. The wind ripped with a force that Raven had never summoned in her life. Still, Kalik resisted, spinning violently in the ferocious elements.

"Harder! Fight harder!" bellowed Pen in another ferocious roar. With every last ounce of strength that Raven and Snapper had, they obeyed Pen. Summoning power that they didn't even know that they had, they channeled a greater force of energy at the witch. Holding their stance, the children did not back down. Pure power flooded against Kalik.

A sudden explosion of ash, smoke, and light mushroomed out like an atomic bomb. Where Kalik had once been were tiny pieces of clothing and gray matter that were shattered into the air in a million pieces. They slowly fell to the earth, some pieces blowing slightly in the wind.

"We did it," Raven said suddenly, totally exhausted.

With a sigh of relief, Pen morphed into his human self. Letting his hands fall by his sides, the water subsided, until all that was left were drops of water dripping softly from his fingertips.

"You bet we did," Pen grinned. "We're a force to be reckoned with."

Raven closed her hands and let them rest by her sides as well. The howling wind relented, and a tiny breeze fluttered around her hands.

"Well that's enough heat for now," announced Snapper. She pinched her fingers together. The flames were immediately extinguished, and all that was left was smoke that rose from her fingertips.

Slowly Pen, Snapper, and Raven made their way back down to the earth. The water came down, just low enough that Pen could step back on to the ground, and then it flew across the skies and landed back into the river in a massive splash. The fire shrunk back down to earth, and Snapper gingerly stepped on to the ground. Bending over, she pinched together the earth, where the fire had once touched, and closing her eyes, she envisioned full healing. The ground immediately closed completely, and where two holes had once been, new plants sprung up, sprouting an array of beautiful flowers.

Raven was last. She changed into her playful boyish form. With a few motions of his hand, he had beckoned for the wind to shape itself into a slide that winded itself down in spirals from the sky, like a roller coaster. Although nobody else could see it because it was invisible, he could! And he laughed merrily. Jumping onto the wind slide, he slid, screaming with glee, around and around, all the way down until he hit the ground.

"Show off!" exclaimed Snapper, looking at him with disdain. "Why couldn't you just come down from the sky like everybody else?"

"Because I'm not everybody else!" said Raven. He reached up his hand to the sky and closed his fist. The wind immediately disappeared.

It wasn't long before Hamza and Tameka were at their side. The wind, fire, and water storm had alerted them from miles away. Raven had just changed back into her female form of Sheila as she saw her parents approaching. Raven, Pen, and Snapper told them what had happened.

Rushing into the burial chamber, the moon's light had just begun to seep through the opening of the ancient tomb. Light began to flash and dart in all directions. Snapper, Raven, and Pen shielded their eyes from the blinding light. It refracted around them like rainbow colors shining through a crystal prism.

Snapper was the first to open her eyes slightly once the brightness began to dim. Peering into the blurry light, she caught a glimpse of two tall figures. They were the faces of her mom and dad. The eyes of her mother lovingly and tenderly gazed longingly back at her through the gentle light that now hung around them. Her eyes danced with joy and laughter. The face of Snapper's father broke into a smile and then a laughter that seemed to shake the very foundations of the burial chamber.

Snapper called out to them, "Where is the hydra that had captured you?"

Pen's face lit up. "I think I know!" he deduced. "We must have destroyed the hydra when we destroyed Kalik! Look over by the wall!" he motioned.

Everyone turned, and sure enough, there lay the skin of the three-headed.

"Looks like her pet went down with her when she was destroyed!" commented Raven.

"My baby girl!" Snapper's dad shouted, opening his arms and running toward her. Within seconds, Snapper was once again in her parents' arms.

From the corner of her eye, Raven watched as Hamza and Tameka noiselessly tiptoed into the hallway. They leaned their backs against the wall. Tears ran down Tameka's face as she watched Snapper, still in her parents' arms.

All of a sudden, Snapper's mother caught a glimpse of Tameka on the other side of the room. Lifting her head, she looked into Tameka's eyes. She smiled at her.

Releasing Snapper, she stood up straight and moved quietly to where Tameka was standing. Looking into Tameka's eyes, she shook her head gently, as if to say, 'what would we have done without you.' Opening up her arms, Snapper's mom embraced Tameka. With tears running down their faces, the two mothers clung onto each other.

When Snapper's mother finally found her voice, she whispered into Tameka's ear, "There are no words to express my gratitude. I will forever be in your debt."

Tameka kissed her on the cheek and whispered, "Thank you for sharing her with me. You have given me the greatest gift that I could ever have dreamed of in my life."

"That goes for me as well," piped up Hamza.

Tameka turned her head just in time to watch as Hamza and Snapper's father shook each other's hands and then hugged each other in an awkward but genuine embrace.

"Thank you, Hamza," Snapper's father said. "If you ever need anything from the dream world, you know we would be honored to do it. Now that we are no longer captives of Kalik, we can finally rejoin the land of our ancestors. You can always reach us in the dream world . . .'" He paused thoughtfully. "Or any departed soul can be summoned to the burial chamber on the first night of a season-changing moon."

Hamza smiled back at Snapper's father. "You know," Hamza began, "it should really be Tameka and me offering to do anything for you because we are the ones who are indebted to you for life. Snapper has given our lives meaning. She is the greatest gift that Tameka and I have ever received, except for our other two children, Sheila and Pen."

Suddenly remembering that Snapper had a brother and sister now, Snapper's mother and father looked around for Pen and Raven. Spotting them sitting nearby, watching everything that was happening, Snapper and her parents walked over to where they were.

"You know, Pen and Raven," Snapper's mother began, "Snapper asked us almost every day if we were going to have children."

"Yes," chimed in Snapper's father. "Psychology has proven through various meta-analyses that it is undeniably crucial for children to share a dyadic friendship, and that children without friendships can become inattentive-hyperactive students, misreading social cues. Every person lives within a microsystem inside a mesosystem embedded in an exosystem, all of which are a part of the macrosystem. In fact, the essence of the bioecological model of development shows us that . . ."

"Honey!" intercepted Snapper's mom, rolling her eyes and groaning. "Sweetheart, it's a reunion, not a psychology lecture. Please stay focused."

Pen and Raven stared in disbelief at Snapper's father.

"Oh my god!" whispered Pen to Raven, once Snapper and her parents had turned to speak to Hamza and Tameka once more. "There are two of them."

Raven giggled. "He's Snapper in a man's body!" she announced, laughing now. She couldn't imagine spending the day with not one, but two walking dictionaries. Snapper was clearly in her element. She was delighted that someone would finally appreciate her verbal dictionary diarrhea. Pen and Raven just giggled.

The light slowly faded. The bodies of Snapper's mom and dad became translucent. Like angels, they began to float. The stars shone out in the night sky. They seemed to pull Snapper's parents toward them. As they floated through the opening of the chamber and up into the sky, Snapper's family watched in awe. Their bodies became one with the stars.

Soon, all that was left was the flame burning in Snapper's hands. Although she was sad to see her parents leave for the dream world, there was a smile of relief on her face. She knew that they were safe now. Kalik and her sisters could no longer harm them. Hamza and Tameka walked over to Pen and Snapper. Taking them in their arms, they embraced their children. It had been a long and wearisome night. Looking around, Tameka could not see Raven in the room. Seeing her expression, Pen, Snapper, and Hamza stepped back.

"Raven?" called out Pen softly. No answer.

Snapper made the flame on her fingers brighter and walked slowly around the room. Pen followed behind her, scouring the area for any clues as to where Raven could have gone. Puzzled, they looked at each other.

"I don't get it," said Pen. "Where did she go? She was right beside me while you were talking to your parents, Snapper."

Snapper shook her head, confused.

Walking once more to the spot where they had been sitting, Pen suddenly spotted a piece of paper lying on the ground. Walking to it, he picked it up. Snapper ran over to where he was and held up her light.

Holding the paper up to the light, Pen read it aloud:

"Dear Snapper and Pen Mom and Dad,

I'm glad Snapper's parents are safe, and they can be at peace.

I am Raven now, and as Raven, I have new responsibilities and duties to fulfill. It is my job to protect the innocent. There's a crisis in Africa. I have been summoned by the witches and chiefs of many tribes. I will need your help, as well as the druids. There is a great evil there that has been awoken. I will be back to call for all of you.

Love, Raven"

SYNOPSIS

Just when Sheila, Snapper, and Pen are beginning to adjust to their lives, adopted into a new family, an old adversary emerges. Kalik, an evil sorcerer who they thought was vanquished, reappears. Unknown to the children, she has come back with her two evil sisters to destroy them. These three dark shadows lurk and scheme a plot to steal the children's magical powers.

A coven of good witches deep in the heart of Stonehenge have mysteriously disappeared. Their bodies were never discovered—only the remains of their spell books lay scattered. Glimpses of these witches have been spotted at the ancient burial chamber long forgotten on the northern shores of Ireland.

Snapper, Sheila, and Pen find themselves on a quest to rescue them. Along the way, they are given magical gifts by mystical druids to help them on this quest. They will need to rely on one another, their magical training, and Raven's help if they are going to go up against the three deadly dark shadows!

CPSIA information can be obtained at www.ICGtesting.com
Printed in the USA
LVOW07*0952091016

508014LV00014B/292/P

9 781499 083187